We hope you enjoy this book. Please return or renew it by the due date.

You can renew it at www.norfolk.gov.uk/libraries or by using our free library app.

Otherwise you can phone 0344 800 8020 - please have your library card and PIN ready.

You can sign up for email reminders too.

June '21

D1330684

BY MATTHEW HARFFY

The Bernicia Chronicles

The Serpent Sword
The Cross and the Curse
Blood and Blade
Killer of Kings
Warrior of Woden
Storm of Steel
Fortress of Fury
Kin of Cain (short story)

A Time for Swords

A Time for Swords

Novels

Wolf of Wessex

FORTRESS OF FURY

THE BERNICIA CHRONICLES: VII

MATTHEW HARFFY

HEAD of ZEUS

An Aries Book

First published in the UK in 2020 Head of Zeus Ltd
This paperback edition first published in 2021 by Head of Zeus Ltd
An Aries Book

9 7 5 3 1 2 4 6 8

A CIP catalogue record for this book is available from the British Library.

ISBN (PB): 9781786696366
ISBN (E): 9781786696397

Typeset by Siliconchips Services Ltd UK

Printed and bound in Great Britain by
CPI Group (UK) Ltd, Croydon CR0 4YY

Head of Zeus Ltd
First Floor East
5–8 Hardwick Street
London EC1R 4RG

www.headofzeus.com

Fortress of Fury
is for everyone who has read, reviewed and recommended
my books.
Thank you for helping me to realise my dreams.
If you keep reading, I'll keep writing. Deal?

NORTHERN ALBION

Cair Chaladain

Sea of Giudan

Din Eidyn

Magilros

DÁL RIATA

BERN

RHEGED

Gill

Caer Luel

MAN

HIBERNIAN SEA

0   25 miles

0   50 km

N

ALBION
AD 647

PICTLAND

DÁL RIATA

BERNICIA

HIBERNIA

DEIRA

ELMET

GWYNEDD

MERCIA

WEST SAXONS

CANTWARE

FRANKIA

Berewic

anford

Lindisfarena

Bebbanburg

NORTHUMBRIA

R. Cocueda

R. Wenspic

Morðpæð

The Wall

Legend

○ Settlements

ᛤ Fortresses

† Holy sites

—— Roman roads

R. Tine

R. Wiur

NORTH SEA

Ediscum

Ingetlingum

Catrice

R. Sualuae

DEIRA

R. Usa

Eoferwic

Place Names

Place names in Dark Ages Britain vary according to time, language, dialect and the scribe who was writing. I have not followed a strict convention when choosing what spelling to use for a given place. In most cases, I have chosen the name I believe to be the closest to that used in the early seventh century, but like the scribes of all those centuries ago, I have taken artistic licence at times, and merely selected the one I liked most.

Æscendene	Ashington, Northumberland
Afen	River Avon
Albion	Great Britain
Bebbanburg	Bamburgh
Beodericsworth	Bury St Edmunds
Berewic	Berwick-upon-Tweed
Bernicia	Northern kingdom of Northumbria, running approximately from the Tyne to the Firth of Forth
Caer Luel	Carlisle
Cair Chaladain	Kirkcaldy, Fife
Cantware	Kent

Cantwareburh	Canterbury
Catrice	Catterick
Cocueda	River Coquet
Dál Riata	Gaelic overkingdom, roughly encompassing modern-day Argyll and Bute and Lochaber in Scotland and also County Antrim in Northern Ireland
Deira	Southern kingdom of Northumbria, running approximately from the Humber to the Tyne
Din Eidyn	Edinburgh
Dor	Dore, Yorkshire
Dorcic	Dorchester on Thames
Dun	River Don
Dyvene	River Devon
Ediscum	Escomb, County Durham
Elmet	Native Briton kingdom, approximately equal to the West Riding of Yorkshire
Engelmynster	Fictional location in Deira
Eoferwic	York
Frankia	France
Gefrin	Yeavering
Gillisland	Gilsland, Northumberland
Gipeswic	Ipswich
Gwynedd	Gwynedd, North Wales
Hefenfelth	Heavenfield
Hereteu	Hartlepool
Hibernia	Ireland
Hii	Iona
Hithe	Hythe, Kent
Ingetlingum	Gilling, Yorkshire
Inhrypum	Ripon, North Yorkshire

Irthin	River Irthing, Cumbria
Liminge	Lyminge, Kent
Lindesege	Lindsey
Lindisfarena	Lindisfarne
Loidis	Leeds
Maerse	Mersey
Magilros	Melrose, Scottish Borders
Mercia	Kingdom centred on the valley of the River Trent and its tributaries, in the modern-day English Midlands.
Morðpæð	Morpeth, Northumberland
Muile	Mull
Neustria	Frankish kingdom in the north of present-day France, encompassing the land approximately between the Loire and the Silva Carbonaria.
Northumbria	Modern-day Yorkshire, Northumberland and south-east Scotland
Pocel's Hall	Pocklington
Rendlæsham	Rendlesham, Suffolk
Rodomo	Rouen, France
Sandwic	Sandwich, Kent
Scheth	River Sheaf (border of Mercia and Deira)
Sea of Giudan	Firth of Forth
Snodengaham	Nottingham
Soluente	Solent
Stanfordham	Stamfordham, Northumberland
Sualuae	River Swale
Tatecastre	Tadcaster
Temes	River Thames
Tine	River Tyne
Tuidi	River Tweed

PROLOGUE

PROLOGUE

Eoferwic, AD 646

Beobrand was yet some way from his destination, but he halted his progress, holding himself still and silent in the darkness. His hand fell to the antler hilt of the seax that hung sheathed from his belt. Perhaps Coenred had been right. Maybe he should not have ventured out alone into the cool night-time shadows of the muddy streets of the walled settlement.

But surely he was safe here, in the heart of Deira's capital. He listened for a long while, feeling foolish for his nervousness. Curse Coenred and his anxiety. The young monk had sown the seeds of fear in his mind and now every shadow held an imagined lurking danger.

A baby wailed, the sound thin and plaintive in the distance. All else was silent. The night was dry and, looking up, there were no clouds to cover the sharp, cold light of the stars and the curved bright blade of the rising moon.

Shaking his head at his own temerity, he pressed on. Much had changed in Eoferwic these last years, with new buildings being erected and old Roman ruins being repaired and returned to some semblance of their former glory. Some of the houses he passed were unfamiliar to him, but he knew the way well enough.

He would be at the church soon, and his heart quickened at the prospect of being alone with her, even if just for a few moments.

Ever since that evening the week before he had scarcely been able to think of anything else. Her soft hair and the pliant lips that had brushed his filled his mind, blurring the rest of his thoughts behind the heat and brilliance of their memory.

When the message had arrived earlier that evening, Beobrand had struggled to appear uninterested. The missive had been brought by a hooded man, who slipped back into the darkness as soon as he handed the scrip of vellum to Attor who was guarding the door. The wiry warrior had brought the note to Beobrand. They had peered at the scratchings on the stretched calfskin by the light of the candles in the hall, but neither Beobrand nor any of his gesithas knew how to read the markings that were usually penned by monks and priests. So he had sent for Coenred, who had been able to decipher the meaning of the words easily.

"It is Latin," he had said, running his finger over the smooth sheet of vellum. "The writing is clear, the letters well-formed."

Beobrand had not wished to know the quality of the penmanship. He had already decided who must have sent the message. She knew how to write and would have surmised he would turn to Coenred to explain the note's meaning. And they both knew that Coenred would keep their secret; that he would be discreet.

Beobrand still harboured a simmering rage at Coenred for stumbling upon them the week before. He felt his face grow hot at the memory. Who knew what that night might have held in store if the young monk had not blundered into that quiet corner of the newly built monastery at Hereteu? But in helping them meet secretly this night, Coenred could redeem himself. After all, it had been an accident back in Hereteu, happenstance that had seen them interrupted by the monk after the briefest embrace.

"What does the message say?" Beobrand had asked, his words coming breathlessly, such was his excitement. He could hardly believe how she made him feel. He was as giddy as a child thinking of her. He had pushed thoughts of her deep down

4

within himself for a long time. Years. But all of his passion and longing had resurfaced, the flames of his desire rekindled by the merest brush of her lips and a warm whisper in his ear.

Coenred had looked at him, the expression on his face pinched. His delicate fingers had stroked the vellum, flattening it unconsciously as he stared at Beobrand.

"The words are simple enough, old friend," he'd said. "*Meet at the church at moonrise. Come alone.*"

Joy had flooded through Beobrand. It was already dark and the moon would be up soon. He'd turned to leave, but Coenred had pulled him back, his slender fingers tugging at the woollen sleeve of his kirtle.

"Beo," he'd whispered urgently, "do not do this thing. Think of the kingdom if nothing else. Even if you care nought for your own life, think of her. Think of her son... The king's wrath will destroy you, should he find out what is between you."

The young monk had been pale in the flickering light of the candles, his eyes glistening. Beobrand had shrugged off his grip and wheeled on him, anger rising. What did Coenred know of how he felt? It had been so many years since he had dared to feel anything like this. A small voice whispered within him that this was madness, that his friend was right. But Beobrand would not listen. He could not forget the scent of her, the lingering touch of her lips. He would not ignore the chance to be alone with her now.

"But nobody else knows of this apart from you," he'd said, his voice a harsh whisper, as threatening as a blade being rasped over a whetstone. "So the king will not find out. Will he?" He'd fixed Coenred with a baleful glower. "Or are you planning on telling him?"

He was almost at the church now. The newly built stone structure was surrounded by open ground. He would be able to see its bulk when he rounded the next corner, but again, something made him hesitate. He stopped once more, breathing silently through his mouth. There was no sound. No wind stirred. The distant infant's crying had ceased. So what caused his neck to prickle so? Could Coenred have been right? He had urged Beobrand not to go, or at least to take some of his men with him. "It could be a trap," he'd said.

Beobrand had dismissed the younger man's fears. Who else would have written the message to him, if not her? Few people could write and who, save for her, would believe that he would be able to find someone to read such a message?

And yet, like an animal sensing unseen hunters, Beobrand's muscles tensed and bunched, ready for action. He was not so blinded by his lust that he could ignore his instincts; they had kept him alive for too long. He sniffed the air, but could smell nothing save the shit-stink of the mud-slicked streets. Cautiously now, he edged his way forward, keeping his left side close to the wall of the building he was passing.

He paused and listened.

Was that the whisper of a voice ahead? He could not be certain. Fingers of dread scratched down his back and he suppressed a shiver. He was sure of it now, there was danger out there in the darkness.

Silently, he slid his seax from its sheath, wishing now that he had listened to Coenred. He had slipped out alone from the hall where they were staying. Cynan, the tall, trusted Waelisc gesith, had questioned where he was going, rising to his feet as if to follow, but Beobrand had waved him away.

"Can't a man piss in peace?" he'd answered and vanished into the night.

Gods, he was a fool. Alone and with nothing more than a seax to defend him should it come to a fight. Still, he was a match for any man who was stupid enough to attempt to steal his purse. Taking a deep breath, he stepped out from the shadows between the buildings and into the open area before the church. The moon had risen above the shingled roof and the night seemed

6

almost bright after the deep shadows of the sheltered streets.

Beobrand swept his gaze around the cleared ground. The entrances to streets yawned black as raven's beaks. Nothing moved. He could see no sign of her, or anyone else, near the church. How had he been so foolish? To think she would have come alone, into the dark streets of Eoferwic. He should turn away now, head back to the warmth of the hall and the camaraderie of his men. But instead, he stepped into the silvered moonlight, making his way towards the church. If there was even the slightest chance she might be there, he could not leave.

He sighed resignedly when the men stepped out from the shadowed lee of the building. He was unsurprised, though he knew not who they were. Still, he had many enemies and he should have known better than to trust that his wyrd would allow him to find happiness in a secret nocturnal tryst. Cursing himself silently for a fool, he rolled his head, loosening the neck muscles. A pitiful sense of disappointment washed over him, but as quickly as it came, it was smothered by a searing fury. He had come here seeking a love he knew was forbidden to him, a connection he had only dreamed of, but now he faced unnamed assailants in the night. Death and blood were all he would find here.

Two men closed with him from the church and a quick glance behind showed three more blocked his retreat. In their hands all of them held long, savage blades, steel edges gilded in the moonlight.

Despite the odds against him, Beobrand grinned savagely, his teeth flashing in the dark. He would be hard-pressed against so many, armed only with a large knife as he was, and yet he felt no fear. He had walked so long with death that it seemed like an old friend to him now. Something in the glint of his eye and the broad smile on his face gave the two men before him pause. They faltered, and in that instant, without any warning, and scarcely aware what he was going to do, Beobrand surged forward. Absently he heard the men behind him begin to run to close the distance. He ignored them. They were too far away yet to be of concern.

He sped forward with a speed that had undone many an adversary.

One of the men seemed completely frozen, whether with fear or merely shock, Beobrand did not know, or care. He rushed forward, clasping the wrist of the man's sword-arm in his mutilated left hand and, without slowing, dragging the deadly edge of his seax across the man's throat. The blade was sharp and it severed flesh, arteries and cartilage until it scraped against bone. Hot blood gushed over Beobrand's hand and the man fell away from him, his wrist slipping from Beobrand's left half-hand as the would-be killer gurgled and choked on his lifeblood.

The second opponent had been quicker to regain his wits and it was all Beobrand could do to parry the scything blow that flashed out of the darkness to his right. Sparks flew and the man grunted. Beobrand shoved him away and took several rapid steps back, past the body of the dying man, moving so that the church was now to his rear and all four remaining enemies were facing him.

The four men drew closer together, unconsciously looking for protection and safety in their numbers.

"Are you all ready to die tonight?" Beobrand asked. His tone was even, as though he were asking them about the state of the weather, but the rattling cough of their dying comrade lent the words a deadly seriousness.

None of the men responded. Instead, as if they had realised the error of their positioning, they began to put space between themselves, spreading out. Beobrand knew they would attack soon. And, if he stayed in the open, in all likelihood he would die. They had the numbers to surround him again and no matter how skilled, he would eventually succumb to a cut from behind. He would not be able to watch all of them at once.

Before they had time to organise themselves, Beobrand jogged backward towards the church. They chased after him, clearly not ready to allow him to escape so easily. A moment later, the cold stone of the church loomed behind him and Beobrand offered them another grin. If he could keep his back to the building, he could only be attacked from the front and flanks. That was something, and all the edge he could find.

No sooner had he reached the church than the man whose sword he had parried jumped forward, feinting at Beobrand's head. Beobrand anticipated the man's next move, shifting his weight to one side. The man's sword slid harmlessly past Beobrand's chest, leaving his arm exposed. Beobrand flicked out with the seax, drawing a long, deep cut along his attacker's forearm. Blood welled black in the night and the man's sword clattered to the earth.

Beobrand snatched up the weapon, transferring his seax to his left hand. His grip was weak on that side, where he had lost the last two fingers years before. But he was still glad of the seax nestling in his half-hand. His left hand might be weaker than his right, but it was still strong enough to hold a weapon; to cut, and to kill.

The injured man clutched his arm, blood oozing between his fingers. He withdrew from the fight, swearing underneath his breath in a tongue Beobrand did not understand.

Beobrand turned his attention to the remaining three assailants. The largest of the three, a broad-shouldered man with a shaved head that shone in the moonlight, stood directly in front of him. The other two, each smaller and lither, moved to either side.

Beobrand tested the heft of the unfamiliar sword in his hand. It was heavier than his fine blade, Nægling, and less well-balanced. But it would suffice. He watched the three men slowly sidling closer, leading with one foot and then sliding the trailing foot to meet the first. They held their blades high and steady.

9

These were not ruffians looking to rob a stranger's purse. These were sword-men. Killers.

And there were three of them. If they attacked at once, Beobrand knew he would struggle to fend them off. They had him, if they fought as a unit. All he could hope for was that they were not well-trained, that each man would attack as he summoned up the nerve to do so.

"Come on then, you bald bastard," Beobrand hissed. "Aren't you going to try your luck?"

For a heartbeat, he met the dark eyes of the large man before him. Beobrand willed him to throw away his caution, to leap forward to be skewered on his blades. But an instant later, without warning, as if they had one mind between them, the three attackers bounded forward together and Beobrand knew he might not live to see the dawn.

Sparks flickered again in the dark as Beobrand's borrowed blade clashed against the bald man's sword. For an eye-blink Beobrand held the central man's sword against his own and flicked his attention to the assailant on his left, as he was half a step closer than the attacker on the right.

The man was swinging his blade in a great downward arc which would surely have slain Beobrand, if it had connected. Beobrand watched the blur of the blade as it descended towards him. Unbidden, his mouth twisted in a vicious grimace. He was born for this. Thoughts of love and the warmth of a woman had fled like spit on a forge. Now there was nothing but the night, cold steel and the hot blood of his enemies. This was the dance of death, and Beobrand knew every step.

Raising his seax, he deflected the huge sword-blow with an almost casual nonchalance. He kicked at the man's bent knee and, off-balance, the sword-man stumbled back with a groan.

The bald man was putting his weight and strength behind his blade, attempting to overpower Beobrand. The man was strong. But Beobrand was known as one of the greatest swordsmen in

Albion and it took more than strength to defeat him. Twisting his wrist, Beobrand sent the man's sword away and down and in the same motion, he delivered a back-handed cut across his wide chest. There was not a great amount of force in the blow, and the sword he had retrieved was not as sharp as Nægling, yet still the blade did its work. The man's kirtle parted and blood blossomed, soaking the wool dark in the gloom.

As he turned to the third enemy, Beobrand knew he was too late. He was faster and more skilled than most men, but he was still mortal. While he had fought off the first two attackers, the third had closed and even now his sword was whistling towards Beobrand's midriff. There was no time to bring a blade to bear, so Beobrand threw himself to the side. He hit the rough stone of the church hard. An instant later, the man's sword clattered against the building and a burning pain engulfed Beobrand's chest. Some of the force of the blow had been absorbed by the limestone, but Beobrand had been cut enough times to know the wound was bad. His right side was hot and wet. He swung his sword instinctively, sending the man back a pace. Beobrand staggered, then righted himself, planting his feet firmly on the damp ground and resting his back on the cold stone of the church.

The three men rallied. None had received a killing blow. They were wary, but they knew they had him now. They did not taunt or jeer as some men did in combat, either to unnerve their opponent or to give themselves courage. They closed with him in silence, the only sounds their panting breaths that steamed in the night.

Beobrand smiled thinly. To think that after all the battles and skirmishes, fighting in shieldwalls alongside ealdormen and kings, he would meet his end here, alone in the dark, slain by enemies he did not know. He shuddered, recalling a screeched curse in a cavern far off in his memories. The cunning woman, Nelda, was long gone, but she had cursed him to die alone. It seemed in the end her magic may have lasted beyond her death.

Gods, all he had wanted was to see the woman he desired alone again. To think that in seeking love he had found a lonely death.

He spat.

Lifting the sword and seax before him, he beckoned to the men.

"Come on, then. Don't be shy now. Finish what you've started, you craven whoresons."

Beobrand tried to see their eyes in the darkness, for to see a man's eyes was to read his intentions. But the night was too dark, and the men's faces were inscrutable. Even so, he watched them. His blood trickled down his side. He saw the minute tensing of their stances the instant before they attacked and he moved to meet them.

The bald man came first. He sprang forward with a probing lunge of his blade. Beobrand swayed to his left, meaning to strike the man's extended arm. He would slay at least one more of them before the end. But the man faltered, his steps suddenly slow and leaden. He looked down at his chest, mouth agape, eyes blinking stupidly. It was as though he had succumbed to Beobrand's earlier cut, but surely that had been a mere flesh wound.

And then he saw it.

Moonlight glimmered from a blood-smeared spear-point that protruded from the bald man's sternum.

The other attackers looked on in shock at their comrade's sudden death. They peered into the darkness, searching for this new unseen threat.

Beobrand did not hesitate. With a bellow of rage, he leaped to his left, his sword cleaving the skull of the distracted swordsman. Brains and bone splattered in the night and he was dead before hitting the earth.

Swinging back to his right, Beobrand saw a shadow spring from the darkness. There was a brief flurry of blows, a clangour of blades and then a wheezing exhalation. The third attacker slid to the ground, a gaping gash pumping his life into the mud.

A strongly built, dark-bearded man wearing nothing but a plain kirtle stepped into the moonlight. His legs were pale and his bare feet splashed in mud. He grasped a sword in his right hand. Its blade was dark with blood. His teeth gleamed.

"Lord Beobrand," he said, "you are out late this night. I thought you might like some company."

"Lord Wulfstan." Despite the agony in his side, Beobrand could not help grinning at the Deiran thegn. "I thank you for your hospitality, but I was enjoying a pleasant chat with some old friends."

Wulfstan chuckled. Beobrand did not know the man well, but they had shared the mead benches in their lords' halls on several occasions. Wulfstan served Oswine of Deira, whereas Beobrand was oath-sworn to Oswiu of Bernicia. The two kings were allies, so those in the kings' retinues often feasted together. It seemed that much of the life of a king was spent in feasting. Beobrand snorted at the thought.

"Well, I am sorry if I interrupted," Wulfstan said. "I merely thought that as you are a guest in Eoferwic, I should offer my services."

Beobrand allowed himself to slump against the church wall as a wave of giddiness hit him.

"I thank you. Let it not be said that Beobrand of Ubbanford cannot hold his own in a conversation, but I must admit that the debate was getting somewhat heated."

Wulfstan stepped closer, concern on his face now.

"Who were they?"

Beobrand shook his head.

"I know not. But wait," a chill gripped him, "there were five of them. There are only four corpses. I wounded a fifth man. Where is he?"

Both alert again, they scanned the darkened mouths of the roads that led to the church. There was no sign of the fifth attacker.

"Your other friend seems to have tired of you," Wulfstan said, tugging his spear unceremoniously from the bald man's back. It was lodged hard, trapped between muscle and bone so that Wulfstan had to hold the body still with his foot while he pulled at the ash haft. Finally, Wulfstan grunted and the spear came free with a sucking sound like a kiss.

Beobrand's head was swimming. He must have looked close to collapse, for Wulfstan handed him the spear.

"Lean on that," he said. "And on me, if you need to. I will send my men to deal with the bodies. Perhaps the morning will shed some light on who they were."

His chest was a screaming agony now, but Beobrand gritted his teeth, using the spear-haft for support, and followed Wulfstan away from the church.

"What were you doing out alone?" Wulfstan asked.

"I could ask you the same," Beobrand replied with a smirk. "At least I am dressed."

Wulfstan looked down at his kirtle and white, muck-spattered bare feet and legs.

"Ah, yes. Perhaps the less said about that, the better. My wife is back at my hall, but the nights are still long and cold at this time of year, if you take my meaning. Gossip travels faster than a bird flies, and it would not do my goodwife, or me, any good if she should hear of how I sought warmth."

Beobrand smiled ruefully. It would seem Wulfstan's night had been more pleasant than his.

"I would not dream of uttering a word," he said. "But I am glad you decided this moment to go for a stroll."

Wulfstan laughed.

"Indeed. I have had more than enough exercise and excitement for one night. It is a wonder I can still stand." He winked. "Now, let's get you to a fire and someone who knows more than I do about tending wounds. I fear that you and I are both only skilled at the taking of life, not the preserving of it."

They trudged slowly towards the road that would lead them to the hall in which Beobrand and his gesithas were staying. Beobrand finally accepted that he might fall without Wulfstan's help and so he clasped a hand on the Deiran thegn's shoulder.

"I am in your debt, Wulfstan," Beobrand said, between teeth gritted against the throbbing that radiated from his wounds. "If you are ever in need of my aid, I will not forget this."

"Let us not talk about debts," replied Wulfstan. "We are just friends enjoying an evening stroll."

Beobrand shook his head in the darkness, smiling despite the pain.

"Very well," he said. "Let us speak no more of this, but know that you have my word. Should you have need of a friend—" He hesitated. "A friend with a sharp blade. Call, and I will come."

In the depths of the town, several dogs began to bark, answering each other's angry calls one after the other. Running steps echoed in the night. Wulfstan drew his sword again, and with a wince, Beobrand readied himself for whatever further assault the night had in store.

A moment later, Beobrand let out a long breath.

"Put aside your blade, Wulfstan," he whispered. "These are my men."

Attor, the fleetest of foot, reached them first, his two long seaxes already in his hands, ever prepared for battle. He was followed by Cynan and the grim-faced Dreogan, the soot-stained lines on his cheeks making him sinister and otherworldly in the darkness. The brothers, Eadgard and Grindan, were close behind and Beobrand was comforted to see that Eadgard carried his huge axe slung over his shoulder as he strode towards them. The last of the group were Fraomar, Halinard the Frank and Coenred. Young Fraomar was fast. Beobrand knew he must have held himself back to keep the young monk safe. Beobrand frowned at Coenred.

"Forgive me, Beo," the monk said. "Your men were worried about you." He took in the dark stain on Beobrand's kirtle. His eyes widened. "It seems they were right to be concerned."

Attor and Cynan both began to speak, their tone anxious at the sight of his injury. Beobrand cut them off.

"There will be time enough to talk later. Coenred, I have need of your healing skills, even if I cannot count on your silence." He sighed and offered the monk a nod to soften the harshness of his words. He could not truly be angry with Coenred when his fears had been proven not to be baseless.

"The rest of you," he continued, "if you would like to make yourselves useful, bring back the bodies of the men we killed by the church. And make sure you pick up all of their possessions. Perhaps in the light we will recognise them. I would know who means to slay me."

"Pardon me," said Halinard, his words strongly accented.

"Yes, Halinard," snapped Beobrand, anxious now to be back inside in the warm. Already his hands were shaking terribly and it was all he could do to keep them still by gripping the spear-haft. Halinard was a good man, but he spoke slowly at times. When he had come back with them from Rodomo a couple of years previously, he could not speak a word of the Anglisc tongue, but he was an intelligent man and had picked it up quickly. Still, he stumbled over some words and Beobrand was in no mood for patience.

"Pardon me, lord," Halinard repeated.

Beobrand sighed.

"Out with it, man."

"It is just that I ask you if you take that sword from one of the men who want kill you?"

Beobrand looked at the sword he had retrieved from one of his attackers. It was not a fine sword, but its pommel was an unusual shape, set with garnets and bearing two rings. Runes were carved on the hilt. Beobrand nodded, watching Halinard intently.

"Then you not need to question who was it who send these men for you to kill," Halinard said.

"You know this blade?" asked Beobrand. It was not a great weapon, but it was as distinctive as a face. A warrior would never forget it.

"Yes, lord," replied Halinard. "It is the sword of a man called Bavo."

"And who is this Bavo?"

Beobrand felt suddenly cold. There could be only one reason for Halinard to recognise this weapon and to know its owner. He thought of the evil web that had ensnared them in Frankia. They had almost lost everything in that faraway city, and they had left behind a brooding and powerful enemy.

Halinard's features were grave, as if he too were remembering his life in Rodomo. Beobrand and the Frankish warrior had a connection they never spoke of. Both of them had daughters who had become the playthings of monsters.

Halinard spat into the earth, as if clearing the taste of evil from his mouth.

"Bavo is a man of Vulmar."

ANNO DOMINI NOSTRI IESU CHRISTI
IN THE YEAR OF OUR LORD JESUS CHRIST
647

PART ONE
DANGEROUS DECEITS

Chapter 1

They chased the raiders westward as the sun slid down through a crimson sky towards the desolate hills and moors of western Bernicia. Far beyond the horizon, before the land dipped into the sea that separated Albion from Hibernia, Beobrand knew there rose great snow-capped mountains. But that land was days' ride away and they would run their quarry to ground long before they saw the craggy bluffs and peaks of Rheged. He glanced over his shoulder at the score of warriors that rode hard behind him. Given their pace and the freshness of their steeds, they might well catch the men they pursued before sunset. He hoped so. He did not wish to lose them in the night. They had burnt a steading, killing folk whom Beobrand had sworn to defend. And they had injured one of Beobrand's gesithas. These Mercians must pay.

Beobrand squinted into the lowering sun. He could make out no details in the glare. A prickle of unease scratched the nape of his neck. Could they be riding into an ambush? With a twitch of the reins, he slowed his black stallion, Sceadugenga, almost imperceptibly. Beside him, Cynan shot him a glance and guided his mount closer.

"What is it?" asked the Waelisc warrior. He rode his bay mare effortlessly, and as always, when Beobrand watched the man ride, he marvelled at how one who had been so unsuited to horseback at first had gone on to become the best horseman of his warband, and arguably in the kingdom.

Beobrand was no great rider, but he had the finest of horses. Sceadugenga was no longer young, but the horse was still hale and strong and there was a deep understanding between horse and rider. Beobrand knew it was foolish to care for a beast, but the bond he shared with Sceadugenga was unlike anything he had felt with other animals. The stallion and he had been through much together and it often seemed to him that the animal knew what he was going to command before he even knew himself.

"Something is not right," Beobrand said, raising his voice over the thunder of the horses' hooves on the summer-dry ground.

"You think it a trap?" said Cynan.

Beobrand frowned. With his half-hand he swiped the sweat from his brow.

"I know not. But let us ride with caution. Keep your eyes open." Looking over his shoulder at the column of riders, Beobrand noticed that a couple were straggling some way behind the rest. "Take the lead, Cynan. I would check on Brinin."

Without waiting for a response, Beobrand pulled Sceadugenga's head to one side and wheeled around. His warband cantered past in a rush of warm wind. Dust clouded the air, gritting his eyes and drying his throat. It had not rained for weeks and the earth was cracked and crumbling. He watched the faces of the warriors, ruddy and angular in the light of the setting sun. They were grim men, hardened by years of shieldwalls and border clashes. Warriors all, they had given their oaths to Beobrand and they served him well. In turn, he was generous and they were well equipped. All held spears, and sheathed swords hung from baldrics on most of them. A few wore helms, but most were bare-headed in the heat, their helmets bouncing where they were tied to saddles. Each man had a black-daubed shield strapped to his back. Years before, some of the men had asked Beobrand what his banner should be. Warriors needed a symbol to rally behind, they'd said. Beobrand cared nothing for pictures or banners made of the pelts of animals, such as those carried aloft by other warlords. His warband had but one purpose when they marched – to kill their lord's enemies – and they should not need a standard to remind them of who they served. They had decided on the colour of death for their shields and thus the infamous Black Shields were born, feared and respected the length of Albion.

One of the riders who had fallen behind was the youngest member of Beobrand's gesithas. The instant Beobrand rode close he knew the boy could not continue to keep up the pace of this pursuit. The puckered skin of a long raw scar stood out starkly against Brinin's milk-pallid face and his eyes were dull and pinched with pain. Beobrand remembered clearly the tumult of crashing waves and the chaos of battle on a distant Wessex beach where the young man had received the wound that had so brutally marked his otherwise handsome face. The man who rode alongside Brinin was Halinard. The Frankish warrior offered Beobrand a sombre nod of welcome. Words were not needed. Beobrand could see immediately that Brinin would soon collapse if he was not allowed to rest.

Sceadugenga fell into step beside Brinin and Halinard's horses. The grey mare Halinard rode nickered in greeting at Beobrand's black stallion.

The strip of cloth that Fraomar had ripped from a kirtle and tied about Brinin's right arm was soaked dark with blood. Brinin swayed in the saddle like a drunk. Halinard rode as nearby as he could, clearly meaning to catch the boy if he should topple.

Anger flared within Beobrand.

"I told you to only see what was causing the smoke, didn't

I?" he snarled. "Didn't I give you an order not to attack any enemy you might come across; to ride back and tell us what you had found?"

Brinin did not reply, but the misery on his features was plain. Beobrand understood all too well the fire that burnt in young men, the fury that would not allow them to turn away from a challenge.

"Gods, boy," he yelled, his anger yielding to exasperation, "I should never have let you ride with us. If you should die, how will I be able to return to Ubbanford? I will not be able to face Ardith with tidings of your death." Beobrand was known as a brave man and had no qualms facing armed men in combat to the death. And yet he could not stomach the thought of having to give his daughter the news of her husband's death. She had begged him not to allow Brinin to go with the warband on their annual patrol of the frontier to the south. Ardith had pointed out that Brinin was Ubbanford's smith and so could not be spared. But Beobrand liked the boy and could see in him a need to prove himself that he recognised. It would do the lad no good to be forced to remain at home with the womenfolk, children and greybeards. And so he had allowed him to come. And how had Brinin repaid him? By ignoring his command and riding in recklessly to attack a party of Mercian raiders. In doing so, he had not only picked up a bad slash to his arm, which could yet become elf-shot and diseased, but he had held them up in the pursuit of the marauders. They had needed to wait while Fraomar had done his best to staunch the bleeding and to bandage the wound. Now, weak and pale, and on the verge of tumbling from his horse, he was slowing them down again.

Beobrand sighed.

"Halt!" he shouted, so that his voice carried to the front of the column.

A moment later, he saw Cynan rein in his mare. The rest of the warband pulled up.

Tugging his reins, Beobrand slowed Sceadugenga and brought him to a stop. Brinin rode on, seemingly oblivious of Beobrand's command. Halinard spurred close, catching the young man's reins. The horse whinnied, shying away, but Halinard held firm and soon had both his horse and Brinin's under control.

Beobrand jumped to the ground. He grunted at the tightness in his right side. The wound he had received the previous year in Eoferwic had healed well. Coenred had sewn up the gash with horsehair and applied a poultice of bread, honey and mead to it. It no longer hurt, but the skin around the scar was tight and pulled uncomfortably when he stretched.

Halinard dismounted and together they lifted Brinin down from his saddle. They laid him on the dry grass beside the dusty road. Brinin's face was awash with sweat and his eyes were unfocused. His head lolled and his limbs were as weak as a babe's.

"Halinard, stay with him. Fetch water from the stream we passed not long since. Keep him warm and his wound clean." Fumbling in his saddlebags, Beobrand brought out a kirtle and threw it at the Frank, who snatched it from the air. "Use this to bind the cut. It's clean." Udela had told him to carry extra clothing. He knew he would not need clean kirtles on the patrol and had told her as much. She had insisted, and in the end, he had stuffed the things into his bags, content to be done with the woman's nagging. He was glad he had allowed her to win that argument now. He knew little of healing, but he had heard Coenred say many times that clean cloths were vital if injuries were not to become poisoned.

With a clatter of hooves, Cynan pulled his mount to a halt beside them.

"We're leaving Brinin behind?" he asked. His tone was flat, with no hint of emotion, but Beobrand sensed his disapproval.

"It is either that, or we lose the bastards that killed Leofing and burnt his hall."

Cynan nodded.

Beobrand swung himself up onto Sceadugenga's back, careful this time not to stretch the skin over his ribs.

"We will return as soon as we can," he said to Halinard. "Keep him safe and we should be back on the morrow."

Halinard looked up at him with a thin smile.

"You will stay safe too, lord," he said in his strangely accented voice.

Beobrand did not answer. He hoped Halinard was right and they would be safe. But as he turned away from the pale, feverish face of his son-in-law and pulled Sceadugenga's huge head around to face once more the red fire of the setting sun, he shuddered. Something was not right here. Why were Mercians attacking so deep within Bernicia? How had they passed through Deira without being apprehended?

Cynan kicked his horse into a canter, calling out to the waiting warriors that they were to ride again. Beobrand followed him, allowing Sceadugenga to carry him without guidance. His gesithas were seasoned warriors, well-drilled and disciplined, and they did not grumble as the column began to move once more.

Beobrand peered into the distance. Thickets of beech stood out starkly against the molten iron glow of the sky, deep shadows puddling beneath them. Soon, they had settled back into the rhythm of pursuit. The thrum of hooves, the jangle of harnesses and the slap of linden boards against broad backs.

When Halinard and Brinin had galloped back from Leofing's hall, they had told of no more than ten men, Mercians by their account. After a brief skirmish, in which Brinin had slain one of them, the Mercians had fled westward.

They could not be very far ahead and Beobrand's warband's mounts were fresh, only recently having left Ubbanford. They had been on their way south to the borderlands, where they'd expected to lend their numbers to those of Deiran warbands, acting as a deterrent to summer raids for cattle from Mercia.

He pushed the worries about Brinin from his mind. Halinard would tend to him and there was nothing more that Beobrand could do for him now. He should be pleased that they had stumbled on these Mercians. They were on familiar territory, on fresh horses, and they outnumbered their foe.

So why was he unable to shake the unnerving feeling that despite all this, and the comforting warmth of the sun on his face, he was leading his men towards darkness and death?

Chapter 2

Beobrand trudged over to where Fraomar was guarding the horses. The dew from the long grass soaked his leg bindings. The horses were tethered and calm, dipping their heads to tear at the lush grass.

He peered toward the western horizon where the land climbed to a rocky outcrop. A buzzard soared above the hill, circling with languid grace on the warm air that rose from the sun-drenched earth below.

"Where are they?" Beobrand whispered to himself.

Before dawn, fearing an ambush and trusting to his instincts, he had sent Attor and Cynan to scout ahead. It shouldn't be difficult to follow the Mercians, as they seemed to have decided to stick to the old track that led into the south and west. But should they deviate from the path, Attor could track any creature over all types of terrain. He would not lose them. Beobrand had given them strict instructions not to approach their quarry. He sensed that the enemy was near and he did not want to ride recklessly into a trap.

They had made camp in a gully where they were sheltered from the path by a stand of alder. They had ridden long into the gathering dusk before eventually accepting, when the last light had bled out of the sky, that they would not catch their quarry that night. They had lit no fire and the men had whispered in the darkness, chewing on their dried beef and sipping water from their leather flasks. There had been no clouds and the night was still and cold. Beobrand had been unable to sleep. Wrapping himself in his cloak, he had closed his eyes, but his mind had been in turmoil.

There was much about this Mercian raid that unnerved him. It was unusual for their enemies to strike this far into Bernicia. The borderlands of Deira, where the barren peaks of the Pecsætna rose, windswept and forbidding – that was where the Mercians would risk a foray to steal cattle. Not north of the Wall.

Bitter memories of another Mercian incursion beat like bat wings in his mind. He remembered the destruction and death left after Halga's raid. In the wake of that attack many of Beobrand's folk had been slain. Reaghan had been one of those who had lost her life, struck down by a treacherous Mercian blade. Beobrand sighed in the darkness to think of her. Reaghan had been a good woman, and what had he given her? In the end, like so many others in his life, she had died blood-soaked and in agony.

She had been dead for years now and as always when he thought of her, he felt a gnawing sense of guilt. He did not miss her; could barely conjure up the image of her, apart from a vague recollection of thick auburn hair and her pale fragile form. She had cared for him and warmed his bed for years and yet all he had given her was her freedom from thralldom. Could he have provided more?

Pushing thoughts of Reaghan from his mind, he scanned the land to the west, shielding his eyes with his hand. The sun was high in the sky already. They had been waiting a long time and the uncertainty of what might be happening over those hills was stretching Beobrand's nerves to the limit.

"Gods," he said, "where are they?" He had not expected Attor and Cynan to take so long, and with each passing moment he felt the chance ebbing away of catching the Mercians who had injured Brinin and razed Leofing's hall.

"I am sure they will be back soon," said Fraomar.

Beobrand started. He had not expected an answer to his question and he smiled ruefully at the young warrior.

"The horses are all saddled and ready?" he asked, in an attempt to hide his nervousness. This waiting, relying on others to put themselves at risk for him, this was the worst part of leading men. Bassus always told him, "You can't do everything yourself. And the men need their hlaford alive. If you go running into every fray, you will sooner or later get yourself killed and warriors without lords are not happy men." Beobrand spat. Bassus' words were true, but he would never be content to command his men to fight for him, if he were not willing to take up shield and sword himself.

"The horses are ready, lord," Fraomar said, with a twisted smile. "Just as they were the last time you asked."

Beobrand snorted. He knew he made the men nervous with his pacing, but he could not shift the feeling that something was amiss. He wondered how Brinin and Halinard fared. And were Cynan and Attor even now engaged in a fight with the Mercians they had pursued?

"Good," he said, "you have done well."

He gazed up at the bright sky. The morning haze had burnt away and the sun would soon be at its zenith. Unable to contain his anxiety any longer, Beobrand raised his voice and shouted, "Time to mount up, men. I had expected Cynan and Attor to return before now. Let us ride and see what we can find."

His gesithas, evidently as anxious as he to find out what had befallen their comrades, jumped to their feet. They quickly slung rolled blankets and bags behind saddles, and pulled themselves up onto their waiting mounts. Beobrand took Sceadugenga's reins from Fraomar and swung himself up onto the stallion's back.

"We ride with caution," he said, surveying the sombre faces of the men around him. "Something is wrong here. If evil has betided Cynan and Attor, we will avenge them." There was a grumble of anger at the thought and Beobrand felt a sudden stab of fear, as if having said the words gave them heft, made the possibility more real. He reached for the Thunor's hammer amulet at his throat and spat into the dew-sparkled grass.

It felt good to be moving and Beobrand welcomed the breeze on his face as he led the horsemen out from the shadow of the alders and up the steep bank to the track and its cracked and crumbling earth and pebbles.

They had ridden for only a matter of moments when relief flooded through him.

Two riders crested the hill to the west. They were riding hard and they were too distant for him to make out their faces, but he recognised Cynan's bay mare. He spurred Sceadugenga forward, his gesithas in his wake. The warband and the two outriders met in a cloud of dust beneath the searing summer sun at the foot of the slope.

"I thought you told us to return before midday," Cynan said, grinning. "The sun is not at its zenith and yet we find you on the move."

"We were getting bored waiting," Beobrand said, returning Cynan's smile with a levity he did not feel. "So, what have you seen? Did you catch up with the Mercians?"

"You could say that," Attor said, reining in his steed. The flanks of both horses were lathered in sweat. Cynan unstoppered a flask and drank deeply.

"Tell me," Beobrand said.

"We picked up their tracks easily when they left the path," Attor replied. "They were riding fast and made no attempt to hide their sign. What we found in the vale of the Irthin explained why."

"What did you find in the valley?"

"This was no mere raiding party, lord," Cynan said, taking up the story from Attor and handing the slim scout the flask of water. "We were warned of their presence by the smoke of many fires. We saw them from far afield and at first we thought perhaps they had put more steadings to the flames, but there are no halls or farms thereabouts."

"What made the smoke?"

"A warhost," Cynan said, all trace of humour gone from his voice now. "We left the horses and climbed the bluff where we could look down into the valley and there we saw a great company of warriors."

"Mercians?"

Cynan nodded. His face was grim.

"Hundreds of them."

Beobrand grew cold despite the heat of the day. Such a horde of warriors would have amassed for only one reason: to invade Bernicia.

"And it's worse than that," said Attor.

Beobrand frowned. What could be worse than a host of Mercian warriors on Bernician soil?

"Tell me."

"Men of Powys and Gwynedd are with them."

"You are sure of this?"

"I am certain. We saw the black lion of Powys and the white eagle of Gwynedd alongside Penda's wolf pelt banner."

"So," said Beobrand slowly, trying to make sense of what he was hearing, "the Mercians we have chased from Leofing's hall…"

"Outriders," said Attor. "From what we could see, the host was not on the move. Perhaps the attack on Leofing's hall was not planned. I do not think Penda would welcome his presence here being made known to Oswiu or his thegns."

Beobrand's head was spinning. Again he cursed Brinin for a fool. Still, perhaps it was his very impetuosity that had led them to discover this host.

"The lord of Mercia will know now that his men were

pursued," he said. "Penda will be forewarned that the element of surprise is no longer his."

Attor nodded glumly.

"I know not how it is that Penda has been able to gather his forces here, but we cannot allow him to travel further within Bernicia unchecked." Beobrand scratched the back of his head beneath his long fair hair. It was wet with sweat. Staring into the distance of the horizon, he wondered whether he merely imagined the smudge of a grey feather of smoke there.

"What would you have us do, lord?" asked Fraomar.

Beobrand turned to him. Fraomar met his gaze with an open, intelligent stare. He was a good man, quick-witted, and the rest of the gesithas looked up to him, despite being younger than most of them.

"You are to take the men, Fraomar, and check on the movements of Penda and his warhost."

"Lord," replied Fraomar, his pleasure at being given command clear on his face.

"You are to watch them, in secret, if possible. Should small bands ride out and you think you can take them, do so. If you can weaken the host in any way, do it. But I leave it to you to keep my warband intact. That means no undue risks. Watch them. Harry them, if you can. But do not throw your lives away. If they try to attack, to draw you out, you are to retreat, marking their position and the direction of travel, so that Oswiu and the fyrd can find them. You understand?"

Fraomar nodded earnestly. Beobrand trusted him to do what was needed.

"And you, lord?" asked Fraomar. "What will you do?"

"I will return with Cynan to where we left Brinin and Halinard. We shall take Brinin to Bebbanburg. The monks there can tend his wound, and I will warn King Oswiu of the approach of the Mercian and Waelisc host."

Cynan opened his mouth as if to say something, but a stern glare from Beobrand silenced him before he spoke. He nodded, his face expressionless.

"The moment Penda's host is on the move, send word," Beobrand ordered.

"To Ubbanford, lord?" asked Fraomar.

"No. I will remain at Bebbanburg while the fyrd is assembled. Send a rider there."

Beobrand turned Sceadugenga eastward and kicked the stallion into a canter. He did not notice the glance that passed between Cynan and Fraomar at his words. With a nod to the young gesith, the Waelisc warrior spurred his already tired mare after his lord.

Chapter 3

Cynan soon caught up with Beobrand. They had not travelled far. The stand of alders where they had spent the night was still in sight.

"Lord," Cynan called. "My horse needs rest."

Beobrand turned in his saddle. For an instant, his face was dark with anger, but after a heartbeat, he sighed and pulled on his reins to slow his fine black stallion.

"Must we halt?" he asked.

"Yes, lord," Cynan replied, keeping his tone meek. He knew Beobrand well. Impatience would be eating at him. Any provocation now could spark his wrath into flame. "At least for a time," he continued. "Mierawin needs water and some grain. And I will brush her down."

Cynan knew that Sceadugenga could run all day without seeming to tire, and his own steed, the mare he called Mierawin, was as fine a piece of horseflesh as could be found in Bernicia. And yet he had ridden her hard all that morning, and to push her further without respite would likely see her winded, lame, or worse.

"If we rest in the shade of the trees a while," Cynan said, "we can ride on in the afternoon and reach Halinard and Brinin before sundown."

Beobrand stared at him for a moment, and Cynan could sense his simmering ire at being slowed. Cynan met his gaze, riding easily beside him. Beobrand was no fool. He knew that to push on without thought for the horses would almost certainly see them reach their destination more slowly than if they rested Cynan's mount.

With a curse, Beobrand spat and yanked Sceadugenga's reins, guiding him back to the alders where they had camped. Glancing behind, Cynan saw a haze of dust lingering in the air over the hill. The only reminder of the passing of the warband that had disappeared over the brow of the rise and ridden into the west.

They rode into the cool shade beneath the trees and Cynan was not surprised when Beobrand slid from his saddle without a word and stalked off down to the small brook that trickled over slick pebbles in the gully. Cynan let out a slow breath, glad he would not have to contend with his lord's anger for the time being. Beobrand had ever been prone to dark moods and flares of anger, but recently things had become much worse. Ever since the attack in Eoferwic the previous year, he had been on edge. Where once he would have sat contentedly drinking, riddling and playing tafl with his gesithas, now he would often pace the length of the hall. He had also taken to more frequent rides on Sceadugenga. He would saddle the stallion himself before dawn and ride far over the hills and moors of Bernicia. He wished to be alone, Cynan knew, but he had taken it on himself to protect his lord and he always rode after him, no matter how much Beobrand protested. Cynan would follow from a distance and keep Beobrand always in sight. Beobrand often ignored him now, accepting Cynan as his shadow, and sometimes entire days would go by without them uttering a word.

Beobrand had much to concern him, Cynan knew. He had the responsibilities of a thegn. He was hlaford to the folk of Ubbanford and Stagga. And his relationship with his sworn lord, Oswiu, was troubled. There was no secret there. He had made many powerful enemies, and following the attack in Eoferwic, it appeared even those far away over the Whale Road were seeking to kill him.

In the summer after the attempt on Beobrand's life by Vulmar's servants, the seaman, Ferenbald, had sailed up the Tuidi in the sleek ship, *Saeslaga*. He bore trade goods from Cantware and Frankia: pungent incense, wax-sealed earthenware pots of sweet wine, aromatic spices, fine linen, and pottery. But more importantly, he brought tidings.

"I have been to Rodomo," he said to Beobrand in the great hall of Ubbanford. His unruly mane of hair and bushy beard gave him the appearance of a shaggy bear, rather than a man. "I did not remain long there."

"What of Feologild?" asked Beobrand. "Does he yet hold our treasure, or has the old bastard sold it all for profit?" When they had fled from Rodomo, pursued by Vulmar's warriors and pirates, they had left behind a dragon's hoard of gold and silver in the warehouse of Feologild, a merchant from Cantware.

"Feologild did not sell your treasure, Beobrand," Ferenbald said, but despite what should have been good news, his features did not reflect pleasure. He frowned and cast his gaze downward. He sighed. "Feologild is dead. Accused of treason, he was tried and found guilty. He was executed publicly before the steps of Our Lady of the Assumption in Rodomo."

Cynan could remember clearly Beobrand's expression at hearing this. His brow had knitted, his jaw clenched. His face was thunder and his knuckles had grown white where he had gripped his drinking horn with savage fury.

"Vulmar's doing," Beobrand said, his tone dripping venom. It was a statement, not a question.

"Aye, and there is more," Ferenbald said. "You must guard against a murderer's blade, my friend. Vulmar has offered a man's weight in silver for your head. You are far from Frankia, it is true, but for that prize many men would risk sailing north. You must be careful."

"I always am," Beobrand said, and after a brief moment of silence, without warning, all the men within the hall laughed as one. If there was one thing the lord of Ubbanford was not, it was careful.

When the mirth subsided, Beobrand shrugged.

"Well, when I am not careful, I am lucky. Isn't that what they say? I will not be killed by some Frankish ruffian come to claim a reward for my death. And perhaps you need a faster ship, Ferenbald."

The skipper from Cantware had frowned. The *Saeslaga* was high-prowed, with curving strakes. It was a beautiful vessel and as fast a wave-steed as had ever sailed.

"Indeed?" he asked. "How so?"

"Your tidings are a month too late."

"You knew of Feologild's death?"

Beobrand shook his head.

"No, but five of Vulmar's thugs tried to slay me in Eostremonath in Eoferwic. Next time, they had better send a dozen."

The men had clapped and cheered at their lord's bravado, but Cynan had slept but lightly these last months and he did not allow Beobrand to stray far from his side.

Jumping to the ground, Cynan tethered both horses. He loosened Sceadugenga's girth and then set about currying Mierawin. He removed her saddle and brushed her sides with handfuls of long grass, cleaning away the foaming sweat from her flanks. The animal's skin quivered and trembled beneath his touch.

Cynan was tense. The sight of Penda's host had unsettled him. He had stood in many shieldwalls and was not one to frighten easily. But he had never before faced such a horde. The camp had thronged with hundreds of Mercian and Waelisc warriors. Campfires smoked lazily and banners hung lank in the still air. Attor had said it was a smaller force than they had faced at Maserfelth, but Cynan did not know whether to believe him.

Surely no larger army had ever been assembled. But the mention of Maserfelth, where Oswald had fallen and Northumbria had suffered a terrible defeat, filled him with sadness and dismay. He had missed the battle and still wondered whether things might have gone differently if he had been there. Bassus scoffed at him when he'd mentioned this to him once after they had both drunk too much mead.

"So you think that you alone would have changed the course of the battle where so many others failed?" Bassus' tone had been incredulous.

"Not alone," Cynan stammered. "Bearn was with me. And a score of others... If we could have fought in the shieldwall at Maserfelth, perhaps Oswald would yet live. Maybe Acennan..." He trailed off then, thinking of the man who had trained him to fight. Acennan had been like a father to him, or an older brother. Cynan had loved him as if he were kin and his loss in the aftermath of Maserfelth had weighed heavily on him.

"You are a good warrior, Cynan," Bassus said, refilling both of their drinking horns with the strong mead that Odelyna brewed. "Perhaps you are even a great warrior, but you cannot blame yourself for what takes place in your absence. Such pride is foolishness. You are but a man." He grinned. "And a damned Waelisc one at that!"

Cynan had laughed dutifully at the jibe about his heritage. He knew Bassus meant nothing by his words, but still they stung. Whenever one of the gesithas insulted the Waelisc, Cynan would bite his tongue, choking back the words he wished to shout at them. Surely each man should be judged on his actions, his honour, his oaths. He had ever been faithful to his oath-sworn lord and had stood steadfast in battle, shield to shield with his Black Shield brothers, and still they would jeer at his accent, at the sing-song lilt of his voice.

"To imagine what might have been is enough to drive a man mad," Bassus went on, before taking a great swig of mead. "You can only walk down one path, no matter how many forks you pass in the road. You can never go back and retrace your steps. To think of what you might have missed along the way is foolish."

Cynan finished rubbing Mierawin's flanks and fetched some oats from his saddlebags. He placed some in his helm and offered them to the horse, who dipped her nose into the iron receptacle and snuffled at the contents.

Despite the wisdom of Bassus' words, Cynan often found himself wondering what his life might have been like if he had taken different decisions. He did not regret following Beobrand and Acennan all those years ago. They'd offered him a new life, and he had been accepted and respected as a gesith of Bernicia in a way he could never have dreamed of when he was a thrall in Grimbold's hall.

But one moment plagued his memories. And he was unable to prevent himself from entertaining dreams of what might have been. He recalled the sight of Sulis walking away from him, disappearing into the gloaming of dusk. She had not looked back and he still remembered keenly the sense of loss he'd felt as the Mercian woman, so fragile and broken from what had taken place, had touched his cheek and called him a fool, before walking out of his life. He had thought then about chasing after her, building a life away from Beobrand and his new family of gesithas. But he had not. Cynan knew then what he yet understood. He could not turn away from the oath he had sworn; could not forsake Beobrand, the lord of Ubbanford, the sometimes brutal man who had given him everything.

When they had discovered Sulis, Beobrand could have taken Cynan's life. Gods, he would have been within his rights to do so as Cynan had placed himself between his lord and the trembling thrall woman, refusing to allow Beobrand to mete out justice. And yet, Beobrand had stayed his hand and allowed Cynan to remain with him even after the Waelisc gesith had defied him.

Cynan wondered for how long Sulis' face would haunt his memories. They had never been lovers, but her fragile toughness had entranced him, and the weft of her had woven itself into his thoughts and dreams.

Beobrand was trudging up from the stream. The cloud of ire had lifted and he offered Cynan a thin smile. Cynan nodded, leading the horses down to drink.

Sulis had cast some secret spell on him so that he could not forget her. It was a kind of madness. Or magic, perhaps. But as Beobrand approached, Cynan knew he was not alone in such folly. The men whispered about Beobrand's obsession, but were too nervous of his infamous fury to broach the subject. And yet it was no secret amongst them that they had visited Bebbanburg more frequently of late than ever before. Where Beobrand once was content to stay away from the royal household, now he made every effort to visit. He said it was to see his son, Octa, who was fostered by the king, but they all knew there was another reason. One with golden hair and swaying hips. The allure was evident for all men to see, and yet so was the danger. They feared for their lord and they spoke in worried whispers about what would befall them, should the king discover that which was so clear to any who looked.

Sceadugenga snorted, shaking his mane. Beobrand reached out his mutilated left hand and stroked the stallion's soft nose.

"How long until we can be on our way?" he asked.

Cynan paused a moment, pondering the possibilities.

"After the horses are watered, let us wait a while more. We will have time to reach Halinard and Brinin before nightfall. If Brinin is no worse, we should make good time tomorrow."

Beobrand said nothing, but took Sceadugenga's reins and followed Cynan down to the stream. It was cool by the water, the burbling of the brook soothing. The horses lowered their snouts, drinking thirstily. After a time, Cynan pulled Mierawin up from the burn. Too much of the cold water at once could cause the horse to sicken.

"What is it you would say to me?" Beobrand said, breaking the silence that had fallen between them.

"Lord?" Cynan was ever wary around Beobrand. He was all too aware of how quickly a misplaced word could cause his anger to flare.

"You have wanted to say something to me for some time," Beobrand said. "What is it?"

Cynan sighed. He turned, leading Mierawin back to the trees. It was easier to speak when not looking Beobrand in the eye.

"We are heading to Bebbanburg?"

"You know this to be true. We must inform the king of what we have discovered. The fyrd must be summoned."

"But is the king not in Caer Luel?" Oswiu, with a large retinue of thegns and gesithas, had travelled west the previous month to visit the royal vills and to collect tribute. The journey to Caer Luel was long and there had been no sign of the king's return.

"Of course. You speak true," Beobrand replied. Cynan thought he detected a slight hesitation in his words. "And yet travel to Bebbanburg we must. Ethelwin is there. He will summon the fyrd. And lead the levies into battle, if it comes to that, which I fear it will. Penda is never one to leave without a fight."

Cynan tethered Mierawin to a low branch, leaving enough slack in the reins for the animal to crop the grass in the dappled shade.

"Oh yes, Ethelwin," he said. "The warmaster. Of course."

"What is it you wish to say, Cynan?" Beobrand asked, his voice low and cold. "Speak plainly, man. We are alone here."

"All I am saying, lord, is that there is much at stake. For you, for us all. For Bernicia. With Penda marching once more, there will be no time for distractions."

He risked looking at Beobrand and was met with an icy glare, the blue eyes glinting angrily.

"I know my duty, Cynan," Beobrand spat. "Make sure you know yours."

Cynan held Beobrand's gaze.

"Just be careful, lord. I beseech you."

"You know me," Beobrand said, a half-smile playing on his lips. "I am always careful."

Chapter 4

Seeing the crag of Bebbanburg rising over the North Sea before them, Beobrand could hold himself back no longer.

"See that Brinin is tended to as soon as you arrive," he said to Halinard and Cynan. His daughter's husband would recover, he was sure. The young man was still weak, and in pain, but Halinard had seen to his wound while they had awaited Beobrand's return. The Frank had boiled water and cleaned the cut, binding it with clean cloths and changing them frequently, as they had seen the monks of Lindisfarena do. The gash was still raw and open, but it had none of the stench that came after becoming elf-shot.

Beobrand swept his gaze across the three men. Brinin's face was pale and Beobrand felt a flash of anger at having been held back by the injured youth. Without him slowing them down, they could have reached Bebbanburg a day, or perhaps even two, earlier.

Without waiting for a reply from his companions, he touched his heels to Sceadugenga's flanks and the horse bounded forward, as if the animal shared its rider's impatience. A cloud of birds rose noisily from the land either side of the road, as his passing disturbed them from their feeding.

The wind on his cheeks carried the chill of the sea. His eyes watered and it was all he could do not to let out a whoop of joy at the sensation of speed and freedom as Sceadugenga bore him effortlessly toward the seat of the kings of Bernicia. No sooner had the feeling of happiness come upon him than it was doused with a wave of anger. Not at Brinin for disobeying his order and for slowing their progress. And not at Cynan for his sly, knowing looks and the constant judgement Beobrand could sense in the Waelisc man's eyes. No. The ire that rolled through him, making his hands tremble with its ferocity, was directed inward.

He should have sent other riders to the fortress. To do so, and to remain with his warband, would have been the wisest decision. What would he do here while the fyrd was called? His was not a mind best suited to planning and organisation. He was a man of action. He should have stayed with his gesithas and led them. Instead, he had left Fraomar in charge. The young warrior was competent and capable, and Beobrand trusted him. And yet he knew the men, and therefore the kingdom, would have been safer if he had stayed with his warband to watch Penda's movements.

Sceadugenga's hooves thrummed on the hard-packed earth that would quickly turn to a quagmire after the next heavy rain. The fortress loomed above him, the cluster of buildings atop the rock encircled with a stout timber palisade. Figures were visible on the ramparts. Men were pointing. He had been spotted. A black and red banner fluttered in the brisk breeze that seemed always to blow in from the slate-grey expanse of the sea. Squinting at the flapping cloth, Beobrand made out a black horned bull's head on a field of red. Fordraed's standard. Beobrand frowned, his mood darkening yet further.

He scanned the walls of the fortress as he approached, searching for one face in particular. Cursing to himself, he spat sideways into the wind that rushed past his speeding mount.

Gods, what a fool he was. She was hardly going to be standing on the palisade staring out awaiting his arrival. How had it come to this? He had known Eanflæd since she was a girl. To think that now she filled his mind so completely. It was like a curse. He could not push her from his thoughts and his dreams, no matter how much he tried. Weeks would pass and just when he was beginning to believe he could be done with this obsession, he would find himself riding to Bebbanburg again. Once there, he was always happy to see Octa. The boy had grown tall and strong and would be a man soon. But it was the fleeting moments of conversation with the queen that he cherished; the brief looks over the board in the great hall that he would recall before sleep claimed him at night. Not since he had escorted Eanflæd to the opening of the monastery at Hereteu had they truly been alone, but the memory of the kiss they had shared was a madness. He was like a moonstruck youth and could think of nothing else.

How the gods must be laughing. To have him so helplessly besotted with one who not only belonged to another man, but to Oswiu no less, his oath-sworn lord and his king. Oswiu took great pleasure in forcing Beobrand to serve him. It was no accident that Octa was under the king's protection. With Beobrand's son fostered in his household, Oswiu was able to command Beobrand to do his bidding, and the lord of Ubbanford was a dutiful hound. But if Oswiu should discover the attraction between his queen and Beobrand, he was certain the king's wrath would be terrible. He had seen the man's cruelty before.

And that is why nothing could transpire between them. There had been the briefest of kisses, the occasional flirtatious glance, the brushing of a hand when passing the Waes Hael cup. And there could be no more.

He rode up to the gates, Sceadugenga's hooves clattering and echoing from the high walls. Beobrand glanced upward and his stomach lurched. Looking down from the gate rampart was Eanflæd, daughter of Edwin, wife of Oswiu. Queen of Bernicia. Her head was covered in a plain wimple, but a lock of her golden hair had escaped and fluttered about her face. Her skin was the hue of pearls and as smooth. The rosebuds of her lips parted in a broad smile when she saw him. She raised her hand, and Beobrand could think of nothing save how much he desired to feel the touch of that hand against his. To press his mouth to hers, her body against him. He returned her salute, slowing Sceadugenga to a high-stepping trot as they neared the gates, which were swinging open.

The vision of the queen was lost to him as he passed into the shadow of the fortress.

She had come to welcome him.

His mouth grew dry. War would be upon them soon. Fraomar might already be fighting against Penda and his Waelisc allies. By Woden, his men might already be dead. He should have stayed with them. To come here was rash. Stupid.

But all he could think of was Eanflæd's face, her smile, her raised hand. She had come to welcome him to Bebbanburg and Oswiu King was far away.

It was madness, he knew. And yet, what man could fight against his wyrd? At the glimpse of her, all his doubts and fears burnt away in the flames of her beauty. Wyrd was inexorable and as he leaped from Sceadugenga's back, throwing the reins to a waiting hostler, he turned and watched Eanflæd descend the steps that led to the gate tower.

The shape of her slender legs was clear beneath her dress as the wind pressed the linen against her form. She lifted the hem to avoid tripping on the fabric, and Beobrand's breath caught in his throat as he saw a flash of white ankle. She offered him another smile.

It was madness. But there was no escaping one's wyrd, no matter how cruel.

Beobrand drew in a deep breath of the salty sea air and, with a sigh of resignation, he stepped forward to greet his queen.

Chapter 5

"You are certain that the force you saw was Penda's?"

Fordraed's jowls quivered as he spoke. He peered down his nose at Beobrand, his lip curled in disdain. Cynan tensed. The set of his lord's shoulders told him of Beobrand's anger and Cynan was worried he would lose control of his emotions. Beobrand loathed Fordraed and had struck him in the past.

"I did not see the warhost," replied Beobrand, his voice flat, "but—"

Fordraed cut him off with a raised hand.

"Oh yes, so you said. Just like at Maserfelth. One whiff of the enemy and you turn and run."

A couple of the men seated at the high table sniggered. Most looked on in silence. Cynan took a step forward. Beobrand's battle-fame was well-known and undisputed, and for one such as Fordraed to accuse him of cowardice rankled. It might well goad Beobrand into some rash action he would not be able to walk away from. Cynan drew in a deep breath. The air was warm and still. The great hall of Bebbanburg smelt of fresh-cut rushes and the cold ashes on the hearth. The afternoon was hot and the fire would not be lit until the sun was setting. The huge doors of the hall were open, letting in streams of light and a welcome draught that blew through the building. On the breeze wafted the smell of roasting meat and freshly brewed ale. There were many to be fed and Cynan did not envy the servants and thralls labouring inside the swelter of the cookhouses.

For a moment, Beobrand was silent. He held Fordraed's gaze without blinking. When he spoke at last, his tone was as cool and sharp as split slate.

"I have come here to warn the warmaster of Bernicia that Penda is on the march with a host of Mercians and Waelisc. They are already deep within our lands. I do not come to fight with you, Fordraed. But know this," he lowered his voice to barely a whisper, "if you again call me a craven, you must be ready to back up your words with a sword. Insult me again at your peril."

"Ethelwin is the warmaster," said Fordraed, "but the king has left me in charge of Bebbanburg in his stead. I speak with his voice. Do not threaten me, Beobrand of Ubbanford."

"My words to you are no idle threat, Fordraed. If you cross me, I will gut you like a salmon and Bernicia's fyrd will be no weaker for the loss of the lord of Morðpæð."

Fordraed's face grew crimson and for a moment Cynan thought the fat lord would stand and confront Beobrand. Cynan tensed, readying himself to leap to his lord's aid. Should it come to it, he knew Beobrand would do what he had said. Fordraed was a toad and he remembered with pleasure watching Beobrand punching the man. It was Fordraed who had abused Sulis, and he had mistreated many other women in his time. They had heard tell that he beat his wife, Edlyn, too and it was not only Beobrand who itched for the opportunity to strike the brute again.

Heremod, a burly warrior with plaited beard, began to rise to his feet. He was Fordraed's man and clearly meant to defend his lord's honour.

Cynan could feel the insanity of battle lust creeping into his mind. He was ready for a fight; would welcome the release from this tension. And if he were able to land a blow on Fordraed's fat face, he would relish it.

But it was not Fordraed, nor Heremod, who stood, but Ethelwin. Placing a placatory hand on Heremod's shoulder, Ethelwin pushed himself to his feet. He was a solid man, thick-necked and wide-shouldered. An able man, he was a veteran of many campaigns as attested by a long scar on his forehead and the crisscrossed tracery of blade-memories on his forearms. His nose was twisted and broad where it had been broken and when he opened his mouth to speak, there were several gaps where teeth had been dislodged in brawls.

"Brothers," he said, his voice as deep as the rumble of distant waves. "Now is a time for unity, not division." He swept his gaze across Beobrand, Cynan, Fordraed and Heremod. "I may not be lord here, but I am Oswiu's warmaster and it seems that war is upon us. It is my duty to protect the kingdom. So, you will put aside your petty squabbles as we stand against our old enemy, Penda."

Beobrand said nothing. Cynan did not breathe. Fordraed glowered at Ethelwin, then gave a curt nod.

"Good," said Ethelwin, seemingly satisfied. "Now, Lord Beobrand, tell us again of the size of the force your men saw, and where they are now."

And so Beobrand once more recounted the tale of how they had stumbled upon the Mercians attacking Leofing's hall, the pursuit and then finding the amassed host.

"And it was the Waelisc, Cynan here, who saw them?" Ethelwin asked.

"Aye," replied Beobrand. "Cynan, tell them what you saw."

Cynan stepped forward. He was almost as tall as Beobrand and moved with the natural grace of a warrior. He fixed Fordraed with a defiant stare, willing him to make a comment about his accent or his forebears. But the portly lord did not speak and looked away. Cynan smirked at the small victory.

"It is as my lord has said." Cynan was suddenly very aware of all the eyes in the hall on him. The lilting accent of his words sounded more pronounced than normal to his ears. His face grew hot as he spoke. "There were many of them. Several score. Hundreds, I would say. Attor, who was at Maserfelth, said there were fewer than at that great battle, but this was no small warband or raiding party. We saw banners of Powys, Gwynedd and Mercia."

Ethelwin sighed. Turning to one of the door wards, he said, "Send out riders to all the thegns and ealdormen of Bernicia. They are to bring their men to the fyrd. We will assemble our host at Hefenfelth five days hence. From there we will march to intercept Penda and his pack of Waelisc curs."

Cynan bridled at the insult directed at the people to whom he had been born, but he said nothing.

"Five days may prove too long," Beobrand said. Cynan noticed that he glanced over to where Eanflæd sat demurely. Her expression did not change, but was there a slight hesitation in Beobrand's voice?

"It is the best we can do, Beobrand," replied Ethelwin. "But I will send out a small force of riders to meet with your warband. They will be glad of the extra bodies should Penda move and it comes to a fight before the fyrd can be assembled. Would you lead my horsemen to your gesithas?"

Beobrand opened his mouth to answer, then closed it. Again he flicked a glance at the queen and Cynan could sense the conflict within him. Beobrand had talked to him of his duty. Cynan wondered whether the sight of the young queen from Cantware might not have blinded Beobrand to his own.

"Cynan is the better rider, Lord Ethelwin," Beobrand said. "And he knows the exact location of Penda's host. Cynan should lead your men westward and I will help you to guide the fyrd when it has gathered."

Ethelwin raised his eyebrows, evidently not expecting this answer.

"Very well," the warmaster said. "Cynan, rest and seek out a fresh mount from the stables. You will lead a dozen of my men at dawn."

Cynan bowed his head. He would go to the stables, but he would not take another mount. He would see that Mierawin was well-fed and groomed. With a night's rest, the mare would be a match for any of the horses in Bebbanburg.

He glanced at Beobrand, wondering whether the turmoil he felt was clear on his face, but his lord was not looking in his direction. Beobrand's gaze was fixed on Eanflæd. With a sigh, Cynan turned and strode from the hall.

The bright sunshine and warmth of the day did nothing to lift his spirits as he walked towards the stables.

Chapter 6

After imparting his tidings to Ethelwin and Fordraed, Beobrand visited Brinin. Halinard had come to the great hall and Beobrand followed the Frank out into the heat of the afternoon sun. Together they strode across the courtyard to where Brinin was being tended by one of the womenfolk in a small room near the stables. The clump of the horses' hooves and the calls of the hostlers and thralls tending the beasts were loud in the still summer air. No sea breeze reached this corner of the fortress and the reek of dung, hay, dust and leather was heavy in their nostrils as they approached the hut where Halinard had left Brinin.

A grey-haired woman, bent and twisted with age, rose from beside the cot where Brinin lay. Beobrand recognised her. She had saved his life many years before when he had lost his two fingers in the duel with Hengist. At the sight of her, his left hand throbbed and the memory of Sunniva filled his mind suddenly, without warning. For a moment, he could not breathe, such was the force of the vision. It had been a long time since he had dreamed of her, or even remembered her face clearly. But she had sat by his bedside as he had lain, feverish and on the verge of death. And it was Sunniva who had brought this old woman to see if she would be able to draw the poison from his wounds. The healer had worked her magic with poultices and wyrts and Beobrand had lived. He sighed at the memory. He should have died many times over, and yet it was the beautiful Sunniva who had been taken from middle earth.

The woman stepped forward on spindly unstable legs, shielding her eyes against the glare from the doorway. The vision of Sunniva fled like mist in a wind and her memory was replaced by a deep gnawing sense of loss.

"Ah, Lord Beobrand," rasped the woman. "So the boy is one of yours, after all. I had thought so, but you can never trust the likes of him." She indicated Halinard with a dismissive nod of her wispy-haired head.

"The likes of him?" enquired Beobrand.

"A Frank. A stranger. A Waelisc. I could barely understand a word he was saying, and the gods alone know what thoughts are in his black heart."

"Enough," snapped Beobrand. "This man has sworn his oath to me and has proven himself loyal. I will hear no ill spoke of him or any of my gesithas."

The woman sniffed, clearly unconvinced by Beobrand's words.

"I know you to be a skilled healer," Beobrand continued, his tone softer now, "and I will pay you handsomely for your care, but say no more against this man, or any other in my warband. To insult them is to insult me, and I am sure you would not mean to do such a thing."

He raised himself to his full height, towering over the hunched woman. She seemed unperturbed, merely shaking her head and offering a grin that showed many gaps between her few yellowing teeth.

"You were ever a proud one," she chuckled. "And I am sure you no more mean to threaten me than I meant to insult you. Now," she smiled slyly, "show me that with which you will pay me."

Beobrand said nothing as he fished out a chunk of hacksilver as long and thick as his thumb. He weighed it in his palm for a heartbeat, allowing her to see it in the light streaming in from outside. He placed the silver in her outstretched palm.

She swallowed, her stringy neck bobbing.

"The boy will recover, lord," she said, "but he is weak and tired. I have given him a draught of betony and mandragora and he is already sleeping deeply." Brinin's face was pallid but serene, and his chest rose and fell slowly and rhythmically. "Rest is what he needs most of all, lord. Under my care, no further harm will befall him and he will be up and about soon enough."

As Beobrand stepped out of the gloom, leaving Brinin to the care of the crone, Bebbanburg's gates were dragged open with a grating rasp. A moment later many riders clattered into the courtyard. Clenching his fists, Beobrand scanned the faces of the richly dressed horsemen. Could it be that Oswiu had returned already? Beobrand's stomach churned at the thought. The arrival of Oswiu's retinue of warriors would be welcome in the coming battle, and yet Beobrand could not hide his disappointment.

But it would be good to see Octa. Beobrand's son rode with the king, travelling the land and learning the ways of a thegn. He would be a man soon and Beobrand missed him. He scanned the incoming riders for a glimpse of the boy. The thought of seeing Octa filled him with unease. The few times they met now, it always felt as though his son was a stranger to him. There would be polite conversation between them and little more. Beobrand scowled. Something else he had failed at.

Halinard, standing beside him and shielding his eyes from the brilliance of the sun, asked, "Who they are?"

Beobrand hesitated, seeking out the features of the king of Bernicia. But it was not Oswiu's face he found in the throng of horsemen dismounting noisily in the courtyard. The men all seemed intent on speaking to one rider in particular. He was a tall man, riding a fine white horse, and he smiled broadly to the boy who took his horse's reins. Beside him, a shorter man, strongly built and bearded, leaped from his saddle. With a start, Beobrand recognised both men. At the same moment, the shorter man noticed Beobrand and raised his hand.

"Lord Beobrand," he shouted, his voice carrying over the hubbub of men and horses. "Well met!"

Beobrand felt a surge of relief.

"Wulfstan," he called, "it is good to see you. Though what brings you to Bebbanburg?"

Wulfstan pushed through the men to where Beobrand and Halinard stood.

"Not what, but who," he said. He laughed at Beobrand's quizzical expression. "I ride where my lord King Oswine commands."

"And why come here now?" Beobrand asked.

"I thought you said you were pleased to see me," replied Wulfstan, feigning an expression of sorrow. Unable to keep up the pretence for more than a heartbeat, he guffawed. "Oswine came to see Aidan. He wished to discuss the founding of new minsters in Deira. We have been on Lindisfarena a sennight. Today we finally were allowed a day of enjoyment. God knows we needed it after all those days cooped up with the monks."

Beobrand nodded, trying to keep up with the Deiran thegn's fast words.

"So what is it you have done today?" he asked.

"Why, today the king has led us all in a hunt. We brought down a stag and a hind, so there will be meat for the feast tonight."

Even as he spoke, Beobrand saw bondsmen leading in mules laden with the carcasses of the beasts slain in the hunt.

Clearly a feast had been planned in honour of the Deiran king, before Beobrand had ridden to Bebbanburg with his dire tidings. And despite the sombre mood that had fallen on the people of Bebbanburg, the venison was soon sizzling on spits over the great firepits and the fresh meat was added to the fare that had already been prepared.

That night was a strange mixture of melancholy and joy, celebration and foreboding. The hall was packed with Deirans and Bernicians, eating and talking together. There was laughter and riddles as the night progressed and ale and mead loosened tongues and relaxed tensions. But much of the talk turned to the prospect of war with Penda and his Waelisc allies.

Beobrand sat alongside Wulfstan on one of the higher tables, but too far from Fordraed, Ethelwin and Eanflæd to hear their conversations. The queen sat beside her cousin, Oswine, and they leaned in close, talking earnestly. Eanflæd gazed raptly into her cousin's dark eyes and whenever Beobrand glanced in their direction he felt a stab of jealousy. The emotion was foolish, he knew. Eanflæd was another's wife and the man she talked to was her kinsman. What right did Beobrand have to feel anything? He had no claim to her, and yet he could not rid himself of the pangs of envy at her closeness to the handsome king of Deira.

The queen never once looked in his direction, which did nothing to lighten his mood. And on one of the benches further down the hall, he could not help but notice the dark glares he received from Cynan. As the night wore on, Beobrand drank more mead than was wise and found himself falling into a gloomy humour.

He was not the only one to be so afflicted. There were many serious faces amongst the diners that night. And none seemed more downcast than the usually placid and kindly Bishop of Lindisfarena. The old Hibernian, Aidan, had walked across the mudflats from the holy island at low tide with a small contingent of monks, including Beobrand's old friend, Coenred. They had come for the planned feast, to share in the abundance of the land and to bid farewell to the pious king of Deira, whom men knew Aidan favoured highly.

Beobrand liked Aidan. The old monk had always been good to him, treating his folk with kindness and offering practical, as well as spiritual, support. It was Aidan who had convinced Beobrand to build a church at Ubbanford for the people to shelter in when the monks and priests came to preach there. The bishop was a good man, and it pained Beobrand to see him so disheartened. He watched as Coenred moved close to the bishop and for a long while they whispered. Coenred frowned, shaking his head, but it seemed to Beobrand that the older man would weep. His mouth was downturned, his eyes glistening.

Sweat beaded Beobrand's brow, and he swiped at it with his forearm. The hall was sweltering. The doors were yet open, but the cool of the night did little to bring down the temperature inside.

"It is warm enough that we will manage without anyone to warm our beds tonight, eh, Beobrand?" Wulfstan laughed before draining his horn of ale and holding it out to a young thrall, who promptly refilled it from an earthenware jug. The girl was young and comely, and Wulfstan watched her appreciatively as she hurried away to fill another thegn's cup. "Still, I can think of some things worth sweating a little for. Am I right?"

The Deiran slapped Beobrand on the shoulder. Beobrand regarded him sharply. Had Wulfstan seen the way he looked at Eanflæd? But there was no indication of a hidden meaning in his words. The Deiran's face was open and guileless. Beobrand forced a smile and sipped at his mead.

Seeing Coenred rising from his place beside the morose Aidan, Beobrand pushed himself up and intercepted his friend.

"How do you fare, Beo?" Coenred asked. "Those wounds giving you any trouble?" He was referring to the injuries he had treated in Eoferwic the year before.

Beobrand shook his head.

"The scars are a bit tight. They sometimes hurt when I stretch, but the wounds have healed well. Thanks to you."

"Thanks to the Lord," Coenred corrected.

"Heading outside?" Beobrand asked.

Coenred nodded.

"I'll join you," Beobrand said. "I need a piss."

The night air was still warm, but the relative coolness after the fug of the interior was welcome. The sweat on his neck began to cool and Beobrand shuddered. The stars above Bebbanburg glimmered like pearls cast on a silken cloak of darkest purple.

"What ails Aidan?" he asked.

Coenred gave him a sidelong look before answering.

"The bishop is hale. He is old, but he suffers from no illness. Thank the Lord."

"He seemed content when he arrived, but his mood has soured and I thought he might weep earlier when he was talking to you. He appeared as one grieving."

"Well, he does grieve for those soon to be slain in battle with the heathen Penda." Coenred's voice trailed off.

"There is something else?"

Coenred sighed.

"I fear you would not comprehend that which has upset the bishop."

Beobrand smiled in the gloom.

"I think you of all people know that I am not incapable of feelings, Coenred."

They walked on in silence towards the midden.

In the distance before them, the sound of waves rolling in wafted to them on the light breeze. The rumble of conversations from the hall filled the darkness behind them.

"I am sorry, Beo," Coenred said, his voice quiet. "I meant nothing by my words. It is just that it concerns King Oswine and Bishop Aidan. The Bishop has become filled with sadness."

"But I thought he had been cheered by Oswine's words earlier."

Beobrand had witnessed the conversation between the two shortly after the monks had arrived from Lindisfarena. Seeing that Aidan, white-haired and bowed with age, had walked across the mudflats from the island and then trudged up the steep steps to the fortress, the king of Deira had been outraged.

"Why did you not ride the fine horse that I gave you last Eostremonath? I gifted you the beast so that you could ride it rather than muddy your own feet and tire your legs with journeys."

Aidan had smiled.

"The gift was thoughtful and I welcomed it, but I no longer possess the stallion." Aidan's voice was heavily accented with the music of his native Hibernia, but he had learnt the tongue of the Anglisc well these last years.

"What happened to the beast?" asked Oswine. "What sickness or accident befell it? It was one of my finest horses. I selected him myself, so that he would serve you well."

"Indeed, indeed," said Aidan, nodding. "It is a fine animal, with a good temperament and a pleasant gait. But there was one who had need for him more than I."

"Who was this man who needed your horse?"

"I do not recall the man's name," replied the bishop. "I find my memory is not what it once was. But he was a wretch and his need was great. He was standing by the road begging for alms to feed himself and his family. How could I ride by when this ceorl was so desperately poor?"

Beobrand recalled clearly seeing Oswine's features become clouded. To give away such a gift was a terrible insult. As Beobrand had watched, Oswine had wrestled with his mounting anger, breathing deeply to calm himself.

"My lord bishop," he said at last, "why did you give away the royal horse that was necessary for your own use? Have we not many less valuable horses which would have been good enough for beggars, without giving away a horse that I had specially selected for your personal use?"

Aidan did not hesitate in his answer.

"What are you saying, lord king? Is this foal born of a mare more valuable to you than a child of God?"

Oswine fell silent, a frown wrinkling his handsome features. After several heartbeats, the king's face cleared. He unbuckled his sword, handing it to Wulfstan. And then, to everybody's surprise, the king of Deira dropped to his knees before Aidan.

"Forgive me, father," he said. "I will speak of this matter no more, nor will I ask you how much of our treasure you give away to God's children."

The bishop beamed at the king's words and raised him to his feet.

"Have no regrets, lord king," he said. "I know you to be a holy man and I hold you in the highest regard. Now, come sit at the feast and worry yourself no more over these things."

They reached the midden and the stench caught in their throats, so Beobrand and Coenred relieved themselves in silence. When they had drawn some distance from the latrine, Coenred spoke in a quiet voice.

"Like you, I did not understand why my bishop was so forlorn. For he had said that he was pleased with Oswine's words and had raised him up and told him to eat with no regrets. And so I asked him."

"What did he say to you?"

"You will not like the words he spoke. I fear that the bishop of Lindisfarena may have heard the word of God. He is the holiest of men, and if any were to hear the Lord God's voice, it would be Aidan."

The talk of gods speaking to men made Beobrand shiver, despite the warmth of the night. Looking up at the bright stars, he wondered what gods looked down upon them even now as they spoke atop this crag that jutted into the sky above the cold shifting wastes of the North Sea.

"What did he say?" he asked.

"He said, 'I know that the king will not live very long, for I have never seen so humble a king as he. I feel that he will be taken from us, because this middle earth is not worthy of such a king.'"

Beobrand thought back to the voyage south when they had travelled to fetch Eanflæd from Cantware. Aidan had foreseen there would be a great storm and had given the priest, Utta, a flask of oil to pour upon the waves to calm them. For a moment, Beobrand swayed, remembering how the ship had rolled in the torment, men wailing and bailing out water from the bilge. He had thought he would die that night. Coenred reached out a slender hand to him.

"Are you well?"

Beobrand brushed the offered hand away, more roughly than was needed.

"It is just the mead. It is a potent brew."

Coenred said nothing for a time, turning his face away from Beobrand as they walked back to the hall. The smells and noises rolling out of the opened doors assaulted their senses as they approached. The door wards, grim and silent, as impassive as oaks, watched them from beside the entrance. The tips of their spears burnt and gleamed with the firelight spilling from the hall. A servant bustled from one of the cookhouses, holding a platter heaped with fresh bread.

A touch on Beobrand's arm halted him. Coenred pulled him to one side.

"There will be war?" the monk said, sadness in his tone. "Truly?"

Beobrand sighed. He knew his friend abhorred the violence of men.

"You heard Ethelwin and Oswine. I am no seer like Aidan, but I tell you the future holds war. With luck," he hesitated, "and help from the gods and our allies, we will prevail against Penda. We have done so before."

Earlier in the evening, Ethelwin had addressed the gathered thegns of Bernicia and Deira, informing them of the news Beobrand had brought from the west. The mood had grown sombre, but Oswine had lifted the spirits of all those gathered when he had stood and spoken to them in his quiet, clear voice. He reminded Beobrand of Oswald. He too had commanded men without the need of raising his voice. It seemed the quieter he'd spoken, the more men had held their breath and leaned in to better hear his words. So it was with Oswine too.

"Brothers of Northumbria," Oswine had said and everyone in the hall had fallen still. "We are two kingdoms, Deira and Bernicia, but we are friends and we share much. We share mead, and meat in great feasts." He lifted the green glass goblet he drank from with a smirk. This received a ripple of applause. The men were enjoying the food and drink before them. "We share a love of the one true God and the Christ, His son. We even share the holy men, such as the wise Aidan and Coenred here, who minister to all Northumbrians, from the shores of the Humber in the south to the banks of the Sea of Giudan in the north. I even share kin with your queen." The hall was silent now, with ealdormen, thegns, gesithas, slaves and servants all listening intently. "All of this shared destiny means that when it comes to times of trouble and woe, we do not stand by and watch as our neighbours are attacked. No. We share many things, but most importantly, we share enemies!"

Oswine bellowed these last words, making some of the listeners gasp and start. A couple of the hounds, awoken from where they lounged by the hearth, leapt up and began barking furiously.

After a moment of hesitation, the hall erupted in a cacophony of cheering. Men nodded approval, turning to their bench-fellows, smiling. Beobrand marvelled at the change in the throng. It always amazed him how one man's words could alter what was in men's hearts. This was the true power of a great king. It was not a strong arm or a sharp sword. It was not even gold and silver and a powerful warband. No. It was the ability to inspire, to make men believe that you were the bearer of the truth and that to follow you was not only wise, it was your wyrd to do so.

"At first light," the king of Deira went on, "I will leave with my comitatus." There was a murmur from the audience. "But we do not abandon you. We will hurry south to call our own fyrd to arms and we will join you on the battlefield to face Penda and his heathen brethren. The united men of Northumbria will destroy Penda and his wolves. For are we not followers of the Christ, the truest shepherd? And a shepherd would not allow a pack of wolves amongst his flock."

The mood in the hall had lifted after Oswine's words, the men buoyed by his passion and certainty.

But out here in the darkness of the star-pricked night, Coenred was pale and his nervousness and fear were palpable.

"Be careful, Beo," the monk whispered.

"Do not fear for me, Coenred," Beobrand replied and made to brush past him into the hall.

But the monk snagged his sleeve and pulled him back.

"No, Beo. I do fear for you. I fear for all of us." He held his gaze and Beobrand felt himself growing irritated. He shook off Coenred's grip.

"Penda will not slay me."

"I talk not of battle," Coenred said, his voice low. When Beobrand did not respond, the monk continued. "You know what I speak of."

Angry now, as much with himself as with Coenred for voicing his own worries, Beobrand shoved past him.

"Do not fear for me, monk," he snapped over his shoulder.

Stepping into the flame-licked warmth of the hall, he blinked, and collided with someone making their way out of the doorway. It was a solid, heavily muscled man, almost as tall as Beobrand.

Strong hands gripped Beobrand's shoulders and he pushed the man away.

"Easy, lord," the obstacle replied. The lilting sing-song of the accent was immediately recognisable to Beobrand.

"Out of my way, Cynan," he snapped.

Cynan stepped aside.

"Of course, lord."

How Beobrand wished the man would stop calling him that. Every time he did, it reminded him of Acennan. How he missed the stocky warrior. Gods, how he had failed him.

"But Coenred is right, lord," Cynan continued as Beobrand passed. "And I too fear for you. You must be careful."

Beobrand spun to face him, his ire flashing into searing flame. But Cynan stopped his retort with raised hands.

"I know, I know," he said, a twisted smile on his lips. "You are always careful."

Beobrand, struggling to control his rage, opened his mouth to reply. Cynan cut him off.

"I am tired and I must ride far tomorrow. Good night, lord."

Without waiting for a reply, Cynan turned and left the hall.

Returning to his place at the mead bench, Beobrand's head began to throb. Wulfstan nodded to him as he sat, but the Deiran was focused on a riddle being told by a fresh-faced young gesith called Cuthbert. Beobrand listened absently to the solutions being shouted out by the warriors. The riddler, who looked about the same age as Octa and filled with the same youthful arrogance, laughed, shaking his head and wiping tears of mirth from his eyes at some of the more outlandish guesses.

Beobrand cared nothing for riddles. Life was complicated enough. He reached for his drinking horn and found it empty. Casting about for a thrall to refill it, he noticed that there was a gap at the high table to Oswine's right. Eanflæd had left the feast.

Beobrand looked the length of the hall, but saw no sign of the queen. Perhaps she had seen his place empty and so had decided to retire. And yet, had she not ignored him all night, never once meeting his gaze through the feast's smoky air?

The thrall girl from earlier spotted him searching for mead and hurried to his side. She filled his horn and he took a deep draught of the sweet liquid. His head ached. You should stop drinking, a small voice whispered to him. He knew he would not listen. Not tonight. His mind was a chaos of thoughts, memories and desires. Mead would help him to quieten the tumbling maelstrom in his thought-cage.

He sat, still and solid like a rock surrounded by stormy sea. All about him the feast crashed and roiled. Laughter, song, shouted riddles merged into a dull roar as he emptied his mead horn again and again. The thrall seemed to always know when he would need more, and his vessel was seldom empty. Soon his head spun and his worries felt distant and hazy, as mountains seen through a smirr of rain: still aware of their presence, looming and giant, but indistinct and nebulous in the drizzle.

He could not recall placing his head upon his forearms on the board before him. But sleep came to him in a spinning rush. The words of the men speaking around him blurred into a thick blanket of noise, like waves rolling across a shingle beach. But as he drifted into sleep, words came to him, as clear and distinct as the moment he had heard them whispered into his ear that afternoon when he had arrived at Bebbanburg.

Eanflæd had descended the ramparts and rushed to his side as he'd dismounted. And then, before anyone else drew close, she had leaned in. For a stomach-twisting moment he had thought she meant to kiss his cheek. But she did not make contact with his skin.

He was unable to voice his own feelings for her. He knew that to say the words would somehow give his emotions weight.

Truth. And yet it seemed that the queen was either braver, or more foolhardy, than he.

For her breath had fluttered against his ear like moth wings and he had felt as much as heard her whisper words he was too fearful to say. Words that had echoed in his mind ever since.

"I missed you. I have longed to see you again."

Chapter 7

By the Lord Jesu Christ and all His saints, what madness gripped her?

Eanflæd lay in a tangle of linen and blankets. Her hair was wet with sweat. Sleep would not come to her no matter how long she tried to remain still in the stifling warmth of the chamber.

She could still barely believe what she had done. When Eanflæd had heard one of the wall wards calling out that a fair-haired man approached on a great black steed, her heart had leapt. She had rushed away from the warm corner of the fortress wall where she had been sitting with Godgyth and Ecgfrith. Hurrying up the ladder to the ramparts, she had felt the eyes of the men and women of Bebbanburg on her. This was not seemly. No way for a queen to behave. She could almost hear her own mother's tone of disdain now, as she lay awake in the stuffy quarters. At the thought of Ethelburga, she felt a terrible sadness. It had been years since last she had seen her. Despite her sharp tongue and quick temper, Ethelburga was her mother and Eanflæd missed her. Though she was glad the old queen of Bernicia had not been present that afternoon to witness her antics.

She had watched Beobrand ride his great stallion into the shadow of the gates and then clatter into the yard. She had felt a warmth in her belly at seeing him again, and when he had looked at her with his piercing blue eyes, her breath had caught in her chest. Without thinking, or even knowing what she was doing, she had descended the ladder from the wall and run to him like a wife welcoming her husband's return.

She sighed. She was a man's wife. But not Beobrand's.

Her face grew hot in the darkness. For a moment she had been oblivious of the watching faces. She had wanted to touch him, to hold him, to breathe in his scent. But a heartbeat later, after whispering in his ear that she had missed him, an hostler had asked Beobrand when his horse had last been fed, and the spell of madness had been broken.

She had fled as quickly as she had run to the palisade, praying that nobody had noted how close she had come to embracing Beobrand. She had avoided him for the rest of the day, busying herself in overseeing preparations for the feast. When she had returned to where Godgyth was sitting with Ecgfrith, Eanflæd had been flustered. But if Godgyth noticed anything amiss, she said nothing. Ecgfrith seemed a bit better than he had been for some time. Perhaps the warm air of summer would finally shift the cough from his tiny lungs. She had consulted Coenred, who had mixed up a foul-smelling concoction of swails apple, brimstone, expensive imported Frankish incense and wax. This he had bidden her lay upon a hot stone near Ecgfrith while he slept. But apart from making her and Godgyth feel light-headed and nauseous, it did not seem to have any effect on the infant's wheezing rasp.

She knew she should trust in God, but she could not bear to see her baby boy suffer so. After the Thrimilci feast, when Ecgfrith had been particularly bad, Eanflæd had even asked the old healer woman, Ymma, for help. The crone had supplied her with a paste made of honey, horehound and barley for the boy to eat at night. She spooned a little into his mouth and, for a time, the baby's breathing had seemed easier. He had slept for a whole night without waking and Eanflæd had been overjoyed. In the morning, though, his cough had seemed worse and the tiny baby had hacked and spluttered pitifully. Eanflæd had been distraught. She had gone to the newly built stone church of Saint Peter and prayed for most of the day. She recited the Ave Maria and the Pater Noster over and over, praying that her son would become well again and all the while frightened that she was the cause of her son's illness. She was terrified that it was her lack of faith that had caused the worsening of his affliction. For the babe's cough had started shortly after she had visited the new monastery of Hereteu. And it was there that this madness had started.

She recalled how she had felt. It was the first time she had left Bebbanburg since Ecgfrith's birth and the freedom of being outside the walls of the fortress, and away from Oswiu, had lifted her humour. The days they had spent in the newly built monastery had been filled with joy. She had enjoyed spending time with such committed and dedicated women as the abbess, Hieu, and the other nuns. She had stayed up one night long after Compline talking to her kinswoman Hild, a stern woman of towering energy and insight. They had discussed theology and the lessons to be learnt from the book of Esther. When Eanflæd had finally walked to the small cell where she was to sleep, her mind had been abuzz with the pleasure of sharing her thoughts with these powerful women. At Bebbanburg, there was nobody for her to speak to apart from Godgyth and, even though she felt great affection for the woman, she was one to talk about babies, the weather, and which of the king's thegns were the most attractive, not to debate the finer points of theology and the future of Christ's mission in Albion.

Eanflæd had been so pleased when she had convinced Oswiu to allow her to travel to the opening ceremony of the monastery and as she had padded along the darkened corridor, she almost felt like a different person, like the young passionate woman she had been before becoming a peace-weaver. She had been allowed to voice her opinions in the court of Eorcenberht of Cantware. Even her father, Edwin, had seemed more interested in her when she was a child, than her husband did now. Oswiu scarcely spoke to her since she had sired him an heir. Before then, he had come to her chamber often. She had endured his visits, but she had been secretly pleased when her womb had quickened. Once she'd told him she was with child, his nocturnal visits had ceased and she knew he spent his nights with other women. Despite herself, she found the knowledge of his infidelity angered her, which made her own feelings towards Beobrand all the more unsettling.

That night in Hereteu, she had felt so free. So alive. Far from Bebbanburg and the king. Even the constantly crying Ecgfrith had remained with his wet nurse. It was thus, rested and filled with a sense of purpose and contentment, that she had met Beobrand.

He had been standing in the shadows, staring out to the moonlit trees that grew near the monastery's vallum. He had started when she approached, as if she had awoken him from a dream.

"What were you thinking of?" she asked. The moonlight played upon his face, silvering the scar over his left eye. His features were smothered in shadows, dark and impenetrable.

He sighed softly.

"I was thinking of wyrd."

"Do you think everything is preordained?"

"Perhaps," he replied, "but I think we must all fight against what the Sisters of Wyrd have in store for us. Mayhap we are able to alter the way they weave our threads."

She stepped close to him. He tensed.

"You think, then, that it was my wyrd to be wed to Oswiu?"

Beobrand said nothing. A glimmering from the shadows showed her how his gaze was fixed upon her.

"Should I be able to change my destiny, then?" she continued, reaching out and touching his shoulder lightly.

71

He shrugged – or was that a tremble at her touch?

"I fear it is too late for that now, Eanflæd, Edwin's daughter."

"I am the queen of Bernicia," she said, her voice barely more than a whisper. "Surely if any can change their wyrd, it would be me."

Beobrand smiled.

"If anyone could change the path the gods had set for them, I think it would be you, Eanflæd. You are like the sea, a storm or a raging river. I have never known any woman such as you."

A surge of warmth had flooded her at his words. Like Bebbanburg itself, Beobrand was a vision from her past life. A time when she had been the respected and well-loved daughter of the most powerful king of Albion, not the chattel of the scion of an enemy line, serving merely as a brood mare to spawn heirs to continue the line of the house of Ida.

Without thinking, she leaned in to Beobrand, rising up onto her toes to reach his face with hers. Their lips met and he did not flinch. For a moment, his body grew rigid and then his strong arms encircled her and the kiss grew deeper.

Whenever she thought of that moment, her mind reeled. What madness had possessed her? She was the queen, not some milkmaid who could have a dalliance with a cowherd. Should they be discovered, Oswiu would see them both killed, she was sure of it.

And of course they had been discovered.

No sooner had their tongues touched than they had been disturbed by the choked shock of Coenred, who had stumbled upon them. He'd mumbled an apology, his voice high-pitched and nervous. With a backward glance at her, Beobrand had led the young monk away. The next day, as he helped her into her waggon for the journey to Eoferwic to visit her cousin Oswine, Beobrand had told her that the monk would be discreet.

Clearly Beobrand had been right, for nothing more had been said about the incident. For many days afterwards, she had lived in fear that Oswiu would confront her. When she had heard about the attack on Beobrand in Eoferwic, her first thought had been that it must have been ordered by her husband. But surely he could not have heard of what had happened in the monastery so quickly. And, as the days had become weeks, and then months, the king had never mentioned anything to her. In fact, no whispers of scandal had reached her ears and she had noticed no furtive glances from people who might suspect wrongdoing. Once he had recovered from his injuries, Beobrand had visited Bebbanburg on several occasions. He would spend time with his son, and Oswiu would treat him as a valued thegn of his comitatus. There was a coolness between them, but she knew this had been there long before she'd travelled north from Cantware, and their relationship seemed no more strained than it had been before the trip to Hereteu and Eoferwic.

And yet she would still awaken in the night, terrified of what her actions might have set in motion. Ecgfrith grew sickly, and she was convinced that this was punishment for her sins. For, although it appeared her husband did not know about the kiss she had shared with Beobrand, she remembered it as clearly as if it had happened the day before.

Worse than the fear of the prospect of her husband finding out about her indiscretion, God knew what she had done. And the Lord knew that, even though her heart twisted with shame at the thought, she longed to feel Beobrand's lips on hers again; dreamed of his arms pulling her against his muscular chest. Oswiu had started coming to her chamber again recently, seeking another heir no doubt, and though Eanflæd tried to empty her mind as her husband pleasured himself with her body, as he thrust into her, she could not dispel the thought of what it would be like to open herself to Beobrand, to feel his weight on her, his hot breath on her neck.

Despite her deepest desires, she had been careful. Perhaps it was the Devil himself who sent these thoughts to her and she railed against them. She prayed often and took the Eucharist regularly. She petitioned Oswiu for extra treasure to be spent on the works of the brethren of Lindisfarena. Minsters were now being planned for other sites across Bernicia, in part due to her persuasive words to the king.

When Beobrand visited the fortress, Eanflæd was aloof but polite and had made a point of never being alone with him. And yet she had often felt his gaze on her when feasting in the great hall, and she had flushed beneath his stare, convinced that everyone would notice.

She had been so cautious, doing her best to dispel her desires and seeking to help the Lord's work throughout the land, and then she had thrown it all to the wind when she had rushed to welcome Beobrand through the gates that afternoon. What madness had possessed her?

She lay for a time in her soft bed, wondering at her actions. She could not push Beobrand's face from her mind's eye. At last, resigned that she would not find sleep, she rose. Slipping her feet into a pair of soft calfskin shoes, she pulled a blue woollen cloak from a peg and made her way to the door. It was stifling and stuffy in her quarters, but she knew that outside in the night, the air would be much cooler. She hoped the fresh air would clear her head. She hesitated by the door for a moment, listening to the sounds coming from elsewhere within the fortress. From nearby, just beyond a partition, came Godgyth's light snores. The servant had helped tend to Ecgfrith earlier when he would not settle and she had drunk several cups of mead. Unless Ecgfrith woke with a bout of coughing, Godgyth would not stir. And Ecgfrith seemed to be breathing more easily this evening. Perhaps the warm sunshine had helped.

She opened the door and a peal of laughter somewhere far in the distance echoed in the night. Then there was silence apart from the far-off whisper of the waves washing on the beach and rocks beneath the walls.

She stepped out into the night and took in a deep breath. The tang of the sea refreshed her immediately and she paused a moment to look about her at the shapes of the palisades and buildings that made up Bebbanburg. On the walkways she could make out the forms of guards, silhouetted against the starstrewn sky. The wind picked up and tugged at her cloak. She wrapped it about her shoulders and walked silently across the courtyard. It was dark here, but she trod with ease, sure that the bondsmen and hostlers would have seen to it that any manure left by the horses had been cleared away.

How familiar this fortress was to her. When she had returned here, some three years before, she had felt a wrenching sense of returning home. Every part of the place brought back memories of her childhood. No day passed without something conjuring up a memory from a different time. In the great hall she half-expected to see her father, as she had last seen him, sitting proudly on the gift-stool and addressing his people with his overwhelming charisma. Here in the courtyard the presence of her older brothers was tangible. She had watched them leaping into the saddles of their horses here, full of the excitement of the hunt. Oswine reminded her of her brothers. He had the same earnest energy about him. There, on the steps leading to the great hall, was where her mother would often stand, face resolute, hard and beautiful, overseeing the menfolk readying themselves to leave for the hunt.

Or for war.

Had Ethelburga enjoyed living in this windswept crag of a fortress? She had never contemplated that her mother might not have been content. She had always seemed perfectly in control and it was not until now, having become a mother herself, that she had begun to wonder. Had her mother ever harboured thoughts of desire for any man other than her father? Eanflæd wished she could ask her.

A moment later, she snorted at the thought. No, she was glad her mother was far away in the monastery of Liminge. The austere Ethelburga would never approve of what Eanflæd had done. And she would not understand her daughter's feelings for Beobrand. Why should she? Eanflæd shook her head in the gloom. It was sinful and it was wrong.

The thought of her mother saddened her. She was suddenly aware of how isolated and lonely she felt in Bebbanburg. Every corner held the memories of her kin's ghosts.

Walking in the darkness of the moon-shadow beside the hall, Eanflæd bit her lip.

She had avoided Beobrand's gaze all that evening in the feast. She had surreptitiously glanced his way a few times, but he had not seen her. But from the corner of her vision she had noted him turning to look at her often. It was her fault. She regretted running to the gate and, even more, she was appalled at the memory of her brazen behaviour in going to him and whispering close to his ear.

As she had sat there, talking to Oswine at the high table, her emotions had churned inside her. She could not shake the memory of Beobrand's cold eyes on her as she had descended the ladder from the wall. There was a hunger there that she recognised. As she had reached up to whisper to him, his manly scent of sweat, horses, woodsmoke and leather had filled her nostrils and a wave of yearning had washed through her. She should never have approached him again. If it was her lot to live with this torment, so be it. She had a duty far beyond her personal desires.

How she regretted whispering to him. She should have continued to pretend that the kiss had meant nothing to her; that he meant nothing to her. Instead, she had inflamed his lust with a susurrus of soft words.

When she had seen Beobrand rise from the mead bench and walk out into the night with Coenred, she had taken the opportunity to leave also. She had told Oswine that she needed to check on Ecgfrith. In truth she had been desperate to be free from the desire and the guilt that battled within her. Yet the conflict had continued to rage and she had scarcely slept, lying instead in the sweaty heat of her quarters, twisting and turning over her thoughts even as her body tangled itself in her blankets.

She was pleased for the cooler air out here. The day had been so hot that she could feel the warmth of it coming from the timbers of the hall. Atop the walls would be cooler. She would climb up on the east side of the fortress overlooking the sea. There was always a breeze there. It was her favourite place within the citadel. In the light of day she loved to look out to Lindisfarena, and the distant Farena islands. The sea would be flecked with gannets, guillemots and puffins, and many times she would witness the dark shapes of seals bobbing in the slate waves far below Bebbanburg. On a clear night such as this, she loved to fill her eyes with the dark majesty of God's middle earth and her lungs with the cool salt air.

Perhaps if she spent some time atop the palisade, she would be able to free her mind of this turmoil. Maybe then she could find sleep.

Unbidden, like a wayward child disobeying its parents, her mind turned again to troubling thoughts: this time of the impending war. Many would not be able to sleep that night, she was sure. Men would be thinking about battle-fame in the shieldwall, or perhaps they would think of their loved ones, the wives and children they would leave behind if they fell. She would be safe here, she was sure. Bebbanburg was impregnable. It had never been taken by force and could withstand any assault. No, Penda would lead his horde elsewhere to fight the fyrds of Bernicia and Deira, and she would be left with the other women of Bebbanburg to fret about what might befall their menfolk. And yet, her husband was not here. And she knew all too well that battles could be lost, even if this fortress remained intact.

She had only been seven years old when her father had led

the men of Northumbria south to face Cadwallon and Penda at Elmet. She had watched the warband ride out. Edwin had looked invincible on his huge horse, bedecked in his battle gear.

He never returned.

She remembered clearly the terror of the days that followed. First the waiting and her mother's pacing and sharp temper. Then Bassus' arrival with the dire news of her father's death and the rout of the fyrd. Followed by the headlong rush south to the safety of her uncle Eadbald's kingdom of Cantware. She had not returned here until her marriage to Oswiu.

Beobrand had fought in the battle that had cost her father and her brother their lives. She had met him shortly before and she wondered at the ways of wyrd that he spoke about. He had been just a farmhand then, but he had joined Edwin's warband and now, years later, he was a warlord, veteran of many battles and slayer of countless men. Men whispered that Beobrand of Ubbanford and his Black Shields could not be defeated, but she thought of her father and sighed. All men could be vanquished and all warriors, no matter their prowess, died in the end. A chill ran through her at the thought that Beobrand might be slain in the coming days.

And then, as she rounded the end of the great hall, making her way towards the steps that would take her up to the east palisade, her breath caught in her throat. Perhaps Beobrand was right when he talked of wyrd; that every man and woman's life threads were woven by three sisters who make up the tapestry of their lives. For out of the hall doors stepped a tall figure with a shock of fair hair that caught the moonlight, shining like burnished silver.

She halted, unable to breathe. His back was towards her. If she did not move, he might not see her. Standing still, she made not a sound. And yet, as sure as she knew who it was, she was certain he would turn to her.

It seemed there was no way to fight against one's wyrd.

Slowly, unsteadily as a man who has drunk too much ale, he moved to face her. His ice-chip eyes glimmered from the shadows of his face and she shuddered under that penetrating gaze.

"Eanflæd," Beobrand said, his voice coarse and low, like the far-off wave-wash of the sea.

Chapter 8

Beobrand's mind was as blurred as his vision. For a time he was unsure whether he was awake or dreaming. For was this not Eanflæd here before him in the gloom? And had she not also inhabited his dreams? He shook his head in an attempt to halt the feeling of standing on the deck of a listing ship. In the dim light from the stars and the moon, he could just make out the slender line of her neck, the curve of her high cheekbones, the bud of her lips. Surely this was a wishful dream.

He tried to make sense of what was happening and how he had got here.

He had found himself slumped over the board. The hall had been dark and quiet, the only sounds the snores of other revellers who had succumbed to the drink. He had lain there for some time, his aching head resting on his arms, wondering whether he should heave himself up and look for somewhere better to spend the night. It had seemed like a huge amount of effort and he had almost decided to remain where he was when a new sound came to him. Somewhere from the shadowed recesses of a far corner of the room came the soft, rhythmic moans of coupling. The sounds stirred his passions but angered him at the same time. By Woden, why could he not find the comfort of a woman who would chase his foolish desires away? Fleetingly, he thought of Udela, back in Ubbanford. The groans from the darkness grew faster and more intense. He could not bear to listen any longer. With a grimace, he pushed himself upright. Almost tripping over the bench, he stumbled, catching his half-hand on a timber column, preventing himself from tumbling to the rush-strewn floor. He hawked and spat into the hearth where the embers from the small fire glowed, giving enough shadowy light for him to pick his way to the doors of the hall.

He bumped into the carved column to one side of the double doors. Cursing his own clumsiness and his foolishness for ignoring the voice that had told him to drink less, he staggered outside.

He'd welcomed the cool of the night, breathing deeply of the salt-fresh air that carried a hint of the chill of the Whale Road. For a moment he had stood there, gazing up stupidly at the spray of stars that swam in the blackness of the heavens above him. Through the drunken fug of his senses, he had slowly become aware of someone watching him. Turning, he'd seen Eanflæd standing there in the darkness, unmoving. She was unreal, surely; a spectre, a drunken vision. He blinked, but her form remained. He had half-expected her to vanish like smoke on the wind.

He whispered her name and she reached out a hand tentatively. Her fingers brushed his wrist. He started at the touch and a shivering thrill ran through him.

"Beobrand," she whispered, moving closer.

He could smell her now. He recognised the scent of her skin and her shimmering hair.

"Eanflæd," he repeated, his voice muffled with drink, but loud in the night.

"Hush," she whispered, her tone urgent. "We must not be seen here. Come."

He felt her hand take his. His cheeks grew hot and again he shook his head to clear it. She pulled his hand and he followed her. She led him into the lee of a building. The stable, he thought, and he remembered when they had first met there, all those years before. She had been a child then, and he had barely been a man. As they walked into the moon-shadow of the stable, he smiled to himself in the dark. So much had changed. And yet even then, as a tiny wisp of a girl, he had felt that she had the better of him, that she was mocking him, deciding his path for him. If it had not been for her, he might never have come to the attention of King Edwin. And then what? What would have befallen him if he had not travelled with the king and stood in the blood and filth of the shieldwall at Elmet? He might never have discovered his talent for killing. Might his life have been one of peace? Would he have ever met Hengist? And what of his friend, Bassus? His love, Sunniva? It did not do to think such things. The tapestry of the past could not be unwoven. His thoughts spiralled away from him and he could not grasp the thread of them.

"I am sorry that I came to you at the gate today," she said, her voice sibilant in the gloom. He could not see her face, but she stood so close to him that her breath brushed his cheek. The smell of her intoxicated him.

"Sorry? Why?" he slurred.

For a time she did not reply. He was beginning to wonder whether she would answer when she spoke in a small voice, tinged with sadness.

"I should never have kissed you, Beobrand. That night in Hereteu. It was sinful." She hesitated. "The flesh is weak."

"Where is the sin in a kiss?"

"I am the queen," she hissed. "You are not such a fool that you believe no wrong would come from this."

"This?"

"We cannot meet this way. We must never see each other again. Not alone. I am not a free woman." She hesitated. Did her voice catch in her throat? "I am Oswiu's."

A flame of anger flared within him at the mention of the king.

"Being wed does not stop the king from taking his pleasure elsewhere," Beobrand said, his voice gruff. He could hear the harshness of his words even as he spoke them. Eanflæd tensed. Feeling guilty for hurting her, he said, "Though why any man would want anything more than you, I cannot comprehend."

A silence fell between them. She sniffed and he realised she was weeping.

"Do not cry, Eanflæd," he murmured.

"Why should I not?" she hissed, angry suddenly. "Do not tell me what I should or shouldn't do, Beobrand!"

He stepped away from her fury, unsure of what to say. His head throbbed, but her proximity filled him with a passionate urge to reach for her.

As if she had heard his thoughts, without warning she moved in close and wrapped her slender arms about him. Despite the heat of the night, they both trembled as their bodies touched. She leaned her head into his chest and whispered, "We cannot be together. God will punish us."

Beobrand could scarcely think of anything apart from the softness of her body and the heady fragrance of her hair. His breath became laboured, his body responding to her closeness. He thought of Eowa and Cyneburg. Their love had almost destroyed them. This lust was a deadly madness.

"God cares nothing for what we mortals do," he whispered.

"Do not say such a thing," she moaned against him. "God sees all and He knows that I am a sinner. After Hereteu, Ecgfrith fell ill. That is God's punishment."

"Your son is getting better, is he not? I heard as much today from Godgyth."

"If he is, it is because we have not fallen to temptation again these past months."

Inside the stable a horse stamped, the sound loud and echoing in the still of the night. Beobrand held his breath and when he spoke again, he lowered his voice to the merest whisper. The mead-haze was lifting and in one thing at least, Eanflæd spoke true: if they were caught together, word would reach Oswiu's ears and things would not go well for them. Eanflæd was the queen, and the mother of an heir of Bernicia, but Beobrand was sure that his own usefulness as a fighter and leader of men would be worth little if Oswiu suspected him of bedding his wife.

The horse in the stable quietened and the night was calm again. No footsteps came towards them. And here in the shadows they were invisible to the wardens on the palisade.

"Do you truly believe that your God would harm your child over a kiss?" Beobrand whispered.

"It is a sin. I am married." She hesitated, searching for other reasons they could not be together. "And what of your woman, back in Ubbanford?"

Beobrand thought for a moment about Udela. She lived in his hall now and helped him to manage the land. She was hard-working and grateful to him for having rescued Ardith from Frankia, but he felt little for her beyond a cool affection. With a stab of guilt he remembered the night she had come to his bed a couple of months after he had brought her north from Hithe. She had crept into his chamber without a word. He had sated himself with her, and she had given him the impression that she had enjoyed the coupling, but in the morning she had been gone from his chamber and they had never spoken of it. She had not returned to his bed since that night.

"Udela is not my wife," he said. "I want no woman but you. You have filled my head this past year. I can scarcely think of anything but that kiss. It is as if you have bewitched me."

She made the sign of the Christ rood over her chest.

"I am no witch," she murmured, "but perhaps we have both been cursed." He thought of Nelda's screeching howls from the cave deep within the earth. Was this part of her evil magic? "But we cannot be together," Eanflæd continued, dragging Beobrand's befuddled thoughts back to this warm night and the shivering beauty in his arms. "I am terrified of what might happen."

"Terrified?" he asked, pulling her gently towards him. "Is this so bad? So terrible?"

He bent down towards her, wondering absently whether she might try to pull away. But he found her face upturned to meet his and an instant later their lips were locked together in a frenzied kiss of such passion that when they parted, they were breathless. Beobrand slid his right hand towards her breast. Beneath her cloak he felt the hardness of her nipple through the linen of her nightgown. She moaned at his touch and with his left hand he pulled her hips against him.

For a heartbeat, she clove to him, her own hands urgently exploring his body, but then she tensed. Pushing his hands away, she distanced herself.

"I am so weak!" she groaned. "This cannot be."

Beobrand, his lust burning now, reached for her. Catching her shoulders he pulled her back towards him. Gone were his worries of discovery. His mind was filled with the thought of her. His body yearned for hers. His tongue was slick with her sweet taste. How many months had he dreamed of this and now she was here, soft and tremulous in his rough grasp. He wanted her. And by Frige, he would have her.

She slapped at his hands, the report ringing out in the night.

"No," she snapped. Was there fear in her voice, or only rage? "Unhand me at once."

Her words cut through the mist of desire and he released his grip on her. She stepped quickly away, pulling the cloak she wore tightly about her, covering the plain linen gown beneath.

Ashamed, he dropped his hands to his sides.

"I am sorry," he mumbled. He wanted to tell her that she filled his mind with a rushing torrent of thoughts and desires. He lusted for her. Needed her. Wanted nothing else but to lie with her and forget that the rest of middle earth existed. But he said nothing. Her face was a pale blur in the darkness, but he could tell from the way she held herself, standing stiffly, arms wrapped about the cloak, that even if she had, she no longer felt any of those things. He was a brute and he had frightened her.

He stepped away, colliding with the timber of the stable with a clatter.

"I am sorry," he repeated, his words tasting like ash. "I—"

"This was wrong," she said, her voice strangely calm now. "We must not meet again. It is sinful and we must not give in to the wiles of the Devil."

"But—"

"No, Beobrand," she said, her tone quiet but forceful. "We both know this is madness. We have been lucky not to have been discovered. It must stop now."

Beobrand's head spun. He understood the sense in her words. They echoed his own belief that this was dangerous and mad. And yet he knew that he did not want to be done with this insanity. His mind was a jumble of desperate lust and terrible shame. The thought that his own desire had driven her away dismayed him. He had witnessed too many times the horror of the violence men inflicted on women in the name of sating their yearnings and he had vowed he would never stoop to forcing himself on any woman. He forbid his gesithas from doing so and while the likes of Fordraed scoffed at the perceived squeamish nature of his men, Beobrand knew his warriors respected him for it. The knowledge that he had almost allowed the power of his own urges to overcome him turned his stomach.

"I am sorry," he repeated for the third time. The words were not enough, but he could muster no others.

For a long moment, Eanflæd stared at him in silence. Perhaps she was waiting for him to say something else, but he just swayed on his feet, fighting down the bile that threatened to rush into his mouth.

"As am I," she said at last. And with that, she turned and walked quietly back into the night.

Beobrand watched her go. His mind reeled and finally, the mead and his self-loathing twisting within him, he bent over and vomited.

Chapter 9

Beobrand trudged through the long grass, searching for a particular marker amongst the canted stones and slouching mounds where the men and women of Bebbanburg had been buried for generations. The dew soaked into his leg bindings. The sun was bright in the pale sky behind him, but the day was not yet hot. Beobrand's head was pounding. He had slept little and fitfully, finding himself a place on the floor of the hall near the doors. He had wrapped himself in his cloak, but his mind had been full of dark thoughts, his shame writhing with his sense of loss and failure in a constantly twisting morass of darkness inside him.

Shortly after dawn, thralls and servants had begun to bustle about the hall, repositioning the benches and boards, cleaning up spilt food and spreading fresh rushes on dark, damp patches where drinks had been overturned, or men had relieved themselves or voided their guts. Beobrand had heaved himself up with a groan, and, after sending one of the thralls for a jug of water which he'd emptied in one long draught, he had set out southward. The door wardens had let him slip out of the gates without comment when he had told them his destination. He was a thegn, a lord of Bernicia, and all knew of his history and that of his warrior brother who had come before him. Beobrand wanted to be far from Bebbanburg. He could not stand the thought of seeing the judgement and disappointment on Eanflæd's face. He felt enough shame already.

He'd walked alone over the dunes as the sun rose above the sea. Gentle waves sighed up the sands of the beach and the marram grass whispered in the light breeze that rolled off the water. The sea-cool and the breeze went a long way towards reviving him, and by the time he reached the ancient burial place, his mind was clear, even if his head still felt as though it had been struck by Thunor's hammer.

Two huge crows, disturbed by his passing, suddenly flapped into the morning sky, croaking angrily. He shivered at the sight of them, and then smiled to himself.

They are only birds, he told himself, hearing his old friend Acennan uttering those words in his memory.

Only birds.

Perhaps.

A scratch of unease traced along his spine as he saw where the crows had been perched. They cawed as they circled in the sky above, looking down, as if mocking him.

His brother's grave was overgrown now, covered in long grass and plants. But this was Octa's resting place, of that there was no doubt. He scanned the trees to the west and glanced back at the fortress to the north. Yes, this was the place. In the tangle of sedge, marram grass and saltwort stood a small stone marker, carved with his brother's name and a few other words. Beobrand could not read, but he well remembered the words he had paid to have carved on the gravestone by a mason who had come all the way from Frankia to work on Bebbanburg's church. Coenred had helped him with the inscription, scratching out the shapes of the letters into a piece of wood for the mason to copy. The monk had said it needed more words, but Beobrand was pleased with the results.

Octa.

Beloved.

Battle-famed.

Remembered.

No. It needed no more words. It was perfect. What more was there that needed to be said?

The stone had sunk into the ground slightly, and the plants had all but hidden it, but the chiselled marks were still crisp. It had been years since he had last visited Octa's tomb, he realised with a stab of guilt, but it would take more than a few years of exposure to the harsh elements of Bernicia to dull the engravings on the stone. He did not begrudge the silver he had paid the Frank.

Reaching down, Beobrand tugged the saltwort and clumped grass away from the stone. As he bent, the pain in his head grew stronger and he grunted as he stood and the throbbing abated somewhat. He frowned, gazing down at the words on the slab of stone. This would be here long after his own death, he was sure. It was hard to believe that this was all that marked Octa's life. How quickly people are forgotten. He wondered how long it would be before his own name was lost in memories. A generation? Two? Shaking his head at the thought, he looked at the grave. The shape of Octa's burial was visible in the lusher grass and the slight mounding of the earth. It was a long grave and Beobrand could picture his tall brother lying there, in the darkness, mouldering beneath the earth.

"It's been a long time, Octa," he whispered. The trees in the distance murmured. The crows fluttered down to land on a barrow some way off to the west. They eyed Beobrand balefully. The place always unnerved him. He could not put from his mind the thought of all those corpses, buried in the sandy earth. Did their spirits yet linger here, tied to their rotting flesh and bones?

Beobrand seldom came here. And yet he had walked from the fortress today in search of someone to talk to. Someone he knew would listen and not offer up his own comments on Beobrand's behaviour.

"I have a daughter," he said, feeling foolish speaking to the wind and the crows. "Ardith. She's older than Octa. I didn't know she existed until a couple of years ago. Udela is her mother. Remember her?" He thought that if Octa had lived, he would have scarcely remembered plump, plain Udela. Octa had been older than Beobrand, tall and strong and every part the warrior. When he had left Hithe, Udela had been not much older than Ardith was now. And despite a certain earnest intensity, she was not as striking as her daughter. Ardith had blossomed into a beautiful, if quiet and reserved, young woman.

He fell silent. The women in his life seemed to control his wyrd; their actions, as much as his own, driving his destiny. His mother's dying words had helped to push him to flee from Hithe. Sunniva had brought him joy and love when he had believed he would find none. She had given him a son. And, with her death, had caused him immeasurable pain. The auburn-haired thrall, Reaghan, had grounded him, giving him a focus, when all about him was chaos. She had been a good woman, quiet and attentive, and it was not until after her death that he fully appreciated all she had done for him. It was even she who had, along with Bassus, rid them all of the cunning woman, Nelda, whose curse had filled him with fear for so long and, even now, years after her death, still hung over him like a storm cloud.

Other womenfolk had pulled and twisted at the threads of his life. Cathryn, the stranger who was brutally violated and murdered at the hands of Hengist and his comrades. Her savage death had impelled Beobrand to seek revenge and to vow never to stand by and allow such atrocities to occur again. Cyneburg, Oswald's queen and Eowa's lover, whose impetuous love for the atheling of Mercia had led to men dying in the fight over her, to tortured oaths being sworn in a blizzard at Din Eidyn and, eventually, to Eowa's bloody end at Maserfelth.

And now, once again, he had allowed a woman to rule his mind. His lust for Eanflæd had all but blinded him. It was as if she had whispered instructions to the Sisters of Wyrd to weave his life threads to her bidding. He shook his head and sighed. No, that was unfair. He recalled clearly her trembling form against him in the night, the taste of her, the smell of her hair. She was as powerless as he to ignore the urges they felt. And yet had she not pulled away? Was it not Eanflæd who had insisted they should not be together?

She was right. She was right and she was stronger than he.

Gods, he had been a fool.

"I should never have come here," he said aloud, looking down at his brother's grave. He did not mean he should not have visited Octa's tomb. He should not have come to Bebbanburg. He shook his head and spat. The taste of bile was still acrid and sour in his throat.

The crows called out. Were they laughing at him? Did Woden look on through their black eyes, chortling at the stupidity of his decisions?

The gods love chaos.

He reached up and clutched the Thunor's hammer amulet he wore round his neck.

He knew what he had to do; what he should have known all along. It was as though the morning sun had burnt away the fog of confusion that had clouded his thoughts. It was all clear to him now, and it had taken Eanflæd to break the spell of madness and to show him the way.

"Rest easy, Octa," he whispered.

Perhaps there was yet time. Cynan had left with the men promised by Ethelwin at first light. Beobrand had heard them preparing the mounts in the courtyard and had thought about going out to bid them farewell. But he had not. Instead he had lain on the floor of the hall and listened to the jangle of harness, the stamp of hooves and men's voices. Now he understood why: he had been ashamed to face the Waelisc warrior. Cynan knew what Beobrand's duty was, and it was certainly not to remain in Bebbanburg while the fyrd gathered. The lord of Ubbanford's place was with his men, harrying Penda's force, defending the land.

He spat again, furious at himself. Turning, he rushed back towards the crag of Bebbanburg. The sun was not yet high. He could saddle Sceadugenga quickly and ride after Cynan. With luck he could catch up with them when they halted for a midday rest, or failing that, when they rested at night.

Cursing his foolishness, he broke into a sprint, lumbering away from the graves and into the dunes with their swishing marram grass. With each step, his feet sank into the soft sand. It pulled him down, slowing him, holding him back.

In the distance, the crows croaked in his wake. For a heartbeat it sounded to Beobrand as if they were crying derisively after him, "Too late! Too late!"

Chapter 10

Sweat poured from Beobrand by the time he reached the top of the steps that led up to Bebbanburg's main gate from the sands below. The door wards allowed him entry with nothing more than quizzically raised eyebrows. They must have watched his progress as he ran across the beach beneath Bebbanburg. And though they no doubt were interested in the reason for his haste, he was thankful not to be questioned. He did not wish to explain to these men why he was running as if pursued by wraiths risen from the barrows. He was also so short of breath that he did not believe he would be able to speak.

Gasping for air, he paused and leaned on the palisade. Slowly, his breathing returned to normal. The sun did not reach here, behind the timber wall, and Beobrand's sweat rapidly cooled on his skin. Suppressing a shudder, he pushed himself away from the wall, swiping his arm across his forehead. His long fair hair was slick.

A cart, pulled by an ox and piled high with sacks of grain, trundled to a halt in the open area before the gates. The cart's owner approached the door wards, where they began to talk loudly over some dispute. Beobrand ignored them and made his way around the cart.

"By the Christ and all his angels, Beobrand, you look fit to collapse," said a voice Beobrand recognised instantly.

Fordraed was leaning against a storage hut. He wore a gaudy shirt of the finest red silk and his belt was tipped with an ornate golden buckle encrusted with garnets. Beside him, Heremod watched on, his left hand stroking the plaits of his beard. Despite his apparently relaxed pose, Beobrand noted how the stocky warrior stood straight, his eyes alert. Heremod's hand rested on his worked leather belt, within easy reach of the wicked-looking seax that hung in a silver-bedecked sheath.

Beobrand glanced back at the palisade. The two men were close to the base of one of the ladders that gave access to the walkway. Had they been watching his approach too? It seemed likely. Why else would they be standing here as if awaiting his arrival?

He had no time for Fordraed and his taunts. He made to step past him, but Heremod shifted his position, blocking his path. The raised voices of the carter and the door wards reached him. With the position of the cart, he could not see the men or the gates.

"I cannot tarry here," Beobrand said. "Stand aside, Heremod."

The burly man did not move.

Beobrand turned to Fordraed.

"Tell your man to get out of my way."

"And if I don't?"

Beobrand sighed.

"We need all the fighting men we have," he said. "I do not wish to reduce our number. Nobody would miss you in the shieldwall, Fordraed, but Heremod has some worth. However, I am in a hurry and if he does not move, I will move him." He let the threat hang in the air for a moment. "Come now," he continued, forcing his voice to remain calm, "I have urgent business. Tell him to let me pass."

Fordraed's eyes narrowed.

"Are you threatening my man?" he asked, feigning surprise. "Are we not all on the same side here?"

Beobrand sighed again. His breathing was deep and even once more, but his head ached and he could feel a cold anger building within him.

"Let me past, man," he snapped.

Still Heremod did not move. But he clearly noticed something in Beobrand's posture or tone that warned him of imminent violence, for Beobrand saw that his hand had moved to the seax, his fingers gripping the handle lightly, ready to tug the blade free from its leather home.

"I have to admit," said Fordraed, his tone sickly and honeyed, "I am surprised to find you so active after your antics last night."

Beobrand was suddenly cold, but his face grew hot. What did Fordraed know? Had someone seen him with Eanflæd in the night?

"What do you mean?" he snapped at the fat thegn. "What are you accusing me of?"

Fordraed's eyes narrowed and he shoved himself away from the hut. He was interested now and Beobrand cursed his own stupidity for snatching at the bait Fordraed had dangled before him.

"Why, Lord Beobrand," Fordraed said, "I was accusing you of nothing. But you look like a man who is stretched as taut as a bowstring. Perhaps what you need is a good rut, but maybe there are no furrows available here, eh?"

Beobrand said nothing. He fixed Fordraed with his icy stare, searching for any sign of how much the man knew.

"Or maybe," Fordraed went on, smiling as if they were old friends and conspirators, "you are a man who has something to hide. Or perhaps both." He let the words linger in the air, his piggy eyes searching Beobrand's face for any hint of what was worrying him. "I know you do not hold much store in the Christ

96

God, but you might like to consider speaking to Bishop Aidan while he is here. He is soon to set off for the Farena Islands, I believe. To pray and to be holy. Whatever it is that holy men do alone on lumps of rock in the middle of the sea. But before he goes I am sure he would hear your confession. It really does wonders for the soul to admit all of the sins you have committed. I don't think I could live with myself without confessing regularly." He laughed. "And the best thing is, the priest will never tell another soul. How he manages to keep himself holy after hearing my sins, I will never know." He laughed, a high-pitched, ugly sound that skewered Beobrand's head like a lance. "Mayhap that is why the man needs to spend time alone with God on his island," Fordraed giggled. "To cleanse his being after hearing of all the things I have done."

Fordraed's laughter died on his lips and his eyes suddenly widened. The plump thegn grew very still. Beobrand's sharp seax blade pressed into his groin. Beobrand had moved without warning. His speed was legendary, and he had drawn the seax from its scabbard and closed with Fordraed before Heremod had barely moved. Now, the dark-bearded warrior was jumping forward, his seax blade clearing its sheath as he came.

"Hold still," Beobrand snapped, his voice as hard as iron.

Fordraed let out a whimper and Heremod came to a halt. He was close enough for Beobrand to smell him.

"If you strike me, Heremod, Fordraed here will lose his manhood first, and then, soon after, his life."

Fordraed moaned as Beobrand prodded the tip of his blade into his inner thigh. They all knew that a deep cut there would open an artery. He would spill great gouts of dark blood and be dead within moments.

"And if you do cut me," Beobrand continued, "you'd better make it a killing blow, because otherwise, I'll be taking you with me to the afterlife. I think you'd both make good slaves in Woden's corpse-hall."

Heremod glowered, but said nothing.

"Let him pass," Fordraed squeaked. Heremod glared and did not move. Beobrand could see murder in the man's eyes, so he pricked Fordraed's skin. The fat thegn squealed in fear. "By all the saints, let him pass."

Heremod slowly, deliberately, sheathed his seax and stepped back.

Beobrand's face was as close to Fordraed's as a lover.

"Do not cross me again," he whispered, following up his words with a gentle jab of his seax. Fordraed shuddered. "I am tired of your accusations and your venomous words. You are a snake. A fat snake. And there is only one thing to do with a viper."

Stepping away from Fordraed, he sheathed his seax and then clapped his hands together hard, a finger's breadth from the portly lord's pale jowls. Fordraed let out a stifled cry. Beobrand spun to face Heremod. The man's plaited beard quivered with his rage and his hand had fallen again to the hilt of his seax.

"Don't," Beobrand said.

He stared into Heremod's eyes. Heremod saw a quick death in that blue gaze and, after a moment, his shoulders slumped.

Without hesitation, Beobrand strode past the two men as if nothing untoward had occurred. He noticed with surprise that his headache had gone. His mind was clear and he was certain what he needed to do now.

But as he hurried towards the stables, a commotion drew his attention. He tensed, spinning around, for an instant thinking that Heremod had decided to attack after all. But Fordraed and his gesith were where he had left them. They had also turned to see what was happening.

A man had entered through the gates. The door wards held him back behind their spears and the man was growing increasingly agitated. Beobrand did not recognise him. He wore a light kirtle and plain breeches. His face was heavily bearded and his feet were bare. His lack of shoes and his rolling gait made Beobrand think he must be a sailor. If so, he might just have beached his ship and made his way up the rock-hewn steps which led from the harbour.

"Where is the queen?" the stranger shouted, casting his voice towards Beobrand and the other onlookers. His accent was strangely familiar yet foreign at the same time to Beobrand. The man spoke with the music of someone from his homeland of Cantware. "Where is the queen?" he called again. Nobody answered him. He glanced around him, as if he might see the queen standing before him in the courtyard.

He made an effort to push past the guards, his exasperation at being held back obvious.

His next words chilled Beobrand.

"I bring grave tidings for the queen."

Chapter 11

Eanflæd dipped her head and once more muttered the words of the prayer to Maria, Mother of God. She knew the words without thinking and as she repeated the litany of phrases, her mind wandered to the night before. She was alone in the church. Thin shafts of light filtered through the small windows and it was dark and cool inside the stone building. In the stillness, her murmured words reverberated about her, buzzing like insects.

The words of the prayer to the Virgin were on her lips, but her mind was filled with thoughts of Beobrand. His taste was still in her mouth. The broad strength of his back, the solid slab of his chest against her cheek. Her face grew hot as she recalled his massive hand cupping her breast, his erect manhood pressing against her stomach as he pulled her into his embrace.

She swallowed. Making the sign of the cross, she recommenced her prayers, fighting against the lustful memories that threatened to engulf her. Surely the Devil had decided to torment her, to lead her astray from the path of righteousness with his temptations. There had been a moment in the hot darkness beside the stable when she would have given herself to Beobrand. She shuddered, unaware that her breath was coming in short panting gasps as she thought again of his touch. She would have fallen to the earth and coupled with him there in the darkness, like animals, had it not been for a moment of clarity that surely had come to her from God or His blessed mother.

She had been so close to losing herself in a passion that was more than forbidden. It was deadly. To succumb to her desires, to allow Beobrand to lie with her, would not only consign her soul to hell, but what of her son, should Oswiu discover her infidelity? What of her own life and that of Beobrand? This folly could not be permitted to continue. She would forget this madness. And to atone for her sins she would renew her efforts to help Aidan and the brethren of Lindisfarena to spread the word of God throughout Northumbria.

She had fallen silent again, the words of the prayers withering on her tongue.

But what of Oswiu? Had he not brought his Hibernian princess, the mother of his firstborn, to Caer Luel, so that he could satisfy his own lust with her? What of his vows before God? Why should the king be allowed to flout his promises but not the queen? She swallowed the bitterness that rose in her throat at the thought of Oswiu with the woman she had never met and whose name was seldom mentioned. It was told that Fín, granddaughter of Colmán Rímid, was a rare beauty of the Cenél nEógain of northern Hibernia. She had sired a son, Aldfrid, for Oswiu long before he had returned with his brother Oswald to Bernicia. It seemed he had never forgotten her and had installed her in a hall far to the west. Every few months Oswiu would assemble his retinue of thegns, gesithas, thralls and servants and travel around the land, visiting his vills where the people would come to him and pay their tribute. Eanflæd had noticed that these journeys seemed to last longer than necessary, particularly when he travelled far into the west. None of his men would tell her what he did there and why he was so keen to travel to Rheged. She had at first thought that he might be visiting Rhieinmelth, the mother of his second son, Alhfrith, and she had been surprised at the anger she felt at the notion and then the relief that had flooded through her when Coenred, who often travelled with the king, had told her this was not the case. In fact, he said, Oswiu never visited the princess of Rheged, who now resided at the new monastery at Magilros, along with Oswald's widow, Cyneburg.

It had not taken her long to wheedle the true reason for Oswiu's lengthy sojourns in the west out of Coenred. When she heard the truth, she had been shocked at the searing jealousy she had felt. If she did not love Oswiu, why should his dalliances cause her any pain? And yet there was no denying that she felt an overwhelming and stabbing pain whenever he headed towards Caer Luel.

She had never mentioned her feelings to the king. She knew him well enough not to show him this weakness that could be exploited. Instead, she brooded over his unfaithfulness, while the seeds of her own longing for Beobrand grew, watered by her jealousy and Oswiu's betrayal.

Looking up at the bejewelled rood that stood atop the plain altar, Eanflæd once again made the sign of the cross. She shook her head. Was she truly the plaything of the Devil? Was she merely using her husband's infidelity to justify her own?

She had lain awake much of the night worrying over her feelings, terrified that she would hear Ecgfrith's pitiful coughs as a testament to her sins. God would punish her, she was sure, and she had prayed over and over that he would spare her son. He was innocent in this. "Punish me," she had whispered in the darkness of her chamber. "It is I who should be blamed."

She had finally fallen into a disturbed sleep, only to be woken shortly after by the sound of men preparing to leave the fortress. Beobrand's man, Cynan, had led the small force out at dawn, and shortly after, Oswine had gathered his comitatus and they had ridden south, hurrying to call the Deiran fyrd. She had risen and watched her cousin leave. The sight of Oswine and his thegns riding away brought her own concerns into stark relief. War was upon them. She would pray and push away this madness that had threatened to consume her these past months.

As if in answer to her prayers, Godgyth had brought a smiling Ecgfrith out of her chamber where, she said, he had slept the whole night without once waking. As Eanflæd had hugged him to her, he had coughed a single time, but gone were the hacking, wheezing gasps of recent months. It seemed as though he was truly recovering from the ailment that had so long afflicted his tiny form. His cheeks were pink and his eyes sparkled.

Eanflæd had been overjoyed. God had listened to her prayers. Despite the pain she had felt at rejecting Beobrand's advances, she knew she had done what was needed. It was her duty to her husband, her son, and Bernicia.

Banishing thoughts of Beobrand from her mind, she resumed her recital of the prayer to the holy Maria.

A heartbeat later, the door of the church swung open. She turned, looking to see who had interrupted her prayer. She expected one of the monks, Coenred perhaps, but the shadowy form in the doorway was tall and broad-shouldered, much larger than any of the brethren of the holy island. She recognised him instantly with a flush of anger. It seemed the Devil was not done tempting her. She gripped the rood pendant that hung from a chain at her neck, a gift from Oswiu.

Beobrand walked quickly into the church, his footsteps echoing in the empty room. She took in his muscular chest, powerful arms and the swagger of his step and she swallowed. Her mouth was dry at the closeness of him, but she kept her face blank, her tone stern.

"Lord Beobrand," she said, "it is unlike you to come to the Lord's house. Do you wish to pray?"

He shook his head.

"No, Eanflæd," he replied, his tone both gruff and soft, like the caress of a callused hand.

She swallowed again.

"I am your queen," she replied, her voice as sharp as a brooch pin. "You will address me as such."

Beobrand hesitated, then nodded.

"As you wish, my queen."

"Well?" she snapped. "Why have you come to disturb me?"

"Eanflæd... My queen..." His voice trailed off and suddenly, staring into his blue eyes in the dim light from the tiny windows and the open door, she felt a prickle of fear.

"What is it?" she asked, her voice no longer imperious and commanding, but small and unsure. The voice of a frightened child, she thought. For an instant she was certain that something had befallen Ecgfrith and she stammered, "What—? Is my son...? Is Ecgfrith...?"

"Your son is well," Beobrand quickly replied.

Relief washed through Eanflæd, only to be replaced with uncertainty and fear once again at Beobrand's next words.

"My queen," he said, "a messenger has brought tidings."

"Is it my husband?" she asked. Her mind spun. Perhaps Penda had met Oswiu in battle somewhere to the west. She took a deep breath, preparing herself for the news of her husband's death.

"No, Eanflæd, the news does not concern the king," Beobrand said, his voice not much more than a whisper, so that she drew closer, looking up at him. She did not comment again on his use of her name.

"What then?"

"The messenger sailed from Cantware. I am sorry," his face looked ashen, but he squared his shoulders and continued. "Your mother is dead."

Chapter 12

Cynan shaded his eyes with his right hand as he crested the rise. He held the mare's reins loosely in his left, gripping Mierawin's flanks easily with his thighs. He rode without thinking, as effortlessly as walking. He knew the mare could give him more speed. She could have eaten up the distance, but the men he rode with were mounted on lesser animals. Besides, no point in exhausting the beasts. Their lives might depend on the horses' stamina soon enough.

Below him the old path stretched out into the distance. Some way off to the right, a shepherd was sitting in the shade of some oaks. A small flock of scruffy, shorn sheep milled about the hillside. There was no sign of anyone else on the track or the land that rolled away before him to the west. The horizon was clear of smoke and the telltale pall of dust of a warhost on the move. A quick glance over his shoulder told him the dozen men Ethelwin had sent with him were some way behind. He hoped they were better warriors than they were riders. They were making good progress, the day was dry and bright, but he had to curb his mount frequently to allow the warband to catch up. This had done nothing to improve his dark mood.

Digging his heels into Mierawin's ribs he sent her cantering towards the lonely shepherd. As Cynan approached, the man stood. His face was lined and weathered, eyes dark within the tanned folds of his skin. He reached for his staff, slowly, deliberately, making an effort not to appear menacing. He was clearly no fool. Cynan was young and strong and his attire and gear left no doubt that he was a warrior of some renown, with sword and helm strapped to his saddle and his black-daubed shield slung over his back.

The shepherd's dog, a shaggy brute with straggly grey, black and white fur, rose up from the grass and growled. A whistle from the shepherd silenced the hound and it slunk to its master's side, from where it gazed steadily at Cynan, the threat clear in its dark eyes.

Mierawin tossed her mane and stared back at the dog, nostrils flaring.

"Good health," said Cynan, reining in the bay mare.

"And to you," replied the shepherd, suspicion evident in his tone. "Friends of yours?" His gaze flicked towards the horizon. Cynan turned in the saddle and the leather creaked. The warband were finally riding into view over the hill.

"Yes," he replied. "And yours."

"Mine?" enquired the shepherd.

"Friends."

The man's dark features creased in a frown.

"I doubt that very much, lad. I've never had any friends who rode horses and carried spears and swords."

"We mean you no harm. We ride from Bebbanburg."

The shepherd seemed unimpressed.

"Seen it once. Not as grand as I'd been told."

Cynan frowned. It had been a mistake to ride to this man. And yet he was here now, so he might as well impart his tidings and offer him the advice he had given others they had passed that morning.

"War is coming," he said, his tone blunt and hard. "Penda of

Mercia is marching. If you value your life, take your sheep and head into the hills."

"War, you say?" The shepherd appeared uninterested. "There have been many wars. None have bothered me."

"Well, if Penda marches this way and you are yet here, they will slaughter your flock to feed their warriors. Likely as not, they will slay you too."

The shepherd shrugged. Reaching up one nut-brown hand he scratched at his beard.

"I don't think they would kill me. What would be the point in that? I once saw a warhost." His face softened into an almost wistful expression. "Years ago, it was. Lord Oswald led them. More men than you've ever seen." He cast a derisory glance at the dozen horsemen on the path. "Much more than that lot. He wanted my sheep to feed the men and I sold him some. Paid me in good silver, too, so he did." He smiled to himself at this memory.

"Oswald is dead," Cynan snapped. "The Mercians will not be as generous."

The shepherd continued scratching in the tangled thatch of his beard.

"We'll see. If these Mercians even come this way," he added, sounding dubious.

Cynan sighed. By the gods, why would men not listen to reason? His anger at Beobrand returned to him in a flash. Were all men so stubborn? So sure of their decisions?

"Remain here at your peril," he snarled. "You have heard my warning."

Without waiting for a reply, Cynan swung Mierawin's head around to the west and, with a squeeze of his heels, sent her cantering at an angle to the track that would see them join the rest of the riders.

Glancing over his shoulder he saw that the shepherd had returned to his spot beneath the oaks. Fool. Well, let him ignore the warning. He would regret it when Penda's horde marched eastward. Cynan could picture their outriders spotting the shapes of the sheep on the hillside, veering off towards them. A warhost was always hungry and fresh meat would not be ignored. As to getting paid for his animals... Cynan shook his head at the man's stupidity.

He was almost at the path now. The course he had set had been judged to perfection and Mierawin jumped the ditch easily and bounded up the shallow bank that led to the hardened earth of the ancient pathway. He was just ahead of the men from Bebbanburg. The leader of the band was a gruff, red-faced man called Reodstan. Cynan had known him for years. He suspected Reodstan disliked him. Perhaps because he was Waelisc, or maybe because he was a more famed fighter and rider. Reodstan nodded a welcome to him as Cynan joined the horsemen. Cynan took in the man's sweaty round face with its tracery of red veins over the cheeks and the flat nose. Reodstan's thinning hair was receding, and what was left of it grew long and was held at the nape of his neck by a leather thong. Perhaps, he thought, Reodstan did not like him because Cynan's face was handsome, where Reodstan's was ugly.

"We will halt soon," said Cynan. "There is a river ahead. The horses need a rest." So do the men, he thought, taking in their vacant stares and slumped shoulders.

Reodstan grunted. They rode on in silence.

Cynan knew that many men considered him blessed. He was tall, fair of face, skilled as a warrior and as a rider. He had a ring-giving lord in Beobrand, who was likely the most famous of all the thegns of Bernicia. Cynan should be content with his life, and yet there was something missing. With the battle-fame and riches he had gained over the years, he could have married a woman of worth. He had treasure enough for the handgeld to be paid to a bride's family and for the morgengifu to be given to a bride on the morning after their handfasting. With his fair hair and his fine features that had fortunately been untouched by battle, he could find many an eager girl to warm him at night. He smiled to himself as he rode. He had bedded a good number of maids around Ubbanford. There was one particular girl, Siflaed, the daughter of a miller in Berewic, whom he had ridden to many times the previous summer. They had spent countless nights in each other's arms in Siflaed's father's barn. Cynan had liked her more than the other girls he had lain with. Siflaed was not only comely, with a curved body no man could ignore, but she was quick-witted and made him laugh. But when one night her father had surprised them, Cynan had run from the barn into the dark, wearing nothing more than his kirtle. Such was his panicked haste, he had left his breeches and shoes behind and galloped into the night. It was not that he was afraid of Siflaed's father. But she had mentioned handfasting the night before and after her father's discovery of their trysts, Cynan knew he would have to wed her.

And the thought of that filled him with dread.

What fools women made of men, he thought. Beobrand was probably even now sitting in the great hall of Bebbanburg, sipping mead and making eyes at the queen. And here he was, remembering a girl who had made him happy. A lively, intelligent young woman who would have made him a good wife. And he had spurned her. And for what? The memory of a Mercian thrall he would never see again?

He saw the River Cocueda ahead of them. There were sallows and alders growing along its banks a short way off to the north. It would make a good spot to water the horses and for the men to sit a while in the shade before they continued into the west.

"We will rest there," he called to Reodstan, pointing to the trees.

Not waiting for a reply, he veered Mierawin off to the right. He heard the sound of the horses' hooves change as the rest of the men steered their mounts from the packed earth of the track to the dry grassland.

He sighed. Beobrand was no more a fool than he. The woman his lord lusted for was forbidden to him, it was true, but at least she was there, alive and tangible. Cynan pined for a woman who was little more than a distant dream of a memory.

Gods, he was such a fool. A couple of weeks after the incident at the barn, he had talked to Bassus about Siflaed. Bassus had laughed, deep and sonorous guffaws filling the hall as Cynan had recounted how he had ridden back to Ubbanford with nothing on save for his kirtle.

When at last he had managed to contain his mirth, Bassus had asked him how he felt about the girl.

"I think of her all the time," Cynan said. "When I am with her I am happy."

"Well, it seems to me then, boy," Bassus said, wiping the tears of laughter from his eyes, "that you had best go back and beg her forgiveness for running. Perhaps you should speak to her father too. There are worse reasons to wed a girl than happiness."

Cynan cantered into the shade beneath the alders. The river flowed slow and silent, the sun glittering from its surface. He lifted his leg over the saddle and slid to the ground. Leading the bay mare to the water's edge, he let her drink.

He spat into the river.

The miller would not let him see his daughter when he returned to Berewic. Looking back now, he thought he could have persisted, pressing his case. Did Siflaed even know he had come looking for her? He hadn't seen her, and the miller, all bluster and outrage, had turned him away.

"To think I would allow a daughter of mine to marry a Waelisc dog," he'd shouted after him. For an instant, then, Cynan had turned to the man, his hand dropping to the hilt of his sword. Fear had drained the colour from the miller's face and he had stepped back, subdued by the deadly anger in Cynan's eyes. But after a moment, Cynan had turned Mierawin away and ridden off, never to return. What had he thought he could do? Slay the father of the girl he wished to marry?

The dozen riders led by Reodstan arrived at the stand of trees and dismounted. Some groaned and stretched, evidently less used to riding than their Waelisc guide. Cynan pulled Mierawin away from the water and led her back under the trees.

Siflaed married the son of a fisherman that Eostremonath. Bassus had heard the news from Aart, the pedlar who regularly visited Ubbanford and plied his wares all over the north of Albion. Bassus had patted Cynan on the back when he had told him the tidings, pushing a cup of mead into his hand.

"No use in crying over a woman," he'd said. But when Cynan had met the grizzled man's eye, he saw the understanding there. Warriors such as them cried for little, but women had power over even the fiercest of fighters.

They rested for a short while beside the river. None of the men spoke to Cynan but it did not concern him. These men were not his friends, not the family of shield-brothers he had stood beside in battles all along the borderlands of Bernicia. Besides, he was content to brood in silence over the influence that womenfolk exerted over his, and all men's, lives.

After the horses had drunk from the river, Cynan ordered the men to brush them down. Some of the warriors grumbled, but Cynan had insisted.

"Keep your mounts' backs clean and free from sores and you will thank me for it if it comes to a chase. Would you want to be left on foot when Penda's host comes marching towards us?"

He didn't need to say more and the men copied him in unfastening their mounts' girths and removing their saddles. Then, using handfuls of grass, they brushed them down.

After they had rested a while, filling their waterskins and drinking from the river and eating some of the rations they carried, Cynan told Reodstan to get the men back on their horses.

The red-faced warrior twisted his lips as if he tasted something sour, but he nodded and began barking orders at his men. Soon they were on their way again.

Cynan had hoped they might reach Fraomar and the men from Ubbanford before dark, but the sun was sinking red and hazy towards the earth when he called a halt to their westward ride. They slid from their saddles in a copse of ash and hazel that had grown around the crumbling grey stone ruins of a collection of long-abandoned buildings. The site was commanding. It overlooked the path and had good views of the land in all directions. It must surely have been built by the men from far-off Roma who had once ruled these lands. Now, only the bones of their buildings remained.

The men were exhausted, slick with sweat and streaked with dust, but Cynan was quick to tell Reodstan to set watches through the night.

Most of the men began stripping the saddles from the horses, but a few threw themselves to the earth, too tired to care about their animals.

"Tend to your horses," Cynan snapped at the men who had slumped to the ground. "If you leave them standing shaking in their sweat like that, they'll be no good to any of us in the morning." Groaning, the men rose and saw to their mounts, tethering them beneath the trees and in the lee of the angular rock walls that seemed to rise from the earth. Cynan ignored the dark glances the men cast his way.

Once Mierawin had eaten a few handfuls of oats and had drunk from the stream that trickled down from the high moorland, Cynan secured her reins to the bough of a hazel and then, chewing a strip of salt beef, he wandered to where the first of the sentries had been positioned atop what appeared to be an ancient earthwork. Fleetingly, Cynan wondered at what manner of men had laboured to raise the earth and erect the stones in this place. The sentry, a slender, fox-faced man with darting eyes, was staring into the setting sun, squinting at its glare.

"Do you see anything?" asked Cynan.

"No. There is nothing moving out to the west."

Cynan glanced away from the fiery orb of the sun. The shadows of the trees stretched out long and spindly against the undulating earth, dark fingers pointing into the east. The low sun showed every ripple of the ground, picked out every blade of grass, the leaf of every nettle and the twig on every tree in a ruddy golden glow against stark, black shadows.

"What about from the east?" he asked.

The sentry turned and let out a curse as he noticed what Cynan had seen.

Two riders were approaching along the path. The setting sun glinted from their weapons and battle harness. One of the horses was a huge stallion, as black as the shadows that gave him his name.

Sceadugenga.

"Reodstan," called the sentry, and the florid-faced warrior hurried up to where the two men stood.

Cynan stepped to greet the two horsemen as they pulled their foaming mounts to a halt. The animals had been ridden hard. They were lathered in sweat, blowing and pawing the ground. Both riders slid from their saddles and Cynan took their reins. He unhooked the leather water flask from where it was attached to Sceadugenga's saddle. Leading the tired steeds to the sentry, he handed the man the reins.

"See to Lord Beobrand's horse and that of his man, Halinard."

The sentry opened his mouth as if to refuse. But Reodstan shook his head with a sigh.

"Ordlaf," he said, "see to the horses and send Aethelwig to take over the first watch. You seem to have forgotten that you need to keep your wits about you to act as a sentry."

"But—" started the sentry, his face paling at the slight.

"And, Ordlaf," Reodstan said, cutting off his protests, "tell Aethelwig you will take the second watch. And if I find you sleeping, I will have your balls for a pendant."

With a face like thunder, Ordlaf led the horses under the trees. Cynan walked back to Beobrand, handing him his water flask.

"So, you decided to join us in the end, lord?"

Beobrand took a long swallow of water, then handed the flask to Halinard.

For a moment Beobrand met Cynan's gaze, but did not speak. At last, he nodded.

"My place is with you, not with the likes of Fordraed, cowering in Bebbanburg."

Cynan smiled. That was as close to an apology as he could expect. They followed Reodstan back towards the rest of the men and the tethered horses. Cynan wondered what had occurred back in Bebbanburg.

"And your place is not with women? Not with the queen?" he whispered.

Beobrand stopped short. Anger flashed in his eyes. Cynan swallowed. Had he gone too far? Again, he wondered what had happened.

Then, after a moment, Beobrand slapped him on the shoulder and offered him a rueful smile.

"No, not with her either," he said, and they walked into the camp together.

Chapter 13

Beobrand looked about as the men roused themselves with the first glimmers of dawn. The night had passed uneventfully. These were steadfast warriors, many of whom he knew by name and a few, such as Reodstan, by reputation also. The camp had been subdued, the men exhausted from the day of hard riding, but also unsure of what the dawn would bring. They were riding into the unknown, but certainly into danger. They were not craven, of that Beobrand was sure. Several of these men had stood atop the hill at Maserfelth. Any warrior who had survived that blood-letting knew what Penda was capable of, so to ride towards a host of Mercian and Waelisc invaders took courage. No, these men were not cowards, but they were quiet and nervous as they harnessed their horses in the cool light of the early morning. No man liked to ride towards an unseen foe. Uncertainty eroded strength and resolve, the way waves gouged at the rocks of a cliff.

Looking at the small number of men, Beobrand began to question the wisdom of what they were doing. What did they hope to achieve? Cynan and Attor had said that the host arrayed against them was huge. What could a dozen more men do, even when added to the score Beobrand had left watching the horde? Thirty warriors against hundreds? Beobrand was doubtful they would be able to do anything apart from keeping ahead of the advance, and then warning Ethelwin and those to the east of their enemies' whereabouts and movements. Still, this was useful enough and being forewarned could be key in the coming battle, spelling the difference between defeat and victory.

Beobrand pulled himself up onto Sceadugenga's broad back, keeping the unease and worry from his face. These men were being led by the mighty Beobrand, Lord of Ubbanford, and he knew he had to play the part of the invincible warlord.

"Keep your eyes open and your hands close to your weapons," he shouted to the mounted men. "Today we will surely meet with my gesithas, but we know not what the day will bring. We are close to Penda's warhost and so must ride with care. And remember, we are not coming to attack the Mercian bastards. Not yet! There will be time enough soon to soak the land with their slaughter-sweat. But not today. We are coming to add our numbers to those of my men. We are to watch Penda's host, to see where he is heading. If he moves, we will follow – and, if possible, we will buy time for Ethelwin and Oswine, that they may assemble the fyrds of Northumbria. And when those fyrds of our countrymen are brought together, there will be such a battle that Penda will regret leaving Mercia. The wolves and ravens of Bernicia will be fat from the feeding we will give them."

The men were all staring at him. He could feel the weight of their gaze on him as much as see them in the dawn-dark under the trees. He reached up to the whale tooth hammer amulet at his neck. He felt as nervous and unsure as the men around him, but he fixed his features in a grim mask of determination and confidence. He prayed that Fraomar and his men yet lived.

"If we see the enemy today, I want no heroic deeds for the scops to sing of," he bellowed, making some of the horses shy away from his voice. Halinard was looking at him and he knew they were both thinking of Brinin, lying pale and sweating in a pallet in Bebbanburg, watched over by an old crone. "Listen to Reodstan and me, and obey us without question. I know you are all men of mettle and my Black Shields and I will be proud to ride with you. To fight alongside you, if it comes to it." He met the gaze of some of the men in the gloom beneath the ash and hazel trees. Did they raise themselves up straighter in their saddles under his glower? "Now, enough of words. Let us ride! For Bernicia!"

Kicking his heels into Sceadugenga's flanks, he set off at a canter towards the steel-grey sky of the west. A few of the men echoed his last words in a ragged cheer and with a rumble like thunder, the mounted warband fell in behind him, hooves drumming against the summer-dry earth.

Beobrand had sent Cynan out just before dawn to scout ahead of them and they had not been riding long when he saw a rider coming towards them along the road. The sun had only just topped the eastern horizon, but the day was going to be clear again and it was already warm on Beobrand's back. He did not have the keenest eyes, but with the sun shining full in the face of the oncoming rider, Beobrand could make out the tawny-coloured mare Cynan rode. Beobrand and Reodstan galloped ahead to meet the scout.

"Have you seen Fraomar?" Beobrand asked as they reined in close to one another in the middle of the wide road. "Or Penda?"

Cynan shook his head. Reaching out absently, he patted his mare's neck.

"I have seen neither, lord."

"Then why return so soon?"

"There are folk fleeing from the warhost."

Beobrand frowned.

"So Penda is on the move. I do not blame sheep for running before the wolves."

"But that is why I have come to you," replied Cynan, his expression one of confusion. "The people I have seen did not speak of Mercians, but of Waelisc. Men riding under the banners of Powys and Gwynedd."

"And what of it? We know that the Waelisc have allied with Penda once more."

"Yes, lord, but you don't understand. We know Penda to be west of here. But the families fleeing the men of Powys and Gwynedd I met at a crossroad, where Deira Stræt meets this path."

It was Beobrand's turn to look confused.

He was suddenly aware of the men gathered behind him. They had ridden up in a cloud of dust, reining in and now listening intently to what the Waelisc scout was saying. A horse whinnied. A man hawked and spat. None of them spoke.

"What are you saying, Cynan?" Beobrand asked.

"These refugees are fleeing from the south. They say that their steading near Hefenfelth was burnt."

This made no sense. Could Penda have decided to lead his host southward from where Attor and Cynan had found their encampment? But to what end? To strike Eoferwic, perhaps? But why then lead his force so far into Bernicia, only to send them back south to Deira? No, that could not be right. Had Fraomar engaged the enemy, perhaps forcing Penda to change his course?

"Take me to the folk you spoke to," Beobrand said. "I would hear their tale for myself."

Cynan obediently led Beobrand and Reodstan, followed by the rest of the warband, back along the path. Soon they reached the crossroads he had mentioned. To the right, starkly lit against the brow of a hill, was a cart and a small group of people and animals.

Leaving instructions to Reodstan to hold the men on the track, Beobrand followed Cynan up the slope.

There were nine of them in all. A stout man, his wife, five children and a skinny thrall. The goodwife, thrall and three of the children were doing their best to drive several pigs and geese along the road. It was not easy, though, and Beobrand could see they would be tired soon and would make slow going chasing the animals this way and that. This was clearly a family of some standing. They owned a wide-horned ox that pulled a sturdy cart. The cart was heavily laden with all manner of goods. Beobrand spied a carved stool, a griddle and what looked like the frame of a box bed jutting from the pile of things on the vehicle. The ninth member of the family was sat atop the jumble of goods on the waggon. He was a wizened, bald man, who sucked at his gums and looked at Beobrand with the vacant stare of an idiot.

The cart was overladen and the ox lowed pitiably as the head of the family goaded it with a birch switch. Two of the man's boys, both little older than Beobrand's son, were leaning their shoulders against the cart, pushing with every sinew of their skinny frames. It would not budge.

Without a word, Beobrand dropped from his saddle. Cynan did the same and they both stepped in behind the cart, lending their considerable strength and bulk. With a heave, the cart began to slowly move up the last part of the rise. Moments later it was over the crest of the hill and the boys and the two warriors leaned over, hands on their knees, panting from the exertion.

"I thank you, lord," said the man.

"It is no matter," said Beobrand, wiping the sweat from his forehead. "I pray that you can keep your family safe. But tell me, are you sure that none of the men in the host you saw were Mercian? My man here says you saw only Waelisc."

The man, a head shorter than Beobrand and perhaps twenty years older, paused, squinting up at the thegn of Ubbanford.

"Well, I did not stay to ask them their names, lord," he said, his face grim. "But I have eyes in my head that see well enough, and I stood in the shieldwall at Elmet. I know my Mercian from my Waelisc man." He flicked a glance at Cynan when he said this. "And I say these men were riding under the banners of Powys and Gwynedd. The black lion and the white eagle. There was no wolf tail standard or any other from Mercia that I have seen or heard tell of. If I were a wagering man, I would bet you an ounce of silver there were only Waelisc in the host that moved along the road."

"Host, you say? How many men? Could they have been outriders for Penda's warhost?"

"I do not know how many men Penda has marching with him, but this was no small band. There must have been over a hundred men, perhaps two hundred. Waelisc men all."

"How is it that you were able to see them so well?" asked Cynan, speaking for the first time. Beobrand noted that his lilting musical accent seemed more noticeable than normal.

"Old Eawig had sent word that warriors were coming. He lives to the west of me, near Gillisland. But Eawig has always been a worrier, and sees warbands where there are only a bunch of brigands in search of a soft farm to plunder. Still, I do not like to take chances, so we packed up the cart and I sent my eldest son here," he nodded at one of the boys, "with the family up the path. I waited back in the woods to the north of our land. That mob of Waelisc bastards rushed along the road." He shook his head, his eyebrows arched in incredulity. "Eawig was right. There was a host of them. Like the plague of locusts they were, in that story the Christ priests tell. They swarmed over our house." His voice choked in his throat as he recalled what he had seen. "The stables and the barn. We only finished building the new barn last Blotmonath. They took what we had left behind and then burnt our home." He hesitated, then, as if a thought had just struck him, he said, "They must have seen the tracks of our cart, but they didn't follow us. In a hurry to go further east, they must have been, for none of them set off after us."

"That was lucky for you," Cynan said.

The man glowered at him.

"I wouldn't call seeing your home burnt and your fields trampled lucky."

The family's grief hung in the air like a cloud of flies over manure. One of the girls who was chasing the geese along had halted and was staring at the two warriors. Her eyes were wide and dark, her cheeks smeared with dirt and the tracks of tears. The man sighed and turned to continue leading his kin northward.

"When did you see the Waelisc host?" Beobrand asked.

"Yesterday," he replied, not looking back.

Without another word, Beobrand swung up into the saddle. Cynan leaped up nimbly onto Mierawin's back. They rode back in silence to the warriors waiting on the path. Reodstan nudged his horse forward to meet them.

"Well?" he said.

They relayed the news. Reodstan listened and then hoomed deep in the back of his throat.

"I can think of only two possibilities," he said. When Beobrand did not speak, Reodstan continued. "Either the man is mistaken…"

"I think he knows what he saw," replied Beobrand.

"Or," said Reodstan, his face grim, "Penda and his allies have split the host."

Beobrand had been thinking the same.

"But why?" he asked, as much to himself as to Reodstan.

"I know not," Reodstan replied.

A sudden shouted warning snapped Beobrand's attention away from Reodstan. A man had spurred his horse forward and was now gesturing to the west. Beobrand recognised Ordlaf. Evidently the man had learnt his lesson about keeping watch.

Beobrand followed the man's pointing finger and saw a rider coming fast along the track. Men tugged weapons from scabbards. The horses fidgeted, jostling and stamping.

Beobrand peered at the oncoming horseman, but he was yet too far away to identify.

Cynan, though, smiled.

"Perhaps he will be able to tell us what the king of Mercia is doing," he said.

Beobrand squinted, but still could not be sure of the rider's identity.

"You recognise him?" he asked.

"Of course, lord," replied Cynan, his tone incredulous that anyone would not be able to pick out the face of the horseman at that distance. "It is Attor."

Chapter 14

Cynan spurred Mierawin forward, scanning the horizon for sign of any pursuers. He saw no movement behind Attor save for a brace of startled partridges that burst from the long grass growing beside the road. They flapped angrily into the brightening sky before settling down into the gorse and heather of the moorland.

Attor was as good a rider as he was a runner and a scout. In moments he had closed the distance between them. Mierawin nickered in welcome, and Attor's piebald stallion nuzzled against the bay mare. Cynan could see that the steed had been ridden hard for some time. The stallion trembled and blew.

"Well met, brother," said Cynan.

"It is good to see you," replied Attor. His eyes flicked over the gathered horsemen. Cynan noticed a strip of linen wound tightly about Attor's right forearm. It was stained red. "Though I had hoped you would return with more men."

Beobrand and Reodstan joined them.

"Attor," Beobrand said, with a nod of greeting.

"Lord."

"What tidings?" Beobrand took in the bandage on Attor's arm. "How do Fraomar and the rest fare?"

Attor's face was grim.

"Well enough. When I left, none had fallen."

"You attacked the enemy?" Beobrand asked, his eyes narrowing.

"No, a group of their scouts found us." Attor spat into the dust.

Cynan, feeling sorry for his friend who looked more tired than he had ever seen him, handed Attor his waterskin. Attor inclined his head in thanks and drank. Cynan liked Attor. He was as vicious as a wolf in combat, dogged in pursuit of his lord's enemies and had never once belittled Cynan for not having been born of Anglisc parents.

Beobrand waited for Attor to slake his thirst and then prompted him to continue.

"So what happened?"

"We slew most of them, but a couple got away with word of our position. We have been riding ahead of Penda's host since yesterday. Fraomar is canny and he has managed to avoid open battle, but how long he can hold out, I do not know."

"And what of you?" Beobrand asked.

"I carry tidings to Bebbanburg. And to you, lord," he added with a twisted grin, "if you were yet there."

"Well, I am here, so tell me."

"Penda has split his force."

Cynan glanced at Beobrand, who was nodding.

Beobrand told Attor of what they had learnt from the refugees.

"The man spoke true, lord," said Attor, handing back the waterskin to Cynan. "The men of Powys and Gwynedd headed south and east."

"To what end?" wondered Beobrand aloud.

Attor shrugged.

"We could not fathom it. Fraomar thought about sending some of the men after the Waelisc, but that would have meant separating the warband and there were few enough Black Shields as it was."

Beobrand frowned.

"And yet he sent you towards Bebbanburg with tidings."

"Aye, lord. Fraomar kept the men together to harry Penda as he advanced. He sent me ahead as he said, rightly I would say, that our most important task was to protect you." He hesitated, before adding, "And the king and his family, of course."

For a moment, Cynan was unsure, confused, trying to make sense of Attor's words, picturing Penda's host marching across the land, the Waelisc warriors splitting from the main force and veering southward.

"You think Penda is marching on Bebbanburg?" he asked at last, for this was the only thing that made sense.

"Yes," Attor said. "I know it seems like madness, but we could think of no other destination. Penda is advancing quickly, possibly in the hope of reaching Bebbanburg before the king has had time to prepare for battle."

Cynan's mind was racing now. He thought of the roads and paths of Bernicia. He had ridden them so often over the years that they were as clear to him in his mind's eye as the lines on his palm. As he imagined the different groups of men marching and riding over his adopted homeland, a possibility dawned on him.

He opened his mouth, but Beobrand spoke first.

"Attor," Beobrand said, "where is the fyrd of Bernicia called to arms?" On hearing the question, Cynan knew that he and his lord had reached the same conclusion.

Attor cocked his head quizzically, almost like a hound trying to make sense of his master's words, thought Cynan.

"At Hefenfelth, lord," replied the wiry scout. "The fyrd is assembled in the shadow of the rood that Oswald erected." Beobrand was nodding. Cynan had heard many times of his lord's involvement in the great battle there. A terrible night battle that had seen Beobrand capture Cadwallon, king of Gwynedd. It had been the end of the Waelisc kingdom's hopes of conquest, and the beginnings of the reign of Oswald, son of Æthelfrith; a great victory.

"Yes, and it is well known that the fyrd gathers there," Beobrand said, his voice growing quiet.

Realisation dawned on Reodstan's flushed face.

"By the wounds of Christ," he blurted out, "could Penda have envisioned such a thing?"

"I know not," Beobrand said, his voice empty of emotion, "but he is a wily old wolf. I think he has seen a way to take Bernicia, and to destroy any chance we might have of standing against him."

The pieces fell into place in Cynan's mind and he could see the position of the different forces, like pieces on a great tafl board in the deadly game played by kings: "The Waelisc will crush the fyrd before it has fully assembled or had time to join forces with the warriors from Bebbanburg," Cynan said, describing the situation they were all imagining. "And Penda will cut off the fortress with his main host, besieging it and swelling his ranks with the Waelisc when they are done with the fyrd at Hefenfelth."

For a moment, none of them spoke.

At last Beobrand said, "But we have some things to our advantage."

"What would that be?" grumbled Reodstan. He sounded like a man already defeated.

"We know what the bastard plans." Beobrand turned to Cynan. "You will ride to Hefenfelth and warn the men gathering there. They must not be caught by surprise. I know of no finer rider and you know the paths of this land as well as anyone. Make haste, my friend, and then hurry north to Bebbanburg, for I fear that is where the true fight will be."

Attor's horse shook its head and the slender warrior patted its neck.

"And what of me, lord?" he asked.

"You, brave Attor, will ride on to Bebbanburg just as you had planned. You will give the tidings of these events to Ethelwin there."

"Ethelwin?" Attor said. "What of our lord king?"

"Oswiu is not at Bebbanburg."

"But does not Fordraed command Bebbanburg in the king's absence?"

Beobrand glowered and Cynan was pleased to see his lord's spirit returned. This was not a man befuddled by thoughts of love and lust. This was Beobrand Half-handed, thegn of Bernicia and lord of Ubbanford. This was the warlord of the Black Shields and Penda would rue the day he had marched his men into the land Beobrand called home.

"I care nothing for that fat bastard Fordraed," Beobrand said. "See to it that you speak to Ethelwin. And warn the people in Penda's path. Tell them to flee and to take their livestock with them. Any food they cannot carry, they are to burn."

"And you, lord?" Attor asked.

"We will join Fraomar and together we will retreat back to Bebbanburg, shielding the folk of the land as best we can from Penda and his dogs."

"And what are the other things?" Attor asked.

"What?"

"You said there were some things that gave us an advantage, lord."

Beobrand grinned. His eyes glinted like chips of ice in the morning sun.

"Penda is not the only king with allies. Oswine of Deira has ridden to Eoferwic. He too has summoned his fyrd and they will march north to Bernicia's aid. If we can hold Penda at bay, we will be able to crush him once and for all with the hammer of Deira against the anvil of Bebbanburg."

Chapter 15

Eanflæd picked up the basket of freshly baked bread. It was heavier than she had anticipated and she almost dropped it. Resting its weight on one of the tables that the bakers used to knead the dough, she adjusted her grip and heaved the basket up with an effort. She knew that everyone was looking to her. She was the queen and it was not seemly for her to be seen performing such menial tasks.

Fordraed had confronted her about her behaviour earlier in the day. He had intercepted her as she carried two brimming pitchers of ale to some newly arrived families.

"You should not be doing this," he said.

"What should I not do?" she had enquired. "Help my people? Bring drink to the men who are building shelters for their families? And why should I not do these things?"

"You are the queen." His voice lost its conviction under her withering stare.

"Yes, I am your queen and you would do well to remember that, lord Fordraed," she said, her tone scathing. "And it is a queen's duty to aid her people."

"Oswiu will not like this," he said.

"Well, I am sure none of us like this," she replied, indicating the throngs of men, women and children who had flocked to

Bebbanburg following Attor's warnings of the approach of Penda's warhost. "I also do not like having missed my mother's funeral." She swallowed back the bitterness of the words. Her arms were burning from the weight of the overflowing earthenware jugs of ale. "And these people do not like having to flee their homes to seek protection behind the palisades of Bebbanburg. Oswiu might not like any of it," she pushed past Fordraed and handed the jugs of ale into the eager hands of two women who bowed to her, "but the king is not here."

Ever since Attor had ridden in the previous afternoon, the refugees had been arriving in their droves. It was likely Penda would destroy all in his path and the only safe haven the folk of Bernicia could imagine was Bebbanburg, the impregnable fortress on the rock.

Hefting the basket of bread, she carried it as quickly as she could to where the largest group of makeshift shelters was being erected. The courtyard was abustle with activity. There was the sound of axe and hammer on timber as men quickly threw up makeshift shelters against the walls. The halls were already filled and all the available floor space had been taken the night before, so the newest arrivals would have to resort to building their own lean-tos.

An elderly woman called Seaxburg helped Eanflæd to set down the basket and then to hand out the food. The old woman had a kindly face, despite the lines of worry wrought there. The bread was taken in moments and a sliver of doubt entered Eanflæd's mind. If they were to be besieged here, they would need to start rationing the food. The days were warm and dry, and the bustle of families in the courtyard gave the place an air of a festival. Many of the families had brought animals with them and the yard was swarming with cows, sheep, goats, even a noisy gaggle of grey geese. The sight of so many animals gave the impression that there would be enough to feed them all for a long time to come. But just scanning the numbers of dirt-smeared faces and the grubby hands that snatched the warm loaves from her, she knew they would be hungry soon enough, if they had to remain in the fortress for any length of time. She would speak to Brytnere the steward and Ethelwin about it.

When all the bread had been given out, Seaxburg smiled sheepishly.

"May God smile on you and your son, my lady," she said. "Your father was ever gōd cyning. I see much of him in you, though you are clearly your mother's daughter too. And even more beautiful than her."

Eanflæd thanked the woman and rushed away, lest she see the tears brimming in her eyes. She was an orphan now and she had never felt so alone in all her life. When Edwin had been slain and her family had fled to Cantware, she had Ethelburga, Wuscfrea and Yffi at her side. Now they were all gone. Oswiu was somewhere in the west rutting with his Hibernian whore and Eanflæd had pushed away the only man she wanted. The news of her mother's death had cut into her like a sword thrust. She had still been reeling from the previous night-time encounter with Beobrand, but to have him there before her in the dark interior of the church, telling her the grave news about Ethelburga, had undone her for a time. She had wailed with grief and, after the slightest hesitation, Beobrand had taken her in his arms and comforted her as if she were a child, smoothing her hair and whispering soft words in her ear.

After a long time, her tears had dried and she had looked up at Beobrand's stern features. She would have thrown all of her promises to herself and God away in that moment. He had wiped the tears from her cheeks with a rough thumb and a thrill had run through her at his touch.

"I am sorry for your loss," he said. "Your mother was a great woman." He sighed. "Now," he said, his tone apologetic, "I must ride after Cynan. I should be with my men. It is where I can serve Bernicia best."

A pain gripped her then. It was a physical, nauseating ache in her gut as bad as any monthly cramps. For a moment she wondered if she was ill, but then rage replaced the pain. She shoved Beobrand away and swiped at her tear-streaked cheeks. Smoothing her dress, she took a deep breath.

"Yes, lord Beobrand," she said with a voice as cold as the hoar frost that formed on the high hills in winter, "you should go. Thank you for bringing me these tidings."

He looked at her, blinking stupidly in the gloom. He opened his mouth as if to speak, but she wished to hear no more from him.

"That will be all," she snapped, dismissing him.

He opened his mouth again, then shook his head and strode from the church.

She had not seen him since then. And her initial anger at him had been replaced by a yearning to see him again. She felt alone on this crag of rock. Even now, surrounded by hundreds of Bernicians, many of whom remembered her heritage and looked up to her as the daughter of Edwin, she had no real friends here. She could not truly confide in Godgyth. The woman's tongue flapped like a flag in a strong wind and to tell her any of her deepest thoughts would be to hear them repeated the next day in the hall. There were other women in the fortress, the wives of some of the thegns and warriors, but the only one with whom she had enjoyed any kind of friendship was Edlyn, Fordraed's long-suffering wife. But she could not confide in poor Edlyn. Being wed to Fordraed brought its own woes.

The news of her mother's death, coming so soon on the heels of the night-time meeting with Beobrand, threatened to overwhelm Eanflæd. After he had left the church, she had returned to her chamber and clutched little Ecgfrith to her breast, breathing in his scent until he began to squirm and whimper. All that day she had felt the darkness encroaching, her black thoughts swirling about her like a murmuration of autumn starlings.

The only glimmer of light came from Ecgfrith. His coughing had indeed abated and, after so many months of sickness, colour was coming back into his cheeks. She had been right to push Beobrand away, she was sure. The instant she had made her decision, God had lifted the curse that had hung over her son. There was no doubt that the Lord was rewarding her for her righteousness, for turning her back on sinful temptations of the flesh.

But still, she had wept often in her chamber as she thought of the mother she had not seen since leaving Cantware; the stern woman she would never see again in this life.

When, the next evening, she heard shouts announcing the arrival of a messenger followed by the clatter of hooves in the courtyard, she hurried into the hall to hear the news. Attor, slender, grizzle-cheeked and travel-stained, stood before Ethelwin and Fordraed. She approached quietly and quickly across the rushes to stand in the shadows as Attor spoke. She heard most of the tidings he brought and pieced together what she had missed by the flow of the subsequent conversation.

Penda was heading for Bebbanburg. He had sent part of his host, that of his Waelisc allies, south, probably to head off the fyrd at Hefenfelth. Beobrand and his small warband were riding before Penda, hoping to slow his advance to provide time for the folk of Bernicia to seek sanctuary behind Bebbanburg's walls.

Soon after Attor's arrival, the first of the refugees began to reach the fortress, carrying what possessions they were able and driving whatever livestock they could before them. On seeing the weary families trudging through the gates, Eanflæd cast aside her own troubles, her grief and broiling emotions. Now was not the time for self-pity. Bernicia was under attack and she would do all in her power to help those who were suffering. She was not able to don battle harness, to take up spear and shield and stand with the gesithas in the shieldwall, so she would do what she could.

Eanflæd started by simply lending her hands to the tasks that needed to be done. She carried provisions, entertained children while their mothers helped their men to build shelters, she had even offered to help the servants in the kitchen, but she soon saw that she made them nervous and caused more trouble by being there than if she left them to their work.

Now she saw a way she could truly help and she hurried across the courtyard to the great hall. The door wards dipped their heads to her as she passed into the gloomy interior. Outside, the fortress was a tumult of sounds and smells from countless unwashed bodies. The sheep and goats bleated, the cattle lowed, and the numerous hounds barked their displeasure at the new visitors to their realm. Stepping into the hall, the chaos receded, dimmed by the stout walls to a vague buzzing, easily ignored.

She took a calming breath, smoothing her dress over her thighs. She noticed that the hem of the green dress was mud-spattered, as were her shoes. The dress had been a gift from her mother. For a heartbeat, Eanflæd remained still in the relative peace of the hall. Closing her eyes, she imagined what her mother would have done if she had been there. She let out her breath, opened her eyes, and walked with purpose down the length of the hall.

At the far end of the hall several men stood around a board that had been raised on trestles as if for a meal, but apart from a couple of pitchers, the table was empty of sustenance. Instead, as she approached, Eanflæd saw that the table held several wooden cups and bowls, each turned upside down. The gathered men were grim-faced and sombre, staring at the upturned vessels with great concentration.

Ethelwin leaned forward and pushed one of the bowls towards a group of cups.

"How long until Penda reaches Bebbanburg, do you think?" he asked.

Attor peered at the items on the table, evidently imagining the movement of horses and men across the landscape of Bernicia, rather than cups and plates over the linen-covered board.

"I think he could be here as soon as tomorrow," he answered at last.

"So soon?" asked Fordraed, his voice rising in consternation and fear.

Attor nodded.

"With the numbers of men Beobrand has with him, I cannot imagine he will be able to hold the Mercians up for long."

All the men looked perplexed. Ethelwin sighed and, turning to one of his warriors, he began asking about how best to deploy the men they had on the walls. They were starting to discuss how to divide them into separate bands of men, so that some could rest while others would be on the walls to defend the fortress, when Eanflæd interrupted them.

"Apologies, noble lords," she said.

They all turned to look at her. Her mouth grew dry under their gaze.

"Have you tired of acting as the servant of the peasants?" asked Fordraed, his tone contemptuous.

How would her mother have dealt with this repulsive man? Eanflæd glowered at Fordraed for a moment, raising her chin so that she peered down her nose at him.

"On the contrary," she said, "I believe I can yet serve. But perhaps you were right and the best way for me to do that is not to carry loaves and ale."

Fordraed let out a guffaw and was about to reply, but Ethelwin cut him off.

"My lady," he said, "however you can help would be welcome, but as you can see, we are busy preparing the defences."

"Indeed, lord Ethelwin," she replied, "and I do not wish to keep you from this most important of tasks." She hesitated, unsure how to proceed.

Ethelwin raised his eyebrows expectantly.

"What did you wish to say to us?" he enquired gently.

Eanflæd drew in a deep breath.

"I came to ask about the supplies of salt."

"Salt?" asked Fordraed. "Lady, we have more important things to discuss than the next meal."

Eanflæd rounded on him.

"Do you truly, Fordraed?" Her tone was calm, but her heart raced, the blood rushing in her ears. She let her gaze take in his quivering jowls and the soft paunch that swelled like proving dough over his belt. "You of all people look like you might be worried lest we should run out of provender."

Ethelwin smiled and Fordraed glowered.

"What are you proposing?" Ethelwin asked.

"I believe that Brytnere is overwhelmed. With so many people flooding into Bebbanburg, I think he would welcome help from one who can tally and plan."

"One such as yourself, my lady?"

"Yes," she replied. "I know how to sum and subtract and I was trained in logic and rhetoric by the greatest minds in Cantwareburh. I should help him. But I thought I should seek the approval of my husband's warmaster and the lord he set to govern Bebbanburg first."

"And the salt?" asked Ethelwin.

"If we are besieged here for many days, food will become our biggest problem. We must slaughter the animals that have been brought onto the rock. We'll need salt to preserve the meat."

Ethelwin was nodding, but Fordraed still glared at her.

"When I have seen the stores and we have set about preparing the meat, I will draw up plans for rationing the food. We have plenty of water from Waltheof's Well, but we will need to keep the food in one of the storehouses and I'll need some men to help with the animal slaughter and to guard the stores."

"You think people would steal food?"

She thought of Ecgfrith, the colour in his cheeks, the sound of his laughter. And then, the memory of the hacking cough that had racked his tiny body for so long.

"The men and women here may well be brave and able to resist temptation should it come to it," she said. "But hunger is a strong goad and crying children might well push parents to do something rash. I pray to God that you brave men of Bernicia can defeat Penda quickly, but if we cannot, we must plan for a siege."

Ethelwin stared into her eyes for a time. She met his gaze, unflinching.

"Very well, my queen," Ethelwin said at last. "It is clear that you have thought much on this and I am sure that Brytnere would welcome the offer of help from one with such a sharp mind."

Eanflæd let out her breath, feeling a great sense of gratitude for the old warmaster's belief in her abilities. She started to move towards the hall doors, her shoulders set, her back straight. She had walked a few paces when she halted. She turned back to the men.

"Lord Fordraed," she said, her voice as soft and sweet as honey. "Do I have your blessing to continue to serve the people by helping Brytnere to organise the food?"

He loured at her. From the board before him, he picked up a cup and filled it with ale. Colour flushed his plump cheeks and Eanflæd was certain that he longed to throw the cup at her, such was his fury. She kept her expression open and expectant, a slight smile on her lips as she awaited his response. Fordraed glanced at Ethelwin, but the warmaster merely shrugged and said, "Well, man? We have matters to attend."

Fordraed opened his mouth, but then seemed to think better of it. Draining the cup of ale, he offered her a perfunctory nod, before turning his attention back to the movements of warriors and plans for the defence.

That would have to do, she supposed, as she strode away down the hall towards the bright sunshine and chaos awaiting her outside. What had made her taunt the man that way? But as she walked out into the light, she knew. She was Edwin and Ethelburga's daughter. Royal blood flowed in her veins and she would not suffer fools and bullies such as Fordraed. Her husband might have placed him in command of the fortress, but the fat toad would never command her.

She made her way across the yard. Several of the ceorls stopped what they were doing to watch her pass. Fordraed was of no consequence. It would be strong men, the likes of Ethelwin and Beobrand, who would defeat Penda. Spotting Eanflæd, Seaxburg waved. Eanflæd smiled back. These were good people. Her people. And she would do all she could to help them.

She found Brytnere in the main storeroom. Several thralls were assisting him in stacking provisions. He was a severe-looking man, with short-cropped grey hair and sharp features. A burly man swung a sack of grain onto his shoulder as if it weighed no more than a bag of autumn leaves.

"Over there," Brytnere barked, pointing into a corner where several more sacks were piled high.

The thrall, evidently knowing that it did not do to keep the steward waiting, turned quickly to do his bidding. He almost collided with Eanflæd, who had entered the storeroom silently. He grunted and had to sidestep quickly to avoid knocking the queen to the ground. The man staggered for a moment and she thought he might fall, but he righted himself and flung the sack down where he had been told.

"Sorry, my lady," he mumbled, red-faced and bowing low. He was clearly terrified of what might happen to him. Slaves had been flayed for less than making a queen gasp in fright.

"You have nothing to apologise for, Caillen," said Brytnere, taking in the scene instantly. His eyes were sharp, missing nothing. "The queen should know better than to enter here unannounced. Now, my lady, what can I do for you? As you can see, I am very busy." His tone was brusque and Eanflæd felt the anger at being dismissed so readily begin to rekindle.

"I know you are busy, Brytnere," she said, forcing her voice to remain calm. "That is why I am here."

"Explain," he snapped, and then, as if realising suddenly that she was not one of his thralls, he added with a rueful smile, "my lady."

Despite his gruff tone and his rapid dismissal of her, she found herself warming to the man. She had spent little time with him before, but she realised he was direct and energetic. He certainly appeared to be a man not to be trifled with.

She repeated what she had told Ethelwin and Fordraed. As she spoke, Brytnere's face broke into a broad grin. As his smile widened, she felt her anger swelling so that by the time she had finished speaking she was ready to scream at his insolence. Here was another like Fordraed, a man who thought that no woman was capable of doing more than cleaning, cooking or carrying his children. Even the queen, it seemed, was incapable in their minds of being more than a peace-weaver between kingdoms, a brood mare to bear the heirs of the king.

For a moment, she stood there, seething as he smirked.

"Well?" she asked at last, her tone clipped.

"Well, why didn't you say so?" he replied.

She was confused. What did he mean?

"Say so?" she asked, feeling foolish.

"That you were here to help me," he said, his smile broadening even further, something she would have thought impossible. "You are right, of course. There is too much for me alone to do, what with so many people behind the walls. And you are clearly as sharp of mind as you are beautiful, my lady."

She blushed at the sudden compliment.

"Well, it seems you have already thought about preparing the meat. How about you take Aibne and Caillen here and start organising the killing?"

The rest of the day was a blur of work. Despite the complaints from the owners of the animals, they began the slaughter of the larger beasts. She found barrels of salt and ordered the precious commodity to be rubbed into some choice cuts of the meat before being hung from the beams in the halls. Thinner strips of meat were also prepared to be dangled over the smoky hearth fire. This would dry into a leathery consistency that would last forever, or close enough. Yet more of the salt was mixed with water. Into this brine, fresh meat was submerged.

It was after dark when Godgyth came to her and ordered her to rest. Before going to her bed, she kissed sleeping Ecgfrith's brow. Godgyth told her he had barely coughed the whole day and he had eaten well. A peaceful warmth enveloped Eanflæd as she lay in her bed. War was coming and the future was uncertain, but she had purpose, her son was well and her body and mind were so tired that sleep rushed over her like the tide flooding the sand between Bebbanburg and Lindisfarena.

The next day she awoke early. She ate a few mouthfuls of porridge and was pleased to see Ecgfrith emptying the bowl Godgyth fetched for him. The boy was smiling and bright-eyed and Eanflæd was sure that she could already see him putting on weight.

With a new sense of focus, she once again set about directing the slaughter and preserving of the meat ready for the possible lengthy siege that might follow. She also spoke at length with Brytnere and together they began to come up with the plan for rationing the food. There were many things to consider, but her mind was quick and she revelled in sharing her thoughts with Brytnere who in turn seemed overjoyed to have found someone to not only confide in, but to share the load of catering for a fortress full of people.

It was another long, dry day and still more refugees arrived from the lands to the west. The sun was low in the sky, setting ablaze the few clouds that floated over the western horizon.

Eanflæd wiped the sweat from her forehead as she watched the last of the salting. There had been fewer complaints today. She had addressed the people that morning, and they had resigned themselves to sharing what they had for the common good. But it was still exhausting work for those doing the killing, salting and storing of the meat. Eanflæd, too, was weary. There were so many things to think about that she started to grow dizzy in the afternoon sun and Seaxburg led her into the shade of one of the shelters and made her sit a while, sipping water and eating a small piece of bread.

She soon regained her strength, but knew she must rest before long. There was nothing to be gained if she grew ill from lack of respite or food. She would oversee this last animal's preparation and then she would return to her chamber. There was still much to do, and tomorrow would be another busy day, she was certain.

A shout came from the western palisade and everyone turned to look up at the guards there, shadowed against the red sky.

"Riders approaching!" came the cry.

The gathered throng quietened as the men and women listened intently. Was this the beginning of the anticipated siege? Was Penda's host even now marching towards the gates of Bebbanburg?

Eanflæd remembered climbing the palisade just a few days before, the excitement hammering in her chest at the sight of Beobrand. For a moment, she thought of running to the wall again. Nobody would deny her and she longed to know who came. But it would not do. She was their queen and they looked to her for strength. They were not best served to see a giddy girl desperate for a glimpse of one of the thegns. One of her husband's oath-sworn men. Besides, she told herself, there was no place for Beobrand in her mind or her heart.

She fixed her gaze on the men before her. Sweat drenched

their limbs, and their kirtles and breeches were dark with blood. They knew what they were about now. This was the last of many animals slain and prepared that day, but she watched them intently.

For what seemed a long while, no more word came from the wall. The crowds were subdued, listening for the next piece of news. After what seemed an age to Eanflæd, one of the wardens shouted out again, loud enough for all to hear.

"They are Black Shields."

A murmur went through the crowd. These were the fabled warriors of Beobrand of Ubbanford. Their prowess was legendary and to hear that they would be at the defence of Bebbanburg brought a ripple of relief to the people.

Eanflæd did not take her eyes from the grisly task before her. Caillen had hacked through the final haunch of the skinned ox, and was placing the fresh meat into a barrel, into which Aibne then poured brine. All the while, Eanflæd stared at the activity. Her back was to the main gates and she refused to turn around. Gone was the weakness of the flesh that had so befuddled her. She was the Queen of Bernicia and she had important tasks to carry out to prepare the fortress to withstand a siege. The defence of the wall and Beobrand's Black Shields were not her concern. She straightened and resolutely watched Caillen working.

She did not move at the rasping squeal of the great gates being hauled open. And she did not turn at the clattering of hooves and jingle of harness and battle gear as the riders entered into Bebbanburg.

But she let out a long pent-up breath when she heard his voice.

There was no mistaking Beobrand's tone, still bearing the unusual inflections of a Cantware native. He called for someone to see to the wounded.

Her heart jittered and her blood roared in her ears. She

stood watching the thralls lifting the brined meat into its barrel and did not turn to see Beobrand's return. She was stronger than that. But it seemed she could not contain her relief, for, though she made not a sound, at hearing Beobrand's voice, unbidden, hot tears rolled down her cheeks.

Chapter 16

"They'll be upon us soon," Beobrand said with a sigh.

He leaned on the timber palisade and stared out to the western horizon. Smoke hazed the distance. He stretched, rubbing at the small of his back. It ached from riding. Further along the wall, Beobrand could make out several of his gesithas, all staring into the west. They knew what was coming and their faces were sombre.

Attor joined him on the ramparts. The slim fighter scanned the horizon to the south. He said nothing, but Beobrand knew he was looking for any sign of Cynan and the fyrd.

"How do Eadgard and Fraomar fare?" asked Beobrand. Both men had been wounded in their final skirmish with Penda's outriders. Eadgard had taken a slashing cut to his leg and Fraomar had received a terrible blow to the head. It had come from an overarm hacking swipe of a langseax, knocking Fraomar to the ground and denting his helm. Grindan had leapt to his aid, disembowelling the Mercian. Beobrand had pulled Fraomar to his feet and they had fought on. Eadgard's injury had bled profusely, and after they had slain half of the Mercians and chased the rest away, they had bound his thigh tightly before setting off for the final gallop back to Bebbanburg. They had harried Penda as much as they could, but there was nowhere left for them to hide and so they had run for the fortress. Beobrand cursed silently as he remembered that last frantic ride. He should have seen that Fraomar's injury was bad. But he had not. The young warrior who had led Beobrand's men in his absence had grown pallid and confused as they rode. Beobrand had only understood the gravity of Fraomar's wound when the man had toppled from his mount.

Hurriedly, they had dismounted and rushed to his side. Fraomar was senseless, pale and drenched in sweat. Beobrand had gingerly removed his dented helm and found blood trickling from his left ear. There had been nothing they could do. Penda now knew where they were and would send fresh warriors after them, so Beobrand had ordered them to lash Fraomar to his saddle and they had galloped on. Beircheart had led Fraomar's horse and Beobrand had winced every time the young man's head flopped and lolled against the animal's flanks.

Attor's face was sombre now and he did not meet Beobrand's gaze.

"Eadgard is as strong as an ox," he said. "He'll live." He reached up and touched the Christ rood that hung at his throat. "Fraomar is close to death. He has not awoken and Coenred says he is in the Almighty's hands now. I have prayed for him."

Beobrand nodded, but said nothing. If he had stayed with the men, would Fraomar have been injured? He knew that no good came of thinking so. The past could not be changed. And yet he chewed over the events of the last few days like bitter gristle that he could not swallow.

When they had arrived at Bebbanburg, they had found it thronged with the people of Bernicia who had fled from the approaching Mercian force. It was overcrowded and noisome. Beobrand wondered how long they would be able to hold out against a determined siege. Ethelwin told him that Eanflæd was assisting Brytnere, organising the slaughter of animals, rationing food. Beobrand had seen her as he'd dismounted. He'd recognised her golden tresses and the slender curve of her neck. But she had her back to him and did not turn to face him. She had not come to the hall that night. It was good that she was helping with the preparations for what lay ahead. She was quick-witted and had as sharp a mind as anyone he had ever met. But no matter how cleverly the rationing of the food was handled, if the siege lasted more than a few days, they would soon need to slay their precious horses. That would feed them all for a few more days or weeks. Beobrand thought back to Din Eidyn and the slovenly camp that surrounded the rock and its imposing fortress. It was not an easy thing to besiege such a place, any more than it was a simple thing to be besieged.

The dark shadows of Bebbanburg stretched out across the land to the west. The sun had risen bright into another clear sky and already it was warm on Beobrand's back and neck.

Ethelwin ascended the ladder to the ramparts and looked out silently at the smoke-enshrouded distance.

"Not long now till he shows himself," the warmaster said at last.

They had spoken for a long while the night before. Beobrand had recounted how they had ambushed Penda's outriders, killing many before finally having to turn and retreat to Bebbanburg. No word had come from Cynan, the fyrd or the king. Beobrand had turned over in his mind what might have transpired at Hefenfelth. Could Cynan have been killed? He dismissed the idea. He would not think such a thing. The Waelisc warrior was hale and would return when he was able.

There was a commotion in the courtyard and Beobrand turned and looked down into the shadowed space. Makeshift tents dotted the area and lean-tos lined the walls. One of the goats, evidently due for slaughter but having other ideas, had butted the thrall who had been holding it. The man, taken by surprise, had tumbled to the ground and the angry animal had set off at a run, weaving its way between the shelters. People stepped into the beast's path, but it either charged them or veered away. Eventually, wild-eyed and head lowered for another bruising attack, the goat was cornered between two lean-tos and the palisade. It looked about frantically, desperate for escape. It was oblivious of the guards atop the rampart above and behind it. As Beobrand watched, one of the wall wards inverted his spear, leaned over the rampart and, after taking a moment to gauge his aim, he thrust down into the unsuspecting animal's back. The goat, terrified and in agony, let out a piercing bleating screech, fell to the earth and jerked convulsively as its lifeblood pumped from the wound.

The onlookers cheered at the guard's quick action. But Beobrand sighed. The animal had been surrounded and did not see where the killing blow would come from. Would that be the fate of Bebbanburg? Was that his own wyrd?

Looking away from the dying creature, his eyes met those of Eanflæd. She was staring at him and, for a heartbeat, their gazes locked. Gods, she was beautiful. A moment later, biting her lower lip, she looked away and began directing the thralls to recover the still-twitching goat carcass. The memory of Eanflæd flooded his mind. Her scent, the taste of her lips, the feel of her soft breast, nipple firm against his palm. He shook his head, turning away once more to look out to the west.

Death was coming. Fraomar might yet succumb to his injury. If Bebbanburg withstood the Mercian storm, there would be time enough to think of Eanflæd. Now, he must turn his mind to the walls, to the men who defended them. To the sharpness of their weapons and the strength of their resolve. He glanced at Ethelwin and saw his own anxiety mirrored in the older man's features. The weight of responsibility was heavier than any other burden, Beobrand knew. He would help Ethelwin to shoulder it if he could. The thought of the impending battle, the blood and the death, hung over them like a dark cloud. The only piece of good news he had heard since returning to the fortress was that Brinin was on the way to recovery. He was out of his cot and walking. He would not be able to take up arms for some time, but if Bebbanburg stood, he would live to return to Ardith in Ubbanford.

The thought of Ubbanford further darkened his mood. He had sent Gram with tidings of what was afoot in the land. He had given Bassus instructions to set up a wide perimeter of scouts to the south of his lands. The folk of Ubbanford must not be caught unawares if Penda should send men northward. Beobrand had told Gram to inform the old champion that he must not risk the people. The remainder of his warband must not come south to Bebbanburg, they must stay with the women, children and old folk of Ubbanford and Stagga. He recalled the horrific scenes of burnt timbers jutting into the sky, surrounded by swirling ash and corpses. He would never leave his people unprotected again. He prayed that Bassus would obey him. His son might be safe far away with the king, but Ardith was in Ubbanford beside the slow, wide, meandering Tuidi. He could not bear the thought of anything befalling her.

"Look, lord," Attor said, pointing into the west and bringing Beobrand back to the present. Bassus would have to see to the people of Ubbanford. Beobrand had more pressing matters to attend. He followed Attor's outstretched arm. Attor was older than Beobrand, but his eyes were still keener. Beobrand could discern nothing more than a vague movement beneath the pall of smoke. "Riders," Attor expounded. Squinting, he held up his hands, cupping them around his eyes to shield them from the brightness of the morning sky.

Beobrand waited for the sharp-eyed scout to provide more detail. He knew Attor would see it much sooner than he. After a pause where the men on the wall fell silent, Attor nodded.

"Mercian horsemen. Outriders for the main host. A score of them."

"You are certain?" Beobrand asked, knowing the answer.

"I recognise the leader," replied Attor. Beobrand glanced at him. Did he jest? He could barely discern the figures in the distance. But Attor was not smiling. He turned to Beobrand and shrugged. "That big brute with the long moustaches," he said with no trace of humour in his tone.

Beobrand let out a breath. He recalled the man well enough. He had led the horsemen in the last skirmish. It had been the moustachioed leader who had struck Eadgard.

"The main host will be here by sunset, I imagine," said Ethelwin. His face was stern. "Soon, then, it will begin."

Beobrand could make out the riders now. They were coming at an easy canter. As they approached the scattered buildings that surrounded Bebbanburg's crag, they fanned out into a line and slowed their pace. Perhaps they expected one final ambush from Beobrand and his Black Shields. Beobrand snorted. They would be pleased rather than disappointed when no such attack took place. The steadings, huts and barns were deserted. The inhabitants had long since made their way into the fortress, taking everything of worth with them. Being so close to Bebbanburg's walls afforded them the ability to return to their homes and make several trips with their carts and barrows. So while the Mercians might suspect an attack, the buildings were utterly empty and as still as burial mounds.

They would ride to within an arrow shot of Bebbanburg, Beobrand thought, and then return to await Penda and the amassed host. There would be nothing for them to do now that the Bernicians were safe atop the mound of rock, behind stout walls.

"We should rest while we can," Beobrand said. "I doubt there will be any fighting until tomorrow."

"I wouldn't be so sure, lord," said Attor, his voice hushed. "By Jesu and all the saints, look!"

Beobrand followed the scout's gaze and what he saw made his breath catch in his throat.

He knew not where they had come from, but on the open ground between the last farmstead and the ramp of earth leading up to Bebbanburg's gates, a small group of people were running. It looked like a family. A man with two bundles of rags, one under each arm, and a woman, who appeared to be carrying an infant clutched to her chest. They had abandoned a handcart that had overturned on the path some way behind them. They must have seen the riders, for they were lumbering onwards, pushing themselves hard, without a backward glance. They were coming towards Bebbanburg as quickly as they were able, but from Beobrand's vantage point he could see that the Mercian horsemen would be upon them before they reached safety.

The riders were yet wary, trotting now and still a long way off. It seemed they had not seen the fleeing family, or if they had, they yet suspected a trap. But calculating the distances, Beobrand knew that if they spurred their mounts on, they would overrun the refugees.

As he watched, the running man placed one of the bundles he carried on the ground, and it proceeded to run beside him. It was a child! Now Beobrand could see that the object beneath his other arm was another child, fair braids flapping, just as Ardith's had when he had first seen her in Hithe. The girl child was clearly too small to run and so her father carried her. The burden of both children had proven too much and so his son, a boy of not more than four or five summers, did his best to keep up with his parents.

"Run!" yelled one of the guards on the wall. The call was taken up by others and soon there was a cacophony of encouragement echoing out from the fortress.

Beobrand turned and half ran, half fell down the ladder to the courtyard below. Attor was behind him.

"With me, my brave gesithas," Beobrand yelled. "To the horses!"

"What are you doing?" called Ethelwin after them.

"What I must," Beobrand shouted back and sprinted into the stables, bellowing for the horses to be brought out.

Chapter 17

"Just the bridles," Beobrand shouted.

The two young hostlers blinked stupidly. He had disturbed them in a game of dice and at the sight of him bursting into the quiet of the stables, they had leaped up, overturning a jug of ale with a curse. Beobrand did not hesitate, he moved quickly to the men and grabbed them roughly by their kirtles. One of them, a sallow-faced boy with a wall eye, whimpered. Beobrand dragged them both towards the stalls and, shoving them forward, he repeated, "Just the bridles. There is no time for saddles."

Quickly, he pulled Sceadugenga's harness down from a peg, and threw it over the stallion's huge head. Sceadugenga flinched and rolled his eyes at him, but the horse did not struggle. He took the bit easily in his mouth and remained still as Beobrand fastened the leather strap behind his jaw. As he worked, Beobrand saw the hostlers had begun to follow his actions and were harnessing the horses nearest to the stable door.

"Faster," he yelled, making the horses stamp and snort.

Attor ran into the stable carrying Beobrand's helm, a black shield and Nægling in its scabbard. Beobrand slung the sword-belt over his shoulder and the shield onto his back. He slammed the helm onto his head. There was no time to fasten the ties beneath the helmet.

It would surely fall off, he thought, and as he led Sceadugenga out into the light, the image of Fraomar, senseless and pale, with blood seeping from his ear, flashed into his mind. Beobrand's head ached dully in memory of the blow he had received years before at the great ditch. His helm had saved him then.

He swung up onto Sceadugenga's back. It was easier than usual despite there being no saddle. He was much lighter without his iron-knit byrnie. No armour, no saddle and a helm that would surely slip from his head in moments. He gripped the reins and turned Sceadugenga's great head towards the gates. This was madness. They would surely be killed in the shadows of the wall. And for what? If they did not die, they would be too late to rescue the family.

And yet he could not shake the image of the girl's fair braids bobbing as her father laboured to run to safety. He could not allow them to be slaughtered. And even if he had been able to leave them to their grisly end at the hands of the Mercians, with the defenders of Bebbanburg watching from the walls, it would do more damage to their chances of survival than two hundred more warriors bolstering Penda's horde.

Others of his gesithas were jumping up onto their hastily bridled mounts. He saw Beircheart, Dreogan, Garr, Ulf and Grindan all join him in the courtyard. He was surprised to see a couple of Reodstan's men and the red-faced thegn himself heaving himself up onto the back of a mud-brown mare. None of them was fully armoured and only a couple of the horses were saddled, but in moments, there were a dozen mounted warriors trotting towards the gates.

Beobrand's mind raced. He was trying to imagine how far the family might have advanced. Had the Mercian horsemen seen them? Had they pushed their horses forward into a gallop? Would Beobrand and the other Bernicians be too late to help them? It would be close. They had mounted their steeds quickly and had not tarried to don battle gear, but valuable time had passed.

"Open the gates!" he bellowed in his battle voice. This was the tone he had learnt from Scand, his first lord, a voice that could cut through the clash of blades and shields and the screams of the dying.

The door ward stepped forward, but did not move to open the gates. His face was pale as he looked up at Beobrand.

"Open the gates!" Beobrand repeated, his voice even louder than before.

The man flinched as if stung by a bee, but he did not turn to the gates. He swallowed.

"Fordraed gave the order for the gates not to be opened," he said. "We are safe behind the walls."

Beobrand nudged Sceadugenga forward with a squeeze of his heels. His ice blue stare burnt from beneath his great helm.

"The people out there are not safe," he said, his voice low now, as deadly as a knife under the shieldwall. "They have no time for this." In his mind he could see the horsemen almost upon the struggling family. The Mercian swords glimmering in the sun, the red blood fountaining. "Open the doors," he growled, "or I will open your bowels and then open the gates myself. We'll see how safe you feel then."

For a heartbeat, the man tried to meet Beobrand's glower. But after a moment he withered and turned to the gates.

"Open the gates," he shouted to the other guards. They obeyed without comment, dragging the doors open.

Without hesitation, Beobrand spurred Sceadugenga through the gap as soon as it was wide enough. His back ached as he was jolted against the horse's spine, but he clung on to the stallion and they burst out into the warm morning sunshine outside of Bebbanburg. Beobrand's shield and scabbarded sword slapped against his back as he urged Sceadugenga into a gallop. Behind him he heard the thrum of the other horses' hooves and in a ragged group they careened down the slope.

The first thing Beobrand saw was that the family yet lived. The small group had almost reached the base of the earthen ramp that led up to the fortress's gates. His heart soared at the sight of the five of them stumbling towards him. An instant later, his mood darkened as if a cloud had scudded before the sun. Bearing down on them at a gallop came the mounted Mercians. They were close enough now for Beobrand to make out their scowling faces, the sheen of sweat on their horses' flanks, the glint of sunlight from the wicked spear-points that were lowered towards the backs of the running Bernicians.

Kicking his heels into Sceadugenga's flanks, he urged the stallion on.

"Fly! Fly!" he encouraged the horse. With a whinny, Sceadugenga responded and surged forward.

It would be a close thing. He watched the approaching Mercians intently, anticipating how far they would travel before the Bernician gesithas were able to intercept them. If they did not slow their charge, he could see no way that the family would avoid being slaughtered or crushed beneath the horses' hooves.

"Get off the path!" he screamed, his voice tearing at his throat. The woman stared up at him, eyes wide, mouth open. He waved his arm, indicating they should move to the side. "Get off the path!" he repeated. If they did not move soon, he would have to slow his gallop to avoid crashing into them. The Mercians would have no such qualms. They came on fast, their blades flashing in the morning sun.

For a heartbeat, the woman stared at him with an expression of such overwhelming terror that he was certain she would not be able to understand him. This was going to be a disaster. They would have to halt just short of the family, allowing the Mercians time to kill them and then to turn and ride away.

Beobrand's men had no saddles, armour or provisions. They could not hope to pursue the Mercians towards Penda's warhost.

He twitched on the reins, preparing to pull Sceadugenga up short. He raised his left hand to indicate to the men behind that they were stopping. The stallion's pace began to slow.

With a sudden roar of "For Bernicia!" Beobrand dropped his left hand down and spurred Sceadugenga onwards once more. For at the last possible moment, the woman had understood and pushed her husband from the path, snatching up their son as she did so. They fell into the tangle of bushes and nettles that grew beside the slope, but Beobrand scarcely noticed as he thundered past.

At the same instant, the Mercians, seeing they would not reach the family before the Bernician riders, reined in their steeds. There were a score of them, and their leader, the big man with the flowing moustache, must have thought he could yet win a victory here, before the walls of Bebbanburg. He shouted a command and the Mercians jumped to the ground, and with the speed and precision of seasoned warriors, they formed a shieldwall across the path, ten men across and two deep.

For a heartbeat, Beobrand considered galloping headlong into that wall of linden boards, iron bosses and glittering spears. If he could urge Sceadugenga on, the bulk of the beast would smash through the men like a rock through the hull of a ship in a storm. But even as the thought formed, so he was tugging on the stallion's reins. The horse would almost certainly baulk at the obstacle and besides, the spears would surely kill him and maybe Beobrand too. He was suddenly, acutely aware that he was not wearing his byrnie. Why send his steed to its death and risk his own life needlessly? The family was behind him. Time was now on the side of the Bernicians.

Beobrand slipped from Sceadugenga's back, unslinging his shield and sword-belt. He pushed his arm into the straps that compensated for his weaker left-hand grip and held his shield secure. He drew Nægling and flung the belt and scabbard aside.

Around him the others were reining in their animals in a cloud of dust.

"Shieldwall," he roared. In moments, the dozen of them had locked shields. To his left stood Attor, to his right Reodstan.

"It's been a whole day without a fight," Reodstan said, grinning. His red face gleamed in the hot sunlight. "I was getting bored in there."

Beobrand returned his smile.

"You may be disappointed," he replied. "These Mercians must realise they have nothing to gain from attacking us now. We are too close to our walls."

"Well, it looks as though that bastard with the moustache doesn't agree with you."

Before them, the Mercian shieldwall took a step forward. They came in good order as their leader shouted commands.

He was in the centre of their wall, peering over his hide-covered shield at Beobrand. The shield was painted the colour of blood and bore the shape of a raven daubed in black.

"Time to finish what we started the other day, Beobrand Half-handed," shouted the man. The Mercian shieldwall took another step forward.

"When we saw you last, we slew six of your men and you fled like frightened women," he retorted. "Now we find you trying to ride down women and children. You are not warriors, you are maggots." Then, in a whisper to Reodstan, he said, "It looks as though you will have your fun after all."

A wailing cry came from behind them and Beobrand glanced back. He was pleased to see that the man and woman had pulled their crying children from the edge of the path and were once again hurrying up the slope towards the fortress gates. The boy and the infant were screaming in pain or terror, but they were alive and they were behind the Bernician shieldwall. Beobrand turned back to the Mercian line.

"All we have to do is hold these bastards for long enough for that family to reach safety," he said in a low voice. His words sounded muffled and strange from inside his helm, which, despite his fears, had remained on his head.

"You are my hlaford, Beobrand, and I will obey you in most things," said Attor with a savage grin. "But know this: when it comes to the fight, I will not merely be holding these pig-swivers at bay." He raised his voice so that all could hear him. "I am going to bathe in your blood, you Mercian maggots. I will rip out your entrails and feed them to the crows." Spittle flew from his lips as he brandished his two vicious-looking seaxes and allowed his battle fury to take him. "Come on then, you whoresons. Come and die on my blades!"

And as if answering Attor's screamed insults like a command, as one, the Mercians ran forward, spears outstretched, shields held firmly before them.

"For Bernicia!" roared Beobrand and a moment later, a spear-point came driving towards his face. Ducking, he raised his shield, catching the spear and lifting it over his head. At the same moment he lunged beneath his shield with his sword, hoping to catch an unprotected leg or groin. But the shieldwalls were yet a few paces apart and his blade met with nothing more than air. Sweat trickled down his forehead, stinging his eyes. The spear pulled back and came again, hard and fast at his face. He caught it once more on his shield, but this time on the flat surface of the board. The steel point bit deep into the hide and wood and Beobrand heaved down in an effort to open up his attacker. The instant he lowered his shield, a Mercian sword-blade flickered towards him, the bright sun flashing on its patterned metal. The spear-man before him was hidden behind his board and it was all Beobrand could do to swing Nægling up and parry the sword strike. The two blades clanged together and the impact jarred his hand and wrist.

The two lines had touched now and the chaos of battle surrounded him, filling every sense. There was nothing now save the Mercian enemies. The stink of their sour sweat caught in his throat. His ears were filled with the crash and crunch of shield against shield, the clangour of blade against blade and the howling rage of warriors locked in mortal combat. This was the sword-song, and Beobrand and his Black Shields danced to its tune better than any warband in Albion.

Twisting his wrist, Beobrand sliced into the forearm of the swordsman whose blow he had parried. He felt Nægling's sharp blade slice into flesh, severing sinews and veins and rasping against bone. The Mercian screamed and fell back, to be replaced by another warrior.

With a roar, Reodstan deflected a scything seax blow, then, with a well-timed movement of his shield, making space for him to riposte, he opened the throat of the Mercian.

To Reodstan's right, one of his gesithas fell, a spear lodged in his mouth. As he toppled backward, eyes staring cross-eyed down the length of the spear-haft, his weight tugged his Mercian killer forward. The Bernicians had formed a single line, so the man's death opened up a gap in the shieldwall that the Mercians sought to widen. They threw themselves forward into the breach, screaming and hacking left and right.

Beobrand yelled a warning to Reodstan but he needn't have worried. Beircheart stepped into the gap, leaving behind the fallen Bernician staring up, unseeing, at the spear that yet quivered, jutting from his face. Dreogan roared and moved to Beircheart's aid. In moments, two more Mercians had fallen and the risk to the shieldwall had been averted.

"Forward," Beobrand bellowed, sensing that the Mercian morale was cracking. "For Bernicia!"

The Bernicians yelled their defiance and shoved forward. For a heartbeat, the Mercians slid back a step, but then, with a barked order from their leader, they redoubled their efforts. Their line held and did not falter further.

The shifting of the lines of men had brought Beobrand directly in front of the Mercian leader.

"Ready to die now, Half-hand?" he jeered.

"I'm always ready to die, Mercian cur," growled Beobrand. "It is why I am so hard to kill."

For a moment, Beobrand held the man's gaze. The Mercian's eyes were bloodshot and hot with fury. But was there something else there? Fear, perhaps?

Without thought or warning, Beobrand let himself fall to one knee, raising his shield as he did so to protect his head and torso. With the speed of a striking serpent, he lashed out with Nægling at the Mercian leader's right foot. The blade found its mark and cut easily through the leather shoe. The man howled as the steel severed his toes and a large chunk of his foot. Blood gushed and the leader collapsed. His eyes were white-rimmed in terror now. Beobrand did not hesitate. He trusted that Reodstan and Attor would protect his flanks and he sprang forward. Kicking aside the moustachioed man's shield, he thrust Nægling into one of his terrified eyes.

Attor flicked his langseax forward, catching the axe-bearing hand of a Mercian. The axe had been aimed at Beobrand's helm, but fell harmlessly onto the trembling corpse of the Mercian leader.

Beobrand flashed a grin at Attor.

"Forward!" he shouted again, and the Bernician shieldwall pushed onward with a stamping step. But this time, there was no resistance. With the death of their leader, their appetite for battle had fled, it seemed. Two more Mercians were cut down as they ran to their horses. The Bernicians stood, panting and slicked in sweat, and watched the rest of them mount quickly and ride away. Some, in their haste, had dropped their weapons and shields.

"Shall we go after them?" asked Attor. His face was splattered with bright droplets of blood and his breath was coming short, his mouth open, tongue red. He looked more wolf than man, thought Beobrand.

"No," he said, glancing up towards the fortress. Several shielded men were running down the slope from the gates to their aid. He watched the Mercians gallop away back past the abandoned buildings. Into the west they went, as fast as their steeds could carry them towards Penda's warhost. They left behind the corpses of their fallen and two horses they had not managed to recapture. "We've given Reodstan here enough excitement for one morning."

Reodstan gave him a thin smile, but shook his head as he looked down at his fallen man.

"More excitement than I needed, truth be told," Reodstan said with a sigh.

Beobrand patted his shoulder.

"I am sorry."

"He died protecting people of the land," Reodstan said, his eyes glistening with unshed tears. "He would have wanted it no other way."

Beobrand nodded and a terrible sadness came over him. His hands began to tremble as they always did after battle. Walking to Sceadugenga, he caught hold of the stallion's trailing reins. Gripping a handful of the horse's coarse mane, he swung himself up onto the animal's broad back.

The warriors who had come on foot from the fortress reached them now and Beobrand ordered them to collect the fallen weapons and to strip the Mercians of any armour. Reodstan was seeing to his man's body. His comrades lifted him onto his shield to bear him sombrely from battle.

Sighing, Beobrand slowly made his way back up the slope towards Bebbanburg.

The family was shuffling forward, exhaustion, shock and terror plain on their faces. The children snivelled now, perhaps too tired or frightened to scream any longer. The boy stumbled and fell to the dusty earth. His mother reached for him, then turned at the sound of Sceadugenga's hooves.

"Thank you, lord," the woman stammered, lowering her gaze.

"You have nothing to thank me for," Beobrand replied. Then, leaning down, he held out his hand to the boy. The child's face was tear-streaked and dirty, his cheeks flushed with the heat and terror of the morning. "Take my hand, boy," he said. The boy did not move. "You can ride with me up to Bebbanburg. You will be safe with me." The child reminded Beobrand of Octa, as he had been not so many summers before. The mother pushed the boy forward and Beobrand took his tiny hand and lifted him easily to sit before him atop Sceadugenga.

"See. Quite safe. Would you like to take the reins?"

The boy did not speak, but nodded and held out his pudgy hands to grip the leather straps.

Beobrand smiled. There was comfort in the warm weight of the child against him.

Walking Sceadugenga slowly, Beobrand climbed the rest of the way beside the family. They were silent in his presence.

When they reached the gates, he slid the boy down to his father's waiting arms.

"You are all safe now," he said. He wondered for how long that would be true.

They thanked him again and he shook his head, ushering them through the gates.

He waited astride Sceadugenga in the shadow of the wall until the last of the Bernicians, the stone-faced warriors carrying the body of their fallen brother on his shield, had entered the fortress. Then, with a glance at the western horizon, where a pall of dust and smoke hung like a low-lying fog over the land, he followed them through the gateway.

He had heard the folk of Bebbanburg cheering as the family entered and the warriors returned, but by the time he rode into the courtyard, the celebrations had dwindled and people were returning to their chores and preparations for what they knew would come next. His and Reodstan's gesithas were leading their mounts back to the stables. Beobrand swung his gaze over the few people who were yet watching the gates and his breath caught. Eanflæd was staring back at him. She looked pale and as radiant as ever. For a moment, she held his gaze and then turned away.

He sighed.

"Now you can close those accursed gates," he growled at the door wards.

Without a word, they swung the great timber gates shut and then lifted the huge locking bar into place. It thudded home with finality.

Beobrand turned and led Sceadugenga across the courtyard.

And so it begins, he thought.

PART TWO

SACRED WIND

Chapter 18

Eanflæd looked down at Ecgfrith's sleeping face. He was still and peaceful and, despite the sense of foreboding that hung over her, she smiled to see him thus, quiet and calm, his tiny mouth open, arms thrown out wide. He had gurgled in his sleep and she had rushed to him, fear stabbing at her heart that the sickness had returned. She needn't have been concerned. He had barely coughed now for days and the nights of his constant hacking and crying seemed almost like a nightmare. Perhaps one day the memories would fade enough to lose their sting, but for now, the endless nights of illness were still recent and raw.

"Come, have another cup of mead," said Edlyn, beckoning her back to the stools where they had been sitting before Ecgfrith had let out the spluttering snore that had caused Eanflæd to leap up and go to him. Would she ever be done with this fear for her child? She thought not. With one last look at his chubby face, she returned to Edlyn's side.

"Just one more cup," she said, lowering herself onto the stool.

Edlyn, half a dozen years her senior, smiled, her teeth bright and shining in the rush light's flame. Edlyn was a pretty woman, though often prone to sadness. It seemed strange to Eanflæd to see her grinning now, as the older woman passed her a wooden cup she had filled with mead. She seldom smiled and was usually surrounded by a cloak of sorrow it was hard to penetrate. Only when she played with Ecgfrith or any other child did she seem truly happy, but even at such times, Eanflæd knew that her sadness lurked close beneath her smiles. Edlyn's first babe, a girl, had died three months after birth, and then she had lost another baby before she reached her time. Eanflæd liked her, but her sadness was sometimes overbearing. Eanflæd could not resent Edlyn her sorrow. The thought of losing Ecgfrith gripped at her heart, so she could only imagine the pain Edlyn felt. But to be with her when her woe overcame her was not easy. At such times, Eanflæd longed to be called away, or to have to attend Mass. Anything to distract them from the all-consuming anguish that clawed at Edlyn's soul. And yet, despite Edlyn's company being tedious during her bouts of depression, Eanflæd always did her best to visit her at Morðpæð. Eanflæd knew that Fordraed's patience had long worn out with regards to Edlyn's sadness. When he was not away with the king, or on some royal errand, Fordraed would beat her if she wept too loudly, or if she was surly in her responses to him. Eanflæd had seen the bruises, and helped to wash the cuts on Edlyn's lips caused by Fordraed's fat fists. He cared nothing for Edlyn, and yet she would shake off these assaults.

"It is my fault," she said the last time Eanflæd travelled to the hall at Morðpæð and found Edlyn with a swollen, darkly bruised eye. "I fell."

"You did not fall, Edlyn," Eanflæd replied with a sigh. "We both know the truth of this. Do not lie to your queen." She hesitated, and placed her hand gently on Edlyn's. "Or to your friend."

Eanflæd thought back to that time in the spring. Edlyn told her what had happened, admitting that Fordraed had come to her bed and found her weeping. He had been aroused and drunk. She had made the mistake of telling him she did not wish to lie with him. He had been furious, lashing out and punching her, over and over. Eventually he had left her bleeding and bruised and had taken his pleasure from one of the Waelisc house thralls. He had hurt the young girl so badly she could not work for nearly a sennight.

"The man is a brute," Eanflæd said. "If he were my husband, I would kill him in his sleep." She despised much about Oswiu. He was a bully and cared more for power and himself than for his children or his wife, and he certainly did not love her, preferring the company of that Hibernian whore in Caer Luel. But he had never struck her.

"Do not say such a thing," Edlyn sobbed. "He is my husband. It is his right to discipline me. After all, I am a terrible wife. I have given him no heir." She had cried for a long time then and Eanflæd cradled her in her arms. She wondered whether she meant what she had said. Would she truly slay a man who beat her so? Murder was a terrible sin. Besides, anyone can be brave and bold when they only wield words and not a weapon.

Eanflæd took a sip of the mead, wondering how long the siege might last. Soon there would be no more mead, just the brackish water from Waltheof's Well. She let out a long breath and stretched her back. She was tired and her muscles ached. Over the last days she had thrown herself into the task of preparing the people of Bebbanburg. It kept her mind occupied and it was only in the brief moments of calm when she awoke, or when she lay in her bed at night before sleep took her, that she found her thoughts returning to Beobrand.

A muffled snoring came from the adjoining room. Godgyth slept there. Eanflæd stifled a yawn. Edlyn smiled.

"I know you are tired," she said. "I will let you go to your bed soon. But I just wanted to share a drink with my queen." She paused. "And my friend."

Eanflæd returned her smile and took another sip of the sweet liquid, wondering at the change in Edlyn. A thought came to her.

She is with child again. It can be nothing else. What other thing could fill her with such cheer when outside the walls of the fortress was camped a host of Mercians intent on their destruction?

"I am weary," Eanflæd said, setting aside her cup and unpinning her wimple. Removing it, she ran her fingers through her long tresses. "But I always have time for my friends." She would not speak of her thought of Edlyn's pregnancy. Edlyn's moods swung from day to night in a heartbeat and Eanflæd did not wish to upset her. They often spoke of Ecgfrith and his health, but Eanflæd had long since decided only to broach the subject of children and babies if Edlyn brought it up.

Now, in the gloom, Edlyn seemed happier than she had ever seen her. Again, she was struck by the strangeness of the situation, but she supposed the quickening of the woman's womb would always be cause for celebration, and Edlyn so desired a baby, she would find it impossible to keep her elation hidden, no matter what else was occurring around her.

"What do you think will happen tomorrow?" asked Edlyn, her expression changing abruptly to earnest concern.

Eanflæd shook her head slightly at her friend's mercurial moods. She presumed Edlyn was speaking of the messenger who had ridden up to Bebbanburg's gate that afternoon as the sun was setting. He had shouted up to the wardens that Penda of Mercia would come to parley in the morning. He would speak terms with Oswiu, king of Bernicia. The messenger had not awaited a reply and had wheeled his horse around and ridden back towards the Mercian encampment.

"I know not. But if I were Penda, I would ask for tribute."

"Tribute?"

"Yes, gold, silver, treasure," replied Eanflæd. "Bernicia is rich, but Bebbanburg is too strong to take by force. It would be better for Penda to ask for riches and then take his host back to Mercia."

"He would do that?" asked Edlyn, her voice tinged with hope. "Take tribute and then leave without a fight?"

Eanflæd thought for a moment of the horde of Mercians that had marched from the west. In the darkest part of the night their campfires dotted the land beneath Bebbanburg like so many stars. There were hundreds of them, more warriors than she had ever seen before. And yet, wasn't Bebbanburg impregnable? Prepared as they were, she thought they would be able to hold out for weeks. Could Penda keep his warhost together for so long? Could he provide his men with supplies enough to feed them?

"I think he would be a fool not to ask," she said. "And Penda is no fool. A king does not slay as many men as Penda has if he is foolish." She thought of her father. Edwin had been a colossal figure. He had seemed unbeatable. Invincible. And yet Penda and Cadwallon had slain him and the land had been ravaged. No, Penda was no fool, but he was as deadly a king as had ever ruled in Albion.

"Why do you think they destroyed the church?" asked Edlyn, her mind as fast-moving and inconstant as her moods, flitting from one thing to the next like a butterfly.

Eanflæd frowned and took a long swallow from her cup. Seeing she had emptied it, she held it out to Edlyn.

"Just one more," she said with a shrug.

She had been saddened to hear what had happened to the church. She had been busy with Brytnere going over the lists of provisions – barrels of salted meat, sacks of wheat, smoked fish, hard cheese and all other manner of victuals – when they had heard the buzz of consternation move through the people that thronged Bebbanburg. One of the guards told them that the Mercians had torn down the new church. Eanflæd's heart had sunk when she had climbed to the ramparts and looked out to the west. It was as the guard had said. The timber structure that she had convinced Oswiu needed to be built so that Aidan and his brethren could preach to the men and women of the surrounding area no longer dominated the view. It had scarcely stood for a year and now Penda's wolves had pulled it down and in its stead all that remained was a pile of timber and splintered rubble.

She sighed.

"I don't know," she said after Edlyn had poured more mead into both their cups. "Penda does not worship the true God. He is a sinful pagan. The sight of God's house must have filled him with fear."

Edlyn nodded.

"But does not pulling down the house of the Lord show that his gods are more powerful?"

"In his eyes, perhaps. But the false gods he worships have no power over the Almighty. For is it not written: 'I am the Lord, and there is none else, there is no God beside me'? Penda's false gods are as weak as they are evil."

Eanflæd took a swallow of mead to hide the sudden anxiety that gripped her. Beobrand was also a pagan. Was he also evil? Her hand trembled. She recalled the rush of passion that had washed over her. The heat in her body, her overwhelming desire. She would have given herself to him completely. Could it be that his gods were things of the Devil? Like the Devil, they brought temptation and corruption. She shuddered, but the room was warm.

"The Mercians have also started pulling down the other buildings," said Edlyn, dragging her back from her dark thoughts. "Did you see?"

Eanflæd nodded.

"I wonder why they do not simply burn them all," said Edlyn. "It would be much simpler than pulling them down plank by plank."

Eanflæd frowned. Edlyn was right, it would be easier. But Penda was no fool, she thought.

"Penda has many men in his host," she said. "They will need a lot of firewood for all those campfires."

For a time, the two women sat in silence. The night was as quiet as an overcrowded fortress could be. From outside came the distant murmur of the high tide washing the beach and the rocks below the crag of Bebbanburg. There were other sounds that reached them in the gloom of the chamber. The lilting singing of a woman; a chuckling laugh from somewhere on the walls; a crying infant.

Eanflæd was beginning to doze, her head dropping to her chest, when Edlyn's voice brought her back with a start.

"Will Penda ask for us all to surrender?" she asked. Her voice was quiet, not much more than a whisper in the shadows of the room. Her eyes glimmered, catching the light of the dying rush light.

"I imagine he will," Eanflæd said. "Before he asks for tribute." Penda was cunning. If they surrendered Bebbanburg, all their treasure would be his without a fight.

"I'm sure my husband will not pay him any gold," Edlyn said. "He loves his treasure. More than anything. Except perhaps meat and mead." She smirked grimly in the dark. "He's like a fat wyrm. He would sleep on his hoard if he could."

Eanflæd did not reply, but nodded sadly.

"Will Ethelwin surrender, do you think?" asked Edlyn.

Now it was Eanflæd's turn to smirk and shake her head.

"Look about the fortress, Edlyn." She thought of the long days of preparations, the slaughtering of the animals, the salting of the meat, the drilling of all the men in the use of shield and spear. "Ethelwin is Oswiu's warmaster for good reason and he has prepared Bebbanburg well. And Beobrand and his Black Shields are here too," she continued, managing with an effort to keep her tone neutral at the mention of his name. The sight of Beobrand leading his men in a charge down the slope to protect the family who were at risk of being killed by the Mercian horsemen had lifted the spirits of the Bernicians. Her own heart had swelled with pride at Beobrand's bravery, as if, due to their closeness, she could take some measure of responsibility for his courage. She snorted at the idea.

"Do Ethelwin and Beobrand strike you as men who give in easily?"

Chapter 19

"He is coming with eight men," said Attor.

Beobrand peered into the bright morning, towards the campfire haze of the Mercian encampment. He could see the small group of riders leaving the camp and heading towards Bebbanburg, but once again, he was thankful for Attor's keen eyesight.

"They bear the bough of truce," Attor continued.

Beobrand knew that Ethelwin had already ordered one of the door wardens to cut a limb from an elm that grew some way down the slope from the doors of Bebbanburg. The man had gone out that morning at first light. There were no Mercians nearby, so he had been quite safe as he'd hacked at the tree. Still, he had evidently not enjoyed the experience of standing alone and unprotected between the two forces, for he had all but run back up to the fortress as soon as he had cut off a leafy branch.

Beobrand knew how he felt. He could feel the gaze of the defenders upon him as he made his way down from the wall towards the waiting horses. Ethelwin, bedecked in his battle harness and a fine blue cloak, lowered his head in greeting.

"Penda and eight others," Beobrand said to him. They had decided to ride out with the same number as Penda brought.

Fewer, and they ran the risk of open treachery, more and they would look cowardly.

Heremod cupped his hands, helping Fordraed to climb up into his saddle, before pulling himself onto his own mount. Ethelwin had attempted to halt Fordraed from joining them, saying he was the lord of Bebbanburg in the king's absence and therefore he must remain to lead in case Penda should prove treacherous and anything should befall those who rode to speak with him. Fordraed had insisted that, as the lord of the fortress, it was his place to speak with the voice of the king. He would not be left behind. Judging from the paleness of his cheeks and the glazed fear in his eyes, Beobrand wondered if he regretted that decision in the bright light of the morning.

Beobrand would have liked to have taken Fraomar with him to the parley. His mind was sharp and quick and he would miss nothing, but he had not awoken and still lay, pallid and somewhere between life and death, on the pallet on which Brinin had rested until recently.

Swinging himself up onto Sceadugenga's back, Beobrand signalled to Grindan and Dreogan to mount their horses. Grindan was quiet and thoughtful; stalwart, fast and deadly if it came to a fight, but Beobrand knew he could trust him to keep his head when the insults began to fly. The young man spent much of his time maintaining the peace between others and his axe-wielding giant of a brother, Eadgard. Eadgard was quick to anger and slow to forgive, and when in combat he seemed deaf to pleas of surrender. This made Eadgard a deadly addition to Beobrand's gesithas, but when not in open warfare, his character had made his brother skilled with placatory words. The older warrior, Dreogan, with his bulk, bald pate and soot-scarred face, would be a brooding presence that spoke of violence and death. If it came to a fight, Beobrand knew Dreogan would deal death as quickly and with as little thought as a flash of lightning from a clear sky.

The rest of the group was made up of Ethelwin's chosen thegns, one of whom held aloft the leafy elm branch.

All of the men who were riding to the parley wore polished byrnies of iron and their finest adornments. Golden buckles, bejewelled cloak brooches, blood red garnets on sword-hilts, all glimmered in the rapidly warming summer sun. Beircheart handed Beobrand his great helm and he placed it upon his head, taking a moment to secure the leather thongs beneath the cheek guards. Immediately, the day grew muffled and subdued.

As the gates were opened, Beobrand listened to his own breathing and the muted clatter of the horses' hooves. He urged Sceadugenga forward to ride beside Ethelwin and Fordraed.

"I will do the talking," said Ethelwin, his voice deadened from behind the finely-made grimhelm he wore. The shining metal of the faceplate was embossed with images of warriors and intertwined animals.

Beobrand said nothing.

"I am lord of Bebbanburg," said Fordraed, his tone shrill. "I speak with the voice of the king."

They trotted down the slope, past the point where a couple of days previously, Beobrand had stood in the shieldwall against the Mercian riders. There were signs of the fight. A discarded shoe, a dark stain in the dust, a belt buckle. The corpses had gone, taken away by Mercians during the night after the host had arrived.

Ethelwin turned the carven faceplate of his helm towards Fordraed. The helm glimmered and flashed in the sunlight. The eye sockets were black pits.

"I will do the talking," rumbled Ethelwin's voice once more.

Fordraed opened his mouth, then snapped it shut again. Beobrand had the sudden urge to push the fat lord from his saddle. He chuckled at the thought, gripping his reins tightly and riding forward in stride with Ethelwin.

Ethelwin glanced in his direction, having to turn in the saddle due to the limited vision from within the great helm. The dark eye holes stared at Beobrand for a heartbeat, but Ethelwin did not speak.

They rode on towards the approaching Mercians.

Penda was close enough for Beobrand to recognise him now. He did not wear a helm, but his thick hair was held back with a golden band. His hair and forked beard were streaked with grey, but he was still a man to reckon with. He was hugely strong, tall and broad of chest. Despite the warmth of the day, a great wolf pelt was wrapped about his shoulders, adding to his already considerable bulk. He rode the largest horse Beobrand had ever seen, and still it seemed somehow small beneath the king of Mercia. The men who accompanied the king were covered in their finest harness. Their iron-knit shirts were burnished and gleaming. The rising sun glared against their shield bosses, arm rings, sword-hilts and helms. Many carried brightly painted spears from which dangled emblems and trinkets.

When they were some fifty paces from the Mercians, Ethelwin reined in his steed and signalled for the rest of the Bernicians to do likewise.

"I will do the talking," he said for a third time, his voice low. Beobrand wondered whether he was speaking to them or to give himself courage.

The Mercians came on, walking their horses without urgency. The sun was hot on Beobrand's back and he regretted donning his helm. It would be sweltering soon and if the parley lasted for more than a few moments, he would be forced to remove the helmet, which might look to the Mercians like weakness, or subservience.

Beobrand scanned the rest of the men in Penda's retinue. He thought he recognised some of the helms and shield emblems from previous battles, but he could not be certain. Then, with a start, he saw that he did indeed know the man who rode beside the king of Mercia. The man was almost as broad as Penda himself, and like the king, his beard bore the grey of age. He was hale and strong, but must be several years older than the king. This was Grimbold, father of Halga and Edmonda. Beobrand had rescued the man's daughter and killed his son. He did not imagine Grimbold would think that an even trade.

The Mercians halted a few paces before the gathered Bernicians. A light wind rustled the leaves in the green boughs that were held above both parties. The ornaments that hung from the spears' crossbars rattled against the painted ash hafts. The horses stamped and snorted. One of the Bernician mounts, a brown mare, whinnied in greeting, and a Mercian stallion nickered in reply, earning itself a slap from its rider.

Penda scanned the group of Bernicians with a frown. Beobrand took in the thickness of his arms and the criss-crossed scars that patterned his forearms.

"Where is the king?" Penda asked at last, his voice a deep growl of annoyance. "I do not speak with servants."

Ethelwin rose up in his saddle to address the king of Mercia.

"I am—" he said, but was cut off as Beobrand nudged Sceadugenga forward and spoke in a loud, brash voice.

"Oswiu, King of Bernicia and Lord of Bebbanburg, does not speak to dogs. So he sent us to talk to you." Sweat trickled down his neck beneath his helm. "Whatever you would say, speak your piece and begone, back to the rest of your hounds and bitches."

The Mercians shuffled. Beobrand heard a sword being drawn somewhere within their ranks, followed by a growled order for calm.

Penda grew very still and he fixed Beobrand with a menacing glare.

"You," he said. "I should have known we would find you here, Half-hand. It seems you are always present when we Mercians decide it is time to slaughter some of the sheep that live beyond our lands."

Ethelwin grabbed at Beobrand's arm.

"Beobrand," he hissed. "Silence."

Beobrand shrugged him off and ignored the warmaster's order.

"Aye, many a time I have faced you in battle, Penda," he snarled. "I have lost count of how many of your Mercian curs I have sent to the afterlife."

Penda grinned, showing a mouthful of unusually white teeth.

"But I have not forgotten how many of your lords and kings I have slain. Have you forgotten that number? Have you forgotten that those who have stood before me have all died and I yet live?"

The image of Sigeberht came to Beobrand then, the one-time king of the East Angelfolc's white robes soaked in his lifeblood at the great ditch. Beobrand thought of Oswald's sightless eyes above the torn flesh of his neck, his severed head staring down at the defeat of his people from the sharpened stake upon which it had been placed.

A bead of sweat ran into his eye. He blinked against the sting but did not reach up to wipe it away. He could show Penda no weakness.

"It is true that you have slain many, Penda," Beobrand said. "I too have killed many men. But you are old now and your time is past. If you dare face me in battle, man against man, you will find out why I have survived all this time when others have died."

"You live because you worship the true gods," Penda said, pointing a thick finger at the Thunor's hammer amulet that hung at Beobrand's throat. "But you have chosen to ally yourself with the weak. With the followers of the nailed god. The Christ is a weakling and Woden will crush him."

"So you are craven?" scoffed Beobrand. "You refuse to accept my challenge? I would fight with you, Penda, and then we would see who is weak and who is strong."

Penda spat. He seemed more amused than angry at Beobrand's outbursts.

"I do not wish to speak or fight with lesser men than I. Tell

Oswiu to come out and I will fight him man to man. We can make the square and fight to the death. It is not I who is craven, Beobrand Half-hand, but your king who hides behind the walls of Bebbanburg."

"Oswiu does not speak or fight with dogs," Beobrand reiterated, and by the flush of colour in Penda's cheeks he could see his words had angered him, even though the king kept his expression flat.

"I swear to the All-father," Penda said, his voice as sharp as a sword-blade, "Oswiu will regret insulting me thus." He swung his horse's head around and shouted over his shoulder. "And so will you, Half-hand."

Grimbold stared at Beobrand for several heartbeats before turning his horse to follow his king. A runnel of sweat traced a line down Beobrand's spine and he shuddered. The invocation of Woden's name filled him with dread. He had witnessed the power of the dark magic at Maserfelth. Then he remembered his own whispered promises to the All-father, and the slaughter of the men beside the Great Wall. The memory of the ravens that had watched on as the men had been slain sent another shudder down his back. To mask it, he tugged at Sceadugenga's head, turning the animal back towards at Bebbanburg.

A moment later, Ethelwin and Fordraed pulled their mounts around. The retinue of warriors followed them.

"Did I not say that I would speak for us?" Ethelwin snarled from within the muffled darkness of his grimhelm. His voice rasped and cracked with barely controlled fury. "You should not have said those things, Beobrand."

Awkwardly, Beobrand teased open the knot that held his helm in place. He did not remove the helmet, but the cool air that wafted in as the cheek guards parted was welcome and refreshing.

"Why?" he asked.

"Why?" yelled Fordraed, his voice rising to an angry scream. "Why, you ask! You will get us all killed, you fool."

Beobrand turned his gaze on Fordraed. Despite the warmth of the morning, his eyes were as cool as shards of ice. Gods, how he would love to punch the man. The sensation of his fist slamming into his fleshy face was a sweet memory.

"If you think it is my words that will cause Penda to attack, then it is you who is the fool, Fordraed. The man is a wolf. Any scent of weakness drives him to greater savagery. He has broken the peace with Bernicia, invaded our lands, stolen our cattle, slain our people. There is only one way to tackle the likes of him."

Ethelwin pushed his horse closer to Beobrand. When he spoke his voice was low and clipped from behind the embossed face-guard.

"When a wolf has you cowering in the branches of a tree," he said, "do you poke it with a stick?"

"No," Fordraed said. "You wait for the wolf to tire and to leave you in peace. Soon it will find other prey."

Beobrand slowly shifted in the saddle to stare at Fordraed. He shook his head at the man's craven stupidity.

"If I were in a tree with a wolf below me," Beobrand said, "I would not cower. I would skewer it with a stick or a spear, if I had one to hand."

"And if you did not?" enquired Fordraed.

"If I bore no weapons, I would jump from the tree and gouge out the beast's eyes with my thumbs."

Fordraed did not seem able to respond. His mouth opened and shut like a beached trout. They rode on in silence for a few moments. The sun was glaring in their faces now. Gazing up at the walls of Bebbanburg atop the mighty crag, Beobrand wondered how long they could withstand a determined assault. The fortress was imposing and seemingly impregnable. But even the strongest byrnie had weak links.

Without warning, Ethelwin laughed. His guffaws boomed from within his great helm. After a while his laughter subsided to mere chuckles. Beobrand could no longer hear him laughing, but could see the warmaster's shoulder shaking with mirth.

"What is so funny, warmaster?" he asked.

Ethelwin reached a hand under his helm to wipe at his eyes.

"I was just thinking," he said, barely able to speak through his giggling. "If you fight wolves with your hands, I understand now how you lost your fingers."

Chapter 20

Penda did not wait long to retaliate.

As the afternoon sun dipped into the west, nine people were brought towards Bebbanburg. The four men and five women had their hands bound and ropes looped about their necks. Their clothes had been torn and their feet were bare and bloody. All of them had the despondent, empty stares of the utterly defeated. This was the look of cattle being led to the slaughter. And judging from the white-robed priest who preceded them, and the sharpened stakes that had been hammered into the hard earth, Eanflæd thought these wretched Bernician peasants would face a similar fate to animals at the winter slaying of Blotmonath.

Bebbanburg's walls were thronged with people, though the wardens had prevented all but the men from climbing up to witness what was about to occur. Eanflæd had only been able to make her way up the ladder because she was the queen. Fordraed had tried to prevent her, but she had spun on him.

"Do you forget that I am your queen?" she asked. "I would see what befalls my people."

He had stepped aside, with a face like thunder.

"Well, this is what we get by allowing that fool Beobrand to speak to his betters," he said.

Eanflæd ignored him, but she wondered at his words. Many

agreed with Edlyn's husband, she knew. Moments after the small group of horsemen who had ridden beneath the green bough had returned to Bebbanburg, she had heard of Beobrand's taunts to Penda. There was not a soul in the fortress who did not have an opinion about his actions. There were those who criticised him for his arrogance. Others admired his brash bravado. Some thought the lords should have offered the king of Mercia terms, a payment of treasure to leave their lands. Of all the opinions she heard, Eanflæd thought they mainly fell into two camps: the men welcomed Beobrand's presence and trusted he would help lead them to some surprise victory; the women fretted and worried that his infamous bad temper would lead Penda to treat them more harshly, if he managed to breach their defences.

For her part, Eanflæd thought that nothing Beobrand had said would change Penda's mind. His course had been set when he marched his host into Bernicia and he would not leave without the spoils he had promised his thegns and ealdormen. It was possible, she supposed, that Ethelwin could have offered Penda treasure to lead his warriors away, but from what she knew of the taciturn warmaster, that was something he would never countenance. He had been set the task of defending the realm in his king's absence and defend it he would. Besides, the treasure was not his to give. So, without the king there to make a contrary decision, Ethelwin would stand firm against Penda.

As she looked down from the walls now, Eanflæd wondered whether Penda's latest actions might further sour people's mood towards Beobrand. They would blame him for sure, even though his was not the hand on the priest's knife. Such was the way of things. She glanced along the rampart to where Beobrand stood with his gesithas. He must have sensed her gaze, for he turned to look at her. His features were hard and fixed. She could see the tension in his neck and shoulders, the grim sternness of his jaw. But the afternoon light softened his stony features, bathing all of the onlookers on the wall in its warm golden glow.

Beobrand offered her a small nod of recognition, nothing more, and she wondered what he must be thinking as he shifted his attention back to the events playing out beneath Bebbanburg. Did he blame himself? She had heard from Beircheart, one of Beobrand's gesithas, that Penda had said he would make Beobrand regret his insults. As she watched the Mercian warriors leading the nine bound prisoners towards Bebbanburg, she could not help but question his actions. Deep down, she was certain that Penda had meant for this to occur from the beginning. If not, why did he have these Bernicians captured and ready for whatever cruel fate awaited them? And yet, the seed of doubt was there. Could Beobrand have averted this outcome with a less belligerent response to the Mercian warlord?

They would never know. Yet, she told herself, it was not Beobrand who had led the Mercian warhost to this place, nor was it he who now stood before the cowed prisoners, raising his voice and his arms to the heavens.

Some way distant, perhaps three arrow flights away, stood the amassed ranks of Penda's host. They had come forward, a great shambling horde, to witness their priest's bloody ritual. Nearer to the sharpened death poles, the waelstengs that had been driven into the earth, stood Penda and his closest retinue, his comitatus. Penda was huge, his bulk as imposing as the malevolence in his gaze as he looked up at the faces staring down from the palisade. He grinned and it was as if he was staring directly at her. She shuddered and regretted her decision to come up here. Fordraed was right, this was no place for her. She knew what was going to happen. Why did she wish to see it? Was knowing not enough?

But she was the queen of these people. She would not turn her back on them. She could not forsake them in the moment of their greatest suffering. By the holy Virgin, where was Oswiu? This should have been his task. He should be standing here with the warmth of the setting sun on his face, about to watch the sacrifice of nine innocents.

A man stepped forward from Penda's comitatus. He was tall and slender and wore a fine warrior jacket of red. From his many-coloured belt hung a golden-hilted sword.

"My lord Penda, king of Mercia, overlord of the West Seaxons and chosen son of Woden, father of the gods, bids you bear witness to this blood sacrifice in honour of the All-father. Nine lives are offered, one for each of the nights Woden hung, wounded and suffering, from the world tree."

The man's voice was clear and carried well. He spoke with the musical clarity of a scop and if his words had been other, his tone would have been something to marvel at. No sound came from the walls now.

"And know this, people of Bebbanburg," continued the man, his voice carrying to all the listeners. "The All-father will drink the blood from these sacrifices and grant us victory over you. You may feel secure behind your walls, but walls can be destroyed, and when the wolves of Mercia are victorious, this too will be your wyrd; to have your blood given as tribute to Woden!"

He shouted the name of the father of the gods and his scream was answered by a roaring cheer from the warhost.

"Woden! Woden! Woden!" came the thundering chant.

Eanflæd felt the flesh on her neck prickle. There was magic here. She clutched the rood necklace she wore and whispered the words of the Pater Noster. Her words were drowned out by the warhost's cries.

The priest stepped forward, cavorting and chanting, spitting and screaming as he danced before the strangely docile prisoners. All the while the battlehost's roar rolled towards Bebbanburg, filling her ears with the name of their ancient, evil, one-eyed god of death. The priest skipped close to the nearest prisoner, a young man with a wispy beard. In a paroxysm of ecstasy the priest howled his incantations at the sky and his knife flicked out, glinting in the fire of the sunlight. The young man's throat opened and blood fountained, bright and terrible. The liquid spurted far and the priest danced in its hot rain, besmirching himself in gore until his robe was crimson.

Eanflæd moaned. Her prayers died on her lips. She wanted to look away, but found herself captivated by the horror, unable to turn from the grisly sight before her.

The dying man fell to the earth. The rest of the prisoners seemed unaware of what was happening around them. They stood, heads bowed, mouths agape, eyes vacant, as the priest screamed his imprecations to the gods. Again his blood-slick blade lashed out, slicing deep into the throat of an old woman. More hot blood gouted and she tumbled, twitching, to the ground.

The Mercians continued their roaring scream to their gods and Eanflæd wondered whether the rushing she heard in her ears was from the chanting warriors of Woden, or the sound of her own blood flowing within her.

The pagan priest was now wholly drenched in blood and he spun like a demon, mouth wide, eyes blazing from his mask of gore. He killed two more of the waiting Bernicians and Eanflæd's vision began to darken at the edges, as though she were staring into a tunnel. All she could see now was the priest, his knife and the blood.

So much blood.

The waves of sound from the screaming warriors washed over her. Another victim fell to the man's knife. Blood gushed, adding to the rivers and pools of the stuff soaking the dry earth before Bebbanburg. Her head spun. She should not have come up here. There were such quantities of blood. How much more would be shed before the end; before Bebbanburg fell and Woden's wolves ravaged them all?

A slashing stroke, a spray of slaughter-sweat, a screamed chant to the ancient dark gods.

They would all die here, Eanflæd thought, and her vision

blurred. Darkness consumed her and she felt herself tumbling down, down.

As she fainted, caught by the strong hands of those Bernician wall wards who stood close by, pale and grim in the face of Penda's unholy sacrifices, a terrible thought surged in her mind. Had Beobrand brought this horror upon them? Or, worse than that, had it been her own sins that had brought the Devil to the gates of Bebbanburg?

Chapter 21

Beobrand staggered across a wasteland of ashes and blood-streaked corpses. The sky was roiling and dark. Lightning flickered far off, and the growling rumble of thunder reached him moments later. His feet sank into the soft ground and he stumbled forward, panting and gagging against the metallic slaughter-stench of blood and the acrid stink of opened bowels that hung over the gloom-laden land.

A rustling flapping, loud as a ship's sail luffing in a gale, made him look up. A wheeling black cloud of ravens seethed in the sky. Dominating the storm-swept horizon was a great crag of rock, topped with a fortress, its timber palisades looming impregnable above the plain. He recognised the fortress and the rock. It was Din Eidyn. When last he had seen the Pictish stronghold there had been snow all about in a white cloak.

As if in answer to his thoughts the wind picked up and its icy chill cut at his cheeks and hands, tugging at his cloak and pulling his long hair about his face. He swept the hair from his eyes with his half-hand and saw that the air was now filled with a dark blizzard. The fortress was almost hidden from view, lost in the maelstrom of grey particles that swirled and swarmed about him.

But this was not snow.

As he ran forward, breathing heavily now with the effort of running into the storm, dry flakes of the stuff settled in his mouth, melting to a salty paste on his tongue. It was ash. He spat, cursing. The fire-snow fell thick and covered all the land with a deep blanket. His mind twisted and writhed at the thoughts of what might be burning to create such quantities of ash in this wilderness of death.

A sudden wind came then, like the breath of the gods, parting the clouds and clearing the air of the powdery remnants of the hidden fires of doom. He was closer to the fortress now, but still it was some way off. A sickly, malignant light shone from the heavens and highlighted the rock and the wooden walls that crowned it. There was movement there and Beobrand peered into the distance, trying to make sense of what he saw. Squinting against the glare of the wan light, Beobrand suddenly recognised what it was that was moving there. Scores of warriors were scaling the rocks, unseen by the unsuspecting inhabitants of the fortress.

Beobrand screamed out a warning to the defenders. He was certain they were his friends, his countrymen and his kin, but no sign came to him that anybody had heard him. He waved and shouted, spitting to clear his mouth of the ash, and then shouting again until his throat was dry and hoarse. Still the enemy warriors climbed the rocky outcrops. Soon they would reach the fortress walls and Beobrand was certain they would swarm over them and destroy the men, women and children who were hidden inside.

He ran on, the soft ash-earth tugging at his ankles, seeming to pull him back with every stride. He was the only chance the fortress had. He alone could warn them. Running in a straight line towards the castle, he leapt over the bloated cadavers that lay in his path. His stomach twisted as he realised that he recognised the face on every pallid corpse. There was Acennan, mouth open in horror. There lay his brother, Octa, fair hair soaked black with blood and ash. He saw the grey beard and wise eyes of old Scand. Some way off to his left he noticed a flash of gold. Turning momentarily, he saw the beautiful, unblemished face of Sunniva, eyes wide and staring, lips parted as if to offer a farewell kiss. Beneath her lovely features her throat was a bloody ruin. Her lifeblood drenched her clothes and the ashen sand around her. All of the corpses had their throats slit.

Stifling a scream of terror, he ran forward. He could not help the fallen, but the unsuspecting defenders of the fortress could yet be saved. He ran on, his breath wheezing, sweat trickling down his forehead and back. He was too far away! Too far. And yet he would not give up. With a roar he pushed himself to even greater speed, half wading now through the deep ash field, those dunes of death.

Something caught at his foot and he tripped forward, flailing with his arms for balance. He managed to remain on his feet for a few steps before crashing to the ground. Pushing himself up to recommence his panicked run he found his hands resting not on the sandy ash but on the cold pliant flesh of a dead body. He looked down and his gaze met the unseeing eyes of Eanflæd. Like all the others her throat was in tatters. He could see the bones of her spine inside the huge gash beneath her chin. Blood had splattered and flecked her smooth cheeks, reminding him of the blood that had dotted the snow after his dual with Torran at the foot of Din Eidyn.

So many dead. How had it come to this? Looking up, he saw that the distant warriors had clambered over the palisades of the fortress and the sounds of slaughter came to him on the freezing wind.

He was too late.

Always too late.

Beobrand awoke with a start. His heart hammered and his breath came in short gasps, as if he had been running. For a moment he could not recall where he was and his mind was filled with the tumbling shadow memories of the dream. The horror of the corpses, the bitter taste of ash in his throat and the forbidding fortress, its defenders unaware, overrun by savage warriors who scurried over its walls.

Opening his eyes, he looked about him. The hall was dark and peaceful. Slumbering bodies lay all about him, all but hidden in the gloom. He listened for any sign of battle, anything that might have disturbed his sleep. The night was quiet, not resounding with the clash of blades and the screams of the dying. But the soul-wrenching terror of being overrun was real, clawing at his insides like rats trapped in a basket.

It was just a dream, he told himself, forcing his breathing to come more slowly. Relaxing finally, he sighed and turned his thoughts to the previous evening.

When he had seen Eanflæd fall he had felt panic rise within him. He must have made to push his way along the palisade, for Beircheart had placed a hand on his shoulder and whispered, "She has but fainted, lord. See, the men have caught her and she will be tended to."

Beobrand's mind had still been reeling from the vision of the blood sacrifice to Woden and for a moment he had pulled against Beircheart's grip, angry at the man for daring to hold him back. But Beircheart had kept firm and told him that the queen would be well.

"It is not your place to see to her welfare, lord," Beircheart had said, his tone strangely soft.

At the time Beobrand had thought little of the man's words. He was right, of course, and Eanflæd had been carried down to her chamber. Later, word had come to them that she was well. She had merely swooned and Fordraed had raged in the hall that evening that he had told her not to climb up to the ramparts.

Beobrand had done his best to ignore the fat thegn, and he had forgotten Beircheart's words until now. He lay in the darkness and pondered them, listening to the snores of the sleeping men in the hall. Was Beircheart aware of his feelings for the queen? Was everyone? The idea filled him with dread for both of them, but he pushed the fear away. There were more important things at stake.

After the nine innocents had been murdered and Penda's priest had finished his invocations to the gods, other men had joined him. Hard-faced men with wicked-looking axes. They had hacked the bodies apart, impaling the limbs and heads upon the waelstengs to serve as a grisly reminder to all the inhabitants of Bebbanburg of the blood-price that Woden had claimed.

Beobrand had felt the eyes of the people of Bebbanburg upon him as he climbed down from the walls. They blamed him for the gruesome sacrifice, he knew. Gods, he blamed himself. Would things have been different if he had not goaded Penda so? He did not know. He could never know, but as he watched the nine peasants slaughtered like cattle, he winced with every blow, horrified at the possibility that he had unleashed this fate for them. Attor had tried to speak to him, to say it had not been his fault. But Beobrand waved him away angrily. Attor had not been at the meeting with Penda. He did not know.

Beobrand had paced about Bebbanburg that afternoon, anxiety, anger and self-loathing bubbling within him. His conflict and fury was evident, so no-one sought to speak with him. Instead, people moved out of his way when they saw him coming, his face like thunder and his fists clenched at his sides. They avoided him as one would a bear with a rotten tooth.

For a time he had sat beside Fraomar. The crone had ushered him in without a word and offered him a stool beside the cot. Beobrand had stared down at the young man for a long time. Beneath Fraomar's eyes, the skin was taut and dark. His cheeks were sharp and his face wan. If not for Beobrand's weakness, Fraomar would yet be hale. The young gesith was barely breathing now and looking down at him, Beobrand feared the worst. To see him thus filled him with bitter regret and the torment of his own inadequacy and so he had pushed himself up and stridden from the hut, his mind turning and twisting against all that had befallen them and the role he had played in everything.

And so it was that he had made his way to the eastern ramparts. There were fewer men positioned on this part of the wall and one look at his glowering face told the few wall wardens that were stationed there that the Lord of Ubbanford was in no mood for conversation. He had leant on the timber wall and stared out to the wide expanse of the Whale Road. Seals bobbed in the dark waters, picked out by the bright light of the late afternoon. Lindisfarena and some of the isles to the south were clear in the light of the lowering sun. Gannets, guillemots, gulls and cormorants all wheeled in the air, diving into the waters for fish and screeching their shrill calls to one another. The lives of these birds of the sea continued unaltered by the events to the west of Bebbanburg.

Gazing down at the rocks beneath the palisade, Beobrand saw a guillemot perched in a cleft in the stone. The wind that blew from the North Sea ruffled its feathers and after a moment it flapped its wings and flew out low over the water. Beobrand wondered where it was heading and whether it nested there beneath Bebbanburg or somewhere far away. He supposed it nested farther down the coast where the cliffs were higher and its eggs would be safe from the hands of the boys of Bebbanburg who would easily climb down to pluck the delicacy from the nests, should they be laid so close to the walls. Beobrand had often seen young boys clambering down the rocks in search of the prized eggs of the seabirds, using nothing but their wits and skill. It was dangerous, but the eggs were delicious and the wealthy denizens of Bebbanburg would pay well for them.

As he watched the guillemot speeding away across the rippling surface of the sea, a terrible thought came to him like an icy wind whistling through a stand of trees. He'd remembered another fortress besieged far to the north, in the land of the Picts. At Din Eidyn it had been Oswiu and Oswald who were the besiegers, and it was Beobrand and his gesithas who had turned the tide of the siege.

Hurrying back down from the ramparts, he rushed across the busy courtyard, ignoring the glares of anger and fear directed at him, and made his way to the great hall. Inside the relative calm, Ethelwin and Fordraed were deep in discussion with their closest advisers.

Beobrand strode down the length of the building towards them. Fordraed pointedly ignored him, instead turning to Heremod and whispering something. Heremod chuckled quietly. Ethelwin glanced up at Beobrand.

"Well?" the warmaster asked, his tone terse.

"We must set more watches on the walls at night," said Beobrand.

"We have already agreed the numbers of wardens at night. You know this. We need to allow the men to rest as much as possible. Placing more men on the walls will just mean we have more tired men the next day. And God alone knows how long this siege might last."

Fordraed swung to face Beobrand. His jowls quivered.

"Why should we listen to you?" he asked. "We have all seen where your actions get us. The blood of those innocents is on your hands, Beobrand."

Beobrand took a calming breath before speaking. Fordraed's words echoed his own thoughts more than he was comfortable with.

"I would prevent more people dying, if I can."

"And you think setting more men on the walls at night will do this?" asked Ethelwin.

"It might," said Beobrand. "I cannot tell what Penda is planning, but I found myself thinking of Din Eidyn."

"What has that Pictish fortress got to do with us?" said Fordraed.

Beobrand did not reply. But Ethelwin stroked his beard and stared at him thoughtfully. Beobrand held his gaze, waiting for the warmaster to make a decision.

"I was there at Din Eidyn," said Ethelwin.

"Yes. Many were there to see the great prowess of the mighty Beobrand," said Fordraed. His voice was slurred. Reaching for a jug on the board before him, Fordraed filled his drinking horn and that of Heremod. The braid-bearded warrior emptied the contents of his horn and let out a loud belch, all the while glaring at Beobrand.

"I do not think Beobrand is gloating of his battle-skill," said Ethelwin. "He speaks of how the fortress fell, do you not?"

Beobrand nodded. He sighed, pleased that Ethelwin was listening.

"As I say, I do not know what Penda will do, but we all know that Bebbanburg is formidable. Perhaps even more so than that great fortress of Din Eidyn. The walls might well be impenetrable to Penda, even with the great horde he has with him. And the gates are stout and can be easily defended."

"Then we are safe behind these walls," said Fordraed.

"Nobody is safe facing Penda," said Beobrand. "He is as wily as he is blood-hungry. And if I were him, I might well send my men to scale the walls in the dead of night. The eastern wall is lightly manned. Determined men might climb the rocks from the beach. With some effort they could make their way over the palisade and then open the gates to the Mercian host." He paused, sweeping his gaze across all of the men who sat about the board. "Once those gates are open, all will be lost."

"This is ridiculous," said Fordraed. "You must always be the one turning men to your will. If folk are not talking about you, you are not happy. But this is not battle-fame, Lord Beobrand." Fordraed's voice dripped with sarcastic venom. "No, this is desperation. We are safe behind these walls," he repeated, perhaps wishing to convince himself. "Penda will not send men to climb them."

Beobrand clenched his fists at his side. Part of him, the beast that was chained within, wished to leap across the board and hammer blow after blow into that flabby face. But such an outburst would avail nothing. And so he ignored Fordraed, drew in a deep breath and kept his eyes fixed on Ethelwin.

The warmaster stared at Beobrand for a moment.

"You cannot be considering this," blustered Fordraed.

Ethelwin did not turn to Fordraed.

"You would be prepared to risk the fortress falling because of your dislike for Beobrand?" he asked, his tone flat.

Fordraed hesitated before spitting into the rushes and then drinking deeply from his horn.

Ethelwin nodded.

"I thought not. We will do as Beobrand says."

Beobrand shook his head in the darkness. He was thankful that Ethelwin had listened to him. Fordraed's opinion was of no consequence. How the man had risen to prominence, Beobrand could not understand. He was venal and cowardly, with an unhealthy fondness for causing others, particularly women, pain. He seemed to have the uncanny ability to find himself on the inside of any intrigue. Schemes and plots swirled about Oswiu and not for the first time, Beobrand wondered what secrets Fordraed possessed about the king. Or perhaps the man's slippery ways were of use to Oswiu. Beobrand was certain that Fordraed had been somehow involved in Halga's attack on Ubbanford, but there was no proof of treachery there, save for the assertions of the Mercian, Halga, who was dead moments after uttering the words.

Beobrand had always loathed Fordraed. Ever since Cair Chaladain. He climbed to his feet, careful not to disturb the men sleeping around him in the dark hall.

Picking his way through the cavernous building, stepping over cloak-wrapped bodies, Beobrand made his way to the doors. The nightmare and his worries had dispelled sleep for good and he knew he would find no further rest before the sun rose.

The door wards nodded at him silently as he stepped out into the night. Judging from the moon, and the blackness of the eastern horizon, there was yet a long while until dawn. He must not have slept for long at all, for the nights were short in the Bernician summer.

He walked away from the hall, heading towards the sea-facing ramparts. He was pleased to see there were more braziers burning there than there had been on previous nights. Ethelwin was a good man. Again the thoughts of the conversation in the hall and Fordraed's open disdain riled him. With any luck, he thought, Fordraed would be slain in the upcoming fighting with Penda's host.

He reached the ladder. It was as black as a tomb here, no light from the braziers or the moon reached the base of the wall. He made his way up the familiar ladder, finding the rungs more from memory than from the use of his eyes.

Bernicia would be a more pleasant kingdom without Fordraed. Beobrand snorted at the thought. Trapped as they were, what would remain of Bernicia in a few weeks?

Ethelwin had sent a messenger to Oswiu to tell him of their plight. That had been three days ago now, but even if the rider reached the king, what could he do? His retinue was not large. Travelling in his own lands, he had only taken a score of warriors with him. They could hardly turn the tide of battle against Penda and his horde.

And what of the fyrd? There had been no tidings of Cynan. Each day Beobrand looked to the south expectantly, hoping to see the Waelisc warrior riding at the head of the fyrd, but each day nobody had come. Penda's Waelisc allies were absent too, and where the defenders lived in hope of seeing their fyrd come marching north to relieve them, they dreaded seeing the men of Powys and Gwynedd coming to join the Mercian host.

No tidings had come from the south and they had all begun to fear the worst: that the fyrd had been destroyed and that Oswine would not risk bringing his own warband north to their aid. They would be alone here, besieged and beleaguered, surrounded by a host of enemies.

Reaching the rampart, Beobrand moved towards the nearest fire. Despite it being high summer, the wind that blew from the sea was cold and he wrapped his cloak about his shoulders. Images from his dream fluttered in his mind's eye, and he shook his head to clear it of the remnants of the nightmare and the terror he had felt.

The night was quiet.

Beobrand had spoken to nobody the previous evening, instead sitting morose and unapproachable until the boards were cleared away for men to sleep. Now he found that he was in need of conversation. Anything to free his mind of his worries and the fears that beat about his mind like the cloud of ravens in his dream.

Beside the fire, barely lit by its flickering flames, slumped one of the wall wardens. Sudden anger surged within Beobrand. It seemed Fordraed was not the only one who believed they were in no danger from a night attack. This man was sleeping on duty!

Beobrand lashed out, kicking the man's outstretched legs hard. He expected the guard to leap up groggily, to splutter his apologies. Beobrand was willing to forgive the man this once. He had no desire to make the man's life a misery. He would make him sorry for his laziness, but then he would stand with the man for a while and look out over the moonlit waves. He wanted company, not a fight.

But instead of jumping to his feet, the wall warden's head lolled to the side and his torso slumped over, sliding against the timber of the palisade. Was he drunk? Beobrand dropped to his side. His hand slipped into a puddle of warm liquid. Looking down, he saw it was black in the gloom.

Blood.

As quickly as if he had leapt into the cold waters of the North Sea, Beobrand was instantly alert. The dead man had a seax at his belt and a shield was propped against the rampart. Beobrand was unarmed, so he snatched both up and stood.

Stepping away from the brazier, he peered along the wall. As he watched, a shadowy figure slipped over the rampart and dropped quietly to the walkway. There were other men there, grouped together in the darkness. Steel glimmered in the night from the naked blades in their hands.

A further man clambered over the wall to join the group. They must have secured a rope. Beobrand leaned over the rampart and stared into the darkness. Many men were congregated on the rocks beneath the fortress. The foam of the breaking waves seemed to light them from below with a faint iridescence. Two more men were already climbing up the rope.

Gods, his dream had come to pass and the Mercians were already inside Bebbanburg.

"To arms!" he screamed in his huge battle voice. The men on the battlements turned to face him.

"To arms!" he bellowed again and ran towards them, shield held high.

Chapter 22

Beobrand charged forward. His only thoughts were to alert the people of Bebbanburg to the threat and to stop more Mercians from reaching the ramparts.

"Death!" he screamed and rushed at the men who had gathered on the walkway.

He shoved with all his weight and strength on the shield, oblivious to the fact that he wore no byrnie. The Mercians carried their shields slung over their backs and so were powerless to stop his advance unless they landed a lucky blow.

He barged into them with the crashing force of a wave hitting a cliff. The men tried to defend themselves from Beobrand's onslaught, holding out their hands to halt the oncoming shield. But they were pushed back. One lost his footing, tripping another, who fell with a scream and sickening thud to the hard ground beneath the walkway.

A hand gripped the rim of Beobrand's shield and he raked the seax blade across it, severing fingers. The owner of the hand shrieked and staggered back, losing his balance and tumbling after his comrade to the courtyard below.

Only three Mercians remained on the wall now.

"To arms!" yelled Beobrand again, his voice loud enough

to even rouse the spirits of those buried beyond the dunes to the south.

His opponents retreated momentarily, and a fourth man climbed over the wall to join them. In the dim light from the braziers and the moon Beobrand could see that a hemp rope had been tied to one of the supporting timbers of the palisade. He could not allow any more Mercians onto the wall. He must reach that rope and cut it.

Without warning, he surged forward, punching with the shield boss at the faces of the men before him. At the same instant, he lashed out with the seax. The nearest Mercian was unarmoured and the blade bit deep into his groin. Beobrand wrenched it free and hot blood washed over his hand. The man groaned and collapsed on the walkway.

Beobrand stamped forward, smashing the rim of the shield down onto the man's head.

A sword flicked towards Beobrand's face. He parried it with the seax and sparks flew, illuminating the pale faces of the three men before him.

The rope was close, but the Mercians were defending it ferociously, knowing that their only hope of survival was to buy time for more of their warband to climb to their aid.

"You die now!" Beobrand shouted at them, the joy of battle and victory washing through him. For in that briefest of flashes from the metal sparks, he had seen another face; grim and blunt features over a dark, plaited beard.

Heremod.

Beobrand had no time to wonder why he was on the ramparts, instead he welcomed the man's presence and leapt forward. Whatever he thought of Heremod, he knew him to be a good warrior; a killer with a sure hand.

The man before Beobrand had now managed to unsling his shield and the two iron bosses collided with a resounding clang.

His opponent grunted and tried to slice into Beobrand's thigh. But Beobrand was in his element now, and he knew what his enemy intended almost before he moved. Twisting his shield, he deflected the Mercian's strike and hacked into his unprotected outstretched sword-arm. The seax he had taken from the wall ward was not overly sharp, but it was heavy. It did not sever the man's hand as a sharper weapon might have done, but its weighty blade opened up a deep gash and smashed the bones of the forearm. The man's sword dropped uselessly over the edge of the walkway. The Mercian, frightened now, the fear evident in his wide eyes, backed away.

Heremod had dispatched the other two Mercians with savage blows from behind in the moments it had taken Beobrand to defeat his opponent. Now Heremod sliced his sword in a glittering, blood-spattering arc that took the last man's head from his shoulders. More blood fountained in the cool night air as the headless corpse toppled into the yard.

Beobrand rushed to the rope that was taut, sawing from left to right and creaking as another Mercian climbed up. Beobrand hacked into the woven hemp, but the blunt seax did little damage to the thick rope. Looking over the edge, he could see two men climbing hand over hand. The topmost man was almost at the palisade.

"Get back," growled Heremod.

Beobrand withdrew and with a single blow of his sword, Heremod severed the rope.

The Mercians fell with a wailing cry. Further screams echoed up from below a moment later.

Running footsteps made Beobrand spin round, shield raised, seax resting on the rim.

"Lord Beobrand," said the newcomer, one of Reodstan's men. More men had clambered up the ladder behind him.

"We have secured this part of the wall," Beobrand said. "Check all the ramparts. They may have planned more attacks."

After a moment of hesitation where his gaze flicked to the carnage behind Beobrand and the blood-slick blade in his hand, the man nodded, turned and began to shout orders.

Beobrand turned to Heremod.

"What were you doing up here?" Beobrand asked.

Heremod bridled.

"Some thanks would be nice," he said, leaning down to wipe gore from his blade on the kirtle of one of the fallen Mercians.

"You have my thanks, Heremod, but my question remains."

Heremod grunted. His breath was sour, reeking of mead. He took three attempts to find the mouth of his scabbard. When he finally sheathed his blade, he leaned over the ramparts and, without warning, puked. Yells of outrage and abuse wafted up from the rocks beneath the wall.

Wiping his mouth with the back of his hand, Heremod chuckled.

"That'll teach them." His voice was slurred and he swayed before slumping against the parapet.

"Why were you here?" Beobrand repeated.

"You should know why," spat Heremod. "It was your accursed idea. Extra watch."

Bebbanburg was alive with voices and movement now. Torches were lit and men shouted as each section of the wall was checked. There were no screams or further clangour of battle. It seemed they had survived the surprise attack.

Heremod heaved one of the corpses out of his way, sending it crashing down into the courtyard. Someone swore from below. He ignored the voice and staggered along the rampart to where he had evidently been on guard. He bent unsteadily, and retrieved a leather flask from the shadows.

Returning to Beobrand, he took a deep draught and proffered the vessel.

"Drink?" he asked and belched. With his left hand he rubbed at his eyes, then yawned expansively.

Ire kindled within Beobrand.

"You are drunk," he snapped, "and you were asleep when you were supposed to be on watch." He gripped the wooden handle of the seax tightly. He still held the shield, and the weight of it helped him to hide the trembling that seized his hands.

"Well, I am awake now," said Heremod with a stifled yawn. "No harm done. You woke me. We killed the Mercians. Now perhaps I can get back to sleep."

Heremod made to push past, but Beobrand dropped the shield with a clatter and grabbed the fork-bearded warrior's throat with his left half-hand. Backing Heremod into the rampart, Beobrand lifted the seax's blade to press its point against his inner thigh.

"Because of you," Beobrand hissed, "a man is dead." Heremod stank of vomit and mead. Beobrand's stomach churned. "If I had not come up here, Bebbanburg might well have fallen. More men would have died for certain. You are a disgrace." He shoved Heremod hard against the timber palisade. A wave crashed and sighed on the rocks and sand beneath them.

"But you did come," Heremod said, his breath threatening to make Beobrand gag. "And Bebbanburg yet stands. Now let me go. I am tired."

"I will see you answer for your deeds," said Beobrand, his anger seething within him. "I will take you before Ethelwin and Fordraed."

Heremod scoffed.

"You think my lord will take your word over mine?"

Again he made to break away, but Beobrand held him firm, jabbing the seax into his groin until Heremod gasped.

"Perhaps not. But do you think Ethelwin will not listen to me? He knows me for a man of my word. But you he has seen drinking all the long afternoon and into the night. You think the warmaster will so easily forgive you? It is one of his men who lies dead by the brazier."

Heremod's gaze flicked to the shadowed shape of the murdered guard. Then a cunning thought narrowed his eyes.

"You want to be careful, lord," he whispered, his foetid breath making Beobrand pull back from him. "It would not do to bring this matter before Ethelwin."

"And why is that?" Beobrand asked. There was something in Heremod's eyes that gave him pause.

Heremod leered.

"You would not be wanting everybody, Ethelwin and my lord Fordraed and all in Bebbanburg, to hear of what goes on in the night with certain ladies, would you?"

Beobrand grew suddenly cold.

"What are you speaking of?" he asked, his voice barely more than a whisper.

"I think you know, lord," Heremod said, with a lascivious grin. He pushed Beobrand away from him and this time Beobrand moved backward, lowering the blade of the seax. "I have seen a certain," he paused and licked his lips, "warrior engaged in activity with another man's wife. I don't really believe you would like me to speak of what I witnessed the other night."

Beobrand's mind reeled. He could barely breathe. If Heremod should speak to anyone of what had occurred between Eanflæd and him, they would both be as good as dead. If Bebbanburg survived the siege.

"Is all well here?" came a voice from behind Beobrand.

It was Ethelwin. His hair was dishevelled from sleep but he wore his byrnie and his sword was slung from a baldric over his shoulder. As Beobrand turned to him, he noticed the warmaster's eyes flick down to take in the seax in his hand and his proximity to Heremod. Ethelwin frowned.

"All is well now," said Heremod. "Isn't it, Beobrand?"

Still Beobrand did not respond. The man knew! By Woden and all the gods, Heremod knew their secret.

"Beobrand?" enquired Ethelwin. "Are you hurt?"

Beobrand shook his head.

"No, lord," he replied. "The fighting came as a surprise, that is all. I've yet to catch my breath."

Ethelwin tilted his head, looking at him quizzically.

"Well, it seems you were right, and we all owe you our gratitude. It is a good thing that we set the extra watches. Without Heremod up here, things might have gone very badly indeed. I see that poor Sithric fell."

"He was a brave man," said Heremod, "but the bravest is Beobrand here. If not for him, I might not have lived and the fortress would have been taken." He slapped Beobrand on the shoulder.

Ethelwin nodded in appreciation of Heremod's words.

"What were you doing up here anyway?" he asked.

"I had a dream," Beobrand replied. "I could not sleep."

"So in the right place at the right time," said Ethelwin. "Praise be to God!"

"Yes," said Heremod, shoving past the two of them and making his way towards the ladder, "praise the Lord for people being in the right place at just the right time." The burly warrior winked, a broad grin showing his teeth, and started his descent.

Beobrand watched him leave, a sense of dismay engulfing him.

Chapter 23

Eanflæd bowed her head and prayed. She prayed for the people of Bebbanburg, for its defenders, that they might remain resolute and strong, and for the women and children trapped within its walls. And finally, she prayed for the poor folk she had watched so cruelly sacrificed by Penda's pagan priest.

She had not climbed up to the ramparts since the brutal slaying of the nine victims. She had been told that their heads and limbs were on display as a gory reminder of their killing and she could not stomach the thought of seeing their faces in death.

She shuddered.

The church was dark, with only thin spears of light piercing the gloom from the small windows. Being made of stone, it was marvellously cool and she felt a momentary pang of guilt that others were toiling outside in the midday heat, while she knelt here in the comfort of God's house. But she had gone over the lists of provisions with Brytnere all that long morning and ever since she had swooned on the walls, the man was fearful for her safety and ordered her to rest frequently. He would not be dissuaded and she acquiesced to his demands, feeling sorry for him. She was his queen after all, and he had enough to worry about without being terrified that she might collapse at any moment. She was hale of body, she was sure. It had been the shock that had snatched her senses from her on the palisade. But she worked hard and the truth was, she welcomed a few moments of respite in the cool of the church. Besides, she thought, even though she was resting, she was still offering up prayers, continuing to help see Bebbanburg victorious.

The crashes and shouts of dozens of men thrusting spears and shoving with shields drifted to her, muffled by the stout walls of the church, but loud nonetheless. She wondered what good they would truly do if Penda's wolves breached the gates, as Beobrand had predicted. He had ordered for his gesithas, led by Beircheart, to train all the able-bodied men within Bebbanburg. Now, for most of each day, Beobrand's gesithas barked orders and the ceorls and even bondsmen and thralls who had been permitted to take up weapons, given the extremity of the fortress's plight, practised how to form a shieldwall and to attack with the iron-tipped spears. At the end of each hot day, the men were sweat-drenched and exhausted, and the thought had crossed her mind that the training was as much to keep the men occupied as to truly prepare them for war. She could scarcely believe that this motley bunch of farmers from the lands surrounding Bebbanburg would be any kind of match for Penda and his battle-hardened killers.

Still, keeping them busy was a good thing, and it seemed to keep their morale buoyant too. She knew that the children of the fortress liked to watch the men train. Even little Ecgfrith was content to sit and stare as the men crashed their shields together, grunting and panting as they tested their strength against each other. Godgyth was there with the child now and Edlyn had joined them. The women also seemed happy to watch the sweating men, and Eanflæd shook her head in the gloom at the weakness of the flesh. She had not fallen to temptation these last few days. She had thrown herself into her work with Brytnere and she was always occupied. She had seen Beobrand a few times, but on such occasions she had maintained an aloof air and had not engaged in anything more than polite pleasantries.

And yet she knew that her feelings had not vanished with her decision to put aside her desires for him. Eanflæd prayed that with time, her lust for him would wane. Just as the fortress must endure against the pagan, so she must be unyielding in the face of the Devil's temptations.

But she recalled how her heart had fluttered when she had been awoken in the dead of night to the sound of shouts and the clash of weapons. She had huddled in the dark with Godgyth, trembling beside Ecgfrith's cot, where the boy had yet slept. Eanflæd had prayed, whispering the words of the Ave Maria, all the while fearing that at any moment the door would fly open to reveal the leering face of a Mercian warrior. When the door had swung open, both women had let out tiny screams of terror. But it had not been an enemy fighter, come to violate and murder them. It had been Edlyn, her face flushed with excitement.

"Mercians attacked the walls," she said, breathless.

The fortress was still filled with shouts and movement, as if it were the middle of the day and not the darkest part of the night.

Eanflæd forced herself to calm her breathing.

"What happened?" she asked.

"Some warriors climbed over the eastern wall. Beobrand and Heremod fought them."

Eanflæd's heart clenched at the sound of Beobrand's name.

"Are they both..." Her voice trailed off. She was unable to utter the question, too fearful of the answer.

"They are both well," replied Edlyn. "They killed the Mercians and cut the rope they had used."

"Praise be to God," Eanflæd had said.

A movement in the church caught her attention, a shadow fell across her kneeling form and she turned to see Coenred.

"My queen," he said with a slight bow. "May I pray with you?"

"Of course," she said with a sigh. She liked the monk well enough, but she felt the accusation and judgement in his eyes whenever he looked at her. He never mentioned what he had seen that night in Hereteu, but she knew that he had witnessed her sin and his open, youthful face was always a reminder of her weakness.

He knelt at her side and for a time they were both silent, lost in their individual thoughts and prayers.

She gazed up at the altar and the ornate whalebone casket that adorned it. The box was a thing of great beauty, carved by master craftsmen. Each side depicted scenes from the life of the Christ and also the extraordinary life of the man whose head rested within. One of the images was of a great rood being erected before a stone wall, men kneeling all about. Another was of a dove slaying a raven, while in the distance stood a tree upon which a figure was hanged. The details of the carving were breathtaking. And as ever, when she gazed upon it, she felt a strange mixture of emotions.

"Oswald was a great man," said Coenred, interrupting her thoughts.

"So I am told," she replied. Her tone was terse and she felt a small cut of guilt.

"He was a good Christian king," said the monk. "I have met no finer follower of Christ's teachings."

"You never met my father," she snapped.

"True. I have heard much of Edwin and his bishop, Paulinus. Both great men, I am sure."

Eanflæd bit her lip. Paulinus had always frightened her with his eagle-like nose, brooding eyes and his strange accent. He was a stern man and had never shown her any kindness. As for her father, she could barely remember him. But Oswald was the son of his worst enemy, Æthelfrith, the king who had sent Edwin into exile across the land, fleeing from the threat of murder until at last he had been able to summon a warband and face him in battle, reclaiming the throne that had been stolen from him. Oswald might have been a good follower of Christ, but she could not forget so easily the deep-seated enmity she had always felt towards his family.

And who was it that had ordered her brother and nephew slain? Wuscfrea and Yffi had been sent all the way to Frankia, to the court of Dagobert, and yet an assassin's blade had still found them. Had Oswald sent the killer? Or had it been Oswiu, keen to destroy any claimants to Bernicia's throne, who had ordered the boys' murder?

She pushed the dark thoughts aside. She should look to the future, not the past.

"They say Oswald is a saint," she murmured.

"It is true that he has been responsible for many miracles," replied Coenred.

Eanflæd nodded. She had heard the tales of how the earth where his lifeblood was shed was imbued with the power of divine healing. It was told that a man's horse had collapsed at the spot and the beast had been returned to good health. After that, people from all around would go to Hefenfelth and take the soil from the spot. It was said that with all the earth that had been taken, a great hole had formed. And only a pinch of the stuff in a cup of water was enough to cure paralysis or even the flux.

"Do you think if we pray to him, he will bring us victory?" she asked.

"Who can say? But I think there can be none better to listen to our prayers. He was the king of Bernicia, a devout man, and Penda was his sworn enemy. Perhaps Penda's terrible unholy sacrifice before the walls will aid us and not him."

"How so?" she asked, suppressing a shudder as a finger of fear traced down her spine.

"I have thought much on this. But I think that the agony of those nine unfortunates, slain as they were in the same manner as Oswald was sacrificed..." He shivered, making the sign of the cross before continuing. "I think their cries in death might have been heard by Oswald, and not Penda's pagan gods. For is not the head of the saintly king here? And would not the holy king of Bernicia, brother to your own God-fearing husband, wish to protect Bebbanburg, his home and the fortress that takes its very name from his mother?"

Eanflæd frowned. She imagined the head of Oswiu's brother, wizened and dry within the casket. She had found Oswiu in the church the year before. He had been kneeling, with the casket opened before him. The king had been angry with her for finding him thus, vulnerable and weak. Tears streaked his cheeks and he had slammed the casket shut. Instinctively, she had looked away from the interior of the finely carved box, not wishing to see something that would lurk in her memories forever. She was glad of her decision and wished she had been as wise and not gone up to the ramparts to witness Penda's pagan blood-rite. But after her lapse in Hereteu and that fleeting kiss, her sense and wisdom seemed to have fled her. She knew she would never be rid of the images she had seen, looking down from the wall in the afternoon sunshine. The gaping throats, the vacant staring eyes, the cavorting priest drenched in crimson.

"Was he truly a good man?" she asked. The monks venerated Oswald, but he was Oswiu's brother, and she knew that her husband was no saint.

Coenred was silent for a time. His eyes were distant, as if he looked far into the past. Outside, the training men shouted as one, a great roar of shared experience, followed by a clash of shieldwalls meeting. The sound made Coenred start. She wondered what the monk had been thinking of.

He met her gaze and his eyes were sad. He sighed, and nodded.

"He was good," he said. "I truly believe that."

"Well then," she said, her mind suddenly made up, "if Oswald might have the ear of God, let us pray to him for victory."

For a moment, they knelt in silence and then Coenred cleared his throat and began to lead them in prayer. He asked the spirit of

Oswald to deliver them from the evil of their pagan aggressors; to shore up the walls of Bebbanburg that they might not splinter and fall; to grant their warriors victory when the final battle came.

Eanflæd nodded, her eyes closed now, that she might wholly concentrate on the monk's words and lend her full support to his pleas to Oswald and to God. When he had finished his prayers asking for Bebbanburg's deliverance, Coenred went on to intone the Pater Noster. Eanflæd spoke the words along with him and their voices echoed within the dark womb of the stone church.

When they reached the line, "*et ne nos inducas in tentationem*", Coenred paused momentarily and Eanflæd felt her face grow hot. Was this a reproach? Or a warning, perhaps? Or maybe it was his way of offering her solace; placing emphasis on those words in the prayer about not being led into temptation, that they might give her strength to fight her own internal battles.

Whatever the reason for his hesitation, Coenred quickly continued with the prayer and she found herself wondering whether she had imagined the added resonance he had given that particular line. But before they could finish the oft-spoken prayer to the Lord Almighty, heavy footsteps interrupted them, followed by a voice they both knew well.

Eanflæd sighed. Of course, it had to be him.

"My queen," Beobrand said, his voice ringing out in the quiet of the church. Eanflæd shuddered at the sound. "*Ne nos inducas in tentationem*," she repeated under her breath. Making the sign of the cross over her breast, she twisted to look up at the thegn from Cantware.

The light from the open door shone in his hair, wreathing his face in glowing gold. His blue eyes met hers and she drew in a long, ragged breath. The light delineated the broadness of his chest, the shape of his muscled legs. Her throat grew dry. Suddenly aware that she was kneeling before Beobrand, she rose, brushing her hands over her dress.

"Lord Beobrand," she said, her tone brisk, "what is it that cannot wait until we finish our prayers?"

"I know what Penda is planning," he said, as if that answered her. Then, seeing her questioning expression, he added, "I need your help."

With an effort, she looked away from Beobrand's silhouetted form.

"What is it you need from me?" she asked. At hearing her own words, she almost laughed, half-frightened at what he might say by way of reply.

But if he had thought of another meaning in her words, he did not show it. Without so much as a smile, he said, "Come. I will show you."

With that, he strode from the church without looking back. With a quick glance to Coenred, who offered her a thin smile and a nod of encouragement, Eanflæd followed Beobrand out into the light.

Chapter 24

"There can be no doubt now," said Ethelwin, shielding his eyes with one wide hand. "You were right."

Beobrand nodded. His eyes watered from the quickening breeze that blew from the north. They stood atop the ramparts near the gate and looked down at where Mercian warriors were dragging yet more timber up the slope. There was already a huge pile of broken beams, shattered fence posts, wattle walls and splintered shingles heaped against the gates.

Initially, they had been unsure what Penda had planned for all the dwellings he had ordered to be destroyed in the land around Bebbanburg, but as the Mercian warriors had begun to laden the remnants of the buildings into ox-drawn carts, goading the beasts towards the fortress, Beobrand had finally understood.

The night-time raid had been thwarted. The attackers had been slain on the ramparts and had failed in their attempt at opening the gates from within. But if they could not be opened through stealth in the darkest reaches of the night, Penda would need to find another way.

At first, the Bernician defenders had loosed arrows down at the approaching waggons, and in this way they had killed a handful of men and two oxen. The men looking on from the battlements had let out a huge cheer as each arrow had struck home, and yet the work had continued. The slain men and beasts were hauled away, and groups of warriors carried the timber in smaller quantities the final paces to the gates. Some of these Mercians held shields aloft to protect their comrades and, whilst every now and again a Bernician arrow would find its mark, the pile grew throughout the day.

Men hurled down rocks and even a few spears at the enemy warriors who were slowly, but with the constant determination of ants, building Bebbanburg's funeral pyre.

It soon became clear that no matter how many missiles they cast down at the Mercians, the defenders were not going to stop the construction of the huge mound of wood at the gates of the fortress. That the very means for the destruction of what they had believed to be invulnerable should come from the homes, farms and new church they had abandoned, made the knowledge of Bebbanburg's impending defeat all the more bitter.

"Do you think they will fire it tonight?" asked Ethelwin.

Beobrand looked towards the setting sun. The land hazed into the distance where the hills met the burnished bronze sky. It would be dusk soon. Down the slope there were still three more carts piled with the wooden bones of Bernician buildings.

"It will take them a long while yet to bring all of that up here," he said. "I think they will wait for tomorrow. But we must be ready to fight tonight. Penda is never easy to predict." Beobrand bit back the sour thought that the only thing he could foresee when it came to Penda was that the Mercian king usually won his battles. He scanned the horizon in all directions. There were only the merest wisps of cloud far away out over the deep blue of the sea. He watched a pair of puffins skimming the waves' surface, their tiny wings beating fast. "But I do not think Penda will wait beyond tomorrow. This dry weather cannot last forever."

Ethelwin nodded, his features grave.

"It seems Penda is not a patient man."

Beobrand shook his head.

"No. Of all the things he might be, patient is not one of them. A long siege is not the way of the man."

"I imagine he does not like being here," said Ethelwin, "with his back to Bernicia and Bebbanburg and the sea before him. Perhaps he has heard that Oswiu is not here and fears he will be attacked from the rear."

"Or maybe he knows that our fyrd is destroyed and he just doesn't want to remain here any longer than he has to. Warriors that are camped in one place for a long time will only cause trouble. It is hard enough to herd sheep, but it is quite some task to keep a pack of wolves in peace."

They watched as a group of Mercians jogged within range of arrow and spear to toss some more logs onto the pile at the gates. Four men held their wide circular shields over them as they came. A single desultory stone flew from the ramparts and clattered harmlessly from one of the linden boards. A couple of the defenders yelled insults at the Mercians, but no damage was done to them, and they hurried back down the slope to collect more tinder for what the men had started to call Bebbanburg's bone-fire. They had long since ceased to shoot arrows at the attackers, and Beobrand had rebuked the men for wasting their spears and so now, the wall wardens watched grimly as the heap of splintered rubble grew.

Ethelwin turned and gazed down to the courtyard. A crowd of men, in the plain clothes of ceorls and bondsmen, sweated and grunted under the watchful gaze of Beircheart, Attor, Dreogan and Halinard. In the shade of the wall, Beobrand noticed Brinin. The young man was pale and clearly not able to lend his hands to the work, but the sight of him on his feet pleased Beobrand. Fraomar yet lay in an unwaking slumber and neither Coenred nor the crone could say anything that might give Beobrand comfort. He could see in their faces that they both believed Fraomar would die, it was just a matter of how long his spirit would cling to this world.

"Will we be ready?" asked Ethelwin, dragging Beobrand's thoughts back to the gate and the work being done in the courtyard.

"As ready as we can be," Beobrand said.

Beircheart and his gesithas had drilled the men of Bebbanburg into a semblance of a fighting force. Beobrand knew that when the gates were breached, as they most certainly would be, and the crashing terror of battle descended upon them, many of those men would be slain. But some would stand strong. A handful might even discover they were that rare breed of man who rose to greatness in combat. Who could tell what would happen when the shields clashed and the steel spear-points ripped into flesh? Only the gods could see a man's wyrd. In the short time they had, his gesithas had done the best they could with the men. The Black Shields were the most notorious warriors of Albion and the men looked up to them with awe and not a little fear. But these farmers would do their best when the time came, he knew. Not to impress the lords of Bernicia and the Black Shields, but to defend their loved ones. If their spirit did not break, they would each fight with the strength of many men. For there can be no man more dangerous than one whose kin is standing right behind him.

For an instant, Beobrand thought of Octa and Ardith. He was glad his son was far away with Oswiu and that his daughter was safe in Ubbanford.

Safe?

If Bebbanburg fell, who would be truly safe in Bernicia? But Bassus would see the folk of Ubbanford safe. The old champion had warriors to defend them. Beobrand hoped that word had reached Bassus of what was occurring here, and that the one-armed warrior would lead the people into the forested hills to the north, where Penda and his wolves would not find them.

He pushed thoughts of Ubbanford, his friends and his children from his mind with difficulty. The only thing he could do to keep his people safe was to survive this battle and send Penda back to Mercia in defeat. Scratching at the sweaty hair that draggled at the nape of his neck, he sighed. Could they win here?

Beobrand watched as Eanflæd stepped out of the shadows and spoke quietly to Beircheart. The black-bearded warrior immediately bellowed orders, which the men followed instantly, without question. No longer were the ceorls and bondsmen being taught the ways of the shieldwall. Now they were helping to move the shelters away from the entrance to the fortress and then, some way in from the gates, they were constructing a secondary defence across the cleared ground. It was for this task that he had asked for Eanflæd's help. She was organised and knew all of the people within the fortress by name after arranging the preparation of the provisions. She was their queen, but she was also the daughter of old king Edwin and she was beloved. The folk obeyed her without question and she had a knack of making difficult decisions seem easy.

Earlier that day, he had been amazed when she had ordered the guardhouse that stood near the gates to be pulled down. Fordraed had argued against it, but Eanflæd had been resolute.

"Would you rather keep the guardhouse and lose the fortress?" she had asked.

Ethelwin had told her to do what was needed.

Beobrand had wanted to laugh at the expression of disbelief on Fordraed's flabby features. But he had kept his face sombre and stern. This was no time for levity.

Eanflæd seemed to become more beautiful the more obstacles were placed in her path, and she appeared to be glowing now in the afternoon sunshine. She glanced up at them and Beobrand felt as though his heart had stopped when her gaze lingered on him for a moment. Her expression did not alter, and Beobrand held his own face as still as a mask. But his neck and cheeks grew hot and he was sure that his discomfort was obvious to all. If Ethelwin noticed anything, he did not say.

Under Eanflæd's and Beircheart's supervision four men were wrestling with a great beam of oak. After a deal of effort they finally rested it on one of the waggons that had been added to the makeshift wall.

"That defence won't hold them for long," Ethelwin said.

"With any luck, it will hold them long enough for our archers to make them pay dearly," Beobrand replied. He hoped he was right.

Those men who possessed bows would climb up to the ramparts and rain down arrows into the Mercians after they had broken through the gates. The attackers would be caught with the smouldering remains of the gate behind them, the wall of rubble and carts before them. The air above them would be filled with the bitter sting of arrows and when they finally managed to pull down the barricades to make their way further into the fortress, they would be met by the shieldwall. Beobrand and his Black Shields would be there, along with Ethelwin, Reodstan and all the other thegns and gesithas in Bebbanburg. The shieldwall was the last line against Penda's horde and Beobrand knew that it would be a terrible thing. Blood would turn the earth to marsh and the screams of the dying would echo from the palisades. It would be the essence of nightmares. There would be nowhere for them to turn after that. They would fight to the last man. Beobrand looked down at Eanflæd and his throat closed. Gods, he thought. So many would die here.

He had looked out at the great warhost of Penda and no matter how he tried, no matter the plans and defences they placed in the path of the attackers, nor the savage power of men defending their wives and children, he could not imagine how they could win this fight.

He cared nothing for his own life – he should have died many times before – but the thought of these women and children being trapped within Bebbanburg's walls filled him with a dreadful horror. Would Eanflæd be spared? She was the queen and of more value than a plaything for blood-soaked warriors to sate their lust on. Could Penda exert that much control over his baying wolves once they had scented and tasted blood?

Beobrand shuddered.

He looked down at her as she talked to the men who toiled to move yet more rubble, dragging a heavy basket of debris to the barricade. They wiped the sweat from their foreheads and smiled at her words. Beobrand could not hear what she said, but he recognised the love in the men's faces. A lock of her hair had slipped from beneath her wimple, and absently she pushed it back under the linen with a dainty gesture of her slender fingers. Gods, how he wished he could go to her; to hold her in his arms and one more time kiss her perfect lips. He drew in a deep breath and did not move.

With an effort he pulled his gaze away from Eanflæd and found himself staring into the eyes of another.

Heremod.

The fork-bearded warrior was perched atop one of the waggons, sliding a whetstone along the edge of his sword-blade. As their eyes met, Heremod grinned and set aside his weapon to pick up a cup. He raised it in Beobrand's direction in a mocking toast before draining its contents.

Despite the heat of the afternoon sun that burnt from a clear sky, Beobrand's skin prickled like that of a plucked goose.

Heremod finished his drink and offered Beobrand a knowing nod before turning his attention back to his blade. For a moment longer, Beobrand watched the warrior as he sharpened his sword. Every now and then, Heremod's dark eyes flicked up to observe Eanflæd and Beircheart.

"Will it be enough, Beobrand?" Ethelwin asked. His voice was hollow and forlorn. The warmaster was no fool and Beobrand was sure he had seen in his own mind the events that would come to pass. The burning of the gate, the thrum of bowstrings, followed by the cries of pain of the Mercians injured before the barricades, the bloodletting at the shieldwall and then the terrible surge of rage from the Mercians as they broke through the last resistance to swarm into the buildings of Bebbanburg in search of treasure and the pliant flesh of the womenfolk.

He offered up a silent prayer to Woden that if it came to that, he would be slain before the screaming started.

"There is no other option," Beobrand said. "It will have to be enough."

He turned and made his way down the ladder into the shade of the courtyard.

Chapter 25

Beobrand rubbed his callused fingers against his eyelids. His eyes felt gritty, as if he had stood staring on a windswept beach. His body ached with tiredness and he knew he should sleep. But whenever he closed his eyes and slumber began to embrace him, visions of death swelled up in his mind like so much scum on a bubbling broth. Faces of men he had killed swam in the darkness. He could not remember when he had killed most of them. These were nameless men – Mercians, Waelisc, Picts, Franks. He would never learn of their names, hear tales of their lives, of their loved ones. But their final moments on middle earth were forever seared into his memory. Their wails of anguish echoed in the dark on nights such as this. He longed for sleep but was terrified of the dreams, and so he sipped sparingly at the cup of ale he had brought with him for his vigil and thought again of what the dawn might bring.

Come the sunrise, he would see more death. Of that he was certain. There would be flames and fear and the foul stink of blood and spilt guts. Who would he lose tomorrow? Dour Dreogan? Beircheart with his swagger and finely combed beard? Attor and his twin flickering seaxes? Would the brothers, Eadgard and Grindan, fall in the shieldwall? What of Halinard? All were dear to him, oath-sworn and loyal and he would do his best to keep them alive. But to die in battle was a warrior's lot. They would welcome it more than a straw-death, old and wizened, or infirm like Fraomar, drifting into the afterlife with not so much as a murmur.

He gazed down at the frail features of the young gesith and again felt the desperate pang of regret and guilt. Fraomar's skin was taut over his sharp cheekbones, his eyes sunken and dark in the dim flicker of the rush light.

The old crone snored quietly from the pallet at the rear of the hut. She had barely acknowledged Beobrand when he had stepped into the hut. Grindan had been sitting with Fraomar and Beobrand had ordered him to get some rest.

"You'll need your strength tomorrow," he told him. "I have a feeling Penda won't allow us to dawdle in our blankets in the morn, so drink sparingly."

Grindan rose.

"You need sleep too, lord," he said.

"There will be time for sleep when all this is done. Tonight I will watch over Fraomar."

Beobrand sat on the stool beside Fraomar's bed. The smell of sweat, piss and sickness was heavy in the air.

Grindan paused in the doorway and Beobrand looked up at him. Grindan's face was a jumble of shadows, the clear purple expanse of the sky rolled away forever behind him.

"It is not your fault, lord," he said, his voice not much more than a whisper, as if he was uncertain whether he wanted to be heard or not.

For the briefest of moments, Beobrand felt the stirrings of his infamous rage within him. But it was as if the kindling of his anger was damp, for the sparks did not take. Instead of the incandescent fury Grindan had feared, Beobrand merely sighed.

"When all is said and done," he muttered, "it matters not who is to blame. All that matters now is what we do next. I will sit with Fraomar. You will spend time with Eadgard and your shield-brothers. And see that you all get some rest. I will have need for your strength," he forced a lopsided smile, "and wits tomorrow."

Grindan nodded and made to leave.

Beobrand called him back.

"One more thing," he said.

"Lord?"

"Tomorrow, things will be hard. If the shieldwall should falter…"

"We will stand with you, lord. We will hold fast against the Mercian scum."

Beobrand held his hand up for silence.

"If the shieldwall should break, I need you to swear to me that you will go to the queen's chambers. Eanflæd will be there, with her gemæcce, Ecgfrith, Edlyn and the other women and children."

"If the shieldwall breaks, we will fall by your side, lord," Grindan said. His eyes glittered in the darkness.

"No!" Beobrand snapped. "If I fall, you must go to the queen and protect her with your life. You, your brother, any of you that yet draws breath. Protect the queen and her son. That is my will and I demand it of you. I am not important. The queen and Ecgfrith are Bernicia. They must not be taken by Penda. Do you understand?"

Grindan hesitated.

"I have your oath, do I not?" pressed Beobrand.

Grindan swallowed.

"Yes, lord."

"And you understand my command?"

"Yes, lord."

Beobrand held him in his frosty gaze for several heartbeats.

"Good. Now tell the rest of the men my wish. There may not be time for such talk on the morrow."

Grindan nodded glumly and slipped into the gathering gloaming.

The talk of Eanflæd's possible fate had brought on a terrible sadness in Beobrand. The last he had seen of the queen was when he had climbed down from the walls and made his way across the courtyard behind the new barricades.

As he walked, he could feel Heremod's eyes on him all the while. He ignored the man, but deep inside he knew that if they survived the upcoming battle, things could not remain as they were. There would be a reckoning. Beobrand would not allow the man to stand over him with the blade of his secret ready to fall at any moment.

Eanflæd had moved away from Beircheart and the men who were putting the last baskets of rubble on the barrier. She had stepped towards Beobrand and he had longed to reach for her. Her cheeks were flushed from the heat and her exertions, her eyes bright. She wore the plainest of dresses and her hair was covered by a linen wimple. She was achingly beautiful. The desire to pull her into his embrace was almost too much to bear, but he felt Heremod's gaze on them and the fortress was thronged with men and women.

And so he had lowered his gaze as he had approached and muttered, "Good day, my lady."

Her eyes had grown wide, but she had offered him a small smile and replied, "Lord Beobrand," before turning back to her work.

He had discussed with Ethelwin the idea of placing guards outside the quarters in the great hall where the queen, the womenfolk and the children were to reside during the battle. But the warmaster said they could not spare any fighting men. The injured and the old would remain with them. They would be given spears and shields, but both men knew that they would be no match for Penda's warriors.

Looking down at Fraomar, the fragility of their existence

gripped at Beobrand's heart. Dismay flooded through him at the thought of Penda's ravening wolves hacking their way into the hall. They would cut any defence down and be on the women in moments. He rubbed at his eyes again, in an effort to stop his mind from conjuring up the thoughts that threatened to flood in. Fresh images came to him then. Cathryn's pleading eyes in a freezing forest clearing. Tata's bruised and broken body on the altar of Engelmynster. Sunniva's haunted beauty. Reaghan's delicate features, wreathed in her unruly auburn mane. Her eyes held a melancholy sadness he had never been able to reach.

And from the depths of his memory came the horrific screams of anguish that had filled the night at Cair Chaladain. That was the night he had vowed never to allow his men to sully womenfolk or to do battle on the innocent. Such was not the way of the brave, but of the craven.

At the thought of all the women he had failed over the years, and what would happen to Eanflæd, Edlyn and the others tomorrow if the Bernicians could not hold the Mercians back, tears welled in Beobrand's eyes.

The weight of the fortress and the land of Bernicia was crushing down upon him. How could he save them? Gods, who was he? Just a farm boy from Cantware. Men looked up to him as a great warrior, but he knew the truth of it. Here, in the darkness, with the stink of sickness in his nostrils, he could admit to the truth. He was nothing. Oswald had been right. It was just luck. All of it.

Or mayhap it was his wyrd, whispered a tiny voice deep inside him. If this was his wyrd, he wished he could be done with it. Tomorrow would bring more pain and suffering, fear and frenzy as men killed and died choking on their lifeblood.

This is what Penda's sacrifices had brought. It was everything the All-father cared for. More blood and more mayhem. Woden loved chaos. Whether the Mercians won or lost, it made no difference to the gods. How they must be laughing.

The full burden of the situation pressed down on him like a great rock and, unnoticed, tears streamed down his cheeks.

"Do not weep, lord," came a thin rasping voice.

Broken from his self-pitying sorrow, Beobrand opened his eyes with a start. Wiping at his cheeks with the backs of his hands he looked about, embarrassed at his show of weakness.

But there was nobody there. The wheezing snores of the old woman still emanated from the rear of the hut. There was no other sound. No-one was there save for him and Fraomar.

"Do not weep," the voice repeated, and with a shock, he looked down to see Fraomar's eyes open. They were liquid and febrile in the gloom, but Beobrand's heart swelled with joy to see the young man awake. "I am not dead," Fraomar croaked.

"I can see that," Beobrand said, his anguish of moments before evaporating like dew in morning sunshine.

"But I am thirsty."

"Of course," Beobrand said, his voice cracking into nervous laughter, such was his happiness. He reached for his cup of ale and gently helped Fraomar to drink, lifting his head but being careful not to touch the place where the Mercian warrior's blow had struck.

Fraomar took two great swallows of the drink before Beobrand pulled the cup away from his lips.

"Easy now," he said. "I don't want you making yourself sick."

Fraomar lay his head back onto the mattress and winced.

"It would appear too late for that," he whispered, a faint smile playing on his cracked lips. "I feel as weak as a kitten."

"We feared we had lost you."

Fraomar smiled again.

"From the pain in my head, I cannot say I am pleased to have returned to the land of the living. What happened?" He frowned, looking about the darkened room. "And where are we?"

"Bebbanburg," Beobrand replied. "You took an almighty

blow to the head. Without your helm, you would have been food for the crows."

Fraomar looked confused. He closed his eyes for a moment and let out a long, shuddering breath.

"I remember none of this," he said at last, a tremble of unease in his voice.

From the shadowed depths of the hut, the old woman stirred. Rising to her feet with a groan, she hobbled over to look down at Fraomar.

"When the head takes such a blow it will often forget the moment when it was injured," she croaked. She leant low over the young man, pulling up his eyelids with her gnarled, arthritic fingers and peering into his eyes. "You almost died, young man." She pushed herself upright with an effort. "If you should forget a few days from your past, it is a small price to pay for life, I would say. No?"

She bustled to the back of the hut and began to pull pots and flasks down from a shelf there.

A sudden terror seemed to grip Fraomar then and his eyes widened. "I had command of the warband. Are they...? Did I...?"

Beobrand placed a hand upon the young warrior's shoulder.

"You did not fail me, or the men. They are well and they are here. See? You have not forgotten everything."

He offered a smile of encouragement, but Fraomar ignored it.

"But why are we in Bebbanburg?" he asked.

As if in answer to his question, there was the sound of a commotion outside. Shouted voices, followed by the continuous, rhythmic wail of a hunting horn. Beobrand was startled by the sound. So soon? Had Penda decided to attack at night?

Moments later, the door to the hut swung open. Grindan was framed there and Beobrand saw that it was no longer night – he must have dozed on the stool for longer than he had realised.

Gone was the infinite star-dappled dome of the night sky behind Grindan. It was replaced with the flat, grey wolf-light of the dawn. Cool air wafted into the room. Was that smoke Beobrand could smell?

"It is time," Grindan said. "The fire has been lit. We must ready ourselves for battle."

Beobrand rose. Now was not the moment for pity. He shrugged off his night-time fears and doubts like a man stepping out of a wet cloak. He squared his shoulders and his eyes blazed in the gloom.

"Welcome back your shield-brother," Beobrand said, grinning broadly despite the impending battle. "Now we have one more thing to fight for."

Grindan dropped to his knees beside the cot and grasped Fraomar's hand.

"My friend, I thought we had lost you."

"So I hear."

"The bastard that did this to you is no more. I saw to it myself."

"You must tell me the tale, for I can remember none of it."

"Truly? I will do my best, for it was a fight worth remembering." Beobrand pulled Grindan to his feet.

"The tale will have to wait until we have defeated the Mercians one more time," he said. "Fetch men to help you carry Fraomar to the great hall. He must wait there with those unable to fight."

The old woman looked up from where she was grinding leaves and roots into a foul-smelling paste in a wooden bowl.

"He cannot be moved. He must yet rest until his head and senses settle," she said.

Beobrand looked down at Fraomar. He was as pallid and frail as his uncle Selwyn had been shortly before death claimed him.

"He cannot stay here," Beobrand said, his tone as rigid as the rocky crag upon which Bebbanburg sat. "And neither can you. You will both go to the hall. Grindan, get others to help you now. And see that Brinin goes there too. I will go to the gates. Meet me there."

Grindan nodded and hurried away.

The wizened woman began to protest further, but Beobrand silenced her with a glare.

"I will not argue with you, woman," he said. "If the shieldwall breaks you would have no chance here. Pack up what you need to see to Fraomar and anything that will aid in treating wounds. I am counting on you to keep him alive."

"It seems whether we live or die rests more in the strength of your sword than in the skill of my hands," she said, shaking her head, but Beobrand was pleased to see she began scooping up pots, utensils and flasks and placing them in a sack. As she started plucking down wyrts that hung from the beams, he turned to leave, satisfied that she would do his bidding.

"Lord," croaked Fraomar, "you have not told me what is happening."

Beobrand clutched the man's hand for a moment. It was dry and cold. The smell of smoke, acrid and unpleasant, was stronger now.

"There is no time," he said. "Pray that we will be victorious and you can hear the tale tonight in the hall. Otherwise, I will tell you of it in Woden's corpse-hall."

Without waiting for a response, Beobrand rose and strode from the hut into the dim pre-dawn light.

Chapter 26

The wind blew the thick smoke into Beobrand's face. Embers from the conflagration were snatched up by the breeze and flung, stinging and spiteful, into the faces of the men who stood behind the barricade. The sun was high in the sky now, and the summer warmth was added to the searing heat from the fire at the gates, making the men there sweat and curse.

They had constructed this second line of defence some way back from the gates, to make enough room for the attackers to enter the killing ground they had cleared, but Beobrand had not counted on the strong wind or the sheer ferocity of the blaze. The sky above the gates flickered and swam and the dark plumes of smoke rose high into the pale sky.

A sudden gust of wind sent a huge shower of sparks and burning debris into the air, to drop amongst the defenders and the rubble barrier. On seeing the size of the fire and how the wind was fanning the blaze towards them, Beobrand had ordered buckets of water to be brought and placed at intervals along the barricade. The sweltering men drank from them and used the water to douse any flames that caught amongst the tinder-dry wall they had constructed from the remains of the guardhouse.

Beobrand climbed up the ladder to the palisade on the western side of the fortress. He had removed his helmet, but sweat ran down his neck and back and his face and hair were slick. When the gates fell and the battle started, it would be like fighting inside a bread oven.

The palisade here was busy with bowmen, ready to unleash their arrows down upon the Mercians when the gates finally fell. Something else he had not predicted was how long the gates, stout oaken slabs reinforced with iron, would take to catch and burn. But now, after a long while of waiting as the sun rose and the heat from the fire grew, the doors were smouldering. From his vantage point, he could see that the Mercian host must also have noticed the development, for the armoured line of warriors had moved closer to Bebbanburg's entrance. Their priest leapt and screamed before them, but Beobrand could not make out the words from this distance. The fire's roaring voice swallowed all others, lending its rushing howl to the wind.

Beobrand glanced to the left and saw the bird-picked remains of the unfortunate sacrifices still hanging like scraps of smoked meat dangling from a hall's beams. It seemed that Woden had answered the priest's calls. The wind had blown constantly and hard all that morning towards the fortress's gates, pushing the flames into the piled timber and against the oak doors, and funnelling the scorching heat into the courtyard, forcing the Bernicians to retreat, soot-stained and sweating in the face of the fire's ferocity.

Far away, towards Gefrin in the west and Ubbanford and Berewic in the north, clouds were forming on the horizon. Could they bring rain? But they were far off and the gate would be destroyed well before any possible rain reached them.

"Not long now," he said to the nearest archer. "Those gates will crumble soon, and then you know what to do."

The man nodded, his face sombre and pale beneath the dark smudges of soot. Up here, the heat was less terrible, but the men had not rested. Buckets had been passed up hand over hand from the well below and the water had been sluiced against the palisade and walkway as close to the gates as they could reach.

The Mercians must be prevented from destroying the wall too. If they could be trapped within the courtyard killing ground, there was a chance. If they were able to swarm over a broken wall, all would be lost.

"We will not fail you, lord," the archer said. "We'll make those bastard Mercians regret coming to Bebbanburg."

"Good man," Beobrand said, clapping him on the shoulder.

He glanced once more at the gates, trying to gauge how long until they fell. Earlier he had come up here with Attor, and the sharp-sighted scout had told him he could see that some of the Mercians bore hooks attached to long poles. They had used these to pull down the buildings around Bebbanburg and now it seemed they would help the gates to topple when they were weakened enough by fire.

"Be ready," Beobrand said, raising his voice so that all the men gathered on the ramparts could hear him. "The gates will soon fall. After that, let your arrows fly true."

The men did not respond with a cheer and he could think of no more rousing words for them. Looking over at the far wall on the seaward side of the fortress, he saw that Ethelwin was also addressing the men there. He knew that the warmaster had been worried about the enemy scaling the walls once more, and so had set guards around the palisade at regular intervals. If they saw any Mercians seeking to take advantage of the distraction at the gates, they were to sound their horns and a group of warriors from the second rank of the shieldwall was under orders to rush to their defence. Beobrand thought it unlikely that Penda would try the trick again. He had rolled the dice and lost and he would know the defenders would not be caught unawares. But Beobrand could not deny that it was a possible place for an attack and so the men needed to be vigilant.

Ethelwin began to climb down the ladder from the east wall. No cheer came from the men there either. Looking at the gates which were now fully robed in throbbing, pulsating flames,

Beobrand could understand that they did not feel that victory was within their reach. This was the impregnable seat of power of the kings of Bernicia. But the king was not here with his people, and the fortress was about to be breached, its gates consumed by a ravenous fire that the men saw as the pyre of the kingdom.

"Stand strong and make your arrows count," he said, before climbing down to the courtyard.

He glanced over at the buildings of Bebbanburg. The stables, the halls and storage huts, the new stone church and the great hall. How strange it was to see the buildings so peaceful while across the summit of the rock, a great fire raged and warriors bristled with spear and sword, ready to kill and maim.

He thought of all of the people in that hall. Fraomar, weak and confused from his injury, would lie in his pallet surrounded by women, children and grey-beards. He would listen to the clash of weapons outside and feel a terrible helplessness and shame at not standing with his brothers. And what of Eanflæd? The thought of her, slender and beautiful, fierce but powerless against Penda's warriors, brought a lump to his throat.

The defence must not fail. He could not allow it to. The shieldwall would stand and somehow, with sheer determination and the knowledge that they were defending their loved ones, their home and their queen, the Bernicians would win. He could not bear to think otherwise.

Shortly after the fire had been lit and the sky was still dark, with the merest hint of gold out over the sea, Coenred had come to him at the barricade.

The monk's face had been pale, but he held himself tall and Beobrand had smiled to see his friend. Coenred hated battle and killing, but he was no coward.

"How can I help?" the monk asked.

"This is not the place for you," Beobrand answered. Coenred dropped his gaze, his cheeks flushed. "But I welcome your offer of aid," Beobrand continued, placing his half-hand on his old friend's thin shoulder. "Go back to the great hall. Prepare your bandages and poultices. Whatever you need to heal wounds. Your skills will be required before the day is old. And the women and children will need your strength." He hesitated for a moment. "And your faith."

Coenred seemed pleased at the words. Or perhaps he was relieved that Beobrand had sent him away from the shieldwall and the barricade.

"I will do whatever I can to help God's flock," he said. "May the Lord watch over you." He made the sign of the Christ rood in the air. Turning, he moved back towards the great hall.

"One other thing, Coenred," Beobrand called to him.

The monk halted, turning to his old friend. Coenred's long hair drifted about his face in the wind. In the early morning gloom, he looked as young as when he had nursed Beobrand to health all those years before.

"Yes?" he said.

"Pray for us," said Beobrand.

Coenred had stared at Beobrand for a long moment, as if weighing his words. At last, he had nodded and left.

A great rending crack snapped Beobrand's attention away from his memories.

The left gate had split. A cloud of sparks gusted into the smoke-heavy sky and the thin cheer from the Mercians reached him where he stood at the centre of the shieldwall behind the barricade.

Some of the men picked up their shields, others checked their swords. There was a murmur from the gathered warriors as they retrieved discarded helms and rose to their feet. The gate would not stand for much longer, and then the Mercians would pull away what debris they could and swarm into the fortress.

"Ready yourselves," cried Ethelwin. "Soon we shall give those Mercian whoresons a taste of Bernician steel." A desultory sound went up from the men, more groan than battle-cry.

"Are you well, lord?" Attor stepped forward, close to Beobrand.

Beobrand had not moved. He was watching the flames and the smoke and thinking of the clouds he had seen to the north and west. And somewhere in the depths of his mind, he wondered if Coenred might be on his knees in the hall, praying to his Christ god.

And perhaps the Christ was listening.

Beobrand had seen the power of the new god over weather before. At Hefenfelth Oswald had prayed beneath a great rood and a storm had come to conceal their approach as they had attacked the Waelisc. Bernicia had been victorious, and all the warriors there had felt the power of the new god who had delivered the triumph to this young, Christ-following king returned from years of exile.

"Lord?" Attor reached out a hand, touching Beobrand's arm and bringing him out of his reverie.

"Attor," he said, not removing his gaze from the blaze at the gate, "what do you see?"

"The fire has almost had its way with those gates," Attor replied. "They will soon fall. Best to be ready for when they do." He made to hand Beobrand his great helm. Beobrand ignored the proffered helmet.

"Look carefully," he urged. "What has changed?"

Attor stared at the flames and the smoke. Another snapping, splintering crash came from the left gate, and a part of it fell to the ground in a sudden shower of sparks. At last, understanding dawned on his face.

"The wind," he said, awe in his voice. "It is changing direction."

As he spoke a strong billowing gust whistled across the courtyard, away from the Bernician shieldwall. The heat from the fire abated considerably with the shift in the wind. Beobrand wondered whether it would swing around again, once more sending embers, ash and sparks and the intolerable waves of heat at the defenders. But rather than turn against them, the wind blew ever harder into the north-west. The flames and heat were now pushed away from them and towards the awaiting Mercian ranks.

"How do the Mercians fare?" bellowed Beobrand at the archer he had spoken to on the palisade.

"They've had their beards singed by the change in the wind, lord," he called back. "They are retreating back from the fire."

Beobrand closed his eyes, picturing the sloping path that led down from the gates. The ramp was narrow, with broken rocks and bushes at either side.

Could it be? Was this how the Christ God had listened to Coenred's prayers? The wind gusted, harder than ever, cooling the sweat on his neck and tugging his long hair about his face. The flames, smoke and heat from the fire were pushed into the faces of the Mercians. The left gate, with a moaning wail, crashed from its hinges. It toppled outward, onto the burning heap of timber that the Mercians had built outside Bebbanburg's entrance. Burning splinters and sparks flew up, to be carried on the gusting wind towards the attackers. Through the heat-shimmer and smoke, Beobrand could see the Mercian line wavering, pulling back from the fire that now assaulted them with each billow of wind.

Beobrand grinned, suddenly consumed by an idea of such audacity that it left him breathless. But why not? There was little to lose and much to gain. And what warrior gained victory by being cautious?

"Bernicians," he boomed in his loudest battle-voice, "do not fear. I know you believe all is lost. But no! The winds have changed and victory will be ours."

A rumble went through the line.

"Look, my Black Shields stand with you today and we will not be defeated by this Mercian rabble. Do you doubt me? Do you doubt Beobrand of Ubbanford?"

A few of the men nearest to Beobrand muttered a reply. His

gesithas hammered their blades into the black shields they bore and let out a roar.

"No!" they shouted.

Gradually the rest of the men took up the chant and soon the fortress reverberated with the word.

"No! No! No!"

"We will have victory today!" Beobrand screamed, his voice rising above the chanting. "Are we sheep to await our slaughter here?"

The booming response grew, as if the spark of his idea had kindled the spirit of the Bernician warriors.

"No! No! No!"

Ethelwin shouldered his way through the gesithas to Beobrand's side.

"How does the change in the wind alter anything, Beobrand?" he asked, placing his mouth close to Beobrand's ear so that he alone would hear the words.

"Waiting here, thinking about the attack that we know will come, it has sapped the men of their spirit. They have felt powerless. But listen to them now," shouted Beobrand, the joy of battle gripping him as it always did. "Do they sound powerless to you? They long to fight, to bleed Penda and his dogs for what they have done."

Ethelwin looked at him, an expression of confused dismay on his face.

"We must take the fight to the Mercians," Beobrand said.

"But the fire," Ethelwin replied. "We are trapped within Bebbanburg."

Beobrand's grin widened, the savage madness of bloodletting calling to him.

"We are not trapped," he replied. "We are caged beasts. And I know how to release us."

Chapter 27

"This is madness!" cried Ethelwin. "We will destroy the gates!"

A few of the men turned at the warmaster's angry words. Beobrand pulled him in close enough that he could smell the man's sour sweat.

"Think, Ethelwin," he hissed. "A divided warband is a weakened warband. The men have taken heart, would you destroy their belief by questioning me in front of them?"

Ethelwin held Beobrand's gaze. His brow was furrowed, his eyes glaring. Beobrand did not turn away. The moment dragged out. The wind blew strongly across the courtyard.

Fordraed's nasal tone cut through their battle of wills.

"What is the meaning of this? Surely you will not listen to this fool." Fordraed was stuffed into an iron byrnie; his jowls, swelling above his collar like rising dough, quivered as he spoke. His hair was plastered against his head and beads of sweat bejewelled his face. A droplet formed on the end of his nose and splattered onto the rings of metal that encased his bulging belly.

For a heartbeat, Beobrand thought that Ethelwin would back the fat lord; that he had pushed his luck too far with the warmaster. Ethelwin stared into his eyes for a moment longer, before giving him the smallest of nods and rounding on Fordraed.

"The gates are already destroyed," Ethelwin said. As if to accentuate his words, the right gate collapsed in a flurry of bright sparks and ash. "And I have learnt to listen to lord Beobrand. You might do well to do the same. If not for him, we would have no fortress to defend."

"But this is madness," spluttered Fordraed.

"No," said Beobrand, raising his voice again so that all should hear him, "this is not madness. This is the will of God! I know those of you who believe in the Christ have been praying. I also told the monk, Coenred, and Utta the priest to pray. And God has heard your prayers. He has sent this great wind to aid us. See now how it pushes back our enemy?"

Peering through the gateway, beyond the flickering furnace of the collapsing fire, he could see the Mercians had retreated even further to avoid the terrible heat and flying debris from the flames.

"We will take the fight to our enemies. To God's enemies. But we must be quick about it. I will lead with my Black Shields and I know you will be right behind us, brave Bernicians. With your strength and courage, and with the power of God on our side, victory will be ours."

A movement caught his eye and, looking up, he saw two crows flapping slowly, labouring into the brisk breeze. He shuddered. With his words he had pitched Woden against the Christ. Most of the Bernicians worshipped the new nailed god so these were the words they needed to hear, but he wondered what powers he might have unleashed by uttering them.

He shook off the feeling of doubt. There was no time for that now. The time had come for action. For killing. To bend his wyrd to his will.

"Listen to the warmaster," Beobrand bellowed. "He knows what you are to do."

He had quickly laid out his plan to Ethelwin and now he must trust that the man would lead the warriors as he had instructed. There was no time for discussion.

While he had been talking, Eadgard, Dreogan, Grindan and Halinard had wrestled the largest waggon from the barricade, swinging it around to face the burning doors. Attor had run to fetch rope and now, with Beircheart's aid, he proceeded to lash some boards taken from the barricade to the shafts that projected from the front of the cart. This was where a mule or donkey would be saddled to pull the vehicle, but today there would be no animal before the cart.

Attor had understood Beobrand's meaning immediately and his eyes had glinted with the savage exhilaration of the idea.

Ethelwin was shouting orders at the men in the courtyard, pulling them together into a narrower force, five men across. He positioned his own warriors, hardened fighters of many shieldwalls, at the front and Beobrand saw Reodstan and his gesithas jostling to take the foremost rank. Beobrand saw all of this in a moment, and, trusting to Ethelwin, he turned his attention to his comitatus.

"Soak your cloaks," he said, dipping his own woollen cloak into the nearest bucket and then swinging its sodden weight over his shoulders. Like all the men, he had discarded the garment as the sun came up, but now they would be glad of its protection against the heat and sparks from the fire. As an afterthought, he dipped each of his feet into the bucket. His gesithas copied him.

"More water!" he screamed, and boys carried the empty buckets to be refilled. All along the line men were drenching themselves in water. He wondered whether it would be enough; if damp cloth, wet shoes and leg bindings would provide protection against the inferno at the gate.

Was this foolishness? He looked at the shimmering air where the gates had stood. Had he thought of this idea himself, or was it perhaps the Christ God who had planted the seed in his mind? He thought of the crows and the waelstengs with their grisly totems. Or was it Woden, the grey wanderer, who had turned his mind to this course? He would never know. There was no time left for pondering. The flames were receding. The wind yet whistled through the gates towards the Mercians, but soon the fire would die down and any chance of a surprise attack would be lost.

"Are you ready, my brave gesithas?" he asked, scanning the grim faces of his men. All of them nodded in return, slinging shields onto their backs to leave their hands free. "Then let us kill some Mercians."

Leaning their shoulders into the waggon, they groaned with the effort, pushing it forward. Attor stood at the front, lifting the shafts with the boards strapped between them. The waggon rolled forward and Attor pushed the shafts to one side, aiming the cart directly into the burning gap in Bebbanburg's defences.

"Heave!" yelled Beobrand, shoving his weight against the wood of the cart. Eadgard, seemingly oblivious of the wound to his thigh that must still be painful, was beside him, lending his massive bulk to the effort, and the waggon, free now of the debris around the barricade and unimpeded by the shafts that Attor had lifted from the earth, hurtled forward.

They sped towards the fire, the wind at their backs, pushing them along. Despite the shift in the direction of the wind, as they drew closer, the heat became oppressive, overwhelming. It sucked the air from their lungs and blistered their skin.

Gods, thought Beobrand, he must have been moonstruck. They would be burnt alive!

He heard an inchoate scream of rage filling the boiling air around him, unaware that the sound came from his own mouth. The smoke stung his eyes and he could barely make out lithe Attor sprinting to the front of the waggon, pushing and pulling the shafts to guide it between the flaming columns of the gateway. They were moving too fast, thought Beobrand, suddenly fearful that Attor would be pushed into the flaming rubble of the doors and the bonfire by the weight of the speeding cart.

But with the uncanny agility that made him so deadly in combat and able to wield a blade in each hand, the wiry warrior darted to one side at the last possible moment. At the same instant, he dropped the shafts to the ground.

They instantly dug into the earth and the boards he had lashed between them drove into the burning remains of the conflagration with a bursting cloud of sparks. The waggon slowed with the impact and Beobrand roared, pushing with renewed energy. Attor spun around and joined the rest of the gesithas behind the cart, adding his own strength to that of his shield-brothers. Together, with a shared shout of defiance, they surged on, pushing the waggon onward, churning up the embers and flaming timbers before them as they passed through the gateway.

For a moment the heat was so intense that Beobrand could not breathe. He felt his hair singe. Heat seared through his wet shoes where he trod on blackened broken beams that flickered like a smith's forge. His throat was afire and he could not see. The air writhed and danced. Sparks and ash and flames filled his world. A burning brand flicked up, sizzling against the back of his left hand.

Gods, what had he done? Had he led them all to their doom?

And then they were through.

The boards on the front of the cart had done their job, carrying before them great piles of the burning wreckage that had been heaped before the entrance to Bebbanburg. Sparks and embers flew into the air, to be carried by the wind into the faces of the surprised Mercians.

It felt cool here, after the furnace crackle of the fire, and Beobrand sucked in great lungfuls of air. His hand was a stinging agony, and his eyes were streaming. But he yet lived.

With one final effort they sent the cart speeding onward. The sloped ramp before the gates turned to the left and so the cart bumped and creaked towards the bend where it careened over, toppling into the rocks and nettles there, and resting at a twisted angle. All along the path in its wake lay the remnants of the fire that the cart had snagged and pushed before it.

With a glance back towards Bebbanburg, Beobrand saw that Ethelwin was leading the first of the Bernicians out through the shattered gates.

Some paces down the slope the Mercians stood, shield to shield, a thicket of spears bristling above them. Penda's wolf banner waved tall above the throng, the pelts and tails flapping in the wind.

"Shieldwall!" Beobrand bellowed, and without pause his gesithas unslung their shields and drew their blades. They carried no spears, but Beobrand was not prepared to lose the moment of advantage their sudden appearance through the flames had gained them.

Breaking into a run, knowing that his men would obey without hesitation, he shouted again.

"Boar's snout!"

Eadgard, with a barely perceptible limp, his huge axe grasped in both meaty hands, took the centre, with Grindan to his left and Beobrand to his right. They would hit the Mercians like a spear-point of men and shields. Eadgard's axe would be the tip, cutting through the enemies like a scythe through barley.

Ten paces from the Mercian line, their black shields touched and Eadgard let out a bellow like a wild beast.

"Death! Death! Death!" yelled Beobrand, and the others joined him in the murderous chant.

All thought had left Beobrand now. He fixed his gaze on a wide-shouldered man before him wearing an open helm. The man's eyes were bloodshot and his cheeks were covered in stubble the colour of new thatch. The Mercian's eyes narrowed as he saw Beobrand charging towards him.

"Death!"

Three paces before they reached the Mercian line, the man lunged with his spear, as Beobrand had known he would.

Catching the spear's blade on his shield easily, Beobrand deflected it over his shoulder.

Beobrand let out a vicious laugh. Gone was all fear. He felt not the pain of the burn to his hand or the sting of the smoke in his eyes. His doubts had been dispelled by the surging, terrifying joy of battle. All that remained was the enemy and Beobrand's overwhelming desire to slay every one of them.

"Death!" he howled, his face contorted into a mask of rage.

And the shieldwalls collided with bone-shaking force.

Chapter 28

Beobrand slammed into the Mercian warrior, pushing him backward. The weight of the amassed boar-snout charge carried Beobrand on. As the broad-shouldered man before him stumbled, falling back in the face of the Black Shields' assault, Beobrand lashed out with Nægling. The sword's fine blade bit into flesh and bone. The enemy's face was instantly smothered in blood and the Mercian collapsed to be trampled by the Bernician advance.

Blood sheeted up from Eadgard's axe blows, showering down on Beobrand. It was warm and viscous, yet strangely soothing after the onslaught of the flames. The metallic taste of slaughter clogged his throat. Beyond the huge axe-man, Grindan blocked a spear aimed at his brother's chest. To the other side of Beobrand, Attor parried and riposted with his two deadly seaxes. He screamed a torrent of abuse at the Mercians and they seemed to cower before him.

Beobrand hacked Nægling's blade down onto a shining helm. It clanged against the metal, skittering down and smashing the man's collarbone. The Mercian fell to his knees and Beobrand thrust his sword into the man's throat.

All was death and chaos now. Beobrand and the line of black-shielded warriors stamped forward. A hand grasped at his ankle and he sliced down with Nægling. They would leave none alive as they passed. Their advance slowed now, halted by the sheer mass of Mercians thronging the sloped path. Beobrand was dimly aware of shouted orders from the Mercian leaders, perhaps from Penda himself. The bellowing voices called for the men to stand strong.

This was the crucial time, Beobrand knew. If the Mercians could rally, they might be able to push the Bernicians back towards Bebbanburg. The wind howled, the heat from the fire buffeting him forward, as if a great hand was pushing him, urging him on.

"For Bernicia!" Beobrand screamed.

With renewed vigour his Black Shields surged forward once more, slashing and cutting, shoving against linden board and iron shield boss. Eadgard battered a man's shield aside, splintering the wood and shredding the hide covering. The Mercian was defenceless against the force of the attack. He had dropped his spear and was frantically trying to free a seax that hung from his belt. His fingers gripped the bone handle, pulling it from the leather sheath, his eyes blazing in triumph. A heartbeat later, he was grasping at the stump of his forearm, his face white, his eyes wide. Eadgard's axe had taken his hand and the seax had fallen into the dust, still gripped in his now-severed fist. Dismissing the injured Mercian, the axe-man stepped past him and set about hammering his way further into the enemy ranks. Thus it always was with Eadgard when it came to battle. He became filled with such a fury and thirst for killing that he ignored all danger. Beobrand had thought they might be able to train him to be more thoughtful, to use his wits in battle, but after a time, it had become clear this would never happen. And so they put Eadgard's terrific strength and focus to good use and he relied on others to protect him. Grindan always stood at his side, shield ready, his sword-blade flickering with great skill.

But now, Grindan was locked in a struggle with a man almost

as large as his brother. Grindan was not small, but the Mercian before him was a full head taller and Grindan was fighting to keep his feet as his massive assailant leaned on his shield. Another of Beobrand's gesithas, Ulf, a burly, straw-haired warrior, clung to Grindan's belt, lending his weight in the battle, but even with Ulf's help, Beobrand could see it would be a close contest.

His gaze flicked back to the man Eadgard had maimed. Blood spurted from his stump, but rather than tumble to the ground to allow death to claim him, as it surely would, the man's face was set and grim, his teeth showing in a savage rictus of rage. Beobrand recognised the man's expression. He had seen it many times before. It was the face of a true warrior. The man knew he was slain, but he would not be dismissed so easily from middle earth. He would take his slayer with him to the afterlife. With his left hand, the dying man snatched the seax from where it lay at his feet, pulling it from the fingers of his own cleaved fist. The Mercian spun around to stab the knife into the advancing axe-man's back. Beobrand admired his single-mindedness, recognising himself in the man's actions. He was almost sorry that the Mercian would have to die without tasting this final victory. But there was no time for sympathy in the shieldwall. Beobrand hacked Nægling into the warrior's exposed neck. Blood spurted from the severed artery, spraying over Eadgard's heaving shoulders. Truly defeated now, the dying Mercian slumped to the blood-soaked dust of the path.

Oblivious to what was occurring behind him, Eadgard moved onward, his axe rising and falling before him, sending up clouds of splinters from shattered shields and a misting of blood from sundered enemies.

The man holding back Grindan finally fell. Ulf had stabbed at his feet beneath the shieldwall, and a vicious sword thrust from Grindan had finished the task. The Black Shields advanced.

Beobrand rushed forward to defend the axe-man, grunting as another spear gouged the hide and wood of his shield. Sweat ran freely down his face now, mingling with the soot and blood. His mouth was filled with bitterness. He spat over his shield into the face of the Mercian there.

The walls were locked together; a heaving, groaning mass of bodies, wood, leather and metal. Now the real bloody work of the shieldwall would begin; the grinding down of wills and flesh in a maelstrom of killing that would see some men weeping for the release of death and others howling with the gleeful ecstasy of slaughter.

Beobrand slid his sword down so that he could stab it under his shield. He rammed it forward, feeling it connect. But it did not cut. It scraped harmlessly against the long skirts of the iron byrnie his opponent wore. The man roared in anger, pushing hard against his shield and probing beneath the wood in an attempt to disembowel Beobrand with a wicked-looking seax. The links of Beobrand's iron-knit shirt were well forged and the seax did not penetrate, but as the Mercian pulled the seax back, its sharp blade scored a line across Beobrand's knuckles. Cursing with the pain, Beobrand punched his shield boss forward. It clanged against his assailant's and Beobrand lowered his shoulder behind the board and shoved with all his strength. The Mercian slipped back a pace and Beobrand stabbed Nægling down into the man's right foot. The warrior screamed and Beobrand twisted the blade free. Retreating a step, he glanced down at his right hand. Blood welled from the fingers that clenched Nægling's grip. It stung as if his hand had been dipped into boiling water, but the cut was not deep and his fingers were still strong.

The shieldwall lurched forward suddenly, catching Beobrand unprepared. Beircheart slammed into his back, pushing him once more into the Mercian shields.

Beobrand knew instantly what had happened: the rest of the Bernician host had joined them and were pressing from the rear, anxious to wet their blades in the blood of the hated Mercian besiegers.

"Sorry, lord," Beircheart grunted, trying to push back on the tide of bodies that pressed them forward.

Beobrand did not reply. The Mercian before him was still reeling from the cut to his foot. But due to the crush of men behind him, he was unable to back away from the Bernician advance and the tall thegn with the ice blue eyes who loomed above him. Beobrand used his height and weight to lever the injured man's shield down, then, with the speed of a striking serpent, he swung Nægling up and over the shieldwall, lancing the patterned blade's tip into the man's face. The sword penetrated the Mercian's left eye and cut a great flap of skin from his cheek. The man dropped like a slaughtered bull and Beobrand stepped forward.

"Let me take the first rank," shouted Beircheart, and Beobrand nodded, slipping to one side and allowing the gesith to take his place. This was done in an instant and was only possible because of the countless days they had practised the move back at Ubbanford. Bassus was a hard man to please, and the men all resented his barked orders and incessant repetition until it came to the blood and death of battle, and then they loved him for it. Beobrand felt himself being carried forward and he saw that others of his gesithas had swapped their positions with those who had taken the brunt of the charge. Eadgard was still in the centre. He would not retreat and his axe glittered in the morning sun as it cast droplets of blood high into the hot air above them. Grindan too, remained in the front rank, protecting his brother's flank with relentless skill and tenacity.

For a moment, Beobrand felt a stab of guilt at having stepped back from the fighting. But that was foolishness and pride, he knew. He was formidable and would stand through the long day, dispatching all who stood before him, but Bassus, Bernicia's old champion, had trained him and the rest of the warband well and they knew that to conserve their strength would aid them better than expending it all in a continuous onslaught. The

Mercian host would not break easily and they would surely be dancing to the sword-song until the sun passed its zenith. In this heat, they would not be able to withstand such a prolonged assault without rest.

The press of men was terrible. The heat and the cataclysmic crash of metal on metal assailed their senses. They jostled and shoved, all the while sweating beneath their war gear till their bodies were slick, their clothes drenched. Beobrand and the rest of the Black Shields threw off their sodden cloaks. They had saved their wearers from the worst of the fire, but now the heavy wool weighed them down. The discarded garments were trampled along with the dead and dying Mercians.

Someone cried out for water, and what seemed like an age later, flasks were passed forward to the front ranks of the host. Beobrand drank sparingly, the warm liquid doing little to refresh him. Handing the leather flask to Attor, he prepared to take his turn once more at the front of the line where Eadgard still hacked and hewed with his hefty axe.

And so the day wore on. Beobrand sheathed Nægling, uncaring of the blood that would congeal in the scabbard. His arm was leaden and his bloody fingers ached. He tugged his seax from its sheath and set about stabbing and chopping with its shorter blade. It was more suited to the butcher's work of that long, dusty, broiling day than the lengthy blade of his sword. After a time, he was overcome with such tiredness that he barely bothered to raise his tattered shield, only lifting it at the last possible moment. He fought with an economical efficiency. Now was not the time for taunts or to win battle-fame by showing one's sword-skill. This was the charnel house of battle and Beobrand killed without thought, relying on his skill and experience to find the gaps in the enemies' defences. There was nothing else now, save for the clamour and stench of the battle.

They fought for a long time like that, mouths too dry to spit and arms heavy, muscles screaming from the exertion and breath burning in their lungs. Before them, the Mercians fell, only to be replaced by fresh warriors. To one side of Beobrand, Dreogan received a slashing cut across his face, sending streams of crimson washing over the soot-tattoos on his cheeks. He fell back and Garr took his place. Beobrand cursed, wondering whether Dreogan would survive. Beneath the blood, the gesith's skin had been pallid. Garr too looked pale and exhausted under the battle-grime that smeared his face. They were all on the verge of collapse.

Gods, they had fought with the strength of wild boars, but they were but men. Soon they would be too slow to block the spear thrust, too tired to parry the striking sword. Beobrand's mind was dazed. He tried to picture the warhost he had witnessed outside Bebbanburg's gates. He imagined how many Mercians they had slain. Their broken bodies were heaped on the sloping path and many had been pushed to the side to tumble into the nettles and rocks. But however many they had killed, he could not believe they would vanquish them.

The host of Bernicians led by Ethelwin might carry the day, but at what cost? Beobrand and his Black Shields would fall, he realised that now. He had not considered that the narrow pathway would mean that there would be no Black Shields standing by the end of the battle. But now he could see no other outcome. There was still a host of Mercians before them, and the amassed Bernicians behind meant there could be no retreat.

He thought then of the crows he had seen in the sky. Was this Woden's doing? How the All-father loved mayhem. Beobrand had oft felt like the plaything of the gods. Was this what they wanted? To see him crushed before the walls of the great fortress where his brother had died? Perhaps Ethelwin or Eanflæd would find his corpse and bury him beside Octa.

Had he led his men from behind the walls of Bebbanburg to their deaths? This was his doing. But if the Bernicians seized the victory, was that not enough? Songs would be sung of this day;

of the warriors smashing through the burning gates and hacking their way to victory. The numbers of dead would not matter. At least his queen would be safe. He was willing to die for Eanflæd.

The thought of never seeing her or his children again filled him with a bitter sorrow. The sudden sadness was like the wind that blew across the embers of the fire at the gates. But the wind of his woe kindled the sparks of anger that lay deep within him, fanning them into a raging furnace of fury.

If he was to die here, he would make the Mercians pay with seas of blood.

"My brave gesithas," he yelled, his voice cracking in his parched throat. "Are we truly going to let these Mercian curs hold us here?"

"No!" came the ragged reply from Attor and Beircheart, both of whom were sweat-slick and blood-grimed. Their arms and faces were red with gore as if they had bathed in the entrails of their enemies.

"Come, see there! Penda's standard is near," Beobrand shouted. "Let us take it. Now!"

And with that, Beobrand sprang forward, stabbing and slashing with his seax, punching with his splintering shield. His Black Shields joined him, and he sensed Ethelwin's warriors pushing forward too, lending their bulk to the renewed charge.

Eadgard did not seem to pay any attention to his lord or the men behind him, but he must have heard Beobrand's words, for he let out a huge roar and began to batter his axe into the foemen as if they were so many saplings.

Together, the Black Shields pushed forward. One pace. Two. Three. Beobrand rammed his seax into a bald man's mouth. Such was the force of the blow that the man's shattered teeth scratched against the cuts on Beobrand's hand. He twisted the blade, wrenching it free with a great gush of blood.

He was screaming incoherently now, his rage filling him with a feverish strength that could not endure. The fire would soon burn out, but until it did, Beobrand would slice through everyone who stood before him. Stamping forward, almost losing his balance on the soft flesh of the man he had just killed, he pushed with his shield, catching the edge of a Mercian board. The man was defending against Eadgard's ferocious axe, leaving himself open to Beobrand's attack. Too late he saw the approaching thegn, his eyes widening in fear as he watched death coming for him. Beobrand laughed and plunged his seax under the man's arm. The Mercian's mouth opened in dismay, but Beobrand could not hear his screaming over his own battle-cries.

Eadgard and Grindan stepped forward, slaying two Mercians in as many heartbeats. Attor's blades flickered, parrying a scything strike and then severing the man's fingers.

"Come and die on my blades, you piss-guzzling goat-swivers!" he screamed. "Die! Die!" He spun and took another Mercian in the throat.

Garr somehow managed to trip the enemy before him as he tried to back away from the savage attack of the black-shielded warriors. The Mercian, a young man with a wispy beard and no moustache, sprawled in the blood-choked dirt before Garr. The man's head was bare, his helmet having toppled as he fell. Without hesitation, Garr hacked into the crown of the Mercian's head, splitting it and spilling yet more gore onto the dust.

They were close to Penda's banner now. If they could keep up this pace, they might yet slay the Mercian king. But Beobrand could already feel his strength waning. The breath wheezed in his throat.

"One more push," he cried, stepping forward.

And then he noticed there was a gap of clear earth before him. The Mercians were backing away, looking anxiously at the blood-drenched warriors and casting furtive glances behind them.

"See, my brave warriors," said Beobrand, barely able to get the words out, such was his shortness of breath. "The Mercian scum are retreating. They run from us."

He bent over, leaning against his knees while he tried to catch his breath.

Taking advantage of the brief respite in the battle, Ethelwin and Reodstan pushed forward.

"Lord Beobrand," Ethelwin said, his eyes wide at the carnage he had witnessed, "you and your men have broken them."

"And now, we will finish them," Beobrand panted, pulling himself up to stand straight.

"It is our turn now, my friend," said Ethelwin. "Drink and then follow us, for there is much slaughter still to be done this day."

"We will not rest," said Beobrand. "You will need every shield, every blade."

He looked at where the Mercians even now were shuffling further away from them.

"Aye, it is true, Beobrand," Reodstan said, his red face gleaming in the summer heat. "But they no longer outnumber us as they did."

Beobrand shook his head.

"We have slain so many?" he asked.

Reodstan laughed.

"You and your Black Shields have killed more men than I would have believed possible had I not seen it myself, but that is not what I meant. The Mercians are pulling back as a new warhost is come to the field."

"What?" asked Beobrand, his mind spinning.

"A host is approaching from the north and west."

"A host? The Waelisc?" Beobrand's stomach twisted at the thought of yet more enemies before them. If the men of Powys and Gwynedd had returned to bolster Penda's forces, they were all doomed. He could think of no way they might stand against

256

such a host. The triumph he had believed was theirs turned to ash in his mouth.

"No, lord," Reodstan said, the ever-rushing wind threatening to rip the words from his mouth. "Not Waelisc. They ride under the purple banner of Bernicia. Oswiu is returned."

Chapter 29

Cynan hesitated, watching as the threescore horsemen spurred their mounts across the open ground towards the outcrop of rock. The rock, topped with its walled fortress, rose like a clenched fist lifted in defiance to the great Whale Road beyond.

Bebbanburg.

Oswiu had returned, his purple banner streaming over the horsemen who were galloping away from Cynan, towards the battle. His place was with them. Mierawin had plenty of wind left and with a squeeze of his heels, she would carry him easily across the flat land to where the unsuspecting Mercian host thronged.

Looking up from the enemy encampment he could see that the smoke had lessened. It was more of a smudge on the horizon above the fortress now, rather than the huge greasy plumes that had urged them on to greater speed, beckoning them eastward like a great beacon.

The slope up to Bebbanburg was crowded with men and he could see standards and banners raised above them, snapping and flapping in the wind. The fighting was fierce before the gates. It was too far to make out details, but the stiff breeze brought snatches of the clamour of the battle to where he watched. Beobrand would be there, he was sure. Again he thought of digging in his heels and chasing after Oswiu and the mounted thegns who were racing towards the rear of the Mercian ranks. His place was there, with his lord and his shield-brothers, cutting a bloody swathe through their foe-men.

And yet he was torn. What of the men behind him who trudged down the slope from the west? Were they not also his shield-brothers? He spat, cursing in his native tongue and pulling Mierawin's head around. Kicking her flanks, he sent her galloping back towards the approaching men.

He surveyed them as he rode. They were a mass of drab clothing, tan and brown wool and linen, not the gaudy leather warrior coats, colourful woven belts, arm rings, gold and garnet brooches and paint-daubed shields of thegns and their gesithas. These men carried boar spears and axes, not fine pattern-bladed swords with shining pommels and hilts. These were fyrd-men. Behind him the fate of the kingdom was being settled in a great clash of kings. And Cynan was to trudge to the battle with this motley group of ceorls.

And yet they were brave. That he could not deny. And they were stalwart and doughty.

When he had arrived at Hefenfelth they were amongst the last men left standing. The Waelisc host had swept down on the gathering fyrd. The men of Bernicia had been taken by surprise. Still waiting for men to come in from the steadings and villages, they had been sitting around fires, drinking and laughing like men at a Thrimilci feast. They had not expected to be attacked. The Waelisc had cut them down before they had managed to mount any kind of defence. Many had been slain before they truly knew what was happening, and many more had scattered, fleeing into the forests south of the Wall. Cynan had no idea what had happened to them. Perhaps the Waelisc had hunted them down and slaughtered them all later. It seemed that the bulk of the host had travelled south after dispatching the Bernician fyrd.

A few of the wealthier men – ealdormen, thegns and gesithas who possessed their own heregeat, their war harness and horse – had managed to mount their steeds and escape northward. Some of them now rode towards Bebbanburg alongside King Oswiu, eager to prove themselves worthy subjects, men of bravery rather than the cowards they appeared for fleeing the field at Hefenfelth. Cynan spat again, thinking of how the men who should have been leading the fyrd had run away. Still, at least they were there with the king now. Others had vanished, drifting back to their halls, or riding as far as possible from the Mercian warhost and battle.

Not so the rabble of men before Cynan. They may not have byrnies and swords, but they had heart.

Reining in Mierawin before them, he pointed into the east. The air was hazed above the fortress and the smell of smoke was on the wind.

"Our king rides to smite his enemy. Penda is caught between the anvil of Bebbanburg and the hammer of Bernicia. You have walked far these last days. I know you are footsore and tired. But would you stand here and watch as those men who ride with the king forge their battle-fame? Or would you hear your names in the songs of tomorrow?"

He scanned their faces. They were dirt-smeared, their eyes dark with weariness. But there was something else, a pride he saw in them. One man, perhaps twenty summers old, with unruly curls of fair hair that he'd tied at the nape of his neck, raised his head, jutting his jaw out defiantly.

"You, Fægir," Cynan said, "what say you? Would you have the name of Fægir be known to all men after the glorious victory today?"

"And to all women," Fægir said. The others laughed. Fægir never ceased talking about his conquests though Cynan had heard Eoppa, one of the older men who came from the same settlement as Fægir, say it was all fantasy. "He is married to his childhood sweetheart," he'd said. "Never so much as sniffed another woman's cunny. If he did, Agatha would cut off his sloes."

"If we are to help win this day," shouted Cynan, "we cannot tarry here, waiting for the king's servants and the thralls." Behind them, still far away in the hills to the west, came the waggons and carts that carried the king's goods and the tribute that he had collected from his royal vills.

"I would dip my blade in Mercian blood," Cynan continued.

"I would like to dip something," said Fægir with a smirk.

A gust of wind shook the gorse and grass about them, bringing with it the sounds of the distant battle.

"This is no time for jests," Cynan said. "Death awaits some of us this day. This is no game." The smile slipped from Fægir's face.

"But you men know the stakes. I have seen your worth. I could have gone with them." He nodded towards the backs of the horsemen. "But you followed me at Hefenfelth and I would not desert you now. And you all saw what happened when the men of Powys and Gwynedd struck. You can never predict how a battle will end, who will run and who will stand. The king might yet have need for your spears."

He could see some of the men nodding agreement. One slender man with balding pate and skin as brown as a nut stepped forward.

"I have not walked all this way just to let those rich bastards take the glory now," he said. "Come on, lads. Let's show those Mercians that they cannot come onto our land without paying a dear price."

Cynan grinned at the man. He liked Ingwald. He was direct, intelligent and bold. He had been responsible for rallying the men at Hefenfelth and getting them into their strong position against the Waelisc. It was Ingwald, as much as Cynan, who had seen these men survive that blood-soaked day.

Cynan recalled the scene he had ridden into that afternoon. It had only been three days ago, and yet it seemed like weeks.

He had reached the meeting place north of the Great Wall as the sun was low in the sky. It was quickly obvious to him that he had arrived too late. Tents were aflame and corpses were strewn about the encampment. Most of the Bernician force had been killed, or had fled. And then he had seen them: a knot of fyrd-men beneath the huge timber cross that Oswald had erected years before. The rood had been raised on the top of a rise and now a group of men were congregated on the hill, shields locked, spears bristling from their defensive wall.

Cynan had halted Mierawin, taking in the situation in a moment. None of the Powys and Gwynedd warriors had spied him, coming as he did from the west. It seemed to him that most of the Waelisc host had moved on, leaving behind it a ruin of death and devastation. One small group remained. They numbered perhaps three dozen and had encircled the spear-men who stood in the shadow of Oswald's cross.

The sun glinted from the Waelisc weapons, their burnished byrnies bright in the afternoon glare. These were warriors of renown, men wearing silver torcs and bearing steel blades. Before them stood what appeared to be farmhands with nothing more than plain willow shields and hunting spears.

Anger flared within him as he thought what the fate of the men on the hill would be. The Waelisc would toy with them awhile, but against trained killers, there was little chance for the Bernicians, unless the Waelisc warriors tired of their sport and rode on.

Without being aware of making a decision, Cynan spurred Mierawin towards the gathered Waelisc. As he cantered across the scattered remains of the camp, he checked his sword was loose in its scabbard. Crows and magpies, gorging themselves on the still-warm flesh of the fallen, flapped angrily into the air as he passed. They croaked at him, furious at having their feast interrupted.

He approached the gathered Waelisc men at a trot, making no pretence of concealing his identity. The men carried shields bearing the image of a black stag on a white field. He cursed. He did not know to which lord the sigil belonged. Most of the men seemed bored. They leaned on spears, apparently content to hold the Bernicians on the hillock with their presence. One man, stockier than the rest, with hair that was greying at the temples, sat astride a dappled horse. He shifted his position at Cynan's approach. He opened his mouth, but Cynan cut him off before he could speak.

"What is the meaning of this?" Cynan snapped, using the Waelisc tongue.

The mounted man sat more upright in his saddle.

"Who are you?" he asked.

Cynan ignored the question.

"Do you lead here?"

"These are my men." The man puffed out his chest. "I am Madawg, do you not recognise me?"

"Of course," Cynan lied, nudging Mierawin close to Madawg's steed. "You are to take your men from here and follow the others. You are not to tarry further."

Madawg frowned and Cynan was suddenly aware of the number of enemy warriors who were within striking distance of him. What had he been thinking? He should have ridden far from Hefenfelth when he saw that the fyrd had been destroyed. This was madness. And yet, here he was.

Madawg's eyes narrowed.

"I was told to finish this lot before following the host," he said. "Why the change?" He hesitated, peering at Cynan, who felt his face grow hot in the afternoon sun. "Who are you?" repeated the Waelisc lord.

Cynan's mind was blank. He could think of no answer that would convince the man. As he hesitated, Madawg's suspicions grew. His hand dropped towards his sword-hilt. There was no more time to think.

Cynan urged Mierawin forward and at the same instant drew

his seax from its sheath and plunged its sharp blade into the stocky lord's neck. Madawg jerked and twisted, wrenching the seax from Cynan's grasp. Even as the man's twitching body tumbled from the horse, his blood splattering the animal's dappled flanks, Cynan swung his leg over Mierawin's neck and slid to the ground.

The time for talking was over. He had thrown the dice and now must see where they landed.

Slapping Mierawin on the rump, sending her away from danger at a run, he unslung his black shield from where it hung over his back. The Waelisc warriors around him were wide-eyed in shock, but already they were moving, raising weapons and spears. He would not last for more than a few heartbeats alone here, surrounded by enemies.

"For Bernicia," he bellowed, his voice as loud as his lord Beobrand's in battle. "Would you stand on that hill and watch me die, brothers?" His desperation ripped at his throat. The five Waelisc who were nearest to him had lifted their shields and were circling warily. They would rush him soon, and then all would be lost.

Without warning, a tall man with black hair and clean-shaven, smooth cheeks leapt towards him. He was a handsome man, perhaps a year or two younger than Cynan.

"You have slain my father!" he screamed as he flew towards Cynan.

One of the older Waelisc warriors tried to hold the young man back, but he shrugged him off, swinging his sword furiously at Cynan. Instantly, Cynan could see that the man was strong, but no killer. His swiping cuts were savage and filled with fury, but whatever training he had with the blade had vanished, replaced with his anger at his father's murder.

Cynan caught one of the man's powerful swings on the rim of his shield, then stepped inside his reach, punching him hard in the face with the pommel of his sword. The man fell back and Cynan finished him with a cut that severed the arteries in his throat. Blood arced hot and strong into the warm air. Cynan jumped back, risking a quick glance behind him. There were no enemies there. But the rest of the Waelisc had been stirred into action at seeing their lord and his son cut down.

They seemed to have forgotten the men on the hill, instead turning and congregating before Cynan. He was but one man, but he had slain two of their number in moments and his sword was slick with gore. This must have given them pause, for they formed a shieldwall before him.

"By the gods," shouted Cynan using the Anglisc tongue of the Bernicians, "these Waelisc whoresons are scared of one man!"

He kept his eyes firmly on the warriors in the shieldwall before him, but from the edges of his vision, he saw movement from the hill. He smiled grimly to himself. Well, he had thrown the dice. He would soon see whether luck was with him this day.

The Waelisc in the shieldwall felt a tremor of fear at seeing the lone warrior before them. The man's shield was black as death, his byrnie glinted in the sun and his sword was dripping with the blood of one of their number. But it was the grin on his face that slid a sliver of uncertainty into their minds. For one man to stand before so many and smile, he was clearly moonstruck. And a mad adversary can be the most deadly of all.

Cynan let out a roar of defiance and charged at the shieldwall. The Waelisc flinched at the sound of his bellowing cry. A heartbeat later, another sound came to them: the howling scream of anger from the fyrd-men who had watched their friends and countrymen slaughtered by the Waelisc host.

The fyrd-men, invigorated at seeing Cynan's actions – and, Cynan learnt later, rallied by rousing words from Ingwald – surged down the slope and hammered into the rear of the Waelisc line at the same moment that Cynan struck the front.

It was chaos for a time. The afternoon air was misted with blood and throbbed with the clash of weapons and the wails of the dying. Cynan fought like a warrior from a scop's tale. His blade flashed and sang, glittering in the bright sunshine as it cut through flesh and sinews. Later, Eoppa said that none of them could believe what they had witnessed. The fight was over in moments, but in that time, Cynan had taken the lives of five more men and all he had to show for it was a thin cut to his right arm and a bruise on his cheek where a shield boss had struck him.

The fyrd-men had unleashed their pent-up fury and fear and had laid about them with savage abandon. Ingwald had killed three men himself, and Cynan discovered later that the man was a veteran of Maserfelth. He was as brave as he was intelligent and strong. A natural leader of men in battle.

Within a few bloody heartbeats, over half of the Waelisc were dead or dying and the rest were fleeing. Some managed to break away from the fighting and catch hold of their mounts. They galloped away to the south. Fearing they would return with reinforcements, Cynan urged the Bernicians to grab whatever weapons they could carry and to follow him.

That night they camped in the hills north of the Wall and Ingwald told him that seven of the fyrd-men had lost their lives in the fight beneath the cross.

Cynan had sighed.

"I am sorry," he said, feeling a dreadful tiredness enveloping him like a cloak.

"Do not be sorry, lord," Ingwald said. Cynan had told him he was no lord, but the men refused to listen. "We would surely all have perished if you had not ridden to our aid."

Cynan had thought much about it as they had made their way north, past the empty shells of halls and the signs of the passing of the great Mercian host. In the end he had decided that Ingwald was right. He had saved the fyrd-men. But whenever he thought of what he had done, or when the men spoke of his battle-skill and boldness, he felt hollow and cold. He could scarcely believe his actions. Did he value his life so little? Then he thought of Beobrand; his scarred face and the ice cold eyes. The single-handed attack on the Waelisc warband was something his lord might have done, Cynan thought, and he was unsure whether to be proud or saddened.

He had led the men northward at first, thinking to put as much distance as possible between them and the Waelisc host. But after the first day it seemed they were not being pursued and he decided to head towards Bebbanburg by a roundabout route that would take them through the hills towards Ubbanford and then south-east. In this way he hoped to avoid Penda's warhost. What he would do when they reached Bebbanburg, he had not decided. He needed to see how things were when they arrived. Perhaps they might be able to slip past the Mercians and make their way into the fortress. But why sneak into a besieged citadel?

In the end, the decision was taken from him.

That morning the day had dawned clear and bright once more, but a wind had picked up from the east. They had set out at first light, but as soon as they had crested the first hill, a dark stain of smoke had risen into the sky, high from where Cynan judged Bebbanburg to be. They pressed on, still unsure what they would do when they got there, but unable now to turn away. Perhaps, thought Cynan, he should lead the men to safety. If the fortress burnt, that would mean Penda had won. Beobrand and the Black Shields would be dead.

And yet he led them towards the smoke that darkened the sky in the east. They trudged along all that morning, and Cynan longed to kick his heels into his mare's ribs and gallop towards Bebbanburg. But he knew this was foolish. Besides, the men needed him.

After midday the thrum of a large group of horsemen reached them from the west. They were coming on fast and Cynan had felt a knot of fear in his throat. Could these be the Waelisc warriors, finally tracking them down?

He ordered the men into a defensive square, such as they had formed beneath Oswald's rood.

"A strong shieldwall will turn away charging horsemen," he said.

The men obeyed without question and Ingwald prodded and goaded them into position. As the riders came into view, they were a wall of overlapping shields, bristling with spears that glinted in the sunshine. Cynan felt a strange welling of pride at the sight.

The horses came towards them at a gallop and Cynan's throat grew dry. There were at least fifty of them, spears, helms and harness gleaming. It was true that a shieldwall would turn horses away, but against so many warriors Cynan knew the fyrd-men would fall.

It was Oswiu himself who recognised the Waelisc warrior. The king raised his hand and signalled for the riders to slow their headlong charge.

Cynan let out a long ragged sigh.

As the king approached, Oswiu's standard-bearer riding before the king, holding aloft his great purple banner, Ingwald whispered to Cynan.

"Behind the king I see Alfhun. He was one of the first to flee when the Waelisc attacked."

The king reined in before them in a flurry of dust and Ingwald lowered his head and said no more.

"What news, Cynan?" Oswiu asked, his words clipped, no time for greetings.

"We come from Hefenfelth, lord king."

"The fyrd?" Oswiu asked, flicking a glance at Alfhun.

Cynan swept his arm behind him to encompass Ingwald and the small band of men who followed him.

"You are looking at them."

"By Christ's bones!" Oswiu shouted. "And the Waelisc host? Alfhun spoke of a great host from Powys and Gwynedd."

"It seemed they headed south, I know not to what purpose."

Oswiu's face was thunder.

"And what of Bebbanburg?" he asked. "Fordraed sent a messenger. The fortress is besieged. We have ridden like the wind since we saw that smoke this morning."

Cynan swallowed.

"You know as much as I, lord," he said. "We were hurrying to see if we could aid Ethelwin and Beobrand there."

"Well, follow us," said the king. "With God's grace we will be in time to send that bastard Penda back to Mercia with his tail between his legs."

Watching now, Cynan saw the king's mounted warband pass through the scattered tents and campfires, past the ruined remains of the church and the halls, houses and barns, to reach the rear of the Mercian host. He could not make out any more from this distance.

"Come on, men," he shouted and without a word, they pushed themselves onward. Their panting breaths were loud, their faces streaked with dirt and sweat. The day was hot and as they drew closer to the battle before the gates of Bebbanburg, the sounds of combat grew louder and reached them more frequently.

A ragged cheer came to them, though whether from the attackers or the defenders, Cynan could not tell.

They hurried on, and Cynan wondered whether he should not call a halt. The men were close to collapse and what good would this dishevelled band of farmers and freemen do anyway?

The writhing, shifting movement of the warriors before the walls changed somehow as he watched. Something had happened and another collective roar reached him.

Cynan raised himself up as high as he could on Mierawin's back. Yes, he was certain of it. The Mercians had been routed.

"The Mercians are fleeing, lads," he said.

He had half expected a cheer from the breathless men, instead he received a groan from Ingwald.

"By Tiw's cock," he said, "all that and now we are going to miss the fight?"

Some of the men grunted in agreement, others were too tired to speak.

Cynan smiled at them. They were good men.

"Never fear," he said. "I'm sure there will be lots of work for strong men. That fortress is not going to rebuild itself."

More groans.

"And don't rest too soon," he said, flicking his gaze back to the men scattering away from the slope before Bebbanburg. "There is nothing more dangerous than a beaten dog."

A group of a score or more horsemen was leaving the battle at a gallop. They headed towards them, riding the exact reverse of the route Oswiu and his horsemen had taken only a short time before. Then he saw the long, trailing streamer of the purple banner fluttering above the riders and realised it was Oswiu.

Why would the king ride back to them? Perhaps he came to rebuke Cynan personally for not joining the battle. The king had never liked him. Cynan thought it was because Oswiu hated Beobrand, but he could not tell if the king simply disliked him for some other reason – being Waelisc, perhaps.

Something about the approaching riders nagged him, like a word he could almost remember but that eluded him the more he strove to think of it. He peered at the oncoming horsemen for a moment longer. The sweat on his brow cooled in the wind. A flock of gulls wheeled and shrieked in the sky.

Then it hit him.

"Shieldwall!" he bellowed. "Form the square!"

To his great credit Ingwald did not ask for an explanation, he instantly turned and began to push and cajole the men into line. Cynan jumped down from his saddle, slapping Mierawin away.

He would join the shieldwall. As he'd told the men, it was the best defence against charging horsemen. He slid into the wall beside Ingwald.

"Not ours then, I take it," Ingwald said, with an enquiring look.

"No. Look there," Cynan replied. "See that big warrior with the wolf pelt around his shoulders?"

"Aye, he looks like a mean bastard."

The horsemen were close enough now that they could feel the ground beneath their feet tremble. The sound of the hooves was like the rumble of Thunor's chariot.

"He is," said Cynan. "That is Penda of Mercia. And that is his standard."

He pointed to the wolf tails flapping beneath a crossbar that a brawny warrior carried aloft behind his king. Another man held Oswiu's purple banner and it trailed over the group of riders.

"They must have snatched the banner," Cynan said.

The riders were upon them and for a terrible instant he thought they meant to drive their steeds onto the shieldwall. The horses' eyes were white-rimmed, their nostrils flared, their ears flat. The men roared with rage, their faces grim and grimy from the battle.

"Hold firm!" Cynan shouted.

"Hold firm!" echoed Ingwald.

Just before the first horse would crash into the shieldwall, the riders pulled their mounts to the side, passing within an arm's length of the Bernician spear-tips. It was a thing of folly and bravado and Cynan could not help but be impressed by the Mercian riders' audacity.

They thundered past, lifting up choking clouds of dust in their wake. Cynan turned to watch them with the rest of the fyrd-men.

Without a word, Ingwald stepped out from the mass of men. His spear was in his hand and he weighed it a moment, following the movement of the horses closely. Taking three fast paces, he let fly the spear and all of the men gazed into the sky. The spear's haft wobbled slightly as it left the man's hand and Cynan lost track of it momentarily in the bright sunshine that limned the clouds that were forming in the west. And then he saw it again, streaking down out of the sky and plummeting into the back of the rider who bore the stolen banner. He rode on a way, until his horse slowed and he left the pack of riders. Cynan saw the rearmost Mercians turn to see what had befallen their comrade, but they did not slow or return. Instead, they rode on into the west as quickly as their steeds could carry them.

The man bearing the purple banner toppled from his saddle and at last the fyrd-men let out a cheer.

"Ingwald! Ingwald! Ingwald!" they chanted.

Cynan called Mierawin and the bay mare trotted over to him. Swinging himself up onto her back, he rode to where the man had fallen. He retrieved the banner and snagged the reins of the man's horse. It was a fine-looking stallion, dark brown and sleek.

He led the beast back to the waiting men. There he handed the reins to Ingwald.

"Yours, I believe," he said.

"Lord, I could not. I am no lord to ride while others walk."

"I've told you, Ingwald, I am no lord either."

"Go on," shouted Fægir. "At least one of us will get to ride something!"

The men laughed, relief washing over them. They had survived the day, when it had looked as though it might end in battle and death.

Reluctantly, Ingwald climbed up onto the stallion's back. Cynan handed him the purple standard.

"No, lord," said Ingwald, his weathered face turning even darker. "I cannot. You must take it back to the king. It is not my place."

But Cynan would not relent. He pushed the shaft of the banner into Ingwald's hands.

"It is the place of the brave man who captured it," he said. "Oswiu is a stern man, but he is a ring-giving lord and I would have you receive the honour that is due to you."

Ingwald sighed.

"Will you ride with me then, lord?" he asked.

"I am no lord," Cynan said, shaking his head. "But yes, I will ride with you, Ingwald. And you will bring back that which the king has lost and you will take your reward."

And so they rode together through the charred gates of Bebbanburg, followed by a score of smiling but exhausted fyrd-men.

PART THREE

FOE-MAN OR FRIEND?

Chapter 30

Eanflæd sipped from her goblet of wine. It was sweet and rich. The warm liquid trickled down her throat, soothing her body and softening the thoughts and fears that had scratched at her mind all that long day. Around her the hall was a chaotic confusion of sounds and smells. Raucous laughter rang out from the younger gesithas, their spirits high from the thrill of living through the bloody battle before the gates of Bebbanburg and fuelled by copious quantities of ale and mead. Singing lilted from the far corner of the great hall, where Cædmon, a scop with a good strong voice, recounted tales of heroes of legend. Closer to where she sat, the queen could hear the quiet sobbing from a huddled group of weeping women and children whose husbands, fathers and sons had been cut down by the Mercians.

There was sorrow here, but the sounds of sadness were all but smothered by the hubbub of a great hall filled with men and women who wished to celebrate their survival and the victorious return of their king.

Oswiu's angry voice pierced the noise of the hall like a spear-point thrust into an unarmoured chest and again Eanflæd felt the confusion within her at her husband's return.

"You would seek to blame Beobrand for the destruction of the gates?" Oswiu shouted. His face was crimson. He had drunk many glasses of the ruby-coloured wine from one of the green glass beakers so beloved by his brother. Fordraed stood before the high table. Oswiu had not invited him to sit at his side, a clear insult and rebuke at the state of the fortress that the king had left in Fordraed's care. Now it seemed the fat lord sought Oswiu's forgiveness.

"You ask for me to blame another in your stead, is that it?" asked the king, leaning forward and lowering his voice to a deadly growl.

"Yes, lord," sputtered Fordraed, his face a crumpled mask of misery. "If not for Beobrand, the gates would not have been destroyed—"

"Do you think me a fool?" screamed Oswiu, spittle flying from his lips in his rage. He slammed his fist into the linen-covered board before him, making the cups, trenchers and knives jump and clatter.

"No, lord king. It is just that—"

"Was it Beobrand whom I left in command of Bebbanburg?"

"No, lord," Fordraed said, his voice catching in his throat in the face of his king's fury.

"And was it Beobrand who set the blaze at the gates?" Oswiu's voice was low and cold now. Eanflæd shivered to hear his tone, his lack of bluster now showing the true depth of his ire.

"No, lord, but—"

"And was it not Beobrand who led the charge that broke the Mercian shieldwall?"

Fordraed flicked a venomous glance at Beobrand who sat near the king at the high table, in the carved chair that should have supported his portly form. Fordraed swallowed.

"It was, lord."

Eanflæd had been purposefully avoiding looking at Beobrand as the feast progressed, but now, with the attention of all those gathered there on the lord of Ubbanford, she gazed at him. He had washed the blood, soot and dirt from his face. His left hand was bandaged and the skin beneath his eyes was dark. He looked exhausted. As his eyes met hers she felt a flutter of excitement in her belly. She looked away, angry at her own weakness. Her mind and emotions were in as much turmoil as the cacophony of the feast around her.

"And when I joined the battle," said Oswiu, his voice dripping with scorn, "and the Mercians lost heart, fleeing into the west like so many whipped dogs, I found you clean and unharmed, as if you had spent the day resting in the hall with the women and children. Are you injured, Fordraed?"

"No, lord."

"Then why were you not fighting for Bebbanburg?"

"There were too many men..." Fordraed stammered. "The press of men prevented me..."

"It did not stop Beobrand and Ethelwin from reaching the enemies of Bernicia," said Oswiu. "They were in the front, leading the brave men in the defence of the realm and the fortress. And they will bear the scars to prove it."

Eanflæd glanced back at Beobrand and found his gaze still locked on her. When she had seen him after the battle, smeared with battle-grime and gore, walking stiffly into the courtyard, her heart had soared. Moments later, Oswiu had passed between the charred remnants of the fortress gates and she had been shocked at the flood of relief that had washed through her. Her husband was returned and Bernicia had its king back where he belonged. At her side. He'd seen her and raised a hand in greeting and she had further surprised herself by going to his side and offering him a kiss of welcome.

"I am sorry, my lord," Fordraed said, his voice barely a whisper. He was clearly defeated, humiliated before Oswiu's onslaught. Despite her loathing of the man for his contemptuous attitude towards her and the violence he directed at Edlyn, she felt a stirring of sympathy for him. Oswiu had decided who was to blame for the near-destruction of Bebbanburg. And she knew it was impossible to stand against the anger of one's king.

Thinking on Oswiu's arrival that afternoon, perhaps it was not so strange that she should be pleased to have her husband come back to her and their son. She pushed aside the pang of jealousy she felt when she imagined him with his Hibernian princess. But what right did she have to anger? Had she not embraced and kissed another man? She was not innocent and could not cast stones. All that interminable day, she had prayed hard for victory, for the safe return of her husband and to be rid of the temptation of Beobrand. When the men had cried out that the Mercians were fleeing, she had rejoiced. Her prayers had been answered, but then a chill had stabbed at her, as if a dagger of ice had been plunged into her heart. Had God responded to her plea to be free of temptation by having Beobrand slain in the battle?

It was only now that she understood. In His wisdom, the Almighty had answered all of her prayers at once. With Oswiu's return from the west, Bebbanburg was saved, and her husband's presence acted as a reminder of her sacred vows before him and God. Oswiu was her son's father and her king. She would put aside her foolish attraction to Beobrand and focus her attentions on her husband. That is what her mother would have counselled her to do. The thought of Ethelburga brought the sting of tears to her eyes.

"You should be sorry, Fordraed," Oswiu said, lifting his glass goblet to his lips and drinking deeply. He seemed somewhat mollified, as if all he had wanted was an apology from the man. "Now, take some food and then get back out to the gates."

"Lord?" Fordraed seemed bewildered and confused.

"As you said, the gates are destroyed. Until they are rebuilt, they must be guarded. As you are not fatigued from the fighting, you will organise the defence of the gates. Take your men and see to it."

Fordraed looked as though he would protest, but then he seemed to sag, his shoulders slumping.

"Yes, lord king," he muttered and walked out of the hall like a man dazed after being punched.

Oswiu, clearly done with the matter of Fordraed and the gates, turned to Ethelwin. The grizzled warrior's head was wrapped in a stained strip of cloth. He looked tired, but his cheeks were flushed and his eyes bright. Where Fordraed had become the object of the king's ire, his warmaster had become a hero, praised by Oswiu for his stalwart defence of the fortress.

"How's the head?" asked Oswiu.

"It is but a scratch," replied Ethelwin.

"A scratch indeed," said Oswiu, laughing. "When I met you before the gate you were awash with blood."

"Head wounds are always the worst," said Ethelwin with a lopsided smile. "The smallest cut will gush like a waterfall in spring."

Oswiu slapped him on the shoulder. Draining his goblet, he held it out absently for more wine. Eanflæd signalled to the waiting thrall, a plain-faced slip of a Waelisc girl. Rising, the queen took the silver jug from the slave and then poured the wine into her husband's empty glass beaker.

His gaze flickered over her breasts and down to her slender hips as she leant over him. When she finished pouring the wine, she found Oswiu's dark eyes staring at her face. He smiled and stroked his rough fingers over the back of her hand.

"Thank you, my queen," he said, his voice thick with some secret emotion.

She dipped her head.

"My king."

Returning to her seat, she could feel Beobrand's eyes on her, but she refused to look in his direction. She would obey her husband and God's will. Ecgfrith was now well and the fortress was safe. God was good and she would do her duty. She thought of the last time Oswiu had come to her bed. It had not been so bad. He was not rough as she had heard some men were. He openly admired her beauty and spoke sweet words to her. Perhaps he would give her another child.

"Any news from the riders?" Oswiu asked Ethelwin.

"Not yet, lord. I do not expect tidings so soon."

Oswiu nodded.

"Yes, of course. But I cannot help but worry."

Immediately after the battle at the gate, Oswiu and Ethelwin had sent off mounted men to follow the scattered Mercians and to see that they left Bernicia. Most of the riders who had come with the king to Bebbanburg he sent into the west to protect the waggons and carts they had left behind.

One of the reasons for his ill-temper, Eanflæd knew, was that he was fretting about whether he had done the right thing. Had he sent enough men to harry the retreating Mercian host? Were the riches he had brought back from Caer Luel and the surrounding vills to the west even now in the hands of his enemies?

"Tell me again," he said, suddenly turning back to Eanflæd, "what did your cousin say?"

At the other end of the hall, Cædmon finished one of his tales and the men around him cheered and hammered their cups and knives into the board in a thunder of appreciation. Oswiu frowned. Oswine was another matter of concern to him and another person to blame for what had happened in his absence. It was not Oswine's fault that Penda had attacked Bebbanburg, nor that Bernicia's king was far away at the time. But she swallowed down her harsh words of reprobation. They would do no good, only harm. Oswiu had long disliked Oswine and she did not wish to throw fat onto the flames of her husband's anger.

His antipathy could all too easily turn into hatred. She waited for the cheering to subside before replying.

"As soon as he heard of the approach of Penda's host, Oswine rode south, my lord. He said he would summon Deira's fyrd and march to our aid."

Oswiu brooded, his brow furrowed and his eyes scowling. He took a deep draught of wine.

"Well, I do not see your cousin here," he said. "If not for my return, Bebbanburg might well have fallen." He reached for a piece of salted beef. There was so much salt meat now, they would be eating it for weeks. He chewed for a while, then spat a gobbet of gristle onto the reeds. Two hounds scrabbled for the morsel, snapping and snarling. "Penda is a wolf," Oswiu continued. "He would have ravaged the place. And what would have befallen you, my queen? Penda would have taken all that is mine."

"If the flock is prey to wolves, perhaps the shepherd should not stray so far from his sheep," she snapped, suddenly angry. As soon as she had uttered the words, she regretted them.

For a moment, Oswiu's face clouded and she feared he would erupt in a blaze of anger. Instead he smiled and reached for her hand.

"You speak the truth, Eanflæd," he said, caressing the soft skin of her palm with his fingers. "I should not have travelled so far from you, my lamb. Leaving you and Ecgfrith here was a mistake. I accept your rebuke. It is a husband's duty to be at his wife's side. And a king's to protect his folk."

She could feel the warmth of his touch, see the desire in his eyes. She did not know how to respond to his words without causing him offence, so she lowered her gaze.

To her surprise, Oswiu stood suddenly and raised his hands. Murmurs and whispers rippled across the men and women gathered in the great hall as they turned to look towards their king. From outside, through the open doors, came the sounds of merriment from the ceorls and their families who had sought shelter behind Bebbanburg's walls. Eanflæd thought of the women and children whom she had come to know these last days. Good people, strong of character and quick to help others. For much of that long terrifying day, with the sounds of battle wafting to them on the hot breeze and the smell of smoke from the great blaze at the gates seeping into the hall, she had huddled at one end of the building with Edlyn and a handful of those God-fearing women and prayed with Coenred and Utta. A titter of feminine laughter drifted in from the courtyard and Eanflæd wished she could be out there, with those women who were simply pleased their men had returned to them. They did not have to be concerned with the anger and jealousy of kings. But, she thought, as the hall grew silent to listen to Oswiu speak, were not all men kings in their own homes?

"Men and women of Bernicia," Oswiu said, his voice clear and carrying throughout the hall. "My brave people. I am sorry for the pain and fear that befell you in my absence. A king's place is with his people, and I thank God that he brought me back to Bebbanburg in time to see off Penda and his pack of dogs."

Some of the men jeered, loudly and drunkenly insulting the Mercians. Oswiu waited for them to quieten.

"It is not an easy thing to be gōd cyning. My brother Oswald, may the Lord watch over his immortal soul, was the man I long to be. Holy and just, but swift to take vengeance when crossed." He paused, perhaps allowing them time to think of the king Oswald had been. "To be a king demands difficult decisions," he went on. "I must visit all the folk of this great kingdom of Bernicia and pray to God that the men I leave behind will prove brave and strong enough to defend what is ours." Again he paused, sweeping his dark gaze over all those gathered before him on the mead benches. "And so it was here!"

He shouted these last words and then the hall echoed with the men's cheers. The sound rose and washed over Eanflæd like a wave. When it had died down, the king continued.

"The stout hearts of you men, led by lords Ethelwin and Beobrand, and with the foresight and planning of Brytnere and my beautiful queen, has shown me Bernicians are the best folk in the whole of Albion. By God, in all of middle earth."

Again they cheered.

"Thanks to all of you, and the prayers of the brethren of Lindisfarena and the most holy Bishop Aidan, and of course the power and grace of God, Bebbanburg still stands." Oswiu nodded in appreciation at Coenred and Utta and the two men who sat with them: a sombre-faced young monk named Wilfrid and his teacher, the grey-haired and dour Cudda. The two of them had trudged across the wet sands from the isle monastery at the first low tide after the battle. They bore tidings of how Aidan had seen the smoke from where he was praying in solitude on one of the lonely Farena islands. The bishop had exhorted the Almighty to send a sacred wind to blow the flames back onto the enemies of the Christ-loving Bernicians. The warriors who had been at the gates spoke of the sudden change in the direction of the wind and already people were whispering that it had been a miracle.

Eanflæd noticed that the novice monk, Wilfrid, was gazing at her and she offered him a small smile. He had come to Bebbanburg earlier in the year and she had seen the potential in him. He was young and possessed a fiery temper, but there was something about him, an intensity that almost reminded her of Beobrand. It had been her idea to send him to Lindisfarena, where he would be taught by old Cudda. In the way of the monks, Wilfrid's hair had now been shaved to the crown of his head, altering his handsome features, but doing nothing to diminish the blazing intelligence in those pale eyes.

"But I will say," Oswiu continued with a grimace and a wink, snapping Eanflæd's attention back to the king, "I do wish my queen had not been so thorough. She could have saved some of the meat from salting." The men laughed and Eanflæd blushed.

"We have won a great victory today and you must not think

I am a mean lord, for there will be a time for the giving of gifts. I will reward every man who fought today, and to every widow, I will likewise give treasure, for their men have given the greatest gift to their lord and king and it shall not be forgotten. And I do not forget those who have done me service. Like you there, Ingwald." Oswiu pointed to a thin, bald man sitting at the lower tables next to Beobrand's man, Cynan, the Waelisc. "I will not forget that you brought me back my banner or that you saved many men from destruction at Hefenfelth with your courage and quick thinking."

The men around Ingwald cheered and clapped. The man himself looked abashed to be mentioned by the king. Cynan reached over and gripped Ingwald's shoulder, grinning with pride, as if the man were his kin.

"But all of this will be for another day when we have all rested. I have been away a long time and I have missed my lady wife. While I am lord and king to you all, I am husband to her, and I must not neglect her further."

The gathered warriors whooped and hollered at their king's suggestive words. Eanflæd's face grew hot. Oswiu held out his hand to her and said in a quiet voice, "Well, my lamb. I think it is time you gave the shepherd a proper welcome home."

His eyes glinted with lust and Eanflæd's mouth was suddenly dry. She could sense all the people of the hall staring at her, waiting for her response. For a moment she was unable to breathe. She did not take her eyes from Oswiu's, but she knew beyond all doubt that Beobrand's gaze was fixed on her, ready to gauge her reaction.

She took a deep breath. She was a wife and a queen. Her life was not her own. She knew her duty.

Reaching out, she grasped Oswiu's hand and allowed him to pull her to her feet. Leaning in close to him, she could smell his sweat and the lingering scent of dust, smoke and blood.

"I will have water brought to our chambers. Let me bathe you, my lord," she whispered, "and then we shall see if you are strong enough for the welcome you wish for."

His eyes widened and he licked his lips.

She led him from the hall to the sounds of whistles and lascivious shouts from the warriors. Edlyn nodded at her, offering a faint smile as they passed. Eanflæd straightened her back as she walked past Beobrand, not looking at him but feeling his gaze on her like heat from a flame.

Chapter 31

Beobrand stared out over the roiling darkness of the North Sea. Below him, the waves growled and hissed as they hit the rocks. Far off, a flicker of lightning lit the world for an instant before the night slammed back, darker than ever. He waited for the sound of thunder, but the distant rumble was lost in the crash of the waves. He took a deep breath of the cool, fresh air. That evening, clouds had rolled in on the strong wind and a storm had raged above Bebbanburg. The downpour had put out the final remnants of the fire, leaving behind steaming, blackened timbers and corpses draped in sodden clothes, eyes staring into the night sky, awaiting the arrival of foxes and wolves.

The stench of fire and death was strong near the gates and Beobrand was glad that the wind had continued to blow in from the sea, bringing with it nothing more than the tang of salt and the memory of endless horizons.

Another flash of Thunor's fire came and went in an eye-blink, leaving a ghost image glowing in his vision. He rubbed at his eyes. He was weary. His hand throbbed where it had been burnt and his arms and shoulders ached. Reaching his hands behind his head, he interlaced his fingers and pulled his head forward. His neck gave a satisfying crack and he grunted. Gods, he needed to sleep. But he knew sleep would not come easily. The faces of the men he had killed that day flickered in his mind's eye, as if his thought-cage was lit by its own lightning and with each flash a new face was revealed, black with blood, eyes staring, mouths screaming. No, sleep would be slow to arrive and when he was finally too tired to remain awake, he was fearful of the dreams that would come with slumber.

Would Eanflæd be in his dreams?

Thinking of her brought back the tumult of battle as his emotions fought one another for supremacy. He desired her, he could not deny that, but to see her beside her husband, serving him wine as a good wife should, had filled Beobrand with conflicting feelings of sadness, envy and – strangely, he thought – even a tinge of pride. Surely she did what was right for herself, her son and her people. Begrudgingly, he realised she was also doing what was best for him. If they had continued with the madness they had courted so recklessly, Oswiu would have had him killed, of that he was in no doubt.

And yet, as they had stared into each other's eyes briefly at the feast, and when she had passed so close to where he sat that he could make out her scent, he had been almost overwhelmed by his lust.

He cursed and spat over the palisade into the night.

Watching her leave the hall with Oswiu had been nearly unbearable. But bear it, he must. Oswiu was his king, his oath-sworn lord, and Eanflæd his queen. There was nothing else to be said or done.

Gods, how he wished he had brought some mead or wine up onto the ramparts. Perhaps the drink would help to ease the troubles that tumbled in his mind. If he drank enough, sleep would finally find him.

To the east, lightning lit the clouds and sea again.

Up here, above the noise of the men who still revelled in the hall, and far from the stench of fire and battle at the gates, he could imagine he would be able to drink and forget for a time. But he knew that no matter how much he drank, how befuddled his mind became with mead, his problems would still be there in the stark light of morning. And the faces of the men he had killed would still haunt his nightmares.

He thought of the night he had found Heremod up here, breath foul with the sour stink of drink. Did Fordraed's man drink to forget? Even if he did, Heremod would not forget what he had seen one night in the darkness between Bebbanburg's buildings, of that Beobrand was sure. A quiet, dark part of him had hoped that the accursed man might be slain in the battle, taking their secret to the afterlife with him. But Beobrand had seen the warrior in the courtyard as the sun dipped into the west. The man had been swigging from a flask of ale. When he saw Beobrand he'd grinned, his teeth white against the face and beard that were slicked with blood. Unlike Fordraed, Heremod seemed to have managed to find his way into the thick of the fighting and Beobrand felt a grudging respect for that.

Of course, Heremod had survived. The gods would not allow him to die without wreaking mischief by revealing his secret. And was it truly a secret? Was it possible he had not spoken to Fordraed or anyone else of the tryst he had observed?

The sound of a woman's moaning drifted up from below. Beobrand glanced down into the courtyard. In the shadows beneath the wall, he could just make out the figures of a man and a woman. She was leaning against the timbers of the palisade, her dress hitched up around her waist. The indistinct form of a man writhed and grunted behind her. Beobrand's face grew hot and he looked away, over the courtyard. Men and women still laughed and talked down there. And no doubt others coupled in darkened corners. It was a strange night of celebration and mourning. But Beobrand had seen it before, after a battle. After so much death and horror, people wished to wallow in the things that brought them pleasure. Many a woman would be with child come morning. With a pang of jealousy, he wondered whether Eanflæd would give Oswiu another heir. Was she even now lying with the king, taking him into her? Crying out with pleasure as he thrust inside her?

With difficulty, Beobrand pushed the thoughts away. Again he wished he had brought some drink up here to dull his senses and his thoughts.

In the courtyard, children shrieked and ran about in the darkness. A mother shouted at them that it was time to sleep. They laughed and disappeared into the shadows. The children had picked up on the feeling of festivity and were enjoying the night of freedom after so many days of gloom and impending doom where all of the adult folk had walked about with frowns and scowls upon their faces.

He recalled his own sudden surge of joy that afternoon when he had seen Octa. At first he had not recognised his son. The boy had grown tall, though he still looked slender beside the burly thegns and gesithas who sat at the boards alongside him. As Beobrand had walked the length of the hall towards the high table, Octa had turned to speak to the young man beside him. It was Alhfrith, Oswiu's son. They laughed and Beobrand saw who it was talking to the atheling. He was shocked that he had almost walked right past his own son. Still, it had been months since he had last seen the boy.

"Octa," he said, beckoning his son over to speak with him.

Reluctantly, Octa rose and joined his father, but when Beobrand asked how he fared, the boy did little more than shrug and say he was well enough.

Beobrand had pressed for more information. Where had they ridden? Had he been in the fighting before the fortress?

Octa spoke in terse phrases and Beobrand found out little apart from learning that the king had led them as far west as Caer Luel and that he had ordered the atheling and some of the other warriors to hang back from the fighting. Beobrand had been thankful to his king for that, but the encounter had done little more than sadden him. His son was as a stranger to him and soon he had let Octa return to Alhfrith and the other warriors of Oswiu's retinue.

As he'd stood there, contemplating whether it was every man's wyrd to see his sons grow to despise him, a hand had clapped him on the shoulder. It was Cynan and that meeting was happier by far. The Waelisc man was headstrong and oftentimes angered Beobrand, but he was steadfast and loyal and Beobrand had been overjoyed to see him return safely to Bebbanburg.

"They grow up quickly, lord," Cynan said.

Beobrand nodded and sighed.

"They do that."

"He is not much younger than I was when you and Acennan brought me out of Mercia," Cynan said.

"Truly? Gods, it seems like yesterday." Beobrand thought of all that had happened in the years since then. The time had passed more quickly than he could believe. So much pain and suffering. So much loss. He tried to picture Cynan as he had first seen him, a scrawny thrall, beaten almost to death by Wybert and his friends. The man who stood before him in the great hall of Bebbanburg was hard to recognise as that weakling youth who could barely stay seated on a donkey's back. Cynan was now a warrior of renown, tall and strong, skilled with blade and the best horseman in Bernicia.

"And look at you now," said Beobrand, smiling broadly. "You are not only a formidable man in a shieldwall, but a leader of men, it seems." He arched an eyebrow and Cynan laughed.

Beobrand had seen when Cynan had ridden into Bebbanburg with the man called Ingwald beside him. Ingwald had carried Oswiu's silken purple banner. He had timidly presented the cloth wrapped loosely about its wooden shaft to Oswiu and the king had been jubilant at its retrieval. Shortly after, several weary warriors in the drab clothing of farmhands had marched into the courtyard. Cynan had greeted them with smiles and words of praise and the men had beamed at the reception.

"They are fyrd-men, lord," said Cynan. "I rode to their aid at Hefenfelth and they have followed me ever since. I daresay they will return to their own homes now that Penda has fled." He laughed suddenly, seemingly embarrassed. "They call me 'lord', though I have told them I am no such thing."

Beobrand slapped him on the back and laughed with him.

"It is no easy thing to lead men," he said. "If these fyrd-men follow you and call you their lord, you have done something few men can do – gain their trust with your actions."

Standing now on the palisade, he thought he should have said more to Cynan. Perhaps he should have told him he was proud of him; that Acennan would have been proud too. Seeing the way the men looked at the young Waelisc warrior, Beobrand was not so sure they would all disappear back to their farms and steadings. When they returned to Ubbanford, he would have to decide what to do with Cynan. He would speak to Bassus about it. If men followed the young gesith, perhaps he should give Cynan some land. He could build a hall of his own. Mayhap the time had come for him to find a wife. Beobrand knew he yet pined for the madwoman, Sulis. The mere thought of her angered Beobrand, and he would never understand how Cynan could have become so enthralled with the thrall.

He looked down into the darkened courtyard. Lightning lit the sky, giving a brief glimpse of the men at the far side of the fortress. Fordraed, Heremod and the rest of the fat thegn's comitatus were guarding the gates.

Beobrand smiled without humour. Who was he to judge a man for the woman he desired? Again he thought of Heremod and what he knew. Gods, what a fool he had been. The man was certain to take what he knew to Fordraed, or even to the king himself. Beobrand shivered. The wind was cold off the sea and he had not found his cloak after the clash of shieldwalls, but it was not the chill air that caused him to tremble. If the king learnt of Eanflæd's indiscretion, Beobrand could imagine all too well the fury that would grip him and what such a rage could lead a man to do.

If only Heremod had taken a spear or sword thrust in the heat of the day's fighting. Beobrand shook his head, ashamed of his own thoughts. The man was a brave warrior and had stood against the enemies of Bernicia. He did not deserve death. But no matter how he picked at the tangle of worries about the queen and what Heremod had witnessed, Beobrand could not unravel the knot of them.

He turned back to look to the dark sea once more. Out there the world was a simpler place of rolling waves and blustering winds. He wondered if Ferenbald was out on *Saeslaga* on such a night. He hoped the skipper was safely moored on some friendly beach, where a local lord would offer him and his crew hospitality and shelter. A few drops of rain splattered the palisade timbers. He would need to seek shelter too when the rains returned in earnest. He wished for fresh air, not to stand out in the howl of a thunderstorm. He recalled the storms they had endured on the voyage that had led them to Frankia and almost to a watery death off the southern coast of Albion.

A sudden brilliant streak of lightning sliced the night's blackness. By its light, Beobrand saw a movement to his left. Someone was climbing the ladder to the palisade walkway. For a moment he could not make out who it was, for the flash of the lightning had burnt into his vision. He blinked. The grumble of thunder reached him, loud and deep like boulders falling down a mountain in the distance.

"Lord," came a voice he knew. More raindrops fell, slapping the planks of the battlement.

"Beircheart," said Beobrand. "I thought you would be enjoying the ale and, by now, perhaps the warmth of one of Oswiu's thralls."

He expected the dark-bearded warrior to laugh, or to respond with a bawdy comment. Instead, he frowned.

"What is wrong?" asked Beobrand. "It is unlike you to leave a feast early. You fought well today, you deserve to enjoy the king's table and mead."

"I can enjoy nothing, lord," Beircheart said, gazing out into the darkness. His shoulders were rigid, his fists clenched on the wet timbers of the ramparts.

Unease scratched along Beobrand's back.

"What ails you?"

"Nothing, lord. I am well." He stared out into the dark distance for a moment. "But I fear I am about to do something that may lead to my death. And I do not wish to bring dishonour to you." His voice had grown quiet now and the wind whipped the words away as Beircheart spoke, but the quivering rage within him was evident.

"What is it that you plan to do, Beircheart?" asked Beobrand. He was unsure he wanted to hear the man's answer. But he was Beircheart's hlaford and the gesith had come to him for a reason. Beobrand thought of what he had said to Cynan. It was no easy task to lead men.

Beircheart did not answer.

Lightning cracked into the sea from the angry clouds, illuminating everything with an icy white light. A heartbeat later, the crash of thunder rumbled around them. Beobrand looked at the man. Beircheart's face was tight, his jaw muscles bunched. Without warning, he cursed and punched the rough wood of the rampart, but still he did not offer a response. Beobrand's unease grew. The wind gusted and a fresh squall of rain fell. He stared at Beircheart's forlorn features. Another storm was coming, of that there could be no doubt.

"Well, Beircheart?" Beobrand asked.

At last, the gesith turned to face him. He was sombre, his eyes dark shadows.

"I am going to kill that bastard Fordraed," he said.

Chapter 32

Wind and rain lashed Bebbanburg for most of the night. The sky was stabbed with lightning and the crash of thunder overhead awoke Eanflæd.

She lay in the warm safety of her chamber and listened to the roar of the storm. Beside her, Oswiu snored. He lay on his back and his mouth was open. She could barely make out his form in the gloom. The only light came from beneath the door. A lamp burnt outside where Godgyth slept with Ecgfrith.

Eanflæd sighed as she gazed at the straight line of his nose and the shape of his strong jaw. Oswiu's arms and torso were heavily muscled and she knew he was a handsome man. He was also the king and her husband and she had made the decision that she must be true to her vows.

When they had come from the hall, she had told Godgyth to fetch some warm water and a clean cloth with which she had planned to wipe Oswiu's body clean of the grime of travel and battle. She had also thought that such an action might bring them closer in some way, stir something within her.

But when Godgyth returned with the water, Oswiu was already sleeping. As soon as they were alone, his desire had grown quickly and he had kissed her, pushing her down onto the bed with his bulk. She had felt nothing. Even as he entered her it was as if this act was being performed by another woman. It had been over quickly. He had rolled over and was soon asleep, exhausted after the travails of the day.

Eanflæd had opened the door quietly, taking the pot of warm water from Godgyth with a whisper of thanks. Closing the door behind her, she had used the water and the cloth to clean herself. She had wiped his smell from her skin and wondered whether his seed would find fertile ground in her womb. If she were with child again, perhaps the feelings she had for Beobrand would finally vanish. At the very least neither her husband nor Beobrand would desire her when her belly was bloated.

She lay in silence beside her sleeping husband and listened to the storm. It took a long time for sleep to come to her again. When it did, her dreams were filled with the taste of the wine on Oswiu's tongue. She dreamed of his weight on her, the feel of him pushing inside of her, the heat of his seed spurting into her. But in her dream, when he rolled away from her, panting from the exertion, the dim light from the burning rush wick had illuminated his hair. As he turned to her, smiling, his hair glowed a golden lustre in the darkened room.

This was not Oswiu. It was Beobrand who lay beside her.

She awoke at dawn, breathless and ashamed.

Oswiu still slept, oblivious to the storm blustering outside and the thoughts that buffeted her mind. She quietly left the chamber. Godgyth was asleep in her pallet and Ecgfrith lay still, his round face calm and undisturbed by the sounds of the wind and rain that rocked the hall. For a moment she gazed down at him, a surge of happiness flooding through her. He had not coughed in days and he was sleeping better than ever. He was gaining weight quickly and his cheeks were pink and healthy. Here was the reason she must push aside her weakness. Ecgfrith was all-important. She watched his chest rise and fall in the gloom and offered up a prayer of thanks to God, the Blessed Virgin and even to Oswald, whose head mouldered in the casket in the quiet of the stone church.

She did not wish to awaken either of them, but her stumbling about in the darkness searching for her clothes roused Godgyth, who sat up, rubbing at her eyes blearily.

"My lady?" she whispered. "Is everything well?"

Eanflæd looked again down at the sleeping face of her son. Nothing else was of importance.

"Yes," she said. "All is well. Help me dress and let us try not to wake Ecgfrith. He is so peaceful."

Godgyth found her plain green gown and helped her attach the brooches and wrist clasps. Ethelburga had given it to her when she had left for Bernicia and the touch of its fine linen brought to her the memory of her mother's serious, lined face as she had said farewell. Neither she nor Godgyth spoke and when she was dressed, Eanflæd whispered her thanks and went out to the hall.

There was already movement there. Thralls and servants, a constant of life in the fortress, bustled about, readying the room for people to break their fast. Someone had thrown open the doors and Eanflæd could see great sheets of rain falling from the leaden sky. Grey light filtered into the hall, mingling with the smoke of the newly kindled fire on the hearthstone. Soon the benches and boards would be brought out, but for the time being many of the revellers from last night's feast yet lay in cloak-wrapped mounds around the floor. Someone coughed, a hacking phlegmy rasp, and Eanflæd started. Would she ever hear such a sound and not think of Ecgfrith? She reached up and touched the crucifix that hung between her breasts. God was good. She had prayed and turned away from the Devil's temptations of the flesh. Her son was well again and he would not succumb once more to illness, she was certain of it. She just needed to remain resolute.

Looking about the hall she regretted her decision to leave her quarters. She could not venture out into the seething rain, but it would be quite some time before the hall was prepared. She sighed. She had not wished to remain in her chamber for Oswiu to awaken. She had no wish to speak with him or to suffer his advances this morning, if he woke aroused. Perhaps she should go back to Godgyth. She could help her gemæcce to prepare Ecgfrith and by the time he was dressed, the hall would be cleaned and the drunken warriors would be up. Maybe the rain would ease and she could take some air, but judging from the waterfall streaming from the porch and the gloomy wet light, the weather did not look like changing anytime soon.

"Lady Eanflæd," said a voice behind her, and her heart clenched. It was a deep voice and it carried a hint of the south lands of Cantware in its tones. She took a deep breath.

"Lord Beobrand," she said, turning to face him. She kept her face expressionless, but the sight of him made her stomach flutter. She felt suddenly too warm in her green dress and mantle.

Beobrand looked as though he had not slept. His long fair hair, just as she had seen it in her dream, was tousled and unruly, softening his harsh features and partly concealing the scar beneath his left eye. The skin under his eyes was bruised and dark and he seemed somehow thinner than he had appeared not two days before.

It had been a trying time for everyone, but she knew that, true to the tales that were told of him, it was Beobrand who had led the charge through the flames. It was he who had smashed into the Mercian ranks. She had heard others at the feast speaking of his prowess in the shieldwall. Hardened warriors spoke of the lord of Ubbanford in tones of awe, with something like fear in their voices. Seeing him now, his eyes glinting cold in the gloom of the hall and no smile of greeting on his lips, she sensed a ghost of what those men had witnessed. A sliver of ice traced her spine and she fought not to shiver.

A silence grew between them as they stared at each other. Beobrand's scowling face was unreadable.

"I rejoice that you are well, Beobrand," she said at last, wishing to break the awkward stillness.

"The king is also returned hale to your side, my queen," he said. His tone was clipped, sharp.

She blushed.

"And for that I also give thanks to God," she replied.

Beobrand looked beyond her, peering into the depths of the hall. She felt a scratch of annoyance.

"Have you seen the lady Edlyn?" he asked, still absently scanning the inhabitants of the hall.

"No," she replied, a touch of frost entering her voice. "I have not seen Edlyn since yestereve."

"And Fordraed? Do you know where her husband is?"

"I do not." She had dreaded having to speak to Beobrand, fearing that he would question her in some way about her actions. She had felt the fire in his glare the night before, but now he seemed almost uninterested. Good. Once again she offered up silent thanks to God for His deliverance from the madness of temptation that had consumed her. "Perhaps Lord Fordraed is at the gates, where my husband sent him."

Beobrand nodded.

"I will look for him there."

And with that he spun away and strode out of the hall and into the rain. As if drawn after him in his wake, she made her way across the hall and out under the cool of the porch. The door wards nodded at her and pulled themselves up straight. She watched as Beobrand crossed the courtyard towards the gates. He would be drenched by the time he reached them and while part of her wished to follow him, to find out what was so urgent that he would walk away from her without a backward glance, the ferocity of the rain pulled her up short.

Despite the rain, several men were moving about by the gates.

The makeshift barricade had been partially dismantled the previous day and now, as she watched, two men led a waggon pulled by a pair of bedraggled oxen through the gap where the gates had stood. She supposed they were heading out to continue the ghastly task of collecting the corpses of the fallen. The previous afternoon, men had been sent to cut down the poor victims of Penda's pagan sacrifice. And most of the Bernician dead had been collected before dark. But the dozens of Mercians who had perished before the gates of Bebbanburg yet lay in the rocks and bushes, faces contorted, tongues black and protruding from between fish-pale lips. They needed to be taken away and disposed of before the warm weather returned. As soon as the rain stopped, they would become alive with swarms of flies and the stench would be terrible.

In some ways, the rain was a blessing. It would keep the air clean and soften the earth, which would make the job of burying them easier, though no less gruesome. They might have burnt the dead, but for the fact that the Mercians had already destroyed all the timber they could find to set fire to the gates. Besides, Beobrand had said in the hall the night before, most of them would be pagans. They would wish to be consumed by flames so that their spirits could float to the gods and the afterlife. And so it was that Oswiu had given the order for all of the Mercian dead to be buried without any of their belongings. They believed that the goods they took with them in death could be used in the life beyond middle earth and Oswiu would give them no such help.

Beobrand had almost reached the gates and the men surrounding the shattered timbers and the remains of the barricade.

"Where is Fordraed?" she heard him yell, his voice carrying over the tumult of the rain.

But before anyone could answer, a horseman clattered past the gates, the hooves of the beast throwing up showers of muddy water. He paused briefly, speaking to the men at the gate before spurring his horse on towards the hall.

The door wards stiffened and held their spears before them. The horse's hooves thudded wetly across the yard. Behind the rider came Beobrand at a jog.

"Where is the king?" the rider called out, his voice thinned by the hiss and thrum of the rain. The man was young and slender, with a stubble of beard on his thin cheeks.

Eanflæd stepped out into the rain and looked up at the rider. The two door wards came with her, flanking her protectively.

Beobrand reached them. He was soaked, his clothes and hair plastered to his form. In his hand he held an unsheathed sword by the blade. Rain ran down his face like tears, dripping from his eyebrows and nose.

"My lord king yet sleeps," she said.

Beobrand fixed her with a look she could not fathom. Was it sadness? Disappointment? Something else? Ignoring him, she fixed the rider with a stern glare.

"Who are you and what do you want?" she asked, speaking in the imperious tone she had heard her mother employ when addressing men at court.

The rider stared down at her. His cloak clung to him and was draped, sodden and heavy, over his mount's back. She noted the empty scabbard at his side. She assumed the men at the gate had disarmed him and given Beobrand the man's sword.

"I am Wigelm and I bring tidings from the south, lady," he said. He slid down from the saddle and offered a small bow. "I am sent by King Oswine of Deira and I bring tidings for Oswiu King."

Chapter 33

"Enough!" shouted Oswiu. The simmering anger he had been holding back as the messenger spoke finally burst forth. The king slammed his hand flat onto the board before him. Cups and platters jumped and rattled. A pitcher teetered for a moment before settling upright once more. Beobrand was surprised that nothing had fallen from the table.

Wigelm stuttered into silence.

Nobody else spoke and the silence in the hall stretched out. Outside, the rain, less ferocious than before, fell in a constant droning downpour.

Oswiu had made Oswine's messenger wait while the hall was cleaned and arranged for the king to break his fast. Then Oswiu had eaten slowly, forcing the clearly exhausted and soaked Deiran to wait at the far end of the hall before eventually beckoning him forward to deliver his missive. Beobrand found the king's actions petty and without honour. He sighed as the hush dragged on. Oswiu allowed the awkwardness to continue, probably imagining that it somehow gave him more power to have Wigelm uncomfortable. But Oswiu was the king and this man a lowly messenger. These antics did nothing but make Oswiu appear vindictive and weak in Beobrand's eyes.

When Wigelm could bear the silence no longer, he pulled himself up straight.

"My lord king Oswiu—"

"Silence," snapped Oswiu. Reaching for his cup, he drank slowly from it.

Beobrand snorted, stifling a chuckle. Gods, why did he not just let the man finish giving his tidings? Surely they all needed to hear what he had to say.

Fordraed glowered at Beobrand in disapproval. Beobrand ignored him. Fordraed had no comprehension of how close he was to death. If not for Beobrand's intervention, the fat bastard would even now be stuffing his belly with the scraps from Woden's table, if the All-father deigned to offer him a place in his hall, something Beobrand doubted. Wherever the man's spirit would go, without Beobrand's calming words to Beircheart, Fordraed's flesh would now be meat for the ravens.

Beobrand thought back to the night before on the palisade. He wondered for how long Beircheart would hold back and stay his hand. He was a proud man, but Beobrand had his oath and that had saved Fordraed for the time being. But Beobrand recognised the fury in the gesith. He knew not how much longer his words to Beircheart as his hlaford would prevent him from throwing reason and sense away and taking that which he craved: vengeance for one too weak to seek it herself.

Beobrand understood the man's anger well. And yet he had been shocked to hear the words that Beircheart had spoken as the rain had begun to pelt Bebbanburg in the darkness. Beobrand had not known Beircheart still held any feelings for Edlyn. He knew they had cosseted each other once, years before when she was not much more than a girl. Since then, she had been married to Fordraed and she seldom visited her mother, Rowena, at Ubbanford. A few times over the years, Beobrand had seen her at Morðpæð or Bebbanburg, but he paid her little attention.

But it seemed Beircheart paid her closer notice, though quite how much Beobrand was not sure and did not wish to ask.

"She is a married woman, Beircheart," he'd said, the cold wind from the North Sea tugging at his hair and cutting through his wet kirtle. He thought of Eanflæd and shivered at his own words.

Beircheart punched the timber of the rampart again.

"I know this, lord," he said. "But by Woden, she is married to a brute."

"Many women are."

"He beats her," Beircheart said and his voice was so quiet that Beobrand could barely make out his words as the rain splattered loudly against the timbers of the wall. Droplets hissed in the nearest brazier and the flame flapped and danced in the wind.

"Fordraed is her husband," Beobrand said. "It is his right to beat her." His words tasted bitter; weak.

"I know this." Beircheart's voice cracked as he gulped back a sob. "Gods, I know this. He has struck her before and I have done nothing. But I saw her face tonight and…" He looked at Beobrand and there were tears in his eyes. "Her face…" He swiped at his eyes. "Gods, the man is a nithing. He cannot fight men and so he takes out his failures on her."

It was true that a man could beat his wife, but would Beobrand stand by and do nothing if he saw bruises on Eanflæd's face? For a moment he thought of Udela and Ardith. The wind gusted and the rain fell more heavily. It was on such a night as this that Scrydan had met his end. Beobrand could almost hear his erstwhile friend's wailing howls of agony in the wind-rent night.

"I loathe the man too," Beobrand said. "But we are at war. Now is not the time."

This was true, but Beobrand could hear the falsehood in his words even if Beircheart could not. The truth was that he did not know what Heremod would say if his lord were killed in a duel with one of Beobrand's gesithas. Surely, the warrior would tell the king then of what he had seen and Beobrand and Eanflæd would be lost.

"Bide your time, Beircheart," he said, gripping his shoulder. "You must swallow your anger until we are certain of peace. Then I will stand by your side as you challenge the fat bag of turds."

Beircheart sighed and lowered his gaze. Beobrand said no more, allowing him to wrestle with his emotions. Eventually, Beircheart gave a terse nod of agreement.

Looking at Fordraed's pink-cheeked face now, Beobrand felt ashamed. Who was he to prevent Beircheart seeking retribution for Fordraed's brutality towards a woman he evidently harboured feelings for? He did this for Eanflæd, Beobrand told himself, but he could not shake the feeling of guilt that clung to him the way his wet kirtle had the night before.

"So, Wigelm," Oswiu said at last, glowering at the messenger, "you say that Oswine met the Waelisc in battle."

"Yes, lord king." Wigelm had already told them how Oswine of Deira had gathered the fyrd of his kingdom and was bringing them north to Bernicia's aid when they had met the great host of men from Powys and Gwynedd near the River Sualuae. However, he seemed content to repeat himself and was clearly relieved that Oswiu had chosen to break the uncomfortable silence. "Our fyrd met the great host of Waelisc at Catrice and there was great slaughter. May God be praised for our victory."

Utta and Coenred, who were standing at the edge of the gathered throng of thegns and ealdorman around the king, both made the sign of the Christ cross. Oswiu did not move.

"And now you say they are marching north." His tone was cold and flat. "Into Bernicia."

"Yes, lord king," said Wigelm. "They march with all haste to offer their aid in the defence of Bebbanburg from the Mercian host."

"Well, Oswine is too late!" Oswiu shouted, splintering the

calm of the hall. "Did you see the gates? Did you spy the corpses that litter the land before the fortress?"

Wigelm swallowed. Beobrand felt sorry for the man. He merely bore the message and it seemed that Oswine had done all that he could to assist Bernicia.

"Yes, lord king. But know that the Deirans too lost many in the battle at Catrice. I am sure that my lord Oswine King will be filled with sorrow to hear of your losses."

The man was brave, thought Beobrand. For a moment, it seemed as though Oswiu might unleash his fury at Wigelm. He took in a deep breath and his face darkened with anger.

"Will he?" he asked at last, his voice strangely calm. "Will he indeed? We shall see. But he will not see the damage for himself."

"Lord king?"

"Ride south with all haste and tell your king that he is not to lead his fyrd into my kingdom. I will not have another enemy warhost on my land."

"But lord king," spluttered Wigelm, "Deira is not your enemy." He looked about him for support, but none came. The men around the king did not meet the Deiran's eyes.

"Is it not?" Oswiu said, taking a sip from his cup. "We shall see."

Beobrand glanced at Eanflæd. She was staring at her husband in confusion. Her face had turned as pale as curds.

For a time nobody spoke. There was a chill in the air of the hall now, and Wigelm scanned the faces around him, unsure of himself. Oswiu glowered, but spoke no further.

After a moment, Wigelm raised his head and pushed out his chest. Beobrand found himself liking the man instinctively.

"Do you have a message for me to take to my lord Oswine beyond not leading the fyrd into Bernicia?"

Ethelwin stepped forward then. Oswiu glared at him as he spoke, but did not interrupt his warmaster.

"Tell Oswine that we will meet him under the branch of truce.

We will ride south and speak at Catrice," he paused, thinking for a moment, "on the eve of the next quarter moon. And, Wigelm, tell him we do not come to fight but to speak together to understand how best we are to face the threat of Penda and his allies."

Wigelm listened to Ethelwin and nodded. He then turned back to Oswiu.

"Does the lord Ethelwin speak for you, lord king?"

Oswiu's face was scarlet. Again Beobrand was tempted to laugh. He wanted to step forward and clap Wigelm on the back for his courage.

"No man speaks for me," Oswiu said through gritted teeth, his words sibilant and sharp. "But Ethelwin is my warmaster, and he speaks with wisdom. We will ride south and meet Oswine under truce. Tell him to be prepared for our arrival."

Oswiu waved his hand and two of the hall wardens led Wigelm away. When he had left the hall, Oswiu rose and paced away from the board where he had sat for the audience with the Deiran messenger.

"You forgot yourself, Ethelwin," he said. "Do not presume to speak with my voice."

"Forgive me, lord," replied Ethelwin. "I am tired and I should not have spoken before consulting with you. But I am your warmaster—"

"Yes," snapped Oswiu, cutting him off, "and it is your duty to help me in war."

Ethelwin nodded and Beobrand could see that he was searching for the right words to say to the king.

"I see it as my duty to protect you and the realm, lord king. Do you agree?"

"Yes," answered Oswiu, still angry, his cheeks flushed, his eyes dark. "But these are just words. It is all the same. You fight my enemies."

"That I will always do," Ethelwin said.

Oswiu's eyes narrowed and he halted his pacing.

"You think I am wrong to doubt Oswine's good faith?"

"I think it would be rash to start another war if there is no other enemy save one we make for ourselves."

Oswiu frowned.

"And you think talking would be better than fighting?"

"There will always be time enough for killing," replied Ethelwin. "I think words kill fewer men."

Oswiu stroked at the morning bristles on his cheeks.

"We shall see," he said. "We shall see."

Chapter 34

Cynan looked back at the looming presence of Bebbanburg as they rode down the slope and swung around to the left, heading south. The corpses had all been removed and there was little on the muddy track to show where so many men had perished just four days earlier. The long period of hot weather had truly ended with the storm that followed the battle and now the skies were leaden, the fortress a dark, brooding presence against the eastern sky where the sun fought to shine through thick banks of cloud.

The atmosphere within Bebbanburg seemed to have been dampened with the onset of the rain. For the three days since Wigelm had arrived with word of Oswine's defeat of the Waelisc, and Oswiu's response to the news, a pall of quiet tension had draped itself over the fortress. The people busied themselves with the repairs to the gates and walls, and they set about rebuilding the guardhouse. They worked hard, but spoke little and never with cheer. At night the men got drunk and there had been several fights.

On the day after Oswine's messenger had been sent south once more, the mood had lifted somewhat with the arrival of the royal waggons and carts from the west. Cynan had half expected them to have been plundered by the fleeing Mercians, but they rolled into sight in the early afternoon, surrounded by the horsemen Oswiu had sent. It was good news. The train of vehicles brought the tribute from the halls and farms to the west. To lose those treasures and goods would have been a hard blow. That night Oswiu had smiled and ordered Cædmon to tell tales and riddles. For a time it seemed that the sorrowful torpor that had engulfed Bebbanburg had lifted. But the peace was soon shattered when one of Fordraed's gesithas beat Fægir senseless.

Cynan had to intervene, barging through the men surrounding Fægir. The young man, who moments before had been laughing and singing drunkenly with the rest of them, now lay in the wet rushes of the hall, barely able to defend himself while Fordraed's men laughed and jeered, kicking and spitting on him.

"The next man to touch him will feel my steel in his belly," Cynan had shouted and the men halted. They glowered at him and one of them, a rat-faced man named Pusa, spat onto Fægir's bleeding face.

"Sheep-swiving Waelisc scum," he said, looking Cynan in the eye.

Cynan ignored him, but he would not forget the insult. He added Pusa to the long list of men who would one day regret crossing him.

When Fægir came round, he could not recall what had started the fight, or who had landed the first blow. His face was a blotchy mess of bruises, with his right eye swollen shut and one of his front teeth knocked out.

"Well," Ingwald said, trying to cheer the boy up, "at least you have Agatha back home. Now that you've been uglied up, your days of having all the cunny you wish for might be over." The men had laughed and even Fægir had managed a pained smile as they poured more mead for him. But Cynan felt a burning fury at the abuse of his man.

His man.

He knew they were not truly his men, they were but ceorls who had turned to a warrior with a horse, helm and sword in a moment of need. They had not sworn oaths to him and, as he often reminded Ingwald, he was no lord. And yet he felt responsible for them. That Fordraed's men should treat one of them so harshly filled him with a searing anger he could barely contain.

He had gone to Beobrand, hoping he would address Fordraed about it, but like the rest of the folk in Bebbanburg, Beobrand seemed oddly subdued and had dismissed Cynan's ire with a shrug.

"Men fight, Cynan. It's what they do. No use pushing this any further." Beobrand had sipped absently at his ale, his mind clearly elsewhere. "You stopped it getting out of hand. Let it go now." Emptying his drinking horn, he'd wiped his moustache with his half-hand. "We'll need all the fighting men hale. I fear we might soon be at war again, if Oswiu has his way."

And there it was, the reason for the cloak of despondency over Bebbanburg. Word of Oswiu's belligerent response to Wigelm had spread quickly and the people worried that their king had barely led them out of one conflict merely to plunge them into another.

The afternoon of the following day saw the return of the horsemen who had been sent to harry the Mercian retreat. They had ridden, slumped in their saddles, exhausted and bedraggled, through the drizzle. They too brought glad tidings. They had slain several more Mercians and the others had scattered into smaller groups. They had followed Penda and the main force of mounted Mercians all the way into the east until they had crossed the Great Wall near Caer Luel. It would be some time before Penda would again be able to amass enough men to attack Bernicia.

This news brought with it a ripple of positivity, but the prospect of Oswiu once again leaving Bebbanburg to confront Oswine for some perceived slight prevented the people from rejoicing. The rain continued to fall from the slate grey clouds, washing away the gore from the site of the carnage before the gates, but also dampening the spirits of the victors.

Cynan turned in the saddle to survey the line of riders heading southward. The column was stretched out behind him, moving slowly, having to maintain the speed of the waggon that housed Lady Edlyn. They were escorting her back to Morðpæð. Oswiu and his eighty riders would overnight there, before continuing on to the parley with Oswine.

The waggon was covered and Edlyn had hurried across the muddy courtyard with her maid and climbed inside, drawing the leather curtain behind her, but Cynan had caught a glimpse of her slim, usually comely face and had been shocked to see it blotched and bruised. Her left eye was darkened from a blow and one of her high, angular cheeks was mottled and dark as a thundercloud. Cynan had always considered Edlyn a spoilt, foolish thing. He seldom gave her much thought, but the sight of her battered face filled him with dismay. Surely it had been that fat bastard of a husband of hers who had done this. Again he thought of Fægir and how Fordraed's men had beaten him when he could no longer defend himself. Beobrand hated the man, Cynan knew, so he'd turned to see the thegn's reaction to Edlyn's injuries. Beobrand was swinging up onto Sceadugenga's back and appeared not to have noticed. If any of the others had seen her, none of them seemed to care. They prepared their mounts and readied themselves for the ride south. Only one man caught Cynan's eye.

Beircheart was staring at the closed curtain of the covered waggon and his face was thunderous and dark. When he noted Cynan looking at him, he fixed him with a glare, the meaning of which Cynan could not interpret.

Beobrand and his retinue rode alongside Reodstan and his men near the front of the line. Beobrand was mounted on his sleek black stallion, Sceadugenga. Beside him rode Dreogan, his tattooed face now bearing a long, jagged scar that Coenred had cleaned and sewn together with horsehair. It gave Dreogan an even more ferocious appearance than before. The wound was still scabbed and cracked open and bled whenever he spoke. It must have pained him greatly, but the burly bald warrior seemed unaffected by it. Brinin too rode with them, though Beobrand had tried to convince him to stay behind.

He was still pale and his arm was clearly stiff and painful, but the youth had stood before Beobrand in the hall that morning and told him he was coming.

"Would you have the man married to your daughter be thought of as a coward?" he had asked, when Beobrand had sought to deter him.

"I would have my daughter's husband return to her alive," Beobrand said. "There is no dishonour in resting to recover from a wound. Fraomar too must remain here, as his body is not yet strong enough for the ride."

"Would you turn your back on your duty, if you thought it the safer route?" Brinin asked.

Fraomar, still pallid and weak, frowned, perhaps perceiving some insult in the young man's words, though Cynan was sure none was intended. It was just the way of headstrong youth and Cynan had not been able to prevent himself from laughing out loud. Dreogan joined in, cursing as his wound opened and trickled blood on his cheek. Soon all of Beobrand's gesithas were laughing at the prospect of their hlaford ever shying away from danger. Beobrand scowled at them.

"Very well," he said at last. "But stay close to me and don't get yourself killed or you'll have me to answer to." The men had laughed again then, and it had felt good after so many days of sombre gloom.

Despite the mizzle of rain that fell on them, it was good to be gone from Bebbanburg and its oppressive walls. Cynan turned away from the shadowed fortress and looked eastward. There were men in the distance working amongst the remains of the buildings the Mercians had torn down.

Without a word to Beobrand or any of the other horsemen, Cynan kicked his heels into Mierawin's flanks and the bay mare took off at an easy canter towards the toiling figures.

As Cynan reined the mare in, Ingwald put down the shovel he was using to dig new postholes in the moist earth. Stepping past the rubble of the building, he walked to Cynan. He looked up, shielding his eyes against the watery light of the sun behind the Waelisc warrior.

The rest of the men from Hefenfelth looked in his direction, nodding in greeting and also in farewell, as they knew he was riding south with the king. Fægir, a large part of his face the same colour as the rain-gravid clouds, raised his hand. Cynan returned his wave, holding his reins loosely in his left hand. He thought of Edlyn and the bruises on her delicate features and wondered how long it would be until Fordraed faced a reckoning for his cowardly actions.

Pushing aside his thoughts, he looked down from the saddle at Ingwald.

"I will return soon, gods be willing," said Cynan.

"I'll be here waiting, lord," replied Ingwald with a twisted smirk.

Cynan ignored the man's teasing use of the title.

"I know the king has commanded you to help with the rebuilding," he said. "But do not tarry longer than you must. You have families to go to, fields to be tended. Work here for a few days and then you have my leave to return to your homes."

"Your leave?" asked Ingwald. "I thought you were no lord." He laughed at the serious look on Cynan's face.

"I am not your lord or anyone's," he replied, "but if you insist on treating me as such, I give you leave to go back to your home."

Ingwald stared at him for several heartbeats, his face serious now.

"I thank you, Cynan," he said at last. "But I will be waiting here for you. I cannot speak for the others, but I will be here."

"As you wish," Cynan said. "Take care of yourself and the rest of them, Ingwald."

He pulled Mierawin's head around and galloped back to the column of riders. He did not look round, but he was certain that Ingwald and the others were watching him. He wondered what they were thinking. Would Ingwald truly remain here, waiting for his return? Would any of the others? The gods alone knew. He could scarcely believe he had instilled such loyalty in any man.

He rejoined the column of riders, falling into step beside Beobrand and Dreogan.

"All good?" Beobrand asked.

Cynan hesitated, unsure of his answer. He wondered what good would come of this meeting between Oswiu and Oswine.

"Are your men well?" Beobrand pressed.

His men.

Cynan felt a shiver of secret pride.

"Yes, lord," he replied and found himself grinning. "They are well."

Beobrand nodded and they rode on in silence into the south, the line of horsemen and the lumbering waggons trailing in their wake.

Chapter 35

They reached Fordraed's hall at Morðpæð shortly before nightfall. The rain had stopped falling and the sun in the west was a crimson orb, licking the dark clouds with flames of red.

After passing many steadings that had been either completely or partly destroyed, it was strange to ride up to the great hall, its golden thatch glowing in the setting sun, and see it apparently untouched by the recent invaders of the land. The barns, stables and outbuildings were all intact too. The place was silent and had an air of emptiness about it that was unnerving after the many days cooped up with so many behind the walls of Bebbanburg.

As they walked their horses slowly into the open area of ground before the buildings, several crows that had been hidden amongst the long grass in the meadows flapped noisily into the reddening sky. That lush grass would need to be harvested soon, scythed close to the earth to make hay for the livestock. Judging from the length of the grass and the size of the meadows, Fordraed's animals would have plenty of fodder to see them through the far-off winter months of cold and gloom.

The men spoke in hushed tones, not wishing to break the calm of the place. They took the horses down to the stream before leading them quietly back up to the stables. It felt to Beobrand as if they were somehow intruding on such a peaceful place. As if the rest of middle earth had been plunged into battle, flames and darkness and this small corner of Bernicia, nestling in the crook of the Wenspic, with its stand of tall willows whispering in the light breeze, had been forgotten by fame-hungry kings and capricious gods. The arrival of so many horses and people filled the settlement with sound. Even though Beobrand could sense he was not alone in his feelings and all of the men were subdued, threescore horses and their riders were impossible to keep quiet.

After they had stabled the animals, Ethelwin gave orders for the men to take watches during the night. Beobrand was glad. He was on edge and nervous. The land was peaceful and calm, and yet his skin prickled as if he were being watched. He would drink sparingly and sleep with his sword close.

When they had finished with the horses and made their way into the hall, the sun had dropped below the horizon and darkness was pulling itself about them. The feeling of silence and abandoned forgetfulness had been shattered. Fordraed's thralls and bondsmen had returned with the riders from Bebbanburg and they had quickly set about readying the hall for the guests. When Beobrand entered, woodsmoke was billowing up from a hastily lit fire and boards and benches had already been set up.

Those men not assigned the first watch slumped onto the benches, glad to be out of the saddle. Fordraed's steward had either brought mead from Bebbanburg, or else he had found some hidden away in the hall's stores, for a couple of young women briskly bustled about the hall, setting out cups and horns and filling them for the thirsty men.

Beobrand nodded to Cynan and the rest of his gesithas as he passed. He would have preferred to sit with them, but Oswiu had requested that he dine at the high table. He winced to see Dreogan's scarred face. The cut must have caused great discomfort, but the man was as strong as an ox and did not complain.

Dreogan grinned at him, the healing scar and the soot lines of his tattoos giving him a formidable aspect. Beobrand was glad of his presence, and that of the other men. He did not know what would transpire when Oswiu met Oswine, but he could almost smell the approach of more bloodshed on the air. He thought of the stillness of Fordraed's hall and how it felt as though the land itself held its breath, waiting. But for what? Still, whatever the night might bring, or the coming days as they rode south for the kings to parley, he could have no better men at his side.

Brinin glanced up at him, then lowered his gaze quickly, unable to maintain eye contact with his lord and father-in-law.

Beobrand wished the boy had stayed back at Bebbanburg and that Fraomar had been sufficiently hale to ride with them. Brinin was brave enough, but he was just a boy and Beobrand dreaded him coming to further harm. He did not wish to have to face Ardith with tidings of the boy's death. The girl doted on Brinin and Beobrand thought it might break her spirit if something were to happen to him. She was a strong girl, but there was a fragility about her that he hoped one day would melt away like winter frosts.

Seating himself at the high table, beside Ethelwin, Beobrand reached for a cup of mead and smiled to himself. There was no denying the boy's mettle. The men loved Brinin, treating him as a younger brother. How they had laughed at him standing up to Beobrand! They loved boldness and bravery above all else, and Beobrand grudgingly admitted Brinin had both.

Fraomar too was fearless. He had also asked to ride with them, but in his case, no matter how much he pushed, Beobrand would not relent. The man was yet pallid and weak. His strength would return, both Coenred and the old healer woman agreed, but neither could be certain about his memory. Fraomar still seemed confused about what had happened and when Beobrand spoke to him, it appeared to him as though part of the young warrior yet slept, lost in a world of dreams within his mind, while the rest of him moved about, ate, drank and spoke. It was as if Fraomar was a shadow of who he had been. Where he had been forceful and decisive, now he was hesitant and nervous, unsure of himself. To see him so weakened, a thin wraith-like reflection of himself, filled Beobrand with regret and sadness.

"Look after him," he had whispered to Coenred before they left Bebbanburg. "Make him whole again."

The young monk had nodded sombrely.

"It is not within my power to grant your wish, Beo," he'd said. "But I will pray that God will bring all of him back."

Beobrand supposed there was no more anyone could do now. It was between the gods and Fraomar whether the bright, clever, deadly warrior would ever stand in the shieldwall once more, commanding men, leading them to victory.

"What say you, Beobrand?"

The blustering voice encroached on his thoughts. With a sigh of annoyance, Beobrand lowered his cup and turned to the brash speaker.

It was Fordraed, smiling and obscenely obsequious.

"About what?" asked Beobrand. His tone was as harsh and hard as a punch.

Fordraed recoiled, as if he feared Beobrand might indeed strike him.

"Why, about my hall, of course." He spread his arms, gesturing at the length and breadth of the building. Beobrand noted that the lady Edlyn was not present at the table. He frowned at the memory of her bruised face when she had hurried into her waggon at Bebbanburg. He had felt Beircheart's ire and had studiously ignored him, not wishing to give the man any encouragement. It had been all he could do to dissuade him from seeking out Fordraed for a duel. To have both the subject of his desire and his anger with them as they rode south must have tormented Beircheart.

Beobrand glanced around the hall, taking in its stout, carved pillars and the great blackened chain that hung down above the hearth. Shields, banners and other trophies adorned the walls.

"It is comfortable enough," replied Beobrand.

Fordraed beamed.

Gods knew how Beircheart had managed to keep his word to Beobrand and not lash out at this fat fool. Beobrand was ashamed to have held him back. But he could not risk the man speaking out, if Heremod had spoken to him of what he had seen.

"It is," Fordraed was saying, "comfortable and warm, and my steward brews the best mead in Albion. Criba has had no time to prepare food, but I am sure that soon we will dine like emperors of old Roma. The man is a marvel—"

"It seems to me," Beobrand said, interrupting him, "that you are indeed blessed."

"I am, I am," said Fordraed. "Criba is a fine man."

"I am sure he is," replied Beobrand. "But your blessings go further than your steward, Fordraed. Do they not?"

Fordraed's jowls quivered and he tilted his head nervously.

"How so?" he asked.

Beobrand swallowed a mouthful of mead. It was indeed good. He could not let this bastard harp on about his hall and his mead. Even as he spoke, he knew there was risk in what he was doing. If Fordraed knew of his meeting with Eanflæd, now would be the moment he would speak up. But if he did not, perhaps there was a way of silencing him, or at least making Oswiu less inclined to listen to his voice.

"I am known as one who has luck," Beobrand said, "yet I do not believe it to be so. But you, it seems, should accept the title of 'Fordraed the Lucky'."

Oswiu, Ethelwin and the others at the high table were silent now, keenly watching Beobrand and Fordraed. All had been peace and stillness when they had arrived, but suddenly, the hall's air crackled with the pent-up energy that fills clouds before a thunderstorm. Beobrand's enmity towards Fordraed was notorious, and since the burning of the gates at Bebbanburg, the fat lord had fallen out of Oswiu's favour. Fordraed was not popular and the men now watched expectantly to see where Beobrand's comments would lead.

The silence of the king, ealdormen and thegns quickly spread to the rest of the hall and soon, all the men gathered there were staring with open interest at the high table.

"Indeed?" said Fordraed, his voice cracking. "How is it that I am so lucky?"

"You have a young, pretty wife. Though I am sure she feels less than lucky with her lot."

Some of the men laughed. Beobrand ignored them and continued.

"And despite the great battle before the gates of Bebbanburg, you escaped without a scratch. Some might say this is due to your great battle-skill," he paused for effect, letting his words sink in. "But no man who knows you would believe it to be so."

The men in the hall laughed more loudly. Fordraed's face grew dark. He pushed his bulk to his feet, seemingly ready to launch himself at Beobrand. Fordraed turned towards Oswiu, perhaps meaning to seek the king's aid in these attacks on his reputation, but Oswiu was laughing with the rest of them. The king slapped the table and struggled for breath, such was his mirth.

"Why you... you..." Fordraed stammered, turning his attention back to his tormentor.

Beobrand held up his hand for silence and slowly the sounds of merriment abated. Everyone leaned forward to hear what he was going to say next.

"But the thing that truly separates our luck and our wyrd, it seems to me, is that when war was far away in the west at Maserfelth, with no danger to the halls and farms of Bernicia, it was my hall of Ubbanford, and my hall alone, that was attacked by a warband of Mercians. Halga led his men through Bernicia, risking attack all the way, and struck at my home when I was sent south to retrieve the body of our lord king's brother."

"That had nothing to do with me," said Fordraed, his voice high.

"I did not say that it did," replied Beobrand, his voice as quiet and sharp as a blade being dragged across a whetstone. "And yet it was my hall that was burnt!" He raised his voice, barking out the words as if he were shouting over the din of battle. "My people slain! My treasure stolen! My woman murdered!" With each statement, Beobrand slammed his fist into the board with a crash.

"Lord king," spluttered Fordraed, "you cannot allow Beobrand to say these things."

Oswiu narrowed his eyes, frowning.

"Do you presume to tell me what I can and cannot allow, Fordraed?" Oswiu's tone was heavy with threats. Fordraed shook his head. "And does Beobrand speak false? He has done no more than speak the truth."

"But lord—" Fordraed whined.

Oswiu silenced him with a glare.

"Tell us, lord Beobrand," Oswiu went on. "How does your ill fortune separate you from Fordraed here? Much as I enjoy seeing him squirm, I am tired and I would eat some of the wondrous food he has promised us."

"It seems passing strange to me that my hall should be destroyed and my people killed when war was far away, and yet Fordraed's hall should be untouched, when Penda leads his warhost to the very gates of Bebbanburg, destroying all in his path, and sending your people scurrying for shelter to the fortress." Beobrand hesitated for a heartbeat. Now was the moment that Fordraed would speak out against him. If he knew of his secret with the queen, he would use that knowledge now. Taking a deep breath, Beobrand continued, "One could almost imagine that the lord

Fordraed might have sent a message to Penda, to ask him to leave his home undamaged."

Fordraed stepped towards Beobrand, dropping his hand to the seax that hung from his belt.

"Why, you whoreson," he growled.

Beobrand ignored him, instead directing his words at the king.

"Of course, such a thing is impossible," he said. "Fordraed is your trusted man and a lord of Bernicia; he would never enter into an alliance with your enemy. And therefore, looking upon the stable, storerooms, barns and this great hall, all standing intact and unsullied by the passing horde of Mercians, I say that from this day forth, Fordraed, and not I, should be known as the lucky one."

Fordraed fell silent. He glowered at Beobrand. The fat man was breathless and red-faced. Beobrand was certain he would have liked nothing more than to lash out at him. Beobrand had not openly accused him of anything, though surely his words had sown seeds of doubt in Oswiu's mind as certainly as if he had said that Fordraed was Penda's man. Fordraed stood there, gasping and shaking and doing nothing.

In that moment, Beobrand was certain that Fordraed did not know of his night-time meeting with Eanflæd. If he had, he would surely have used that knowledge to deflect the king's suspicions away from him.

For a moment he wondered whether the man would attack him, but just as quickly, Beobrand dismissed the thought. Whatever else was true of the man, Beobrand knew Fordraed to be a coward. If he meant to strike out at Beobrand, it would never be face-to-face in a hall, it would be with a knife slipped between his ribs in the darkness. And more than likely, it would be a blade in the hand of another.

Oswiu held Beobrand's gaze for a long time, stroking his chin in thought. Evidently, the lord of Ubbanford's words had set him thinking. After a time, he nodded at Beobrand.

"Sit down," he said to the furious Fordraed, "you look ridiculous standing there. Be seated," Oswiu smirked at Beobrand, "Fordraed the Lucky."

Chapter 36

In the morning the rain had returned. Despite Beobrand's misgivings the previous evening, the night had been uneventful and with the first light of dawn they were up and mounting the horses in a thin drizzle that fell from a sullen sky.

For the rest of the evening Fordraed had chosen to ignore Beobrand, turning his broad back on him and seeking to make lively conversation with the king. Beobrand drank sparingly of the mead and as soon as the benches and boards were pulled to the edges of the hall, he had wrapped himself in his cloak and slept. He was surprised at how quickly he had fallen asleep. The place was loud with the talk of the men, most of whom were more accepting of their host's hospitality than Beobrand. As the mead flowed, so the noise within the hall grew louder, but Beobrand slept more soundly than he had in days. Perhaps it was the long ride and the sense of freedom that came from being outside the walls of Bebbanburg, or maybe it was the certainty that Fordraed did not know his secret. Heremod was still a risk, but the man appeared content to drink himself into a stupor in the hall that night, and somehow the warrior with his plaited beard seemed at once both more and less dangerous than his hlaford. Heremod was certainly deadlier with a blade, but also, it seemed to Beobrand, less likely to whisper vicious secrets into the king's ear.

But he was still a danger to both Beobrand and the queen, and thoughts of how to deal with the problem turned in Beobrand's mind as he drifted to sleep.

Leaving Fordraed's hall, they pushed on south. Now that they had left behind the waggons carrying Edlyn, the thralls and servants, they made better progress. But the roads were muddy and the days miserable as they passed the Great Wall and crossed the river Tine. These paths were well-known to them, but as they travelled south of the Tine, they noticed that the land did not display the scars of a passing warhost. The fields were full of rippling seas of barley and wheat and the ceorls and bondsmen who worked the land seemed less frightened than the men north of the Wall to see mounted warriors. They rode beneath Oswiu's streaming purple banner, it was true, so perhaps the folk recognised their king. But whatever the reason, where the common folk of the land would usually flee from armed men, now they often spotted clustered groups of people staring at them as they passed.

In the late afternoon, as they approached Lord Ecgric's hall, where they hoped to spend the night, they saw a single man by the crumbling road. He was leaning against the gnarled trunk of an old elm. On the hill behind him were scattered a score of sheep. At his side sat a skinny hound. Both man and beast openly stared at the column of riders as they trotted past. Beobrand reined in Sceadugenga and nudged the stallion off the road. Attor, Beircheart, Dreogan and Cynan all followed their lord, their horses crowding around the man. His dog rose up and growled deep in its throat. Sceadugenga's ears went down and he pawed the damp mossy earth beneath the elm.

Beobrand patted the horse's neck.

"Waes hael," he said to the man.

The old man peered up at him, his eyes shadowed pits within the wrinkled, leathery face. He grunted.

"Have you seen a host of warriors pass this way?" Beobrand asked.

The man nodded, but did not speak. He eyed Beobrand suspiciously, as if the question were a riddle.

"When?" Beobrand said, an edge of frustration entering his tone.

"Now," said the shepherd. His expression was one of bemusement as he nodded towards the passing riders.

Beobrand sighed.

"Not now," he said. "This is your king, Oswiu, son of Æthelfrith."

The old shepherd bowed his head.

"My lord," he muttered.

"No. I am not your king," said Beobrand, wishing he had not stopped to converse with this fool. Cynan stifled a laugh and Beobrand shot him an angry glance. "Did a host of warriors come this way some days ago? There would have been many more of them than there are of us. They were Waelisc."

The man's face lit up then and he nodded.

"Oh, yes," he said, his furrowed face cracking into a broad smile. "We saw them, didn't we, Ræcc? There were as many of them as fleas on old Ræcc here."

"When was this?"

The man removed his woollen cap and scratched at the thinning, greasy grey hair beneath.

"I don't rightly know, lord king," he said. Beobrand did not bother to correct him. Cynan snorted. "It must have been at least a sennight ago…" His voice trailed off as he tried to remember.

"Did they return?"

"Oh no, we would have seen such a host of men if they had come back up the road. We've not seen any Waelisc hosts since then. Reminded me of the old days of Edwin, it did," mused the man. "When Cadwallon brought his great hosts into Northumbria. Terrible days. Terrible. Brigands and ruffians stalked the land that winter. Nowhere was safe."

Beobrand nodded, his mind suddenly filled with distant, dark memories of ice and blood.

"Do you think we will be returning to such days again?" the man asked, looking nervously at Dreogan. The warrior's scar was a raw, vivid red, his tattoos black and menacing.

"No," said Beobrand. "We have heard tell that Oswine of Deira defeated the Waelisc at Catrice. If they have not returned this way, they have been slain or routed and have rushed back westward, I imagine." Beobrand hoped the message about the defeat of the men of Powys and Gwynedd was true.

The man looked set to say more, but the horsemen had already passed and Beobrand did not wish to tarry further, so with a nod, he swung Sceadugenga's head to the south and cantered after Oswiu and his retinue. His gesithas followed him.

They stayed that night in the hall of Ecgric, son of Eacgric. The lord of the hall was old and had always been large, but now he was huge. His barrel of a belly must have been at least twice the girth of Fordraed's. Ecgric struggled to squeeze his bulk into his finely carved chair, where he sat with the king. He had no news of note, having decided to remain in his hall when the summons for the fyrd came.

"Three good men, I sent," he said, shaking his head and wiping his greasy fingers on his fine kirtle. "Not a one returned to me. It is always thus when I send men to the fyrd, lord. I sometimes wonder if they don't just decide to follow another man, rather than dying with dignity for their king and country."

Beobrand thought of the men who had followed Cynan from Hefenfelth and wondered whether Ecgric might not have the truth of it. He chose not to sit at the high table that night, and enjoyed his men's company. One of them – Cynan, most likely

– had told them all about the old shepherd mistaking Beobrand for the king and they had all laughed. Beobrand sighed, but smiled happily enough, despite the nagging feeling that they were riding towards danger. The thought from earlier that day tugged at his mind. Could it be that the tidings they had been sent by Oswine were false? Perhaps the Waelisc host yet remained in wait for them in the south.

A sudden cheering drew Beobrand's attention. One of the men further down the table had won a pile of hacksilver at knucklebones and was hollering and laughing at his good fortune. At the far end of the hall sat Fordraed's men. One of them was staring at him. Peering through the smoky haze and the flame flicker from the hearth and rush lights, Beobrand was not surprised to recognise the bearded face of Heremod. The warrior returned his gaze for several heartbeats before raising his drinking horn to Beobrand with a mocking grin.

That night Ethelwin once more placed guards around the hall. Beobrand took one of the watches, glad of the peace in the cool darkness. There were no sounds in the night but the whisper of the trees and the calls of night animals. At one point in the darkest part of the night, when the rain had stopped and the air was cold and moist, redolent of loam and leaf, a rustling brought Beobrand crashing from a doze into alert wakefulness. His heart hammered and he dropped his hand to Nægling's pommel. A moment later, the shadowy shape of a badger snuffled into view, its white-striped face dimly lit by the moon and the stars dotting the now largely cloudless sky.

There was no further disturbance, and Beobrand began to wonder whether he was not being overly nervous. And yet, as they rode into the clear morning, the land steaming gently about them as the warm sun rose into the duck-egg-blue sky, he could not dispel the sensation that every step they travelled south brought them closer to something terrible. Could Oswiu truly wish to plunge them into a war with their closest neighbour and ally? Oswiu's ambition was every bit as powerful as his brother Oswald's. Both had wished to become Bretwalda, ruler of all the kingdoms of Albion. Perhaps Oswiu saw this as a way to begin making his dream a reality.

At the end of the third day, as they rode down a long slope towards the Sualuae, they saw several horsemen arrayed across the road. The lowering sun shone on the distant water of the river and glinted from their battle gear and their horses' harness.

Beobrand held up his hand to halt the column and moments later Ethelwin and Oswiu rode up to where he set astride Sceadugenga, looking down into the valley.

Oswiu glanced at the gathered warriors.

"They are Oswine's men," he said. "They bear his standard."

They were too far away for Beobrand to make this out, but he saw a smudge of red and gold above the men, which must have been the banner atop a spear. Attor, knowing his lord's eyesight was not as keen as his, nodded in agreement with the king.

"Aye," he said. "I make out a dozen of them. I think one of them is Wulfstan."

Oswiu spat into the weeds that grew in a tangle beside the old road.

"By Christ's bones," he said. "I detest that man. I'll never understand what Oswine sees in him."

Beobrand looked sidelong at Oswiu, wondering at how close Fordraed had been to him all these years. He would much sooner spend time with Wulfstan than with that fat worm.

"We will stay here," the king continued. "Ethelwin, Beobrand, take a dozen men and see what they want."

They cantered down the slope, the sun warm on the right side of their faces. There was no hint of rain in the sky now, and the day was hot and still, the only memory of the rain coming from the humidity that made their garments stick to their sweaty skin.

Halting their band of horsemen before Wulfstan and the Deirans, Ethelwin and Beobrand kicked their mounts forward, ahead of the dozen gesithas who followed them. Wulfstan and another man Beobrand did not recognise did the same, nudging their horses a few paces forward.

"Well met, Beobrand, lord of Ubbanford," said Wulfstan with an open smile. "You are well come to Deira."

Beobrand nodded in greeting.

"We have been awaiting your arrival," continued Wulfstan. "My lord king Oswine has given me the task of leading you to meet him."

"Where is he?" asked Ethelwin.

"Oswine is awaiting your king at Catrice."

Ethelwin nodded.

"We will not follow you there," he said.

Wulfstan frowned. The other man who sat beside him astride a white mare bristled with annoyance. He was fresh-faced and young with handsome features. His byrnie was of the finest quality and his shield was newly painted with a bright red star on a black background.

"What is the meaning of this?" he snapped. "Our lord king extends the hand of friendship and you spit on it."

Wulfstan held up a hand. The younger man fell silent.

"What do you propose?" Wulfstan asked, keeping his tone light.

"Our king, Oswiu, son of Æthelfrith, lord of all Bernicia, would meet under the roof of one who both men trust. He will ride for Hunwald's hall at Ingetlingum. Oswine King is to come there with no more than threescore men. Hunwald is known to them both. There will be no mischief there and our kings can parley in peace."

"Does your king not trust Oswine?" blurted out the young Deiran. Wulfstan placed a hand upon his arm.

"It matters not, Odda," he said. "We are no more kings than we are fish in the sea and therefore it is not for us to determine the ways of those men who are our betters."

Odda scowled, but clamped his mouth shut.

"You will take this message to Oswine?" asked Ethelwin.

"We will," replied Wulfstan.

"Very well." Ethelwin turned his horse back towards the men on the hill. "Until tomorrow then," he said, and kicked his steed back up the slope. Beobrand raised his eyebrows at Wulfstan, who chuckled briefly.

"Till tomorrow," he said. And the two groups rode off in separate directions.

Chapter 37

Beobrand stood silently listening to the quiet of the night. From the distant hall came the murmur of voices and laughter. He was glad to be away from the fug of the hall and the press of people surrounding him. He sighed, wishing he were back at Ubbanford, standing outside his own hall, beneath the looming presence of Sunniva's oak, gazing down the hill to the light of the moon playing on the waters of the Tuidi. It had been too long since he had been home and in all those weeks, he had never truly been able to relax. He had slept well these last nights, the rhythm of the road somehow conveying a unique tiredness to his body that allowed slumber to come easily. And he was glad for the nights of dreamless sleep. And yet his mind was still exhausted. He craved rest and time away from the worries of kings and kingdoms.

He smiled grimly in the darkness. Such was not his wyrd, he knew. He had given his oath to Oswiu and so he would follow where the king commanded. Still, he was amazed by the intrigues of the king and those surrounding him. When Beobrand thought of problems, he saw straight lines, direct paths to follow that would lead to their solution. Not so Oswiu.

Beobrand had been surprised when they had arrived at Ingetlingum to find the lord of the hall, Hunwald, already expecting their arrival. Hunwald had introduced them all to his wife, a serious woman called Frythegith. She had welcomed them and offered the Waes Hael cup, but she was obviously already known to Ethelwin, for she greeted the warmaster with an embrace and tender kiss on the cheek. It transpired that the lady Frythegith was Ethelwin's sister, and suddenly how the decision had been taken to meet Oswine there became evident. The hall was clean and tidy and there was food and drink aplenty. Clearly word had been sent ahead that the king and his comitatus would be staying and it was quickly apparent that the preparations for the King of Deira's visit the next day were well underway too.

Beobrand sniffed the cool night air. There was a faint scent of cooking meat and woodsmoke lingering over the fragrance of damp earth and the verdant, fertile land around Ingetlingum. Oak and ash grew in great thickets along the beck that ran through the settlement and Beobrand thought again of the king's astute decision to meet Oswine here. The path that led to the hall passed through dense woodland, with hills on both sides. It could be easily watched and a large force could not approach unnoticed.

Beobrand's thoughts spun in his mind like so many bats caught in a cavern. They swarmed and flapped but could find no escape and nowhere to settle.

How much of all of this had been planned in advance by Oswiu? Beobrand began to even wonder whether the king had timed his absence from Bebbanburg in some way to give him an advantage over Oswine. But he could not see how that could be. What benefit was there in Oswiu not being at the fortress when Penda struck? Beobrand could think of none, but such was Oswiu's cunning, he would not discount the idea. For a long time, ever since Halga's attack on Ubbanford, Beobrand had believed Oswiu to have been involved somehow. The red-headed giant had implicated the man who had been about to take the throne from his brother, Oswald. What reason did Halga have to lie? He'd believed he was victorious over Beobrand. Perhaps it was as Halga had said and Oswiu had allowed him to attack Ubbanford, but there was no way to accuse a king of such duplicity and certainly no way to prove it. As Beobrand had uttered the words in Fordraed's hall that implied the fat thegn was in league with Penda in some way, the idea had coalesced and hardened in his mind. Perhaps Oswiu had not been involved in the Mercian raid on Ubbanford after all. Maybe it had been Fordraed who had enabled Halga to pass through the lands of Bernicia unhindered. He certainly hated Beobrand enough to want to see his wealth stolen and his home destroyed. Beobrand had never voiced any of his fears about the attack on his hall. How could he? What good would it do? Octa was fostered in Oswiu's household. If Beobrand should speak out against the king, not only would his life be over, but the threat to his only son was all too real.

But in Fordraed's hall something had snapped within him and the words had come tumbling out. Words he had barely dared think before he heard them spoken in his own voice. The suspicion that he voiced at seeing Fordraed's steading untouched when so much destruction had been wrought on the land was clearly in other men's minds too. Ever since that night, the king himself had taken to calling the fat lord Fordraed the Lucky, sarcasm dripping from his tone like venom from a viper's fangs. Now, thinking about how Oswiu had planned ahead to come to Hunwald's hall, Beobrand wondered whether Fordraed was truly guilty of what Beobrand had accused him of. Could it not also be true that Oswiu was done with Fordraed, that he had become tired of him and saw this as a way of distancing himself from the man who had previously been his closest companion? After all, ever since his return to Bebbanburg the king had not ceased to criticise the man.

A vixen shrieked, the sound loud and otherworldly in the darkness. Beobrand shivered, but it was not cold. He peered into the gloom, trying not to imagine the denizens of the forest, goblins and elves, stalking the shadows in search of prey.

Ethelwin had again ordered the men to watch throughout the night. Oswiu, it seemed, was fearful of treachery, but Beobrand thought it unlikely. Oswine was a man of honour. He would face his enemies head-on, not skulking about the forests at night to strike from the shadows. It said much about Oswiu, thought Beobrand, that he believed the king of Deira might attack at night, without warning.

A footfall behind him made him spin around, dragging Nægling from its scabbard. A dark form approached from the hall.

"Easy there, brave Beobrand," said a voice. Despite not seeing the face, Beobrand could hear the smile in the tone.

Oswiu.

"My king," Beobrand said. "The night is so still, your approach startled me." He sheathed Nægling once more.

The king stepped closer and Beobrand saw that two others followed him. Beobrand could not make them out, but he saw the bulk of their shadowy forms. Oswiu's hearth-warriors. He had left them out of earshot, but close enough to come to his aid.

For a while, they stood in silence, each staring out at the night. The vixen screamed again.

"What is that?" asked Oswiu.

"My father would tell me that was the call of a she-fox."

"By Christ, she sounds like a handful," chuckled Oswiu. His words were slightly slurred. As he spoke, the scent of mead wafted on his breath. "I've bedded a few women in my time, but none that would wail like that."

"Perhaps they save that kind of scream for the right man," said Beobrand, keeping his tone flat, but unable to stop himself from delivering the oblique insult.

Oswiu tensed beside him. Beobrand held himself still. At last, Oswiu let out a bark of laughter.

"By Christ's bones, Beobrand, you are brave. There are not many men who would insult their lord king's prowess."

"You have sired many children, lord," Beobrand said. "I am sure there is nothing to insult there." The thought of Oswiu lying with Eanflæd threatened to flood his mind. He would like nothing more than to reach out and grab the king by the throat and shake him, the way a fox would shake a rat.

Oswiu snorted.

"Indeed I have many children, and I am sure I will beget many more. Eanflæd is yet young and is willing enough to help me in that regard."

Was the man goading him? Did he know of Beobrand's feelings for the queen? Had someone spoken to him? Had Eanflæd herself admitted her sins to her husband? It was possible that the Christ god demanded it. Beobrand knew that his followers believed they needed to confess their sins. Perhaps this extended to wives and husbands.

"Children are a blessing," said Oswiu. "Your boy, Octa, is a good lad. Strong and worthy," he paused, "just like his father."

"Thank you, lord," replied Beobrand. He felt awkward in the king's presence. He had been enjoying the peace of the night's watch, and now he was having to remain alert in a very different way, to avoid any trap Oswiu might set for him. This was the longest they had ever spoken alone together and Beobrand wondered at the meaning of the king coming to him here.

"All quiet out there?" Oswiu asked.

"Apart from the foxes and owls, I've heard nothing."

For a time neither man spoke.

"You are a lord of men," Oswiu said, breaking the silence that had settled between them. "You do not need to stand out here in the night."

Beobrand turned to look at his king. Oswiu's face was an unreadable pale blur in the darkness.

"Neither do you, lord king," he replied. "And yet here we both are."

"I am not a good husband," Oswiu said, lowering his voice to not much more than a whisper.

Beobrand held his breath. The king had fallen silent.

"Lord," Beobrand said, hesitantly, unsure of his words, "I do not think I am the man to speak to about being a good husband."

"Ah, yes. Sorry. My brother called you lucky, but you never had much luck in that regard, did you?"

Beobrand thought of Sunniva's golden hair, the touch of her skin. Then he recalled the fragile form of Reaghan pressed against him, always so willing, but forever hiding part of her mind away from him; a part of her he had never tried very hard to find. Both of them were gone now. Nothing more than ash and smoke and memories. He sighed.

"I was not lying when I said I never thought of myself as having the luck Oswald saw in me."

The king seemed not to have heard him.

"Eanflæd is a marvel, you know?" he said.

Again, Beobrand wondered if the king was trying to trick him into admitting something that would get him and the queen killed. He bit his lip in the dark.

Somewhere off to the south an owl hooted.

Beobrand said nothing.

"She is beautiful, of course," Oswiu said. "Any man with eyes can see that."

Beobrand pictured her slender form, the curve of her neck, the intelligent eyes.

"But she is more than that," continued Oswiu. "She has a strength about her. And her mind is as sharp as any man's."

"She is her father's daughter," said Beobrand.

"Of course. You knew her as a child, did you not? Was she always thus?"

Beobrand thought of the tiny girl he had met in the stables at Bebbanburg a lifetime ago.

"I knew her but briefly, lord," he said. "She was smaller then."

Oswiu laughed.

"But she was always one who commanded a room," Beobrand went on. "Even when she was a child. And she knew no fear."

"Ha! Her father's daughter indeed." Oswiu fell silent for a time and Beobrand let out a long breath. He hoped the king would tire of this talk soon and head back inside. But Oswiu did not leave.

"She is still afraid of nothing," he said. "I have never known any woman like her. She is strict and unbending in her faith. And yet I cannot dispel her from my thoughts."

Beobrand almost laughed. It seemed Eanflæd had captivated them both. But Oswiu had an important advantage over Beobrand.

"She is your wife, lord," Beobrand said. "It is no bad thing that you think of her."

"It is when I travel to Caer Luel to see Aldfrid's mother, Fín. By Christ's thorny crown, that Hibernian vixen can do things no royal woman should know of, let alone do." He ran his fingers through his hair and looked out into the darkness, perhaps imagining the feats his Hibernian woman performed. "I have always gone back to her, you know," Oswiu said, "no matter who I needed to bed for the good of the kingdom. But this time, no matter how much Fín tried to convince me otherwise, I could not get Eanflæd out of my mind."

Beobrand said nothing. Again, the irony of the situation was not lost on him. He was now convinced that Oswiu did not mean to entrap him with his words. The king was seeking to unburden himself, perhaps to free himself of these worries before facing

Oswine on the morrow. Had he come here to speak to Beobrand, or would any thegn have done; any ear? Perhaps it was the very fact that they were not friends that had led Oswiu to be so open. Beobrand wondered how the king would feel when the effects of the mead wore off and in the stark light of day he recalled what he had said to this thegn whom he usually despised. One thing was for certain, it would not go well for Beobrand when the king realised he had given his secrets to him.

"When I saw the fortress aflame..." Oswiu said. His voice, barely audible, caught in his throat. "And Penda's host before the gates. I did not think of myself or Bernicia. Do you know what I thought of?"

Beobrand shook his head, but did not speak.

"All I could think of was Eanflæd and Ecgfrith," Oswiu said.

The owl, closer now, called again in the stillness of the night.

"I will not forget the great service you have done me, Beobrand," the king said. He straightened his shoulders and took a deep breath. "I know there is no love between us. There never has been and I doubt there ever will be. But I respect your bravery. Your loyalty. And your honour."

Beobrand's mouth was dry. So this was why the king had sought him out: to thank him for saving his queen and their son. Oswiu was right, Beobrand did not love his king, but he had always been true to his oath. His word was iron and no man could say otherwise. But Beobrand's oath to Oswiu was dust in his mouth. He would have lain with Eanflæd in an instant, no matter the consequences or the broken vows.

"My sword is yours, lord," he said. "With it I will protect your kingdom and your kin. I would give my life for the queen."

He did not turn to look at the king, but he could sense Oswiu's gaze on him. After a time, he clapped Beobrand on the back.

"Some years ago I might have wished for such an outcome; to be rid of you. But now I know the worth of loyal men. I am glad it did not come to that."

Beobrand lowered his head. Oswiu must have thought it a sign of subservient gratitude. Beobrand, face hot with guilt, knew it was shame that meant he could not face his king.

Silence stretched out between them and the moment of intimacy was gone. Awkward now beside the thegn who for so long he had disliked, Oswiu turned to head back to the hall.

"I will not forget," he repeated.

Beobrand nodded his thanks, but said no more. He would be glad when Oswiu had gone, leaving him alone with his turmoil of thoughts and the tranquillity of the night.

As the king stepped away from him, a strange sound came to Beobrand. It was like a muffled cough and it was close by. His waking thoughts did not tell him what the sound was, but some part of him, the deep instinct of the animal, the natural killer within that made him such a formidable warrior, screamed silently that the night was suddenly full of danger.

Without thought, he spun, grabbing the king's cloak and heaving him back. In the dim light of the moon Beobrand made out that where there had been two hearth-warriors to protect the king, now there were three figures. As he watched, steel flashed cold in the night and one of the shadows groaned and fell to the earth to lie beside the first slain hearth-guard.

"Treachery!" Beobrand bellowed, sliding Nægling out of its scabbard.

Before them, two men wrapped in dark cloaks with soot-blackened faces stepped stealthily towards them. Beobrand sensed, rather than heard, movement behind them. Looking over his shoulder he saw the shadows of three more attackers. They had slipped out of the forest, as silent as spirits; as ethereal as dreams. But their swords were real and their blades glimmered, lambent and cold in the starlight.

The men did not speak, but it was clear they came with only one purpose: death in the darkness.

Chapter 38

The five assailants rushed towards them. There was no time for thought. Beobrand was a mighty warrior, but here in the open, alone and surrounded by five attackers, he could not hope to prevail.

But Beobrand was not alone. His conversation with Oswiu had sent his mind reeling. He did not like the man, but the king was a fighter and no coward. Beobrand had seen him standing in the front ranks of shieldwalls, splattered with gore, his sword red with the blood of his enemies. The men of Bernicia did not follow Oswiu solely because of the blood that flowed in his veins, they followed a great warrior king.

Yet Oswiu had not come here to fight. He bore no byrnie and no weapon.

Beobrand thrust Nægling's grip into Oswiu's hand.

"Back to back," he said. "You take those two."

Beobrand pushed the king behind him so that he faced the men who had slain his guards. Oswiu grunted and Beobrand could sense him dropping into the warrior stance behind him.

Beobrand slid his seax from its leather sheath and faced the three shadowy forms that came towards him. They came on fast. The sounds of combat and Beobrand's shouts would bring defenders to them in moments. These murderers would need to be quick about their work.

"To arms!" bellowed Beobrand, and, without waiting for the men to reach him, he threw himself forward with a roar.

They had not expected him to bring the fight to them and the central figure hesitated momentarily. Ignoring the other two men, trusting to his speed and the iron links of his byrnie, Beobrand batted the middle man's sword away the instant before colliding with him. Dropping his shoulder, Beobrand hit the swordsman hard beneath the sternum. Such was the force of the assault that the man was lifted from his feet and flung backward. He went down like a man hit by a charging bull. Beobrand did not slow. A weak blow from one of the others scratched against his ironclad back, but the sword's blade did no damage.

As the man before him crashed to the earth, Beobrand allowed his full bulk to land on him, one knee smashing into his midriff. Turning his seax blade downward, Beobrand hammered it into the man's eye, and then, tugging it free of the skull, he rose in a fluid motion and turned on the others.

In the darkness, he could just make out the solid form of the king defending himself against the two attackers. Sparks flew as blades met, but Beobrand could not tell whether the king or either of the men had been injured.

A blade came singing towards his face and he had no more time to look to the king. With the speed that had made him famed throughout the kingdoms of Albion, Beobrand dodged backward, allowing the flashing blade to pass a finger's length from his face. Lashing out with his left half-hand, Beobrand grasped the wrist of the blade-wielder. Off-balance, the man staggered forward and Beobrand pulled him on, snapping his forehead into the man's nose with savage force. Cartilage crunched and the man sagged. Dropping his seax, Beobrand grabbed the man's kirtle, holding him upright and spinning him into the path of the third attacker. The scything sword strike that had been meant for Beobrand hacked into the neck of the dazed man. Fresh blood gushed, adding a black torrent to the trickle that flowed from his smashed nose.

Beobrand shoved the now dying man at the remaining swordsman. The attacker retreated with a muffled curse. Beobrand did not understand the man's words, but something in them sparked a memory of another such night-time attack.

But there was no time to dwell on that. Behind the man, Beobrand could see that Oswiu had dispatched one of his assailants and was battling furiously with the other man. In the distance, men were shouting. The dogs in the hall were barking and light poured out into the night as men came from the warmth of the building into the darkness, holding torches aloft. It was only a matter of moments now before the defenders would be upon them and then the last two attackers could not hope to survive.

Clearly coming to the same conclusion, the man before Beobrand roared and leaped forward with renewed vigour. Beobrand snatched up the sword that had fallen from the second man's hand and parried the first wild blow. Sparks glinted in the gloom, lighting momentarily the soot-stained, snarling features of his opponent. With a start, Beobrand realised he recognised the man. It was the Frank who had escaped him in Eoferwic.

The Frankish man spat insults at Beobrand that he could not understand and sent a flurry of blows at him. Beobrand parried the attacks easily. The man was strong and had some skill, but he was no match for Beobrand. The attacker grew ever more frenzied as the sounds of the men from the hall drew nearer.

Beobrand stepped back, deflecting yet another powerful strike that would have taken his head from his shoulders.

Oswiu's voice rang out, breathless and high.

"To me! To me!"

The sounds of fighting there had ceased, allowing Beobrand to focus his attention fully on this last attacker; a man who had attacked him once before and fled. He would not escape again. Beobrand watched him in the dim flickering light that came from the approaching torches. The Frank was swinging his blade in great arcs, his movements predictable. Beobrand was sure that he would be able to disarm the man without striking a killing blow. He would question him and find out how many more killers Vulmar had sent after him.

He was dimly aware of the cries of the men who had reached the king. Voices were raised in dismay and disbelief, but Beobrand could not take his eyes from his furious attacker. The torch light was bright after the cool glimmer of the moon and stars and Beobrand blinked. Men loomed behind his assailant, blades gleaming red from the flames.

Too late, Beobrand saw the raised spear in Cynan's hand.

"Hold!" he cried.

But Cynan either did not hear him in time, or chose to ignore his hlaford. The sharp spear-blade plunged deep into the man's throat, pushing him towards Beobrand with an almost comical expression of surprise on his face. Cynan twisted the spear and tugged it free. The Frank staggered forward, still reaching out with his sword for Beobrand. Beobrand stepped back, swatting the man's blade away from his weakening grasp. He fell to his knees, hand outstretched to Beobrand as if in entreaty. But there was nothing the Cantware thegn could do for him. Blood gurgled, dark and bubbling from his open mouth. He slumped forward, shuddered and then was still.

Beobrand spat onto the earth and cursed. Dead men tell no secrets.

"Lord," said Cynan, "are you well?" He indicated Beobrand's forehead. Beobrand reached up with his mutilated left hand. His head was tender to the touch and his fingers came away dark with blood.

"Not my blood," he said.

A new sound that he had not noticed before reached him then. A man, weeping with grief. For a chilling instant of mixed emotions, Beobrand thought that perhaps Oswiu had been slain in the attack.

Striding forward, he shouldered the gathered men aside. Ethelwin nodded to him in grim-faced greeting before commencing to bark orders for the men to search the trees and to be extra vigilant. This might have been a diversion, to distract from a larger assault. Men dashed off into the night and their shouts could be heard echoing in the woods around Hunwald's hall. If there were any more enemies out there, they would certainly hear the Bernicians coming.

The wails of grief continued and Beobrand moved closer to where Oswiu had fought the two attackers. For a moment, the shapes sprawled on the ground confused him. There were four bodies here, not the two that Beobrand had expected. Grindan moved close, holding aloft a burning brand, and the shadowy forms suddenly made sense. Here were the corpses of two men with faces daubed black with soot. Of the other two bodies, one was in fact alive.

It was the king, on his knees, tears tracing lines of anguish down his cheeks. On his lap he cradled the head of the fourth figure. This man's belly was huge, his arms flabby. The face was pallid, eyes wide and unseeing. The dead man's jowls were heavy slabs of flesh, pulling his lips down into a scowl in death.

"Fordraed, my old friend," Oswiu said, stroking the fat man's hair. "I am sorry. I should not have doubted you. You have been true to your oath."

Beobrand shook his head, unsure how this had come to pass. Beside one of the dead attackers, the light from Grindan's torch glimmered on Nægling's blood-smeared blade. Beobrand bent down and wiped the sword on the corpse's cloak. He examined the metal in the flickering flame-light before sliding it back into its fur-lined scabbard.

Oswiu was whispering to Fordraed words that Beobrand could not make out. Beobrand shivered. The king's grief was unnerving. Turning away from Oswiu's pain, Beobrand went in search of his fallen seax.

Chapter 39

Dawn came, bright and fresh, bejewelling the land about Hunwald's hall with glistening dew. The rising sun painted the clouds in the west the hue of a salmon's flesh. A light wind rustled the leaves of the ash and oak trees. The beck burbled over the smooth stones of its bed and the birds sang their chorus loudly in the forest, welcoming the coming of a warm summer's day.

Beobrand stepped out of the hall and rubbed his eyes. He had not slept and tiredness tugged at his eyelids.

In the open area of ground between Hunwald's buildings, several men were mounted and ready to ride. A cart, yoked to a pair of oxen, stood ready beside the horsemen. When he saw Beobrand, one of the riders moved his mount close. It was Cynan. In his left hand he held Sceadugenga's reins. The stallion was saddled and ready.

"Are we sure about this?" Cynan asked, keeping his voice low. "I can see no good coming from it."

Beobrand sighed. He swung himself up onto Sceadugenga's back.

"The king has spoken," he said. "We must do as he has commanded."

He did not wish to converse more on the subject, so he kicked Sceadugenga into a trot. Slowly, the rest of the riders, some half of the contingent that had ridden south from Bebbanburg, followed him. The carter, one of Hunwald's bondsmen, lashed the oxen and with a creaking rumble, the waggon rolled forward.

Like Cynan, Beobrand could see no good coming from this. The night had been filled with death and treachery. Then came Oswiu's grief, which was quickly replaced with a searing anger. The king had become convinced that Oswine had plotted to have him murdered. When they had returned to the hall, Beobrand had sat with him awkwardly for a time, but it soon became apparent that the unusual closeness that there had been between them before the attack had vanished along with any chance there might have been for peace between Bernicia and Deira.

The fire on the hearthstone had burnt down and the thralls, seemingly frightened to approach the grieving king, did not place more logs on the glowing embers.

In the gloom, Oswiu's face was drawn, gaunt and hard. As he sat brooding and sipping a cup of Hunwald's mead, he barely acknowledged Beobrand's presence. Beobrand began to wonder if he had imagined the moments they had spent talking in the darkness. He rose and paced the hall, clenching his fists at his side to control the shaking that always followed a fight. Going to the hearth, he lifted a split log of beechwood and tossed it onto the coals with a shower of sparks. Oswiu, deep in conversation with Ethelwin and Hunwald, muttered and cursed, turning a sharp gaze on Beobrand.

Outside in the darkness, Beobrand could still hear men shouting to one another as they searched for more attackers. He was sure they would find none. To be certain of his fears, he had pulled Halinard close, snatching a guttering torch from his hand and shining its light close to the face of the attacker that Cynan had killed. Halinard's eyes had widened in recognition.

They had gone from one corpse to the next, lowering the flaming torch near their soot-smeared faces. Halinard recognised one more. The other three were unknown to him.

"These two men," he had whispered to Beobrand in his halting Anglisc, "are men of Vulmar."

"You are certain?" Beobrand had asked, gripping his shoulder tightly.

Halinard had nodded.

"I know them."

In the hall, Oswiu's ire had grown, the way a forge fire burns ever hotter as the smith pumps the bellows.

"Oswine believes he can send men to murder me in the night?" he raged. "By God, I was right not to trust him. The man is a serpent!"

Beobrand shook his head.

"Lord king," he said, interrupting Oswiu's tirade. Ethelwin, Hunwald and the king all turned to look at him.

"You have something to say?" asked Oswiu, his tone brittle and curt.

Beobrand swallowed. He knew Oswiu would not wish to hear his words, but he could not remain silent. The fate of two kingdoms might be forged on the fires of the decisions taken this night.

"I do not believe those men were sent by Oswine."

"Nonsense!" cried Oswiu. "He knew we were coming here. He must have planned to kill me at Catrice. Me coming to Hunwald's hall made him change his plans and send his men here." The king had taken a cut to his brow and now the wound began to seep. He reached up and wiped the blood away. For a moment he stared at his red-smeared fingertips. "By the nails of Christ, Oswine will pay dearly for his mistake."

Beobrand's head ached.

"I know not what Oswine's plans are, lord king. But he has always seemed an honourable man to me." Oswiu snorted, but

Beobrand did not stop. He must be heard. "Oswine is not one to skulk in the darkness, to strike with treachery in the night."

"No, he is not brave enough for such things. He sends others to do his killing for him. But he did not count on you, Beobrand, or me." He hesitated and took a shuddering breath. "Or my old friend, Fordraed."

"What do you believe has happened here, Beobrand?" asked Ethelwin.

Beobrand nodded his thanks. The warmaster too could sense that they should find the truth of what had happened.

"My man, Halinard the Frank, recognised two of the men who attacked us."

"Who were they?"

"Vulmar's men."

"Vulmar?" asked Ethelwin. "I know not of this lord."

"Vulmar is a Frank. A lord of Rodomo, in Neustria. I made an enemy of him last year when I took my daughter from his hall."

Ethelwin gazed at him for a time, pondering his words. The warmaster stroked his beard. Slowly, the ghost of a smile came to his lips.

"It is unlike you to make an enemy," he said.

"It matters not who this Vulmar is," snapped Oswiu. "You think you are an important man, Beobrand son of Grimgundi. It has always been thus. But know this, when killers come to murder in the depths of night, it is not for the likes of you. It is the king's blood they want. And who wishes to kill a king but another king? No. They came for me, and it was Oswine's hand that guided them."

"But those men were Franks," said Beobrand, hearing the frustration in his tone. He knew Oswiu would not pay him heed and yet he could not fall silent. "Vulmar has promised a great treasure to the man who slays me."

"By Christ's teeth," shouted Oswiu. "This is not about you!

Fordraed lies dead at the hand of one of those killers. As do two of my most trusted gesithas. If these men were Franks, they came here at the order of Oswine. Of this I am certain."

"But lord," said Beobrand, "consider for a moment that it might not be as you say. Would you truly take us to war over this?"

"It is Oswine, not I, who will take us to war!" Oswiu bellowed, setting Hunwald's hounds barking again. "Now leave us."

Riding now beneath the tall oaks that lined the path, the column of riders trudging solemnly behind, Beobrand shook his head. Perhaps it was best for him that Oswiu did not believe him. If the king thought his beloved Fordraed had been killed in Beobrand's stead, who knew what he might do? The carter's goad slapped against the oxen and the cart trundled up the incline towards the meeting of ways where the path to Hunwald's hall joined Deira Stræt. It was here that Oswiu had ordered them to place the grisly cargo that lolled in the timber bed of the cart.

When they reached their destination, the men dismounted and tied their horses to the trees beside the road. From this point they could see some distance both south and north along Deira Stræt. Beobrand stared south into the morning haze. Far off, too distant for him to make them out clearly, a flock of birds, dark dots against the brilliant sky, took flight. Nearby in the hedges and weeds that grew in a great thicket along the eastern side of the road, dozens of sparrows and finches twittered, flitting in and out of the foliage. Across the wide, cracked and muddy surface of the road, a lone magpie hopped onto a large, moss-covered rock. The bird seemed to stare at the men as they climbed down from their mounts.

There was no sign of Oswine on the road. Of course, Beobrand had tried telling Oswiu that if the Deiran king were indeed guilty of ordering the attack, he would hardly ride to speak with the subject of his plot the following morning. Oswiu had refused to listen, saying that Oswine was bold and brazen.

Hunwald had told them there was a copse of ash close to the road and the sound of axes biting into wood echoed in the warm morning. The young staves from the coppiced trees were stout and straight and would be perfect for what Oswiu had ordered.

"Are you not going to help?"

Beobrand turned to see Heremod standing beside the cart. The bearded warrior scowled at him. Two of Reodstan's men leant into the cart and clumsily pulled out one of the blood-streaked corpses. The head flopped back, and Beobrand saw the death-pallid features beneath the smear of soot that the man had used to conceal himself in the darkness. Beobrand recognised him as one of Vulmar's men.

"I think I did more than my share of the work killing them," Beobrand replied. "It is time now for you to do your part." He left the insult unspoken. Where had Heremod been when his lord was slain? Heremod's face darkened and he turned away, hefting one of the bodies out of the cart with apparent ease. Beobrand knew that Heremod would never forgive himself for Fordraed's death. He had drunk huge amounts of Hunwald's mead and was in a deep sleep when his hlaford, still racked with guilt and worry at the king's treatment of him, had gone in search of Oswiu. Beobrand supposed Fordraed had meant to profess his innocence, to defend his honour and to refute the suspicions that Beobrand had cast on him. Fordraed never spoke another word to the king, but with his actions, leaping to Oswiu's defence, slaying one of his attackers and taking a mortal wound, the fat bastard had cleared his name of any doubt as to his loyalty. But Beobrand saw in Heremod's haggard features and hollow, shadowed eyes that the man blamed himself for his lord's death. The rest of Fordraed's gesithas glowered at Beobrand, their fury clear.

Beobrand walked down the road, away from Heremod and the other men grunting and cursing as they manhandled the corpses from the cart.

"What do you think will happen now, lord?" asked Cynan.

Beobrand took a deep breath. His men had followed him, closing about him protectively, sensing the hatred that oozed from Heremod and the rest of Fordraed's gesithas.

"I think that once they have dangled those corpses for all to see, we shall have an uncomfortable wait for Oswine."

Oswiu had told them to send for him when they spotted Oswine's approach. He had decided he no longer wished to meet with him in the hall. The idea of the two kings facing each other with threescore warriors apiece did not fill Beobrand with confidence of a peaceful outcome. He remembered a similar meeting at Dor. There it had been Oswald and Penda, and it had been Beobrand's lust for vengeance that had almost caused a war. He closed his eyes for a moment, rubbing again at their gritty tiredness. Gods, that had ended badly. Absently, his left hand stroked the handle of the seax hanging from his belt. He recalled how the blade had snagged on Anhaga's ribs, the man's eyes staring at him as he died.

"You think Oswine will come?" Cynan said.

Beobrand opened his eyes and nodded.

"Yes. He had no hand in the attack last night."

"And when he comes?"

Beobrand sighed, staring into the south at where the distant birds still wheeled in the sky, like dark thoughts in a troubled mind.

"We must trust that both kings respect the bough of truce. If they do not, I fear none of us will see Bernicia again."

Behind them, men were sharpening the saplings they had chopped down. Next, they would impale the corpses and then hoist them up, embedding the stakes into the earth. This is what Oswiu had ordered, so that all who travelled past this place would see what happened to those who raised their hands against him.

"You think Oswine will break the sacred pact of truce?"

Beobrand hawked and spat.

"It is not Oswine I am concerned about."

Chapter 40

The sun was past its zenith when the two Northumbrian kings arrived at the meeting of ways near Hunwald's hall. As soon as they had seen the horsemen approaching along Deira Stræt from the south, Beobrand had sent Attor galloping back for Oswiu.

Cynan watched as the Deirans approached. They came on at a trot and would cover the ground quickly, despite the distance. The red and gold banner of Deira fluttered from the long haft of a spear raised above the riders. The sun glittered from burnished metal. The threescore horsemen rode in a tight group, their colourful warrior coats and cloaks, gleaming arm rings and sparkling adornments giving them an air of gaiety and merriment at odds with the sombre expression on their grim faces.

Facing the Deirans on the brow of the hill was a tired group of half their number. The Bernicians had not slept, having spent the night scouring the woods for signs of other assailants. After that they'd had the gruesome task of bringing the bodies of the night-time attackers here and displaying them for the arrival of the king of Deira. Now, the five mottled bodies, stripped of all items of value, appeared to hover, like otherworldly ghouls gazing out over the old Roman road with sightless eyes and gaping, swollen-tongued mouths. They had been impaled on the sharpened stakes the men had cut from the copse, and their feet dangled some way above the grass and nettles that grew beside the road. Soon, Cynan knew, they would become unrecognisable, once the birds and beasts had gnawed at their flesh and corruption had set in. But during the morning, whenever a crow or magpie had landed on the corpses, the men had waved their arms or thrown pebbles, scaring off the birds.

"On your horses," growled Beobrand. He swung up onto Sceadugenga's back and Grindan handed him the bough he had cut from one of the coppiced ash staves.

The Bernicians had separated into distinct groups as they had waited, with Heremod and Fordraed's men sitting away from Beobrand and Reodstan's gesithas. The two bands of men had not conversed, but now Beobrand broke the silence between them. Heremod, his plaited beard quivering as he turned, glowered at Beobrand.

"I do not take orders from you, Beobrand," he said. "You are not my lord."

"I am not," replied Beobrand. "But Oswiu will want us all mounted when Oswine arrives here. The Deirans are all riding. Do you think our king would want us to be lesser than his enemies?"

Heremod glared, but did not reply. Instead, he climbed to his feet and the rest of Fordraed's men did likewise. Soon they had all clambered into their saddles and formed a line across the road, facing the oncoming Deirans. The five corpses on their stakes watched on with vacant empty eyes, a silent, twisted reflection of Penda's blood sacrifices before Bebbanburg.

Cynan sat astride Mierawin on Beobrand's right flank. He watched as Oswine and his comitatus trotted closer. He admired the finery of the warriors' clothes, armour and weapons. These were the greatest men in Oswine's retinue; men of renown and battle-fame. In the front rank he spotted Wulfstan. He wore a red warrior jacket and gold and garnets glinted at his shoulder and on his belt and sword. In his left hand he held aloft a leafy branch of oak that rustled and waved in the breeze. Cynan had seen the man several times before and he had always seemed affable, smiling and jovial, almost comical in his lightness of spirit. But now Cynan understood well why the man was held in such high esteem. This was no light-hearted jester, this was a stern-faced leader and slayer of men.

Cynan looked sidelong at Beobrand with a renewed respect. He had obeyed his hlaford's command to mount up, but it was only now, as the Deirans drew close and their full might became apparent, that he truly appreciated the decision. It seemed natural to Beobrand, but having the men on their horses was clearly better than leaving them on foot. To stand in the road, with shields and spears, and the grisly spectacle of the staked corpses behind them, would have looked like a provocation. Men fought on foot, not from horseback. But at the same time, the horsemen would have felt some superiority garnered from looking down at the Bernicians. And thegns and warriors had the wealth to ride. Ceorls could not afford mounts. By having them mount, Beobrand had at once elevated the Bernicians to the same status as the Deirans, while lessening the threat of their presence.

Cynan thought of Ingwald and the other men he had left back at Bebbanburg. Again he wondered if any would wait for him. If they did, and if he survived this encounter between kings, he must learn to lead with Beobrand's instinctive decisiveness.

When they were still several paces distant, Wulfstan raised his hand. The column halted, dust from their passing hazing the air behind and around them. Oswine scanned the line of Bernicians before him. His handsome face was drawn, his eyes dark-circled. Cynan realised they were not the only ones to be tired. The Deirans had fought for their kingdom and if leading a few men from the fyrd had weighed on Cynan's mind, how draining must it be to have the lives of all the people of a realm on your shoulders?

Oswine's gaze lingered for a moment on the haggard, open-mouthed horror of the faces of the impaled men. Finally, his eyes settled on Beobrand.

"Lord Beobrand," he said. "What is the meaning of this? I was asked to meet Oswiu at Hunwald's hall, and yet you block my path."

"My lord king Oswiu wishes to meet you here and has commanded us to await your coming."

Oswine frowned. The magpie that Cynan had seen several times that morning flapped out of the sky and landed on the matted hair of the central corpse. He recognised the body as the man he had slain with the spear thrust to the neck. The movement of the bird drew the gaze of all those gathered there.

The magpie stared back at them and let out a chattering cry. A scratch of dread ran down Cynan's spine. He straightened himself in the saddle to cover the shiver that had shaken him.

"And who," asked Oswine, with a sombre glance at the staked men, "are these unfortunates?"

Before Beobrand could answer, the sound of a large group of cantering horses reached them. Several of Oswine's retinue dropped their hands onto the pommels of swords or seaxes. They were nervous. Their land had been invaded and now the king of their northern neighbours seemed to have turned against them. The corpses on display had only exacerbated an already delicate situation. Violence was in the air like the stench of a midden. Death could be upon them in moments.

At the same instant both Wulfstan and Beobrand held up their right hands, mirroring each other.

"Easy now," Beobrand shouted out. "That is the sound of Oswiu approaching." He shook the branch in his hand. "We meet under the bough of truce. There will be no bloodshed here today."

Cynan looked at the black of the dried blood on the white skin of the bodies and thought it was too late for such a promise.

Oswine held Beobrand's gaze for a moment, before raising his voice for all to hear.

"We ride under the branch of peace. No man is to draw his weapon. I would hear from Oswiu himself the reason for his actions before we use the branches of truce to light a bone-fire."

With a great commotion, Oswiu, Ethelwin and the remaining Bernician warriors rode out from the wooded path and onto the Roman road with a clatter of hooves and jangle of harness. The men streamed out and jostled for position. Horses stamped and blew. Many whinnied in welcome at the newly arrived animals.

Oswiu, Ethelwin and Hunwald rode along the verge of the road, close beneath the gory emblems, to where Beobrand and Cynan waited. Ethelwin flicked a glance at the corpses and his face pulled into a scowl. Oswiu ignored the bloody totems.

Oswiu and Ethelwin reined in their mounts, but Hunwald continued on until he was close to the king of Deira. There he slid from the saddle and dropped to one knee before Oswine.

"My lord king," he said. "I trust I have done well by you in accepting Oswiu, son of Æthelfrith, ruler of Bernicia, into my hall. I am as ever your oath-sworn man, and I want nothing but peace between our kingdoms, as it has been for generations. You know my wife is of Bernicia, but my loyalty is not split; I am your man, and my sword and life are yours."

"Arise, good Hunwald," said Oswine. "I do not doubt your honour or allegiance. It is as it should be that you show hospitality and honour to my ally and brother."

Hunwald stood. He looked set to respond when Oswiu kicked his horse forward. Beobrand, carrying the bough of truce, followed him without comment. Ethelwin and Cynan joined them a heartbeat later. Wulfstan and a couple of other hard-faced thegns nudged their horses on to stand beside their king. A sharp word from any of them now could beckon death to that joining of paths. Cynan could almost feel Death's wintry breath on his neck.

"You say I am your ally," Oswiu said. "But does not an ally come to his friend's aid in time of need?"

"He does, cousin Oswiu," Oswine said, reminding the king of Bernicia of their kindred through his marriage to Eanflæd. "And I was on my way north to Bebbanburg when my fyrd was attacked by such a host from the lands of Gwynedd and Powys as has not been seen in this land since the battle of Catrice that the Waelisc still sing of. And like that battle long ago, we put them to flight and there was great slaughter."

"While you lingered in Deira," snapped Oswiu, "Bebbanburg burnt!"

Oswine took a deep breath. Colour rose in his cheeks.

"We did not tarry here," he said, his voice clipped and taut as a bowstring. "We fought and shed our blood against the Waelisc horde. There can be no doubt that Penda meant to destroy us both, or at the very least to separate our forces so that he could attack Bebbanburg. The lord of Mercia knows that we are allies, Oswiu, even if you have forgotten."

Sensing its rider's mounting anger, Oswine's horse shook its head and snorted. The king of Deira patted its neck gently, but his gaze did not leave Oswiu's.

"We are not allies, it seems," said Oswiu stubbornly.

Cynan wondered at the king's words. Why did he suddenly feel such hatred towards the king of Deira?

"We are," Oswine replied. "I have forever kept faith with you, brother."

"We are not brothers," said Oswiu.

"Are we not brothers in Christ?"

"Would a brother in Christ seek to slay me in the darkness? Sending his treacherous curs to stab me in the night?"

"What are you speaking of?" Oswine glanced at the bodies on the stakes. "You mean these men? I know nothing of them. They are not mine."

"And yet they are in Deira and they sought me out at the place where I had told you I would be waiting. Are you truly going to deny all knowledge of them, brother?" He filled the last word with venom, so that it sounded like an insult.

Oswine looked at the faces of the dead men and shook his head.

"I would swear on the holy book or the bones of Christ himself, I do not know these men."

"I have seen them before," said Wulfstan suddenly. Both kings started and turned to him, as if they had forgotten they were not alone. Wulfstan peered at the corpses.

"Well, man, speak," said Oswine.

"I do not know their names or from whence they came, but I saw them in the fyrd."

"You are certain?"

Wulfstan nodded.

"They came soon after the messengers went out, but I do not know which lord they served. I remember them because they were always together. They kept themselves apart from the others, but they fought well when it came to the battle. I recall seeing them in the shieldwall. It looked to me as if they had trained together. They were not a rabble, not ceorls with spears, as we so often get sent."

"You say you do not know whom they served?"

"No, lord. I don't remember seeing them with any lord. But they clearly had one, for they each bore blades and byrnies."

Oswine turned to his retinue.

"Do any of you know these men? Do you know their lord?"

Murmurs throughout the gathered men. A few rode forward to look more closely, but all gave the same shake of their head. None knew their names or the man they served. As they each gazed upon the corpses, Oswiu's face grew darker and his impatience and anger could be sensed in the rigidity of his shoulders and the tightness of his jaw.

"Enough of this foolishness," he snapped at last. Several of the horses started and stamped at his shout. "You say these men were amongst the warriors of your fyrd, Oswine. We have all heard this. So they are your men, and they came upon me in the night with naked blades and death in their hearts."

"I do not know them," said Oswine. "None of my men know who they were."

"Enough! They were your men and you sent them to slay me. For too long you have had your covetous eye on my lands, Oswine. But now you have gone too far."

"Oswiu," the king of Deira held his hands with the palms up, "I did not do this thing, and now is not the time to break our alliance. Penda and the Waelisc will make quick work of us if we are not united. Think on it. Perhaps these men were sent by one who wishes to weaken us both. If you were to be killed, Deira would lose an ally and Bernicia would be thrown into chaos at the loss of their king."

"No!" shouted Oswiu, spittle flying from his lips. Again Cynan was shocked at the strength of his loathing towards Oswine. Had it always been there, hidden beneath the surface of the alliance between their kingdoms? "No," Oswiu repeated, his voice calmer now. "From this moment on we are no longer allies. We are foe-men, you and I. Your actions have brought war between our kingdoms, Oswine."

"Cousin," implored Oswine, "do not do this thing. Think!"

"It is done. We will ride from this place in peace, as, unlike you and your treachery, I respect the truce we have between us. But know this, the next time our paths cross, there will be blood." He pointed up to the five bodies that stared down from their perches. "Those will not be the last Deirans I have placed on stakes."

Without awaiting a reaction, Oswiu swung his horse's head around and rode back along the line of Bernicians. Beobrand, Ethelwin and Cynan pushed their horses forward instinctively, to ward off any attack that might be aimed at their king. But none came. Cynan could not believe what he had witnessed. Oswiu must be mad to have thrown away his strongest ally at the time of the kingdom's greatest need. Gods, would they ever be free of war?

A movement caught his eye and he readied himself to pull his blade from its scabbard. But it was not an attack. It was Wulfstan, raising his hands and eyebrows questioningly at Beobrand. The lord of Ubbanford shook his head. The meaning was clear: Beobrand had no idea why Oswiu was acting thus.

Backing Sceadugenga away from the Deirans, Beobrand raised his voice.

"Follow the king," he shouted. "There is nothing more for us here."

The Deirans watched grim-faced and angry as the Bernicians wheeled their mounts around and rode after their king.

Chapter 41

They returned to Hunwald's hall, riding in silence back through the dappled sunlight beneath the trees. Ethelwin ordered the men to stand guard in case Oswine decided they were no longer under the protection of truce. Dismounting before the hall, Beobrand nodded to his gesithas to join the others in watching the road.

"I do not think we will remain here for long," he said to Cynan in a low voice. "Keep the men close and your eyes and ears open."

He handed Sceadugenga's reins to Cynan and followed Oswiu, Ethelwin and Reodstan into the shadowed interior of the building. After the warm sunshine of the afternoon, filled with the chirping of birds, the whisper of wind in the high ash and oak, the burble of the brook and the clatter of hooves and chatter of conversations, the hall seemed dark and strangely quiet. The smell of ash, roasted meat and spilt ale lingered in the still air. As the king and thegns entered, Frythegith hurried forward from the rear of the hall to greet them. Her eyes flicked to her brother, who offered her a small nod.

"Hunwald is well. He is with Oswine."

The lady bowed her head.

"I forget myself," she said, standing tall once more. "Waes hael once more, lord king."

Two thralls leapt up from where they had been waiting at the rear of the hall.

"Bring mead," she said. "And meat."

The slaves rushed to bring food and drink. The newly arrived men sank onto a bench at the side of the room. Frythegith remained standing awkwardly before them.

They sat in silence for a moment, each wondering what would happen now. Beobrand wanted to scream at Oswiu, to yell that the man was a fool to plunge them into yet another war. Instead, he chewed his lower lip and kept his thoughts to himself. If he had learnt anything these past years it was that shouting your anger was not always the best way to make your opinion known. Also, when a king had made a decision, he would not change it because one of his thegns told him it was a mistake. Kings were perhaps the most stubborn of all men, convinced of their own worth beyond all reason.

The thralls returned with a pitcher of mead and cups. Outside, Beobrand could hear Cynan shouting at the men, giving orders. He smiled thinly to himself. The young Waelisc had learnt much since he had taken him in. Beobrand felt a glow of pride in seeing the man grow beyond a good swordsman and rider into a leader of men. He wished Acennan could have lived to see it.

Frythegith filled their cups.

Oswiu stood up abruptly, sending the lady of the hall and the thralls away with a flick of his hand. He glowered at Beobrand.

"Is something funny?"

Beobrand realised he had still been smiling at the thought of Cynan and how proud Acennan would have been of him. He met Oswiu's gaze, changing his smirk for a grave scowl.

"No, lord," he said. "I find nothing to be amused by."

Oswiu frowned.

"You have something you would like to say to me?" he said, his tone as sharp and as deadly as a stake of ash wood.

For an instant, Beobrand considered telling the king exactly what he thought of his decisions, but he shook his head.

"You are my lord and king," he said. "It is not for me to question you."

Oswiu snorted.

"No, it is not. But I can see the judgement on your face as plain as if you had shouted it." He took a swig of mead. "You think me a fool."

Beobrand sighed. It seemed Oswiu would have him speak. He hesitated, picking his words carefully.

"I think that Bernicia can scarce afford a war with Deira. Oswine does not want it. Perhaps it would be best to reconsider, lord."

"What do you know of what Oswine wants?" snapped Oswiu. "If he did not want war with me, he should not have sent murderers to take my life."

Beobrand regretted having spoken, but now there was no way out of this.

"Oswine says he did not send the men. And I have told you, the killers were sent by Vulmar to murder me. Not you, lord king."

Oswiu looked up at the soot-draped rafters in exasperation.

"By Christ's teeth, man," he shouted, "you are nobody! Those men came to slay a king, not a lowly thegn."

Beobrand took a deep breath. He could feel his anger straining at its fetters within him. He gripped his cup tightly and took a long draught, vowing to himself to remain silent in future. No good could come from talking to Oswiu.

Perhaps sensing Beobrand's mounting rage, Ethelwin stood and joined Oswiu in his nervous pacing.

"None of that matters now, lord," he said. "We cannot stay here. We must return to Bebbanburg. There we can begin to make preparations for the coming war." Ethelwin's expression was grim. Beobrand knew there was nothing to be gained from arguing further with Oswiu. Nothing would dissuade the king, so they would need to ready themselves for more fighting, more death.

Shouts from outside. The door to the hall swung open. Cynan was there, shadowed against the golden late afternoon brightness.

"Lord Hunwald has returned," he said.

Moments later, Hunwald strode into the hall. He approached Oswiu and dropped to one knee before him.

"Lord king," he said, "I pray to the Almighty in Heaven that you will still consider me a friend of yours and of Bernicia."

Oswiu took hold of the man's shoulders and pulled him to his feet.

"Of course, man," he said. "I understand that you have given your oath to Oswine. And a man's oath is all, is it not, Beobrand?"

Beobrand frowned, and Oswiu laughed.

"Tell me, Hunwald," he said, "what will Oswine do now?"

"I cannot say for sure," Hunwald said, his nervousness making his words jump and start like fat on a griddle. "But he does not wish to fight the might of Bernicia. His thegns and ealdormen are angry at your words, but have little appetite for battle after facing the Waelisc with such losses."

Oswiu nodded.

"Good, good."

Beobrand watched the two men talking. What game was Oswiu playing? And where did Hunwald fit into it? What piece was this Deiran lord on the great tafl board of kings?

"So he will hold to the truce?" Oswiu asked.

"I believe so, lord king," Hunwald replied. "He will let you ride from here in peace."

"Then we should leave before he changes his mind," growled

Reodstan, his face even redder than usual. Beobrand met his gaze and could see that the man, like him, wanted to be far from this place. Perhaps he too was biting his tongue to keep from shouting out his dismay at Oswiu's actions.

"We will rest one more night here in your fine hall," Oswiu said to Hunwald.

Hunwald was pale, whether from the fear that he was harbouring his oath-sworn king's enemy, or the thought of having to provide food and drink again for sixty hungry men, Beobrand could not tell. Perhaps he was unnerved and anxious about both things.

After the briefest hesitation, Hunwald clapped his hands. Frythegith came from the shadows at the rear of the hall.

"Husband?" she said, bowing before them. "I give you joy at your return."

"See that food and drink is prepared for our guests."

The woman's face was impassive as she bowed once more and bustled away, giving orders to the thralls and servants.

"You have a good woman there, Hunwald," said Oswiu. "I thank you both for your hospitality." He clasped Hunwald's shoulder. "I will not forget it."

The king said no more, but the implication was clear: one day, he would repay Hunwald for his aid.

"Thank you, lord," Hunwald stammered. "I just pray that tonight will be less eventful than yestereve."

Oswiu drained the contents of his cup.

"I too pray that we should get some rest this night." He held out his cup, and after a signal from Hunwald, one of the thralls scurried over and refilled it. "But such a thing cannot go unpunished."

A scratch of unease prickled the back of Beobrand's neck. Was death to the would-be killers and a war with Deira not punishment enough?

As if he could imagine Beobrand's thoughts, Oswiu turned his attention to the Cantware thegn.

"God demands an eye for an eye. A tooth for a tooth."

"We killed the men who attacked us," Beobrand said. "That is five teeth for one."

"Those men were nithings. They were not lords, not men of worth, with halls and thralls of their own. Even their king did not know of their names. No. Their deaths are nothing when compared against the killing of my trusted servant, Fordraed."

Beobrand bit back his retort that the five men might well have weighed the same as the fat thegn. He fought to keep his expression flat. Now was not the time for laughter and jests.

Oswiu paced the length of the hall, clearly pondering his next words. Beobrand could sense they would bring further misery on them all.

He was right.

"Oswine must be made to suffer as I have," Oswiu said at last.

"But lord," Ethelwin said, his tone imploring, "we cannot send men to attack Oswine. Such a thing would be madness. Without honour." Beobrand was glad that the warmaster had spoken out. Oswiu was not inclined to listen to such criticism from Beobrand.

Oswiu swung on Ethelwin.

"You think me mad, do you? A man without honour, you say!"

"No, lord king," replied Ethelwin. "I meant no disrespect. But to do this thing…" His voice trailed off. He did not know how to respond without further angering the king.

"I am no fool, warmaster," said the king. "And I am not moon-touched. You should know this much of me, old friend. I do not mean to send men against Oswine. I will meet him in battle in the end." Beobrand noted that Oswiu had not mentioned being a man of honour.

"I am sorry for my words, lord king," said Ethelwin. "I should not have doubted you."

He patted Ethelwin's arm, clearly forgiving him for his rash outburst.

"We are all tired," Oswiu said, with a magnanimous wave of his hand. "It is already forgotten. But the killing of Fordraed will never be forgotten and I would have Oswine remember it as clearly as I will." He spun to face Beobrand. "When we leave here tomorrow, you will not ride with us back to Bernicia directly, lord Beobrand."

Beobrand's heart sank. All he wanted was to return to Ubbanford, to be far from this king and his plots and intrigues.

"Where am I to go, lord?" he asked, keeping his tone devoid of the emotions that roiled within him.

"You are to take your gesithas, and Fordraed's sworn men, who will no doubt want vengeance for their lord's murder, and you are to ride to Ediscum."

"And what would you have us do when we reach Ediscum?" Beobrand said. A cold emptiness was creeping within him. He was sure he knew what the king would ask of him.

"When we spoke in the night, you told me I had your oath; that your sword was mine."

"Of course, lord king."

"I would put your sword to good use. You are to ride to Ediscum and there, you will kill the thegn and master of that hall. He is dear to Oswine, as Fordraed was dear to me."

Beobrand clenched the muscles in his jaw. He was no murderer, to steal the life from a man for no reason. Whoever this thegn was, he was no enemy of Beobrand's, nor of Oswiu's, as far as he could tell. There was no honour in such killing, no battle-glory to be sung of by scops in mead halls. A man who did such a thing would be forever deemed a craven and a nithing.

Sensing his wavering, Oswiu said in a low voice, "When we

return to Bebbanburg, I will inform Octa that you are well. That I have sent you on an important quest. The boy will be so proud of his father."

Beobrand stared at Oswiu. The king did not need to voice the threat to his son. Was this the same man who had told him of his doubts and weaknesses just the night before? Was it because of that very openness that now he sought to send Beobrand to do this terrible task?

"I have your oath, do I not?" asked Oswiu, staring into Beobrand's icy eyes.

"I am your man," Beobrand said. His voice sounded strangled to his own ears, as if his throat was closing up.

"Good!" said Oswiu. "Tomorrow you will ride to Ediscum and I want to hear tales of how you killed the lord of the hall while his wife and family looked on."

"I am a warrior, lord king," said Beobrand, his voice as hard and sharp as flint knappings. "I do not wage war on women and children. I will fight this man, and kill him if you so command, but I will not hurt his family."

For a long moment, they stared at each other. The hall was silent as the rest of the men there watched this battle of wills. At last, Oswiu looked away and laughed.

"Of course, brave Beobrand," he said. "Everybody knows you have no stomach for such things."

"I do not have the stomach or desire to harm those weaker than I," he said, his voice cold. "I have given my word to my gesithas that we will never raise weapons on those who cannot defend themselves."

Oswiu nodded impatiently.

"Yes, yes. I do not ask that you break your word. Go to Ediscum, call out the thegn and kill him. That is all I ask."

A sharp splinter of doubt pricked at the nape of Beobrand's neck.

"Who is the thegn that resides at Ediscum?" he asked. "Whose hall is it?"

"Why, I thought you knew," replied Oswiu. "It is the hall of that smug bastard, Wulfstan. I have long wished to see that smirking grin wiped from his face."

Chapter 42

Beobrand had not thought he would be able to sleep, such was the storm of thoughts that whirled in his mind. But the moment he wrapped himself in his cloak and lay down, the respite of slumber washed over him as quickly as if he had fallen into a dark, tranquil lake. His body, exhausted from the lack of sleep the previous night, the exertion from the fight and the trials of the day, needed rest, and his worries and concerns could not keep sleep at bay.

Beircheart shook him awake before dawn.

For a moment, Beobrand did not know where he was. The hall was filled with the shadowy forms of men. Many snored, the noise loud and intrusive. He wished to be back in the still darkness of sleep. Despite his fears before sleeping, he did not recall any dreams. For a moment he was thankful that the gods had not sent him nightmares of the dead to haunt him in the night, but then, with a sickening jolt, he remembered what it was he was being sent to do.

Oswiu had trapped Beobrand between two oaths. He could not do that which his king ordered without betraying the promise made to Wulfstan in the dark in Eoferwic when the Deiran had saved his life.

Beobrand took Beircheart's proffered hand and allowed the gesith to pull him to his feet.

"Are the horses ready?" Beobrand asked, his voice a croaky rasp in the stale air of the hall.

"Yes, lord. Everything is as you commanded."

He had told them to be ready to leave before the king and his retinue. Beobrand could not face the thought of conversing with Oswiu again. The path before him now was clear and he knew that the king had enjoyed seeing him squirm the night before.

For a brief hopeful time, Beobrand had believed that Wulfstan would not be at his hall in Ediscum. After all, he was with Oswine. Surely with the possibility of battle the king would be loath to lose one of his most trusted men. Beobrand had told Oswiu he would not wage war on the man's kin and so, if Wulfstan were not there, they could return to Bernicia without shedding any innocent blood. Yet even as he had clung to this thought, Oswiu had called out to him that he should not be concerned that the thegn might not be at home. Gods, it was as if the man could see into his very mind, thought Beobrand. It seemed that before Hunwald had returned, Wulfstan had pleaded with Oswine to allow him to go to his hall. His wife had been in her confinement and word had come to him of the birth of his first son. Having three daughters, he had been overjoyed at the tidings of the birth of a male heir. Oswine had granted his wish and even while Hunwald was with them on Deira Stræt, Wulfstan and his gesithas had ridden off, homeward bound. These tidings had snuffed out Beobrand's hopes of a simple solution to his problem. Oswiu had grinned to see him so conflicted.

Beobrand followed Beircheart out of the hall, stepping carefully over the slumbering occupants. He did not wish to see the king before he left. He would not give Oswiu the satisfaction of seeing him further humiliated.

Outside, the air was cool and fresh. The horses, shadows in the grey pre-dawn light, were lined up in the yard. Halinard, standing by the animals, handed Beobrand a hunk of bread and a cup. Beobrand sniffed the contents of the cup. Water. Suddenly aware of being terribly thirsty, he drank it down in two massive gulps. He took a bite of the bread. It was hard and chewy, but tasty enough. He wished he had kept the water to soften it.

Nodding his thanks, he made his way to the horses. Eadgard was there, waiting with his byrnie. Beobrand held the bread in his teeth and the massive axe-man helped him to shrug into the iron shirt. His brother, Grindan, handed Beobrand his sword-belt, which he strapped on, cinching it tight to take some of the byrnie's heft. He hoped they might have no need for armour and weapons, but they rode through Deira, which was now enemy territory.

None of the men spoke above a whisper and as Beobrand swung up onto Sceadugenga's back, he thought his plan might work. Then a loud voice cut the early morning stillness and he knew that chance had fled.

"Leaving without us?" said Heremod, striding out of the hall. "Do not forget that it was my lord who was slain. Lord Fordraed's sworn men will have their revenge. It is our blood-price to take, not yours."

"It was I whom Oswiu commanded to ride to Ediscum. It is my task."

"Did he not tell you to take us with you?"

Beobrand sighed, his breath steaming momentarily in the cool air. Any hope of reaching Wulfstan without Fordraed's men had fled as quickly as the dew would disappear with the heat of the rising sun.

"Well, if you are coming, gather your gear and follow us. You know the way."

And with that, he kicked his heels into Sceadugenga's ribs. The stallion surged away from the hall, carrying Beobrand at an easy canter into the blackness of the path beneath the oak trees. Moments later, his gesithas were all mounted and following in his wake.

Heremod shouted angrily, his voice echoing in the dawn gloom. Beobrand frowned. It was a small victory. Fordraed's men would be with them soon enough. It would make things even more difficult.

A rider galloped up close. In the darkness beneath the trees Beobrand could just make out Beircheart's savage grin flashing from his dark beard.

"Heremod isn't happy."

"That is none of my concern," Beobrand replied. They rode on for a moment, the only sounds the thrum of hooves on the packed earth of the path.

"And Cynan?" Beobrand asked, shouting over the din of the horses. When Heremod and the rest of Fordraed's gesithas reached them, they would not be able to speak freely.

"He has ridden ahead to scout the way, as you asked."

Beobrand nodded. Realising the gesith could not see him in the darkness, he called out, "Good. You have done well."

When Beircheart had discovered Fordraed's death, he had struggled not to laugh out loud. Beobrand had believed he was the only one to know of Beircheart's hatred for the thegn and his feelings for Edlyn, but when Heremod had learnt of his hlaford's death, he had scanned the faces of the warriors gathered around the king. His gaze had settled on Beircheart. The young man had not managed to conceal his grin and Heremod had taken a step forward, his hand on the hilt of his sword and murder in his eyes.

"You might well smirk, Beircheart," he said. "You are happy at my lord's death, no doubt."

Beobrand stepped between them.

"He means nothing by it, Heremod. We all mourn your loss," he'd lied.

Since then, the two groups of warriors, Beobrand's and Fordraed's, under Heremod's leadership, had avoided each other.

Beobrand had asked Beircheart about Heremod's reaction, but Beircheart had simply shrugged.

"He knows that none of us could abide Fordraed. He is merely angry at his choice of lord."

They rode on without speaking, Beobrand brooding about what would occur when they reached Ediscum. Wulfstan was a good man. He had saved Beobrand's life and in turn Beobrand had given his word that he would return the honour if he could. Now was his time to keep that promise, but he could not simply ride away, turning his back on his king's command. He thought of Octa, smiling and content in the retinue of the atheling, Alhfrith. Would Oswiu truly do him harm if Beobrand disobeyed him? Unbidden, the image of Eowa, trembling in a wind-shaken storehouse in far-off Din Eidyn, came to him. Beobrand would never forget the glee with which Oswiu had struck the atheling of Mercia and, when he had beaten him until he was blood-soaked and moaning, how he had pulled out a sharp blade and cut his face so that he would ever bear the scars, should the memories fade.

Beobrand's face was set into a grim scowl when they reached the Roman road. It was dawn now, and the first glimmers of light limned the five corpses that stared down in accusation from their stakes above the road. They were a stark reminder of Oswiu's reprisals. No, there could be little doubt that Oswiu would make good on any threats.

And so they rode towards Ediscum.

The sun peeked above the forest in the east, bathing the land in a sudden warm glow. There were no clouds in the sky. It would be another fine day.

Beobrand hawked and spat into the weeds beside the road.

Yes, another fine day that would be besmirched with blood and killing.

And broken oaths.

He slowed Sceadugenga to a walk. Heremod would catch up to them soon enough anyway, unless they pushed the horses so hard that the beasts would be dying when they reached their destination.

In conversation the night before, they had calculated that they would reach Wulfstan's hall mid-afternoon. Beobrand was in no rush.

They rode north towards the River Wiur. There, Hunwald had told them, they would find a track to the west. That would lead them most of the way to Ediscum.

The sun was high in the sky, its bright heat making the men sweat beneath their byrnies, when Heremod and the rest of Fordraed's men, ten in all, caught up with them. Heremod was clearly furious, but rather than launch into an angry onslaught at Beobrand, he chose to ride alongside the men of Ubbanford in sullen silence. It was not until they halted beside the Wiur to rest, eat some of the food they had brought from Hunwald's hall and to refill their flasks and waterskins, that Heremod finally spoke.

"If you were hoping not to fulfil our lord king's orders," he said, fixing Beobrand with a baleful stare, "know that I will. I will take the blood-price for Fordraed."

"I do not doubt your intentions," said Beobrand. "And I do not wish to ignore Oswiu's commands."

Heremod glowered at him. His forehead was beaded with sweat and his skin pallid. This was a man who would rather be drinking horns of mead in a hall than riding under the heat of a summer sun.

The sudden thump of approaching hooves made them all leap to their feet. Swords slid from scabbards, spears were lifted from the ground and held out threateningly in the direction of the oncoming rider. The men were nervous, on edge.

The path to the west was partially obscured by a great yew tree and a thicket of bramble. A horse and rider cantered out from behind the vegetation at an easy lope. It was Cynan, sitting effortlessly on his bay mare's back as if he had only been out riding for a few moments instead of since long before sunrise.

The Waelisc warrior reined in before Beobrand. Attor stepped close and handed him an open waterskin. Cynan swilled water in his mouth to clear it of dust, spat and then drank deeply.

"What news?" asked Beobrand.

"The road ahead is clear," replied Cynan.

"Good," said Beobrand.

"How far to Ediscum?"

Cynan thought for a moment.

"Maybe as far as from Ubbanford to Berewic. Not far."

"Mount up, men," Beobrand shouted. "We will soon be at Wulfstan's hall. And remember, and I will not repeat this," he looked pointedly at Heremod and the men he had brought with him, "we will not make war on women or children. Any man who raises a hand against the innocent will make an enemy of me. And believe me, you do not want me as your enemy."

He swung up onto Sceadugenga's back and waited for the others to mount their steeds. Heremod, riding a broad-backed white mare, kicked his horse next to Beobrand.

"I do not like this," he said, glowering at Cynan.

Beobrand chose to misunderstand him.

"I do not like this either, but it is what we have been commanded to do. You know that."

"I mean your Waelisc man," Heremod growled.

"Lots of folk do not like Cynan," Beobrand replied lightly. "And not merely because he is Waelisc. There is just something about him that annoys."

"Enough of this nonsense," barked Heremod, colour rising in his cheeks. "You know full well of what I speak." When Beobrand did not reply, Heremod continued. "Your man, Cynan. Coming from the west."

"He was scouting ahead. We are in enemy land now. We must take care."

"You sent him ahead to warn Wulfstan, did you not?" asked Heremod.

"I did not," Beobrand said.

"If you are lying, I swear on Christ's bones and Woden's one eye that it will be your blood I will take in payment for Fordraed's. He always hated you, it would be fitting for me to send you into the afterlife to serve him as his thrall. He would like that."

Beobrand turned in his saddle and stared at Heremod. His blue eyes burnt cold in the summer sunlight.

"Are you a fool, Heremod?" he asked.

"What?" blustered Heremod. "Why, you—"

"I asked if you were a fool," answered Beobrand, his tone brittle and freezing, like shattered ice. "Or perhaps you have been drinking more than water. Is your mind addled?"

"My flask is filled with water from the river and I am no fool, you bastard."

"Then you must be braver than I thought, for only the bravest of men, fools or drunks threaten me. And none have lived to speak of it for long."

Beobrand kicked Sceadugenga into a canter, leaving Heremod behind. Heremod swallowed, frowning after him.

Beobrand rode at the head of the column as the sun began to dip into the west. The path rolled out ahead of him, leading them ever onwards towards Wulfstan's hall. Towards lies and broken oaths.

And towards death.

For he was sure now that the day would end with hot blood soaking into the land at Ediscum. What Beobrand was not certain of was whose blood would flow and who would live to see the darkness of night.

Chapter 43

The path was well-travelled. For the large part the ground was hard packed earth, firm underfoot. There were some patches of stubborn mud, where the land dipped and trees overshadowed the trail, but these were few. Cynan had ridden this way twice already, so he warned them where it was best to skirt the path. If they had been travelling in winter or spring they would not have made such good progress. With heavy rains the path would become a quagmire and only the bravest or most foolhardy traveller would risk it. But winter was far away. The sun shone warm in the sky above them, and the horses' hooves clacked and clopped against the dry earth as loudly as if it were stone.

Shortly after they had ridden off from where the men had rested by the Wiur, Cynan had moved alongside Beobrand. They had not spoken, but a look had said all that was needed.

It was done. The message had been given, Beobrand's oath to Wulfstan fulfilled.

Cynan was pleased. He liked Wulfstan. The thegn had recognised him when he had galloped up to his hall that morning. Striding out into the sunlight, he had invited Cynan in to drink and eat. Cynan was surprised at the man's demeanour: he smiled broadly and welcomed Cynan as an honoured guest. It seemed that the war between their kingdoms was still just a matter of words between kings.

Even when Cynan had imparted his grave tidings, Wulfstan's smile had not left his lips.

"Do you hear that, men?" he shouted out to the gesithas who were lounging in the hall. "My friend, Beobrand, has been sent to kill me!" He laughed, but his warriors did not smile. Neither did his wife. She approached them, bowing in greeting to Cynan. She was broad-hipped and full-breasted. In her arms she clutched their newborn son, swaddled in a linen cloth. The babe's pink face glowed with rude health and his intelligent eyes, so like his mother's, darted about, watching everything, missing nothing. The lady's round, comely face was full of concern.

"What dark news is this, my husband?" she asked, frowning.

"Never fear, my love," replied Wulfstan with a grin. "The lord Beobrand clearly does not mean to carry out his king's wishes, or else he would not have sent brave Cynan here."

"Beobrand does not wish you ill, lord," said Cynan. "He counts you as a true friend. But he is oath-sworn to Oswiu. He cannot ignore the word of his king." He hesitated, unsure how much to say. "He promised you that one day he hoped he would be able to repay you for saving his life in Eoferwic. That time has now come. He has sent me to warn you of his orders, but know this: he is riding behind me. You should not be here when he arrives."

At last, Wulfstan had grown serious. He looked down at the tiny bundle in his wife's arms. Reaching out, he stroked a finger down her cheek.

"It seems a man can never celebrate anything for too long. I had hoped to spend time resting in my hall with my family. Alas, I fear such is not to be." He sighed. "Give Beobrand my thanks. His debt, such as ever it was, is repaid."

Cynan knew something was wrong the moment they reached the brow of the hill that overlooked Wulfstan's hall. Smoke still drifted lazily from the golden thatch of the building. The doors were wide open. A half-dozen horses were penned in a small paddock near the stables. This was not a place abandoned by its inhabitants.

Cynan had been riding some way ahead of the others, now he paused on the summit of the hill, waiting for Beobrand to join him. Beobrand was soon at his side and for a moment they were silent, both peering down into the valley, the westering sun lending the lush grass, the trees and bushes and the timbers of the buildings, a lustrous glow. Beobrand turned to Cynan, a question clear on his face. Before Cynan could reply, Heremod and the others reached them.

For a time they all gazed down at the cluster of buildings.

"Perhaps I was wrong to judge you, Beobrand," Heremod said, tone gruff and grudging. "It seems Wulfstan is at home."

Beobrand said nothing. With a kick of his heels, he sent Sceadugenga down the slope. Cynan rode beside him, his mind in turmoil. What had Wulfstan done? Why would he remain in his hall when he knew men were riding to kill him? Cynan scanned the area below them, looking for any sign of deception or ambush. He saw none.

They rode slowly down the hill in silence. The air was warm and still. There was a quiet tension in the afternoon, like the oppressive crackle in the air before a thunderstorm. And yet the sky was empty of clouds. But every man could sense it. Something was about to happen. They passed the paddock and the horses there nickered in greeting to the Bernicians' mounts.

The path narrowed between two large oaks, like pillars, or a doorway. The trees were in turn flanked by a dense thicket of brambles. Beyond, the track opened out into a yard before the hall. The doors to the hall had been flung wide and the shadowed darkness inside would have beckoned to most weary travellers, cool and inviting. To the Bernicians, riding with thoughts of violence ringing in their minds, the gloom of the hall seemed forbidding; a place of danger for the unsuspecting.

Still the steading was silent and still. Cynan began to wonder whether Wulfstan had in fact left, for some reason deciding to leave half a dozen horses behind, his hearth burning and his hall open. Before the foolishness of these thoughts could fully register, a dozen men poured out of the dark mouth of the building.

They ran as fast as they were able, encumbered as they were with byrnies, shields, helms, spears and swords. The lowering sun reflected off their polished metal with a brilliance that made Cynan and the Bernicians squint.

Beside him, Beobrand tensed and Cynan knew he was considering spurring his stallion forward, to pass the narrow throat of the path before Wulfstan's men reached it. Cynan readied himself to follow his lord, but he could see they would never all manage to pass through the gap between the oaks in time. Those who did manage to reach the yard beyond would be left open to attack from the spear-carrying Deirans. A heartbeat later, clearly having come to the same conclusion as Cynan, Beobrand hauled on his reins and, swinging his leg over his horse's back, he slid to the ground. Cynan did the same, pulling his sword from its scabbard as he landed. Beobrand had been right to halt and dismount.

Cynan knew then that the Deirans did not wish to fight. They could have hidden behind the trees and bushes at the edge of the path and ambushed the riders as they passed into the yard. Instead, they had awaited them in the cool shadows of the hall, before blocking the entrance.

The Bernicians were hastily dismounting, unslinging shields from where they hung on their backs, placing helms on their heads. Before them, Wulfstan and his gesithas quickly formed a shieldwall. No command was shouted and the Deirans did not speak. These were well-trained warriors. A fight with such men would be bloody; the outcome uncertain.

As Cynan watched with admiration as the Deirans formed into ranks of overlapping shields, bristling with spears, so his black-shielded brothers silently joined him and Beobrand, effortlessly taking up their positions to either side. In moments, where the afternoon of the steading had been quiet and empty, but humming somehow with the hidden energy of an impending storm, now it was filled with armed men, staring grimly at each other over the serried ranks of their linden boards.

Lightning had struck from an empty sky.

What storm would follow was yet to be seen.

Wulfstan, resplendent in a great helm and burnished iron-knit shirt that hung to his knees, stepped from the ranks of Deirans who blocked the path.

"You are well come to my hall, Beobrand," he said. "Though you seem overdressed, if you have come to give me joy on the birth of my son." His tone was light and jovial. He was smiling.

"I give you joy, Wulfstan," replied Beobrand. "And I would that you could enjoy your son's company for many years to come."

"I would like that too," Wulfstan said. "Why don't you put up your blades and come and share mead with me inside?"

"You know I cannot do that, Wulfstan," Beobrand said, a heavy sadness in his voice. He stared at Wulfstan for a long while, then shook his head. "Why did you remain? You could be safely away from here."

Wulfstan nodded, his smile fading.

"Indeed, I could. And I thank you for your message. You gave me time to see my family safely away."

"I would never have harmed your kin," said Beobrand. "It is not my way. And I wished to repay my debt to you."

Wulfstan met his gaze, his expression sombre now.

"And you have, Beobrand. For that I thank you. But I could not ride from my hall like a nithing at the approach of an enemy. What would you have done? Would you have abandoned your home to escape danger?"

Beobrand shook his head.

"I do not wish to fight you or your men."

"You are welcome to ride peacefully from this place," replied Wulfstan. "I have no disagreement with you or yours."

For a moment the two leaders stared at each other, weighing up the options open to them.

"Perhaps we could have a drink and talk things over," Wulfstan said at last. "Mayhap we can avoid any undue foolishness here. I am sure there is a way we can all leave here with our honour and our lives."

"And our oaths?" asked Beobrand, an edge of desperate hope in his voice.

"No!" yelled Heremod, shattering the calm that the two leaders had woven over the men. "We will only leave here when we have claimed the blood-price for my lord." The burly warrior, his plaited beard quivering with his rage, glared at Beobrand. "There will be no parley with Wulfstan, you treacherous cur," he snarled. "I knew it! I knew you had warned him of our coming." Heremod's face was crimson. He shook with the force of his outrage. "Well, I care not if I must add your blood to that of the Deiran."

Beobrand grew very still. Slowly, he shifted his weight, turning his body and shield towards Heremod. Without a command, the Black Shields shuffled quickly into a new formation around their lord. Now they stood not across the pass, but at an angle, partly towards the gathered Deirans, but also able to rapidly defend against an attack from their fellow Bernicians. Fordraed's men shifted nervously, flicking their gaze between Beobrand and his black-shielded gesithas and Heremod.

"I have warned you once about threatening me, Heremod," Beobrand said, his voice cold as winter steel. "I will not warn you again. If it is death you seek, I can oblige, and willingly."

Heremod was defiant, jutting his jaw so that his beard shook.

"Nobody is going to kill Wulfstan here today," Beobrand said, his tone final and carrying to all those gathered in the afternoon sunshine. Cynan felt a trickle of sweat run down the back of his neck.

"You would break your oath? For this Deiran?" Heremod raged, incredulous.

"This Deiran saved my life," Beobrand replied, his voice unnaturally calm in the face of Heremod's anger. "Wulfstan is not my enemy."

"We stood together on the wall at Bebbanburg. Have you forgotten? We fought like brothers against the Mercian scum. Forget Wulfstan," Heremod said, outrage in his voice. "I am not your enemy!"

Cynan sensed the change in Beobrand as he fought against his anger. Death was close now. He could sense it in the harsh tone in the warriors' voices, the sharp smell of their sweat. If Beobrand were to relinquish his hold on his ire, Ediscum would become a place of slaughter.

"You say you are not my enemy," Beobrand said, his voice shaking with emotion, "then perhaps it is you who has forgotten himself."

"What do you mean?"

"You threatened me, Heremod. Do you not recall?" Beobrand's anger was bubbling over now. He was almost shouting. Gone was the calm of moments before. "You said you would speak out about my meeting with Eanflæd."

Cynan gasped as he heard his lord's words. He had long known of Beobrand's affection for the queen, but he had not suspected he had acted on his desires beyond seeking out her company in the great hall of Bebbanburg during feasts. He watched as the shock appeared on the faces of Fordraed's men. Even Heremod was caught unawares. Cynan saw it in the widening of the man's eyes, the way his mouth flopped open and he seemed to rock back on his heels as if punched.

"What? You—" he stammered. "You and Eanflæd? I knew nothing of this."

Beobrand frowned, confused.

"Then why threaten me?"

"I spoke of your man, Beircheart. I had seen him with Edlyn."

For a moment nobody spoke. Beobrand flicked a glance at Beircheart. So he knew, thought Cynan.

"But you did not speak out, even knowing your beloved Fordraed was being wronged," Beobrand said.

Heremod looked down.

"Edlyn deserved better," he said. "She was happy with him." He pointed with his drawn sword at Beircheart. "Fordraed was a brute, but I should have stopped it. He was my lord. He had my oath."

"Fordraed was a fat animal," yelled Beircheart. "Edlyn is well rid of the toad. And so are you, Heremod. Find yourself a real man to follow, not a slug like Fordraed, who beats women and is afraid to fight men."

Fordraed's men let out a low growl and took a pace forward.

"A real man?" asked Heremod. "Like Beobrand here? A man who has made a cuckold of our king? Who has broken his oath to warn our enemy of our coming? This is no man to follow. The king will know of his treachery. Oswiu will see your lord slain and maybe that whore of a Cantware queen with him."

The moment before anyone moved, Cynan sensed it; the crumbling of the bonds that had held the two lines in check. Beircheart and Beobrand leapt forward together. Cynan and the rest of the Black Shields were only a heartbeat behind them.

Heremod roared in defiance and Fordraed's men raised their shields and weapons to meet the attack. The two groups of warriors crashed together and the warm air rang with the thunder of blades striking boards. Moments later, Cynan's heart sank as the first Bernician blood showered into the hot air.

Chapter 44

"Death!" bellowed Beobrand, as he ran forward. "Death!" Even as he screamed the words, bashing his black-daubed linden board into Heremod's shield, his spirit quailed. Twisting his left arm, he managed to lever Heremod's shield down, allowing him to strike with Nægling at the bearded warrior's exposed head. He fought with his famous speed, agility and strength, with instinct more than thought. All the while his mind screamed silently. What have you done? What have you done?

Heremod, no mean swordsman, ducked away from Beobrand's blow. His lips were pulled back in a savage snarl, showing his yellow teeth. With a skilful twist of his wrist, he pushed Beobrand's shield aside, aiming a desperate swing at his shoulder. Beobrand parried the blow with Nægling, absently feeling the thrum of the two blades singing together.

They continued to trade blows, but Beobrand was barely aware of his actions. He could scarcely believe what was happening.

The king had sent them to this place to slay a Deiran in blood payment for the loss of a Bernician thegn. The order was foolish and cruel. No good could have come from it. But as the afternoon was filled with the sword-song of battle and the first hot blood sprayed in the sunshine, Beobrand understood that he had made oath-breakers of them all.

It was he who had led them to this place, and it had ever been folly. If he had meant to break his oath, why not merely run? Had he truly believed he could fulfil both his oath to Oswiu and his promise to Wulfstan? It was pride and madness to have imagined such a thing was possible. And yet here they were, grunting and shouting, the clang of metal and the thump of shields loud in the sun-drenched afternoon heat.

A howling scream and he saw one of Fordraed's men fall back, blood fountaining from a huge gash in his throat. Dreogan, his tattoos and new scar giving him the appearance of some beast of legend, sprang after the falling man, into the breach in the shieldwall. There he lay about him with his sword.

By Woden, Beobrand thought, he had made murderers of his gesithas.

Heremod flicked another swiping cut over his shield, this time aiming at Beobrand's head. He swayed back, lifting his shield to catch the blow on its rim.

"Traitor!" screamed Heremod.

Beobrand did not reply. Heremod spoke the truth. He had broken his oath and betrayed his men's trust.

Another of Fordraed's men collapsed under Eadgard's bludgeoning axe blows. The huge weapon splintered the man's shield and the iron head bit deeply into his chest, bursting the links of his byrnie with the force of the strike.

He had made traitors of them all, and they had followed him forward without question. Pride rippled within him. These were his men, his comitatus, who would stand with him even in the face of death and despair. He had led them to break their oaths with their king, but their oath with him was yet strong.

A renewed vigour filled his limbs and the fog of despondency lifted from him. What was done could not be altered. He could only lead his men forward now. Perhaps all along he had known it would end this way, but with sudden certainty, he understood the path they must follow. If they ever hoped to return to Ubbanford and Bernicia, and if Eanflæd was to have a future, they must kill every last one of Fordraed's gesithas.

This thought flooded him as if with freezing meltwater. There was no other way. As so often in Beobrand's life, death was the only answer. So be it then. By Woden, if he had to, he would wade through the guts of Fordraed's men to save his gesithas and Eanflæd.

And yourself, whispered a small voice deep within him.

Was this the act of a coward? he wondered. To kill rather than be killed. And yet was that not what all warriors did?

Along the line, he heard more screams and was dimly aware of yet more men falling; more warriors dying. But now his focus was fully on the man before him. Beobrand knew the path he had led his gesithas down, and he saw the end would be awash with blood.

The murmuring doubts rising within were drowned out by the chaos and clangour of battle. There was no time now for thinking.

"Come on then, Heremod, you bastard," he yelled. "Come and die on my sword."

Heremod did not hesitate, he shoved forward with his shield, following it up with an overarm slicing cut with his sword. Beobrand had known he would. The man was strong and skilled, but Beobrand was stronger and fought with a fluid natural ability few men could match. With his shield, he deflected Heremod's blade, then, with an almost casual flick of his wrist, he opened the man's throat. Heremod's beard braid fell to the earth, severed by Nægling's sharp blade. A heartbeat later, blood welled at the slowly yawning gash in Heremod's throat. Heremod opened his mouth, perhaps to hurl one last insult at Beobrand, but no sound came. Blood gurgled over his tongue and teeth as he dropped to his knees. For an instant,

Beobrand stared into his eyes. He had seen many men die. Some men died with the hatred of their enmity still burning in their gaze. Most were filled with terror at the end. All he saw in Heremod's glare was judgement and disappointment. A moment later, Heremod slumped forward, resting with his forehead pressed to the blood-soaked earth, as if bowing before Beobrand.

Beobrand stepped back for a moment, taking stock. His men were fighting well. Besides Heremod, three others were on the ground. With a sudden wrenching sensation, he saw that one of his own was also lying on the earth. It was Beircheart, his face the colour of whey. Beobrand shuddered. Gods, was there some magic that had been worked by the womenfolk to beguile them? Why else would they have acted so rashly? What had driven them both to such foolishness?

A loud voice boomed out, rising loud over the clamour of the battling Bernicians.

"For Oswine and Deira!"

Wulfstan.

Beobrand watched in dismay as the thegn charged forward from the oak gateway, his dozen warriors beside him, their spears lowered and shields raised.

Beobrand shouted a warning to his gesithas. Grindan, perhaps hearing his lord, faltered in his attack against a stocky man who wielded a hand axe. Grindan turned to see what new danger approached. None of the others paid any heed, or did not hear Beobrand's yell. They continued fighting, as death rushed towards them.

Beobrand could do nothing except watch in horror as the Deirans rushed headlong into the fray, hitting the flank of the embattled Bernicians with crunching force.

Chapter 45

There was no celebration in Wulfstan's hall that night. Though the warriors had fought and survived, there was no cheer in them. They sat, grim-faced and sombre, sipping ale and mead. The womenfolk and servants had not yet returned and so the board was sparse. No roasted meats filled the air with succulent aromas and the promise of greasy warmth in their bellies. Instead, they gnawed on yesterday's bread, adding some hard cheese and tough, coarsely cut ham. It was mean fare, but none of the men complained. They sat in small groups, talking in hushed tones about the events of the day. What Oswiu had planned to be the first killing in the war between their kingdoms, marked the alliance of two opposing thegns. The surviving gesithas drank and talked and were glad they yet lived when so many had been cut down in the afternoon sun at Ediscum.

Beobrand took a swallow of ale to moisten the bread he was chewing. Finishing the mouthful of food, he pushed his trencher away and rose. Attor and Cynan made to stand, but he waved them back. They were nervous, he knew. He had led them into a dark chasm of treachery and he was uncertain he knew how to lead them out safely.

He felt the gaze of all the men in the hall upon him as he climbed to his feet and moved to one of the gloomy corners of

395

the room. There, on a small pallet, lay Beircheart. The man's skin was leeched of colour, his lips pallid. Beobrand sniffed the air. There was no sickly scent of corruption. If the wound had been elf-shot, that would come later. A spear thrust had split his byrnie and pierced his side before Beircheart had managed to plunge his own blade into his opponent's groin. Attor had bound the wound as best he could, but he was no healer. Beircheart's life was in the hands of the gods now.

The gods!

What a spectacle he had provided them, thought Beobrand. Men said he had luck; that the gods favoured him. Perhaps it was true. Maybe Woden and his kin kept him alive for their own entertainment, he mused bitterly. For surely there was nobody else in all of middle earth who provided them with such amusement.

Beircheart's eyes were closed and he did not move at Beobrand's approach. For a heart-wrenching instant, Beobrand feared he might have succumbed to his wound. He could almost hear the gods chuckling.

But then Beircheart's eyes flickered open and he offered Beobrand a weak smile.

"I have brought you some bread and ale," said Beobrand.

"I will take the ale," Beircheart replied. "My mouth is as dry as a crone's cunny." He started to laugh at his own words, before wincing at the pain. "I should not laugh," he said, with a grimace. "It only makes it hurt more."

Beobrand sighed.

"I can think of nothing worth laughing about," he said. Squatting down beside Beircheart, he helped him drink from the cup of ale. He held out the piece of bread, but Beircheart shook his head and lay back on the cot.

Beobrand stared down at him. Beircheart's skin was wan, shiny with sweat. It was warm in the hall. Beobrand hoped the sheen of sweat was not an indication of the wound rot.

"You will need to eat," he said. "You'll need your strength."

"I'll eat soon enough, lord."

For a moment, neither man spoke. The sounds of the other men were slowly growing louder as the ale flowed. Good. Normally they would be telling tales of the fight, playing games and riddling raucously. To see them so subdued twisted his heart. It was his doing, not theirs. He was filled with a despairing anxiety at the path he had led them down. He longed to be able to talk of what he had done, to unburden his mind, but he was their hlaford, not their friend to ask for comfort for his mistakes.

As so often in such moments, he wished Acennan were yet among the living. His friend had always been able to lift his spirits. But he would never see the stocky warrior again. Not this side of death. When they reached Ubbanford, he would speak with Bassus. The old champion would offer him good counsel. Until then, he would have to swallow his worries and lead his men to safety.

"It seems we both have secrets," he said.

Beircheart closed his eyes for a moment, sighing.

"Indeed, lord," he said, staring up at Beobrand earnestly. "And yours will be safe with us."

Beobrand reached out and clasped his forearm in the warrior grip.

"I know I can trust all of you with my secrets."

"You have our oath," replied Beircheart. "We are sworn to you. We will stand by you no matter what."

Beobrand thought of the fight against Heremod and Fordraed's men. His gesithas had not hesitated to fight against brother Bernicians. Their loyalty brought a lump to his throat, and tears stung his eyes.

"I have never doubted your loyalty, or that of the rest of the men. But I offer you my thanks."

"You have our oath, lord," said Beircheart. "You do not need to thank us."

"Still, I know it is no easy thing to follow one who leads you to break your oaths."

Beircheart stared up at him, his eyes bright in his pallid face.

"Lord," he said, his tone grave and serious, "you have no need to worry on account of the men. They all feel as I do."

"And how is that?"

"The men we have slain knew the manner of lord they followed. Fordraed was a devious toad." Beircheart's face was as hard as granite.

"But Fordraed was dead before we came to this place."

"And what choice did Heremod leave you? Would you kill a friend? One who had saved your life? And if Heremod and the others had been allowed to return to Bernicia, your life would be forfeit. We would never stand by and see that happen."

Beobrand nodded, unable to formulate the words that would express his gratitude. Despite his earlier thoughts, it seemed he had gone some way to unburdening his worries, but even that caused him further unease. He should not be turning to his gesithas for encouragement and comfort. He was their leader and must be stronger than any of them. That was his wyrd, the destiny of a lord.

"Eat that bread and get some rest," he said at last.

Leaving Beircheart, Beobrand walked outside the hall. The doors were open to the warm night air, and Wulfstan had placed two spear-bearing men outside to guard the entrance. Oswiu and his retinue were yet close. It was not inconceivable that the king of Bernicia would send more men to attack the hall. Beobrand thought it unlikely, but it was wise to take precautions.

Nodding to the door wards, Beobrand sensed Cynan following him.

Beobrand sighed. He was accustomed to the Waelisc warrior shadowing him, but he wished for nothing more than a moment of peace. A moment to turn over the thoughts that rattled within his mind; to sift through them as a man winnows wheat from chaff. It was true that Heremod and the others had followed Fordraed, in spite of knowing him to be a brute. And yet, had not his own gesithas followed him blindly to break their oaths to the king? He despised Oswiu, but did he too not follow the man because he had sworn his oath to him? Should a man be judged for the actions of his lord?

Walking into the darkness, he sensed as much as saw bats flitting about him in the summer night air. Moths and other night insects fluttered, picked out by the light spilling from the hall's opened doors. He halted, looking out into the darkness beyond the stables. The hills and trees that surrounded the hall were huge looming shadows in the gloom. Soon enough the sun would rise in the east and another day would begin. What new trials would the dawn bring? No man could say. The future weft and warp of the tapestry of a man's wyrd were hidden to him.

A crunching footfall made him turn around angrily. He had hoped that Cynan might sense his mood and keep his distance. By Tiw's cock, the man was insufferable. But it was not Cynan who stood close to him. He could make out the shadowy form of the Waelisc near the door wards. The man who had walked across the yard to join Beobrand was Wulfstan.

For a time they stood in silence. The first ripples of laughter floated from the hall as the men within began to relax, to feel the tensions of the day slip away.

"Your men fought well today," said Wulfstan. "I give thanks that none was slain."

The Black Shields had fought with great skill and discipline. They were a formidable force and famed throughout Albion for good reason. Bassus would be proud to hear of how they had followed the training he had drilled into them. Few could stand before them. Even Brinin, young and inexperienced, had held his ground and stood firm with the others. Afterwards, Eadgard had slapped him on the back, almost knocking him to the ground. No words were said, and the atmosphere had been sober, but

Beobrand knew Brinin had proven himself to the men and they had accepted the youth into their ranks.

"I thank you too," Beobrand said. "Without your aid, I fear I might have lost some men."

He could not bring himself to say that Wulfstan's gesithas had fought well. Wulfstan had held them back, waiting to see the outcome of the fight amongst the two groups of Bernicians, only falling upon them when the battle seemed already decided. His Deirans had rushed into the exposed flank of Fordraed's men, quickly dispatching the unsuspecting warriors who were too caught up in fighting Beobrand's Black Shields to note the danger from the Deirans. There was little honour in what they had done. And yet, as he said, without their help, more of his men might have been injured or killed, and for that, he owed Wulfstan his thanks.

"How does Beircheart fare?" asked Wulfstan.

"Well enough. Travel will be hard, but with some luck, we will get him back to Ubbanford where he can rest."

"You can leave him here, if you wish. The womenfolk will be back tomorrow, and they could tend to him."

Beobrand turned the idea over in his mind for a moment before shaking his head.

"No. I thank you, but we must be gone from here. Gone from Deira. We are at war, remember?"

A sudden outburst of laughter, followed by a thundering of fists on the boards, echoed out of the hall.

Wulfstan snorted.

"They do not sound as if they are at war."

Beobrand sighed. He liked this man. He had no desire to be his enemy.

"And yet we are."

They stood in silence for a while longer. Beobrand could not shake the feeling of despondency that had draped over him like a wet cloak.

"Those men did not deserve death," he said into the silence. "They were oath-sworn to a bad lord, that is all. Is it not right that they followed their lord's commands? Is that not what we all do?"

"It is the way of things," replied Wulfstan, his tone deep and serious in the night. "But they will not be the last men to swear an oath to a man who was not worthy of it, eh, Beobrand?"

Beobrand said nothing.

He thought of his oath to Oswiu. How he longed to be done with it. For a brief moment in the night at Ingetlingum he had begun to feel something akin to understanding for the king. But then, following the attack and the death of Fordraed, the cruel edge of Oswiu's character had returned, like a man slipping a grimhelm over his face to hide his features, turning him from a mere man to a warlord, implacable and deadly.

He could not escape it. Oswiu had his oath. And even without it, what would Beobrand have done? He owed much of his wealth to the king. And of course, Octa was in his household. If Beobrand should turn against the ruler of Bernicia, what would befall his son?

And if Oswiu should learn of his meeting with Eanflæd? What then? He was certain of his men. They would not spread word of what they had learnt. But even the truest of men spoke to their women. And women did gossip so. The rumour would reach Oswiu eventually, of that he was sure. It was just a matter of time. Besides, Wulfstan and all his men had heard the secret too. Beobrand had already slain to prevent the secret getting out, he would not kill for it again.

"Those men chose who to follow," said Wulfstan, interrupting his spiralling self-pity. "And it was their choice how they followed him. You are sworn to Oswiu, are you not?"

"Aye, and today I have broken my oath to obey him." The thought of it turned his stomach. "If he finds out what has happened here, my life, and that of my men, will be like dust in

401

the wind." He stared into the darkness, glad that Wulfstan could not see the tears that threatened to spill from his brimming eyes. "My word now is worthless," he said, his tone desolate.

"And yet," said Wulfstan, "I still live." He placed his hand on Beobrand's shoulder. "You gave me your word that you would help me in a time of need. Today your promise is fulfilled. I hope no more comes of this madness between Oswiu and Oswine. I would rather be your friend than your enemy."

Beobrand blinked back his tears, cuffing at his eyes.

"No matter what our lords command, I am happy to be your friend, Wulfstan."

The Deiran squeezed his shoulder.

"What will you say happened here?"

"I know not." Beobrand thought for a moment. "I suppose I will tell Oswiu you defeated us and killed Heremod and Fordraed's men."

"Will he believe you?"

Beobrand hawked and spat.

"Probably not, but what man would accuse me of being a liar?"

His own words, full of vitriol, failure and disappointment, were as sharp and cutting as a sword-blade. Without waiting for a response, Beobrand turned away from the hall and the sounds of laughter and camaraderie. These things were not for him. Leaving Wulfstan staring after him, he stalked into the night to be alone with his anguish.

Like a distant shadow, unseen and unheard, Cynan moved silently from the porch of the hall and followed his lord.

Chapter 46

As they rode north, Cynan could see that something had changed within Beobrand. Always a surly, serious man, not prone to merriment and levity, now the lord of Ubbanford seemed somehow less present. He was distracted, as if he listened to words that only he could hear. Whenever Cynan attempted to converse with him, Beobrand reacted as if awoken from a dream. He would then turn his glower to Cynan, offering him the barest response. After a time, Cynan did not approach him, merely keeping close to him in case of danger.

The rest of the men whispered about Beobrand at night. Cynan listened to them, but did not enter into the discussions. The gesithas were not griping and moaning about their lord or his decisions, though well they might have, for the course he had set for them would only lead to misery, thought Cynan. They were concerned for him, worried where his dark state of mind would take him next. For they were oath-sworn to him, and wherever he led, they would follow.

The journey had been without serious incident. They travelled slowly, as Beircheart was too unwell to ride. Wulfstan had given them a cart in which to carry the injured man. It was pulled by one of the horses. First they had tried Beircheart's mare, but the beast had hated being harnessed to the wooden contraption, kicking out and whinnying in distress and anger. Eventually, Cynan had selected Eadgard's sturdy gelding and had him ride Beircheart's mare. The gelding was docile and much more suited to the task of pulling, but Eadgard was no rider and was thrown twice until his brother, a more accomplished horseman, had swapped mounts with him.

Two of Fordraed's men's horses were tied to the waggon, a precaution against any of the mounts going lame. The rest of the steeds Beobrand had gifted to Wulfstan. The story of being beaten by the Deirans would never be believed if they returned with all of the mounts they had left with.

The sun was low in the sky, hazing the hills in the west with a rosy hue. Beobrand rode ahead of them on Sceadugenga. Cynan spurred Mierawin forward to join him. Beobrand did not turn to see who approached. His eyes were dull and he seemed content to allow his black stallion to carry him where it wished.

"Shall we make camp near Gefrin?" Cynan asked.

Beobrand let out a long sigh.

"As you wish," he said at last, without looking at Cynan.

Cynan frowned. Like the rest of the men, he was worried about Beobrand. He had often before seen him descend into a dark humour following a battle. He was prone to dwelling on what had taken place and what he might have done differently. Such thoughts were pointless, but a man could not change his very nature.

But on each of those occasions, Beobrand's despair would turn eventually to anger and hatred at the people he blamed for events. His ire would drive him on and soon he would be forging onward once more.

This time it was different. Something had snapped deep within him.

Beobrand had battled for years against men he considered less than him. Men who lied and cheated. Oath-breakers. Nithings. Cravens. He hated such men and used his anger with them to propel him forward, pushing aside any obstacle that stood in his way.

But now, he could not push aside the barrier before him with his anger, thought Cynan. He could not use his hatred against his enemy. For Beobrand had broken his oath and his word had been as iron. Every man knew it. That iron had been sundered and now Beobrand hated himself.

They rode on. Brinin, who rode in the cart with Beircheart, shook the reins. Eadgard's horse snorted and began to heave the vehicle up the slope. Behind the cart came the rest of the mounted men.

"Are you certain you do not wish to travel with me to Bebbanburg?" Cynan asked.

"There is nothing for me at Bebbanburg," Beobrand said, his tone bitter.

"Octa is there."

"Octa cares nothing for me."

"That is not so, lord," said Cynan. "Octa looks to you with admiration and love."

"Perhaps once," said Beobrand. "Now he has only disdain for me."

Cynan knew not how to answer and so they rode on in silence until they reached a stand of beech and hazel that grew a spear's throw from the road. A small stream flowed beside the trees and the warband of Ubbanford had made camp there many times over the years.

The men went about their established duties setting up the camp. Attor lit a fire, while others collected wood, and water from the stream. Halinard, who they all agreed was the best cook, set about preparing the last of the meat that Lord Ecgric had given them when they had stopped at his hall two nights before.

They ate the stew Halinard made and, as ever, Cynan marvelled at how the Frank could make the simplest of fare taste so rich and fulfilling. By then the sun had slipped behind the hills and the sky had turned a deep purple. Soon the men were wrapped in their blankets and cloaks beside the fire.

Cynan had decided to take the first watch, so that when he awoke, he could saddle Mierawin and head for Bebbanburg. His stomach clenched at the thought of returning there. He was not sure whether he was most concerned over the tidings he must impart to the king, or the other task that drew him to the fortress. Would Ingwald and the men have waited for him? Did he really think he could become their lord?

The night was quiet, a light breeze whispered through the leaves above him. The fire crackled and Dreogan snored loudly. The crack of a twig startled Cynan and he dropped his hand to the hilt of his sword. A massive shadow loomed up in the darkness. For the briefest of instants, Cynan was filled with terror. He had not been listening carefully and now an enemy was upon them! He began to drag his sword from its scabbard, but a voice halted him.

"Easy there, Cynan."

Beobrand.

"Lord," Cynan said, fighting against the breathlessness that had gripped him. "I did not hear your approach. I am sorry."

"We all make mistakes, do we not?" Beobrand said.

"Aye, lord." Cynan was surprised that Beobrand should seek him out to talk, but he was glad of it. Perhaps Beobrand could talk of what ailed him and begin to dispel his anguish.

"Be careful at Bebbanburg," Beobrand said. "Oswiu will not take the news of Heremod and Fordraed's men well." He sighed. "I should take the tidings, but it seems I am a coward, as well as an oath-breaker." Beobrand's voice was barely a whisper.

"You are no coward," replied Cynan.

Surprisingly, Beobrand guffawed, a sudden bark in the darkness.

"But I am an oath-breaker," he said. "That you cannot deny."

"Whatever you did, lord, you would have broken one oath. You did what you must."

Beobrand did not reply for a long time.

"Do not tarry in Bebbanburg, Cynan," he said at last. "If Fraomar is well enough to ride, bring him with you. See which of those men of yours are willing to come too. I feel we will have need for stout hearts and strong arms soon."

At the mention of the men, Cynan clenched his fists in the dark. If any were still there, what right did he have to ask for their service? He was just a warrior. And yet Beobrand had said he would give him land to build his own hall. The idea of it made him giddy.

"Aye, lord. I will not stay long. I will see if any of the men have waited for me and then return to Ubbanford with all haste."

"Oh, they will have waited for you," said Beobrand. "Of that I am sure."

A night creature shrieked in the distance, sending a shudder down Cynan's spine.

"But, Cynan," Beobrand's voice was flat and cold in the gloom, "to lead men is not easy. Think carefully before you accept their oaths. For a man's promise to his lord is both a treasure and a burden."

And with that, Beobrand walked back towards the light of the fire. Cynan watched his lord's shadowy form retreating. Nothing in his words had helped to quell his fears of what the morrow would bring.

HISTORICAL NOTE

As usual with all of the *Bernicia Chronicles*, Beobrand's tale is fiction, but it wends through real historical events, and his life intertwines with those of real personalities.

In *Fortress of Fury*, the main events are the siege of Bebbanburg and the start of the war between Oswiu of Bernicia and Oswine of Deira. The dates of both of these events are unknown, but there is a window of a few years when they must have occurred. We know this because the death dates of certain characters are known and they are involved in some way in these stories. I won't give more away here, as it might spoil future stories. But if you are really interested and cannot wait till future novels, you can of course investigate further.

The oldest sources are Bede's *History of the English Church and People* and the *Anglo-Saxon Chronicle*. If you would prefer a more modern read, you could do much worse than Max Adams' wonderful book, *The King in the North*, which is ostensibly a biography of King Oswald, but as its subtitle, *"The Life and Times of Oswald of Northumbria"*, indicates, the book covers the whole of the seventh century, all the kings of Northumbria and their interaction with the other kingdoms of the period.

It is not only the date for the commencement of the war between Oswine and Oswiu that is not known with any certitude. We also have no explanation of what triggered it. Clearly Oswiu wanted to be king of all Northumbria, just as his brother, Oswald, and their enemy, King Edwin, had been, and so I have settled on Oswiu pushing for conflict when there is already tension between the two kingdoms. In this way, he shows himself to be an opportunistic leader, but, as so often in history, it is the ability to strike when an opportunity presents itself that leads to ultimate victory.

Oswiu's jaunts to Caer Luel to visit one of his previous wives are purely fictional, but the fact that he had a son before he married Rhieinmelth or Eanflæd is true. Genealogical tradition has it that the mother of Aldfrid was a Hibernian princess called Fín, the granddaughter (or perhaps daughter) of Colmán Rímid, an Irish king. Details of when the liaison between Oswiu and Fín and the subsequent birth of Aldfrid occurred are missing from the historical record, but it seems likely they would have met during the exile of the sons of Æthelfrith in which they fought in Ireland on the side of their Dál Riatan hosts.

The description of Oswine and the tale of the horse that he gifted to Aidan, only for the bishop to then give it away to a beggar, come straight out of Bede's *History*. He describes the king of Deira as "a man of handsome appearance and great stature, pleasant in speech and courteous in manner". He was beloved of "everyone by his regal qualities of mind and body" and his "singular blessing of humility" was such that Aidan held him in high esteem. Bede recounts the story of the horse as a special example of how humble the king was and how he would never again question the manner in which his wealth was given away "to God's children". Bede also has Aidan weep and predict that the king's humility would be his undoing.

The novel starts shortly after the opening of the monastery at Hartlepool (Hereteu). It is a time of expansion of the Church across the north, with minsters and churches being founded all over Bernicia and Deira. Despite having different kings, both kingdoms saw their spiritual father as Aidan, bishop of Lindisfarne.

Eanflæd was a devout Christian and became increasingly heavily involved in the relationship between the royal house of Bernicia and the Church. So it seems entirely possible that she would attend the opening ceremony at one of the monasteries, particularly given that one of her kinswomen was there.

Hild was Edwin's great-niece, a woman of influence and formidable strength of character who would soon take over the running of the community at Hartlepool and who would later become the Abbess at the now famous Whitby Abbey. Such was the complexity of the relationships in the ruling families of Northumbria that Eanflæd was also kinswoman to Oswine, who was her second cousin.

Even more surprisingly, an investigation of the royal family trees shows Eanflæd and Oswiu to be cousins; Oswiu's mother was Acha, Edwin's sister, and therefore Eanflæd's aunt. Bede makes no mention of this, however. The marriage took place before the time of Theodore, the Archbishop of Canterbury who reformed the British church at the end of the seventh century, in particular with regards to marriage and consanguinity. I imagine that Bede was not comfortable with these blood relatives marrying, but as with so many other disquieting facts, he chose to ignore it. After all, he could not rewrite the past, but he could turn a blind eye. If there were any concerns about the marriage at the time, it seems that the need to unify the Deiran and Bernician dynasties outweighed them.

In the years following Oswald's defeat at Maserfield (Maserfelth), Penda continued to pose a significant threat to the other kingdoms of Britain. Of course, apart from slaying Oswiu's brother, Penda had already killed several other kings and in 645 he drove Cenwealh of Wessex into exile in East Anglia. And yet it appears that, for a few years at least, he did not choose to continue his aggression towards Bernicia. Perhaps a pact had been struck with Oswiu, or maybe he was just busy with Wessex and East Anglia. But whatever the reason for the relative peace, we know it was broken sometime in the late 640s when Bede recounts the siege of Bebbanburg and the great fire that Penda employs to attempt razing the fortress.

In 2015, in one of the trenches of the Bamburgh Research Project, archaeologists found discoloured subsoil that points to intense burning. This evidence of burning lies very close to St Oswald's Gate, the oldest entrance to the castle, and dates back to the early medieval period. It is speculation, but it is tempting to believe the discoloured subsoil they found is a remnant of the fire that Bede describes.

In his *History*, Bede says that when unable to enter Bebbanburg "by force or after a siege", Penda ordered all the neighbouring villages to be pulled down and carried to Bebbanburg where "vast quantities of beams, rafters, partitions, brushwood, and thatch" were piled high on the landward side of the settlement. It seems unlikely that Penda would have just hoped that a random spark would blow into the castle, or that he would expect the palisades high up on the crag to burn, and so I have described him attempting to destroy the gates by fire. With the archaeological discovery in the subsoil there, perhaps my account of the Mercians' actions is not too far from what actually happened.

It is impossible to know for certain what the layout of the castle was in the seventh century. In later years, there was a second entrance to the south, which in time became the main gate. However, it seems probable that at the time of the *Bernicia Chronicles* there was only one way in and out of Bebbanburg – what would later become known as St Oswald's Gate. Steps from that gate would have led down to a harbour that is no longer present. I have decided that there must also have been a slope of earth and rubble leading down to the landward side of the rock and the settlement and church there. This would make it possible for horses and vehicles to reach the fortress. It also makes for a great location for the Black Shields to burst forth from the flames and embers to launch their counterattack on Penda's forces!

The tale of the wind changing direction after Aidan noticed the fire and prayed is again described by Bede. On seeing the column of smoke, Aidan is said to have raised his hands and eyes to heaven and exhorted, "Lord, see what evil Penda does!" Apparently, no sooner had he uttered these words than the wind shifted away from the fortress and "drove back flames onto those who had kindled them". This is supposed to have so unnerved Penda's men that they abandoned the assault, seeing that Bebbanburg was clearly under God's protection. Now, this says a lot about the superstitious nature of the people of the time, but I thought it more likely they would be dissuaded from their attack by sharp steel and stout linden boards wielded by the brave defenders of Bernicia.

The tales of miracles attributed to Oswald come straight from Bede's accounts. He also writes that Oswald's head was interred on Lindisfarne, and his arms and hands were kept at Bebbanburg. I have chosen for the head to remain in a reliquary in the fortress. Eanflæd and Oswiu praying to his limbs just doesn't have the same emotional clout as them petitioning directly to his saintly – though decaying – face.

There is no historical evidence of Waelisc (Welsh) forces being involved in the assault on Bernicia with Penda, but as they had been allies in previous battles, it is credible.

The Roman ruins, where Cynan and Reodstan make camp on their way westward from Bebbanburg, are the remnants of the Roman fort at High Rochester (Bremenium). It was built to defend the important communication artery that ran north from Corbridge to the Antonine Wall and beyond.

By the end of this book Beobrand has had his allegiances tested to the limit. His famous word of iron has been pushed beyond breaking point and his feelings for his queen have put his, and her, life in jeopardy. He might have earned favour with Oswiu for his part in the defence of Bebbanburg and saving the king's life from assassins' blades, but whatever advantage he has will be short-lived if the king should get any indication of Beobrand's indiscretions with Eanflæd.

And what of his powerful enemy in Frankia? It seems unlikely that Vulmar will give up trying to exact vengeance on the Lord of Ubbanford.

The future looks uncertain, with intrigues and danger lurking over every hill and in every shadow. But with Penda once more plotting against Bernicia, and a war between Oswiu and Oswine brewing, there will surely soon be need for Beobrand's blade and his black-shielded gesithas.

But that is for another day, and other books.

ACKNOWLEDGEMENTS

Thanks must go first and foremost to you, dear reader. I am indebted to everyone who has bought my books and, hopefully, enjoyed them enough to recommend them to others.

As with each book, my trusty cadre of beta readers helped me polish the manuscript before submitting it to my editor. Thanks to Simon Blunsdon, Gareth Jones, Shane Smart, Rich Ward, James Faulkner and Alex Forbes for reading that early draft and helping me to make it better than it would be without their keen eyes.

Extra special thanks to Jon McAfee, Anna Bucci, Simon Kent and Roger Dyer for their generous patronage. To find out more about becoming a patron, and what rewards you can receive for doing so, please visit www.matthewharffy.com.

Special thanks to Paul Buxton for seeking out and sending me maps and pictures of Bamburgh Castle through the ages.

Thanks to Paul Lennon for the chats about early medieval marriages and the interrelated nature of the different royal lines of Northumbria. And thanks to Max Adams for helping to clarify things.

Thanks to all my online friends, readers and writers alike. The Internet is often maligned, but it is a wonderful resource and for someone who works at home alone, the ability to reach out to like-minded people and receive nearly instantaneous responses is priceless.

Extra special thanks to Nicolas Cheetham and all the staff at Aries and Head of Zeus for their continued support and belief in me.

And finally, thank you to my family, especially my lovely wife, Maite. Your support means everything.

About the author

M ATTHEW HARFFY grew up in Northumberland where the rugged terrain, ruined castles and rocky coastline had a huge impact on him. He now lives in Wiltshire, England, with his wife and their two daughters.

@MATTHEWHARFFY   MATTHEWHARFFY.COM